'A ridiculously propulsive page turner. Barbara Bourland has written a 'du Maurier-esque' literary thriller about sexual jealousy and artistic legacy, a gorgeously scathing critique of the New York art scene, and a warning about the deadly consequences of stifling female expression. Could. Not. Put. It. Down' Lisa Gabriele, author of *The Winters*

'In Bourland's decadent twist on the classic campus novel, a group of struggling artists succeed beyond their wildest dreams, but at what cost? Gloriously mordant, and just the right amount of rococo, you have to start your summer with this glittering new read' Courtney Maum, author of *I Am Having So Much Fun Here Without You*

'I love *Fake Like Me*. It's the perfect smart-thriller paradox: you'll be driven to finish the twisting plot, but you will not want the narrator's insightful observations to end. Drop everything to follow Bourland's brilliant young painter to Pine City, the upstate artist colony with its crumbling camp buildings and secret histories. You will not see the art world - or a woman's place in it - the same way again' Maria Hummel, author of *Still Lives*

'With her trademark flair and razor-sharp attention to detail, Barbara Bourland offers the reader an incisive exploration of the tension between the desire to make art and the desire to make money. *Fake Like Me* is satirical, brilliantly realised, and has a twist you simply won't see coming' Louise O'Neill, bestselling author of *Asking For It*

'A convincing account of the tension between the artistic process and the deadly perils of pretension' *Daily Mail*

'A satirical take on the contemporary art scene - smart, witty and eye-opening. This gripping tale throws back the curtain on a world of secrets and intrigue' Liv Constantine, author of *The Last Mrs Parrish*

'A menacing, swirling, hypnotic dance of parties, art, sex, and, ultimately, startling revelations. Readers eager for a glimpse into the New York art scene will be enthralled . . . A haunting, dizzying meditation on identity and the blurred lines between life and art' *Kirkus*, starred review

Praise for *I'll Eat When I'm Dead*

'I can't put *I'll Eat When I'm Dead* down, I LOVE it. Bourland's debut is like *The Devil Wears Prada* meets *American Psycho*' Louise O'Neill

'Anyone who has opened up a woman's magazine and despaired at the content should read this book' Rhiannon Lucy Cosslett

'A whip-smart New York fashion magazine-set crime novel with more edge than all the haute couture shows put together' Sarra Manning, *Red*

'A satire, a murder mystery and an exaggerated exposé of the industry people love to make assumptions about . . . If you want an Agatha Christie update, this is it. We look forward to Bourland's next quirky outing' *Stellar*

'Ambitious but far more brutal. This murder mystery takes a satirical look at the world responsible for bombarding us with destructive images' *Big Issue*

'A smart, satirical take on fashion and media that will have readers snorting with laughter' *New York Post*

BARBARA BOURLAND is the author of the critically acclaimed *I'll Eat When I'm Dead*, a Refinery29 Best Book of 2017 and an Irish Independent Book of the Year. People called *I'll Eat When I'm Dead* "delectable." Wednesday Martin, bestselling author of *Primates of Park Avenue* and *Untrue*, deemed it "a deft, smart, and hilarious debut." *Kirkus* noted that "death by beauty was never so much fun," and the book was featured in *Fortune*, *Us Weekly*, and the *New York Post*, among others. *I'll Eat When I'm Dead* is now available in paperback and is forthcoming in Hebrew from Matar Press in Israel.

Bourland is a former freelance writer and web producer for titles at Condé Nast and Hearst, among others. She lives in Baltimore with her husband and their dogs.

Fake Like Me was written with support from the Wassaic Project in Wassaic, New York, where Bourland was a resident over the winter of 2017–18.

Fake Like Me

Barbara Bourland

riverrun

First published in Great Britain in 2019
This paperback edition published in 2020 by

riverrun

An imprint of

Quercus Editions Limited
Carmelite House
50 Victoria Embankment
London EC4Y 0DZ

An Hachette UK company

A CIP catalogue record for this book is available
from the British Library

Paperback 978 1 78648 645 5
Ebook 978 1 78648 646 2

This book is a work of fiction. Names, characters,
businesses, organizations, places and events are
either the product of the author's imagination
or used fictitiously. Any resemblance to
actual persons, living or dead, events or
locales is entirely coincidental.

10 9 8 7 6 5 4 3 2 1

Printed and bound in Great Britain by Clays Ltd, Elcograf S.p.A.

Papers used by Quercus are from well-managed forests and other responsible sources.

To my contemporaries:

I made this for you,
I made this for me,
I made this for us.

Carey Logan Retrospective Coming to Young Museum

The Young Museum announced today that Carey Logan, the artist known for her hyperrealist sculptures who committed suicide by drowning in 2008, will be the subject of a sweeping retrospective at the museum this October.

Dramatic rumors of an as-yet-unseen final work have churned through Chelsea for months, and the museum confirmed today that the exhibition, BODY OF WORK, will include all of Logan's sculptural and performance works, including the rumored final work. A source from within the institution told The Times that the final work has not been viewed by the curators, and that it will not even be transported to the museum until the exhibition's opening night.

Ms. Logan's vivid, detailed representations of human bodies could be—and often were—easily mistaken for the real thing. Made from combinations of ceramics, resin, paper, ink and oil paint, the sculptures were both a visual pun on the currency of a market where the greatest quantities of money so often change hands over the estates of dead artists, and a running commentary on the subjugation and degradation of women.

Her bodies were exhibited all over the world and acquired by dozens of private collectors. But in 2006, Ms. Logan ceased her sculptural work entirely and devoted herself to an earnest revival of 1970s performance art. In separate performances at the Eliot&Sprain gallery over the two years preceding her death, Ms. Logan choked, passed out, slept and stayed awake for days, all on public view, to mixed reviews.

It is not clear whether her final artwork was also made at Eliot&Sprain, or even what medium it is in.

A source familiar with the work who wishes to remain anonymous was unwilling to provide further details. "It cannot be described," they wrote to The Times in an email. "It is fascinating, highly personal, explicit and extremely upsetting, and must be seen to be believed and understood in its full context."

BODY OF WORK will open October 21, 2012, and run through June of the following year.

1996

Chapter One

The first time I saw the five members of Pine City, I was nineteen years old. They were standing outside what would someday become Team Gallery on Grand Street in Soho, sharing cigarettes and laughing. It seems in my memory that everyone in the intersection turned to look—that cabbies craned their necks through the half-lowered windows of their broad yellow Crown Victorias, that shop owners materialized in open doorways, that even the old women walking arm in arm behind me stopped to gawk—at those five ravishing, obscene young people on a street corner. In person they seemed like these glamorous lightning bolts, something between human and divine, the embodiment of the moment Zeus turned into a swan or a cow or whatever other thing that was not human but was still a fuckable divine being. It was shocking, to me, how they looked.

Pine City was the name of their group—their collective—though they didn't make work together. Three of them had graduated from the art school where I was a currently a sophomore, and all five made the type of nihilistic, shrewdly absurd work that smart young people on drugs will inevitably make, and it was of a kind, it *seemed* like a collective action, so they became famous together—for their work but mostly for being bad, for being attractive and defiant, for making money and lighting it on fire. And like every-body else at the Academy, I was completely obsessed with them.

A poster for Carey Logan's show, *THE BURIAL PROJECT*, had been wheatpasted on the side of the college's non-ferrous metal forge two months earlier. Selling off meals from my dining plan at half price ginned up enough cash for a same-day round-trip bus ticket in and out of Chinatown, and so—there I went.

The walk to Soho took only a few minutes. After rounding the corner at Grand Street, I was almost an hour early, and unprepared for Pine City to simply *be there* in the street.

By contrast, anyone could tell that I was a college sophomore. Baby fat rolled over the waistband of my jeans, pushed uncom-fortably against the sleeves of my thrift-store shirt, and my skin was rosy, flushed even, from crippling self-consciousness. My head swerved. Time slowed, to fractions of seconds, as I moved my eyes to the toes of my shoes. *Who did I think I was?* The answer, of course, was nobody.

I was nobody.

It took one turn of my body to become a shadow—another girl on the street—and I kept walking west on the cobblestone streets of Soho, holding myself as though I knew where I was go-ing. Blocks away I climbed up into an empty loading dock and sat cross-legged, metal-and-glass grating pressing into my ankles. I watched people go by and wrote in my notebook for an hour until the clock turned eight. I did know enough to know that I should wait for the party to get going. I think I ate a banana out of my backpack, and that was my dinner.

It was my first time ever in New York City.

When I returned to the gallery, it was packed. Spidery people poured out of the massive double doors. My first impression was the scent of fading chlorine mixed with Chanel No. 19 and du Maurier cigarettes, and my second was of secrets being exchanged, of whispers floating from lipsticked mouths to earlobes encrusted in diamond-bedecked safety pins. Somebody passed me a cold beer out of a trash can filled with ice, but before I could even say thank you, they were gone, another body in their place: a thin man in a gray flannel three-piece suit. He wiped his nose with his folded handkerchief and it came away with a blossoming red stain. He caught me staring and winked. I looked away, uncomfortable, then watched a wasplike woman—her shoulder blades sharp, like wings—pull up in a cab. She threw a twenty at the driver, the crumpled bill sailing through the divide, then crossed the sidewalk confidently in a low-cut lavender dress before compressing herself into the packed gallery and disappearing.

The overall crowd has glommed together in retrospect into a shiny, pointy landscape of shadows—of willowy, satin-haired city people, fine and crisp, black and white, like a Stockholm funeral. Mostly, I remember feeling mortified—of myself, of my oversize man's shirt and ripped jeans and Chucks and pink hair (*Why did I think this was a cool outfit, I look terrible, grunge is over, grunge is for kids, nobody here is a kid except me*). I would have left early but didn't know how; the Chinatown bus stop was a bedraggled street corner covered in bursting garbage bags and milky puddles of sewage, no exchange office in sight. Later I would learn you could give the ticket to any driver for any bus going your way, and if there were enough seats, you were fine. But that night I didn't know. I thought I would have to wait—so I did.

Someone passed me another beer. Halfway through it, I started to feel a little brave. Maybe it was the contact high of everyone else's self-possession: The people around me, kissing and hugging and drinking and talking, sincerely acted like they owned the entire world. I'd never seen such a concentration of confidence. Now I think that every single moment of every single day, somewhere new becomes the center of the universe, if only for a second—and that night, it was us. Or rather—it was them, Pine City, and I happened to be there.

The show was roaring in the middle of the gallery, but the crowd was so dense I could barely see anything without shoving, which

I couldn't imagine doing, so I remained in the corner until a third beer. Then, emboldened, I pushed through.

I spotted Jes Winsome first. Tall Jes, with her blue-black hair, lounged in the lap of a clean-shaven man in a tuxedo. He fed her puffs of light-blue cotton candy while one of her naked feet sat in a tub of wet, white plaster. Behind her, Marlin Mayfield—lanky, densely freckled—dumped a bottle of pink wine over her white t-shirt and white jeans. She laughed hysterically while Tyler Savage, the one who looked like a professional tennis player, ran his fingers up her stomach. The fourth member of Pine City, Jack Wells, spoke animatedly to a golden-haired teenage girl in a buttery fur coat, pale like butterscotch, that swung around her in a dream.

Finally, Carey Logan, the smallest one, worked around them, mixing quick-dry plaster into plastic tubs at a rapid, balletic pace. Even in that room of overly confident downtown people, her confidence stood out; it was in her movements, in her posture, in her step. There was a surety in her that I envied and coveted immediately. I hadn't seen a lot of women behave that way. Hardly any—certainly none under forty. She was twenty-four years old at the time.

Carey cast forty-two different body parts that night, including mine, though it took me another hour and another beer to work up the courage to get in line. When she got close to me, I realized we were the same build, our hands almost the same size. Yet our bodies held space differently. Where I slumped, she was rigid; where I shrank, she expanded.

"Don't move your hand," she whispered. "Not until I say. Or it'll be ruined."

"You smell like grapefruit," was all I could manage to reply. Her whole face opened up, those round cheeks and tiny pink lips drawing away to reveal a jumbled mouthful of pearl-white teeth, and she gave me a smile so luminous that I thought, for a moment, that we were friends.

"I like your hair," she complimented me back. "It's cool."

"Thank you," I whispered, then immediately felt a rush of embarrassment. I sounded grateful and reverent—*too* reverent. My eyes fell to the floor, and our connection was broken. She moved on to the next setup, the next body part. I remained still and obedient.

All five members of Pine City, Jack Wells, Jes Winsome, Tyler Savage, Marlin Mayfield, and Carey Logan, were *right there*. I resumed my regular slump, receding naturally into the background, where I could watch them from the safest, most invisible emotional distance.

Jes, still perched atop the man in the tuxedo who was diligently peeling the cotton candy from its paper cone and depositing it on her tongue, watched Carey languidly. Jes never smiled—not once—nor did she speak. She was solid, like an object, like a sculpture, and silence suited her. The more conventionally outgoing Marlin and Tyler were caught up with a group of admirers, people more arachnid than human, light drowning in the hard beetle-black of their eyes. Tyler glanced occasionally at us, Carey's subjects, peeking up and down the row before returning to smile at whatever compliment had been laid at his feet. Marlin put her arm on top of Tyler's shoulder and ran her fingers across the shortest part of his haircut, at the nape of his neck.

I wanted to reach out and do that, too.

Jack had turned his attention away from the butterscotch blonde and was hovering behind Carey, watching her mix, and pour, and dip—and whisper. When someone put hands on Carey—on her arm or shoulder or wrist as she leaned in to speak—Jack's eyes narrowed, and focused, until there was distance again. He monitored every conversation, ensuring that no one crossed her boundaries.

I watched and waited as they danced around each other, and her, and the crowd, for twenty-four minutes. I marveled at Carey's particular command of the room. She was the natural center of attention without doing... anything. She did not wear a bedazzled leotard, she did not wear lipstick, she did not dance, she did not perform a display in the usual sense of *woman on display*. All she did that night, other than walk around in worn-out blue jeans and a tank top, was talk to people and mix plaster. Ultimately, it was what would be *done* with the plaster that made the impression: The casts would become the highly detailed sculptures of corpses upon which she'd built her budding career.

Her first, a woman in a bikini with strangulation marks around her neck, *HARD BODY (7 TIMES A DAY)*, won the Young Prize. The title of the work referred to the statistical number of women killed by a domestic partner per day in America, and every piece she had made since then featured what she called "working-class bodies" in various shades of disease and decay. It was that one-two combination—of her simple (almost *simplistic*) way of being, and the extended shadow of her morbid imagination—that went right up the nose and into the lungs, contaminating the crowd.

That night on Grand Street was the most informative night of my young life, thus far. Much of it was semiotic: Up until that show, even in my second year of art school, I possessed very little vocabulary for what being an artist looked like after 1960. I was only a sophomore, after all, and this was before everyone had a smartphone, before the internet was piped into your every living moment. I didn't know how the YBAs had been living or even what Warhol's Factory was. I think at the time I didn't actually know what Jean-Michel Basquiat *looked* like. I hadn't read the *New York Times* on more than three or four occasions, and I certainly didn't know to subscribe to *Artforum* or *Interview* or any of those arty, expensive magazines; I was just a kid, and I was a painter, my world limited to a lineage of painters. At nineteen, my entire frame of reference was essentially based in old photographs of Helen Frankenthaler and Joan Mitchell hanging in the East Village with the vast landscapes of their canvases, their hair set into big curls like I was doing with my own pale, rosy bob.

But beyond my lack of the most basic cultural and historical knowledge, much of my awe was relational. Pine City were three women and two men in a spiral of their own making, five people who were best friends, lovers, partners, equals. It was family and friendship and romance at once. I'd never seen anything like it, partially because I was from a town in Florida where men had pickup trucks and women, if they were lucky, had abortions, and because I was incredibly young—but also because Pine City was genuinely special, and the way they lived was rare.

Four out of five of them were living together (supposedly sleeping in a giant bed made of four other beds) in a triangle-shaped loft at the end of 44th Street in Long Island City. Rumor had it that Johnson Reuchtig, Tyler Savage's blue-chip gallery, would send a bike messenger every weekend with a silver briefcase full of drugs that Pine City consumed in earnest until it was empty. Then JR would deliver an entire shiva buffet from Barney Greengrass, which Pine City would eat before passing out, waking up, and starting the cycle anew. The only one who didn't sleep in the massive bed—Jack Wells—lived on a thirty-two-foot wooden sailboat docked mere steps away from the loft on the East River, and they would sail it around Manhattan shooting rubber bullets at skyscrapers, taking photographs as the glass walls rippled but did not break.

I was so young then, and *very* sheltered, not on purpose, not because someone was protecting me, but the opposite. I stood beneath, still, the shadows of impoverished white Southern swamp masculinity—bitter misogynies that stick to every particle of your consciousness, so that you don't know if it's possible to be anything other than a failure. You don't know if the sun will ever come out.

But they were the sun.

Months later, all of the body parts Carey cast that night would be painted in various stages of decay and buried, on public and private property, without permission, through the entirety of New York State, though I didn't know that at the time. When she returned and set her hand on top of mine, freeing me from the shrinking white dust with a light tap on each finger, someone took her picture. Though I felt the flash on my face, I wondered if I would show up in the image at all.

"Don't steal my fingerprints," I said to her—the joke I'd been working on for twenty-four minutes.

Carey looked at me. "I won't," she said, after a moment. "Hold on." She reached into the mold and rubbed them away, erasing the whorls of my fingertips one by one. "There. Now you can be nobody."

"I'm already nobody." I lowered my eyes, embarrassed.

She placed one plaster-dusted fingernail under my chin, tipping it up. Her eyes went to my hair and back again.

"No," she said. "You're a pearl." She withdrew her finger.

I blushed. "Thank you."

"You're an artist," she said. A statement, not a question.

"I paint," I admitted. "Well—I'm at the Academy. I *want* to be a painter."

"What are your paintings like? Like—*really*?"

"They want to be bigger. But we're not supposed to."

"You're exactly like me," she said. "You try to follow all the rules, but you don't want to."

"I guess," I agreed nervously.

"Hmm," she said. "I think you should let them. The work comes first, you know."

"Um—I'll try it." Nobody had ever given me permission to step outside the rules of the Academy.

"Can I tell you something else that I've learned?" she whispered, eyes on fire.

"Sure." I leaned in.

"These people"—she twirled that plaster-dusted fingernail ever so slightly to indicate the entire room—"these people will make not only your work, but *you yourself* into a commodity. They'll buy you and sell you. Let them. But make sure you always do it on your own terms."

Before I could ask her what she meant, the other four members of Pine City were looking at us—the rays of their eyes burned my skin—and Carey closed up.

"You can go," she pronounced somberly, like a nun at school, and I did.

As I headed for the door, dodging the elbows of a cluster of drunk bankers, their suit jackets off, ties loose, Tyler Savage wrapped an arm around Carey Logan's waist and held her one inch above the floor, like she was floating, and he whispered something. They were steps behind me, and when she laughed, this big, open laugh, I stopped and turned at the sound. They didn't notice me. She placed her hand on his cheek, and then—almost as if it was the first time, and maybe it was—they held each other against the wall and kissed so deeply that I knew I ought to look away.

I didn't think anyone would ever love me like that, or treat me with so much care.

Somehow, I got a ride the four blocks back to the bus stop in time, doubled on the handlebars of a stranger who kissed *me! hard!* before pedaling away without so much as an introduction. And though it wasn't the same as being kissed by someone like Tyler Savage or Carey Logan, I grinned the whole way back to the Academy.

That was when I decided I would move to New York.

Two years later, I packed up my last dorm room and got on that Chinatown bus one final time. I landed in Brooklyn, subletting a friend-of-a-friend-of-a-friend's roommate's room for a year, and slept in a plywood cave on a lofted bed, a set of single-file doll-house steps leading to the cold, dirty floors. I fell in love right away with a guitarist named Ben who lived down the hall. He had the biggest eyes I'd ever seen, and gentle fingers, and he was in love with a girl called Kate who was much prettier than I was. I found a job in a metal bar and spent my first twelve months in New York drinking and chasing Ben while he chased Kate and then eventually this ended in the spring, with me sobbing in the then detritus-park at the end of South 3rd while Ben walked away, shaking his head and apologizing. Five minutes later—tears dripping off my chin as I stared out at the river mournfully—I was approached by two pale, bearded Hasidic guys in their big satin jackets. They asked if I liked to party. We wound up doing coke behind a curtain in the back room of a nearby dive bar, and they told me that God was ashamed of me for being impure, and I was so coked up that I cried again and told them they were probably right. I hadn't picked up a palette knife since arriving in New York, and I hadn't seen hide nor hair of Pine City, or any other real artists, and I'd lost myself. I was miserable and I truly thought that I'd ruined my life, that I had wasted the most precious opportunity I'd ever known, because when you are twenty-two every day feels like a year.

One night I followed one of Ben's friends to an ad hoc music venue in the city to see a sparsely attended folk concert. Cavernous and sticky with old beer, it was a ninth-floor walk-up somewhere off an alleyway in the Financial District, and I loved it immediately. The venue was full of art debris—blowtorches and canvases and weird, incomplete foam sculptures shoved against the wall to make room for the stage—so when I found out that the people who lived in the back were looking for a new roommate, I ran three blocks to the nearest ATM and took out all my money.

Seven hundred dollars in tens later, out of breath from the stairs, I introduced myself to Cady, Atticus, and Jonny, the sloe-eyed twenty-somethings on the lease, and told them I was a large-scale abstract painter looking for a live-work space. They shrugged their sloping shoulders, ambivalent—until I gave them the cash, at which point they hugged me, showed me my room—really, a lightly partitioned drywall area—and gave me a key to the front door.

"Jonny is leaving tomorrow for graduate school. We weren't gonna make rent and it was already three weeks late," Cady admitted, sheepish, blushing. "That's why we were hosting Victory and the Beautiful. Only—they only have ten fans, and we didn't feel right charging more than five bucks. Things were dire."

"You're our angel," Jonny said.

The next morning, I ditched the sublet, in a shitty way, if I'm being honest—I think I left a note on a paper towel and taped it to the fridge—and moved into that loft on Dutch Street in the Fulton district of Lower Manhattan. Cady scored me a job, as a hostess at an upscale West Village restaurant, and Atticus cleared out a ten-by-fifteen-foot space in the living room. He was on one side, making sculptures, and Cady was on the other, painting, too, differently from me. Back in a world of artists—and away from Ben, away from Kate, away from dive bars—I started to make work again. The moment I picked up my palette knife, it was like whoever had been sitting on my chest suddenly stood up. I could breathe.

I work primarily in oil, which has enough variations in tone, hardness, depth, and clarity to rival most spoken languages. It can be thick and weirdly inconsistent like an unpasteurized soft cheese; deliciously smooth and stable like a room-temperature buttercream frosting; or thin and weepy like a salad dressing. It can whip into a knot, pan into the ideal smear, beat into a creamy, airless gel. Stiff enough for peaks and valleys—yet smooths out cleaner and flatter than hot glass. Oil paint is needy: It must be paid attention to as it cures in the atmosphere, slowly, and it's hard to cheat. It lives in the world and follows a linear time of its own devising. Essentially: It is *so much work* that it makes everything else disappear.

The first time I used it, at a community arts class in the ninth grade, I dumped an entire, pudding-consistency cup of the palest teal, a half octave of opacity behind Tiffany blue, onto a readymade canvas, then used a paper-thin metal knife to stretch it flat, into the flattest, densest rectangle, and then—the room around me fell away. I was hooked.

Jonah, the cute desk clerk at Pearl Paint on Canal Street who never smiled at anyone but me, whispered one afternoon that *Pine City bought an abandoned hotel somewhere upstate.* It was to be their private retreat, though he'd heard they might host a couple of artists the following year. Immediately I pictured receiving an invitation in the mail that said *Welcome to Pine City.* I told Jonah I was going to be there someday, and he rolled his eyes. Then I spent a thousand dollars on materials. He didn't roll his eyes at my wrinkled pile of money, rubber-banded from the restaurant. When I left he looked at me with something that was either pity or pride or a mixture of both.

Soon, I had my first show.

It was in Brooklyn at a shitty gallery in Bushwick when I was twenty-three, and I called it *Ohne Titel,* "untitled" in German, which is still embarrassing. Only two of my paintings sold. The other eight I donated to a homeless shelter. The gallery dropped me afterward, making the radically uncreative argument that they had no real way to sell a series of near-identical untitled paintings by a young no-name female painter; it was too difficult, especially as long as I insisted the work remain untitled and that the wall text include basically no information. It was like trying to sell a plain white t-shirt with no brand name for two hundred dollars. *Did I know anyone famous,* they asked, *who could help me? Did I have any well-known friends? Or maybe a group show that made it look like I was a part of a trend* . . . whatever it was, something had to be done about my "identity problem."

Anyone could sell plain untitled abstracts by a young female painter with an *identity,* they insisted. All I had to do was get one.

By contrast, Pine City, now crossing into their thirties, were becoming a reference point unto themselves. Their private retreat upstate had been photographed, celebrated, and fetishized, and their lifestyle was a romantic touchstone. At DIY venues without

toilets or bars, people lined up around the block to see Jes's performances. Marlin's wheatpastes became sites of pilgrimage. Jack and
Tyler's site-specific installations, always mounted illegally at mid-
night, were now left up for a week or two, instead of being taken
down immediately.

And Carey—she had truly blossomed. The combination of her
simple, direct persona and the elaborate morbidity of her imagination was irresistible, and collectors outbid each other again
and again in their clamor to own her corpses. Her gallery,
Eliot&Sprain, held elaborate presentations of her work, releasing
limited-edition illustrated chapbooks describing all the body parts
that had been discovered so far in *THE BURIAL PROJECT*, or
sending invitations so extravagant they could be mistaken for a
wedding for her *FORGIVE/FORGET* show. In that one, bodies
stood upright, dancing with each other, at a party frozen in time.
Dead, but alive; real, but simulated. Working-class, talented beyond
measure, obsessively prolific, and coated in an easily digested political gloss, Carey's professional identity was clear as a bell.

The work itself, however, was what held my attention. It was so
detailed, so labor-intensive, and produced at such a brisk pace—
one show every year, radically rapid for artwork that complex—
that I saw it for what it was: the compulsive productions of a restless
mind. Carey was lucky that the world had decided it was salable;
she would have made it either way. I knew this because I was exactly the same.

I was jealous, and fascinated, and I wasn't the only one. It
seemed that everyone, even people outside the art world, now
knew about their place upstate, knew what they were up to, who
was in love with who, who was being invited. I was desperate to be
their guest. I tried a dozen different ways to find out how to apply,
but they had no listed phone number or website, and nobody I was
friends with seemed to know them personally—only *of* them, like
I did.

I tried walking into Johnson Reuchtig, that cavernous, white-walled cathedral of money on 21st Street and West End Avenue, to inquire at the desk. The gallery girl, her hair two long, shiny brown curtains that swept across the papers in front of her, looked at me with confusion and said with disdain that there was no formal process to apply. It was private property. *I.e.: Get out.* I felt like I'd tried to invite myself to a stranger's summer house by asking when the deposit was due. In the intervening four years between Carey's plaster show and that moment, Pine City had moved so many rungs ahead of me that the distance between us had become officially unnavigable.

Then 9/11 happened. Cady, Atticus, and I were drinking coffee on a rooftop in Dumbo, sobering up after a party, when the first plane hit. We watched the towers fall from the waterfront in silence, then decamped to a bar to watch the news coverage. We weren't allowed back in our neighborhood for weeks. As we waited it out on sofas back in Brooklyn, I felt a creeping relief: Maybe we could never go back, and then I wouldn't have to paint anymore. I could do something else.

But despite a layer of fine, brown dust, the loft was unharmed, and our landlord, scared to lose more income, offered fifteen-year leases when we returned, which we accepted gratefully. Broadly I thought of it as a ticking clock: I had fifteen years to make it.

After the failure of *Ohne Titel*, I fell into a multiyear depression and supported myself with a variety of odd jobs as I tried on different careers, other than painting, but none of them fit. My studio portion of the loft remained covered in that fine brown dust for years. I was *her*, that weird, depressed young temp in your office who when pressed says she's thinking about applying to law school because it's something to say, but she's taking cooking classes, too, and maybe working for an NGO abroad is the next step, helping people, but she's also always wanted to do hair, and you think to yourself as she talks, *I might be unhappy, but thank God I'm not that lost.*

I remained in the audience—went to shows, supported others in their successes—but stopped referring to myself as an artist. When asked about my work, I said I was on a sabbatical from painting. It was a pale, ivory-colored kind of lie. I wasn't ready to tell anyone that I thought I would probably never, ever paint again—that I'd failed so spectacularly, I was too ashamed to try.

In that way I left a door open for myself, because I was afraid to say *I quit* out loud.

That open door was a gift. One day, painting came back to me, for the second and final time.

It was unexpected—I saw a group show of young women photographers at the International Center for Photography, a show that had the startling effect of a hard punch—and then painting blossomed in my chest overnight, like a bruise. When I woke up, feeling the need of it aching beneath the surface of my skin, I made that familiar walk to Pearl and handed over all my savings to Jonah. He smiled and gave me his discount. A good omen. Then I called my latest employer (I was, at that time, the assistant to the assistant of an upscale florist) and quit.

Two weeks later I'd created a rose-gold cataclysm that was nine feet high and eighteen feet wide. In that painting lived an expression of the pink hair on my head and what it cost me over the years. I calculated the time and money spent on my hair (my time being valued at $25.00 per hour) and arrived at a figure of $31,492.00, give or take a thousand. That painting was the pain of earning the money to begin with; the egoistic joy it brought me to spend it on such a temporary adjustment; the time wasted getting my hair yanked and cut and painted and blown out; and the burning on my scalp each and every time it was double-processed back into the trademark pink-champagne cloud that I've worn since my teens in some form or another. A name fell out of my mouth. One year and five more paintings later, I had a show, *Accounting for Taste*, at Parker Projects, a respectable gallery in Chelsea, and my career found its first real foothold.

The first piece of mine to land in a real collection was *31,492*

(Hair Money). Soon after, *7,067 (Tampons and Ruined Underwear Money)*; *6,413 (Fingernail Money)*; *278,388 (Teeth Money)*; *4,875 (Ripping Hair Out of My Cunt Money)*; and *7,049 (Bra Money)* were getting packed up and shipped out, too. Parker sold them all. I got 50 percent. Parker's tax man showed me how to keep most of it. Everything went back into my work.

I had stumbled, if unwittingly, onto one of the art world's invisible rules: Make something people can talk about. According to Claymont Parker, in my case, that meant two specific things: how detailed the paintings were, and the personal nature of the titles. "People are so bored of this masculine disaffected-artist-assistant-factory bullshit," he said. "You're part of a new wave of female artists whose work is *personal*. These paintings are very clearly the product of a young woman alone in a studio. So—*intimate*. Like Carey Logan's sculptures." Armed by his certainty and flattered by his comparison, I barreled forward.

For the next three years, I painted during the week and worked weekends at the restaurant with Cady. Ostensibly these paintings would be my next show, but I was dissatisfied, not for any particular reason other than *The work was not worth my satisfaction*, and so I painted over them, again, and again, and again. The canvases grew heavier—a lot heavier—and I had to support the canvas substrate with plywood to stop it from sagging. The thicker and nastier they became, the more I loved them—yet they were still not done. During that time, Cady and Atticus both moved out; Cady got a Hunter studio (back when you could enroll and keep your studio for a decade), and Atticus moved to the Catskills with his boyfriend. I took over the lease and knocked down all the drywall and started to feel like a real artist—one who could afford all the rent for a space that I actually needed.

I became an adult. For the first time in my life, I *wanted* to socialize. I went to more shows; I saw more work. I applied for a passport and traveled, to Venice and Miami and Switzerland and Berlin and London and even Paris, where my very own left hand was displayed inside a vitrine at the Palais de Tokyo—the skin loose and shifting—in Carey Logan's *72 HOURS* installation. She'd used at least one of the same molds from *THE BURIAL PROJECT*; I could tell it was mine from the fingernails, from their hard, geometric ridges. *I was in a museum*, I told myself, *even if nobody knew about it.* Spurred to action, I went on three residencies, where I made a dozen one-off paintings on commission purely to make money, mostly landscapes, though they were still abstract. I dated, albeit lightly and without consequence. And at last, I was invited to parties that the members of Pine City attended—sure, either they were leaving at the moment I was arriving or vice versa—but I was getting closer. I was working toward stature.

As I changed, so did Carey. She stopped making sculptures and turned to an earnest revival of '70s performance art, using her own body as her primary medium. She slept in a cage, she ate speed until she was passing blood, she choked down hot dogs and smelled the breaths of strangers, all on public display at Eliot&Sprain. Yet, aggressive as they were, the performances completely lacked the magic and power of her sculpture. I could not figure out what she was doing, or why she was doing it, and neither could anybody else. When asked by the *Times* why she changed, she only said, "Because I want to express myself." That was it. It was a meaningless explanation. I promised myself that the next time I saw her at a party, I would introduce myself. I finally had enough of an identity to hold a conversation.

Still: The paintings for my supposed third show languished, growing thicker, and stranger, but never complete.

Then—Carey Logan committed suicide.

The obituary, "Carey Logan, Artist Known for Death Practice, Dies at 37," reported that in the thirteen years since her show on Grand Street, the "dirty-blond Wednesday Addams for the Marfa set" had exhibited at the Venice Biennale as well as the Basel and Frieze fairs; she'd held solo shows at the Kiasma in Helsinki, the mumok in Vienna, and the Palais de Tokyo in Paris. A slideshow of her extremely prolific career showed dozens of sculptures identical to corpses; a marble pyramid engraved as her own gravestone; the tomblike interiors of a house; and her more recent performance work.

Her early life was summarized as briefly as always: A native of Wappingers Falls, New York, Carey Logan had no formal training. An unnamed source referred to a "long-term mental illness" leading to her suicide. Tyler was quoted: "We have been devastated," he said, "by the loss of Carey Magnolia Logan, who was the heart and soul of Pine City."

My immediate thought was: *So soon? Before I truly knew you? How could you go—how could you leave me behind?*

I felt, deeply and urgently, *betrayed*. There were only so many successful female artists who were my age, and even fewer tiny little women making big work, *sincere* work, in a time when everyone else was telling a long joke. Carey was supposed to stay ahead of me. To lead the way. She wasn't supposed to quit. It was, quite honestly, the last thing I expected, even though to the rest of the world it seemed reasonable that a woman whose artistic career focused on death would commit suicide.

Yet what I saw was that Carey had, for reasons that were not clear to me, given up on her compulsive behaviors and traded them for something that broke her in two.

In the weekend magazine they printed more photographs, under the headline "Perpetual Persephone: Carey Logan at Home in Pine City." Greasy-haired, with purple shadows under her eyes, she held a bottle of gin in one hand and the bow handle of a canoe with the other on the shores of a black lake. In the next photo, in a white dress, embroidered so heavily with flowers it looked almost as though she'd been dipped in a cartoon field, she smeared handfuls of ripe fruit over the tattooed skin of a bearded Tyler Savage. After that, she lay on a table, her clothing and skin coated in honey and crawling with clouds of bees, while Jes, Jack, Marlin, and Tyler stood behind her in white beekeeper suits. The last image showed her staring directly into the camera. It was painful to look at. I suppose that's what made her special.

We were supposed to be something to each other, I thought, looking at it. *You said I was exactly like you. You were supposed to show me how to do this. You made it.*

But she was gone.

And so—I was more alone in the world than ever.

Creatively, Carey's suicide opened up the floodgates. The paintings that had smoldered in my studio for three years, now nearly half a foot deep in paint, were finished inside of six months. There were eight of them, all of them at least fourteen feet across and ten feet high. I titled the show *The Distance Between Our Moral Imaginations*. It sold out opening week.

Shortly thereafter, riding high on my own momentum, I changed galleries from (reputable but not sterling) Parker Projects to the fully blue-chip Galerie Milot, a big-dick New York / London / Paris / Hong Kong / Rio ballbuster of a gallery helmed by an actual member of the French aristocracy. It wasn't the Venice Biennale, and it wasn't a solo show at the Palais de Tokyo, but it was the first brass ring I would need to follow the remaining four members of Pine City to the top.

So after that—after over a decade of working and waiting and working and waiting—you'll forgive me for feeling after *The Distance Between Our Moral Imaginations* as though I'd made it. I paid my student loans in full, which felt even better than I'd anticipated, and bought some extremely expensive equipment—a hydraulic lift and scaffold that allowed me to work horizontally—and got into high-end materials, imported small-batch milled pigments and exotic ingredients like shark urine and uncut rubies. For the first time in my life, I had buckets of money, and I put every cent into *Rich Ugly Old Maids*, the show that I was making for Milot.

I spent the next two years on seven paintings: *Humility*, *Obedience*, *Chastity*, *Modesty*, *Temperance*, *Purity*, and *Prudence*. Scheduled to be shipped to the flagship gallery in Paris in three and a half months, they were beautiful and enormous and easily the best things I'd ever made. Loosely based on the seven saintly virtues, they were the paintings that graduated me from recovering Catholic no-collar girl painter into independent adult artist. They were an exorcism of the words that named them, from the guilt that had dogged me through years of wondering how I was supposed to be a person who pursued only her own interests, who was never aligned, who was never part of a family, who did not wake up every day ashamed of herself for being childless and alone. I was not pure of heart, chaste of body, obedient to authority, humble before others, prudent in my actions, temperate in my behavior, or modest in my appearance—and I no longer felt bad about it. I was free from the burden of being only a girl. I had become an old maid, a woman of my own, a master of my medium. They were my crowning glory.

And all seven of them were in my loft on the day it burned to the ground.

2011

Chapter Two

Here is exactly how it happened. It was the middle of May. I was thirty-four. I still lived on Dutch Street, in that same floor-through loft where I had once shoved seven hundred dollars into Cady's palms, where I slept on a king-size mattress on the floor and my living room was made of thrift-store 1970s furniture, dark wood upholstered in gaudy plaids that you could only sink into. I'd never left, because it was big and it was cheap and it was in Manhattan. Though it was mostly illegal, and I thought I might die there—a fifty-fifty shot between old age and becoming the victim of a serial killer—I was fine with either outcome because I didn't want or need any other kind of place to live. The loft was my home, my work space, my everything. It was my whole world.

A professional studio is a beautiful thing and mine was no exception. There were custom shelves and painted pegboards, handmade hooks and clamps, razor-edged palette knives and French enamel trays looped on vegetable-dyed leather. Everything—my awls, my nail gun, my saws, my torches—had been sorted, labeled, and etched with my initials. Handmade boxes (thick cardboard and white masking tape seams) held my history, the archive of my thirty-four years on earth, a lifetime of papers and photographs and additional miscellany from each and every painting I'd ever made. Against the wall in the back were my supplies of propane, ether, turpentine, resin, liquid acrylic, vinegar, ammonia, and so forth— all those wonderful industrial blue and red and orange canisters adjacent to hanging rolls of canvas, paper, linen, stacks of hardwood and plywood, and bags of powdered fiberglass.

I woke up to a bad smell. It was a bouquet of burning rubber, but I didn't think anything of it because 11 Dutch Street had nine floors with nine artists and we were constantly doing things like running currents through wires to make an improvised hot knife, or melting resin in a recycled can on a Sterno burner, or etching copper with nitric acid, or whatever else dumb toxic thing we felt the urge to do. We did wear masks much of the time, but let's face it, fumes travel. On the top floor, I smelled *all* of it.

The morning of the bad smell, I got dressed as best I could, throwing a scarf over my rat's nest of curls and a black romper over a tattered red bikini (*weeks* beyond laundry day). I shoved my socked feet into a pair of wooden clogs and grabbed my canvas backpack, which contained my wallet, my paint-coated cellphone, a small Canon camera covered in oily fingerprints, and my notebook. (These details are important because they became my only possessions a few short hours later.) After locking up, I thumped hard on my prime suspect's door: Ruby, the sculptor who lived one floor below me, was a habitual Styrofoam melter and decade-long abuser of my airspace.

I banged four times and yelled, "RUBY, YOU'RE KILLING US BOTH," for what felt like the thousandth time in my life. Without waiting for her to reply—*it's not like today was the day she was going to change*—I skipped down the rest of the stairs and made my way north, to Pearl, where Jonah had a new delivery of R&F oil sticks. I snapped photographs of colors and textures that caught my eye as I walked: the dun-gray feathers of a dead pigeon, wedged into the waffle grid of a manhole cover. The no-longer-red sneakers on a pair of feet sticking out from beneath a pile of plastic bags and twine on Duane. The hangers left behind in an empty Baby Gap.

At Pearl, I had first dibs on colors, picking out moss and sap green, pale scarlet—fat, cigar-tube rolls, soft, delicious, pure potential. Jonah smiled at me, gave me his discount, asked about my day; our usual routine. Then I bought a coffee, an egg sandwich, and a carton of orange juice from a bodega and headed back home.

It was a day like any other.

I thought that regular day would be spent finishing a painting called *Prudence*—pouring a bucket of glowing resin across her barbaric landscape of grease and detritus, before melting one of my new oil sticks into a puddle using a propane torch from the restaurant depot on Bowery. My mind was already there, up in my studio, as I made my way down Dutch, though I did notice that there were, for some reason, a *lot* of people on my block, and they slowed me down, but I was still thinking about my painting, about what was next. When I arrived at my front door, there was a big guy in a sexy costume blocking my entry. Confetti fell down around him like little paper snowflakes. *Doro must be having a party*, I thought.

"Excuse me," I said to the muscleman in the very realistic fireman's costume blocking the door, in that absentminded city way, *Please move, I am a person too.*

"You can't go inside, miss," he said, all rough around the edges.

"I live here," I said, exasperated, pointing to my name on the buzzer. "Ninth floor."

"Number nine?" he asked. "We've been looking for you."

It was then that I realized his "costume" was in fact very durable and covered in scuff marks—not from being ripped off in a million living rooms, but because, of course, it was real. Everything came into focus at once: the red fire trucks in the street, the rubber of the firefighters' suits, the smell in the air, the flakes of ash dusting the shoulders of his jacket. Smoke poured out the top of my building. My fellow tenants were standing across the street, drinking coffee, shaking their heads. Ruby, red-faced and sullen, was wrapped in a blanket, talking to a blonde with a clipboard.

"What?"

"But."

"How."

"When?"

These were the words that fell out of my mouth. I don't know if the fireman replied. I wore somebody else's skin and none of it was right. My vision narrowed into a tunnel: I could only see the door beyond him and I wanted to get through it. I dropped my bag and felt a hand on my shoulder. The hand squeezed and pulled me away.

"Thank God," Doro said, hugging my inert, alternate-timeline body. "I didn't know where you were. It happened this morning. Ruby had an electrical short. She was asleep. You banged on the door and woke her up. Oh, honey, I'm so glad you're okay."

"Is everybody okay?"

"Yes. Joey looked in your place but you weren't there. We tried, honey, but we couldn't stop it."

"What?"

"It went up, honey. Ruby's place, and your place."

"What?"

"Your apartment burned down. Or *up*, I guess. The fire was on eight and nine."

"What?"

"I know. It's terrible."

"What?"

"*What*, lady?" the firefighter said, exasperated, hands gloveless and turned to the sky. Cooled shavings from the campfire of my home, delicate and ephemeral, fell from the air and dissolved into dirt in his palm. I opened my hand and caught them greedily, smearing the ashes into the crevices of my own reddened fingers.

"What?" I blinked at Doro. She gazed up at me with her moony eyes, concern and pity spilling from every wrinkle of her owly old-lady face. I stared back, hard and unblinking, not understanding. I had five years left on the lease, I kept thinking. Five more years.

How could my loft be gone?

The firemen said that the paintings themselves didn't *burn*, not exactly.

The fire started below, inside the hundred-year-old plaster walls, from an electrical surge. Ruby's air conditioner plugged into the same ragged socket as her open-current hot knife and her soldering iron, both of which were left on overnight. When the current surged, sparks hit the ancient newspapers used as insulation between the plaster and the stone. The walls smoldered from the inside, burning their way out and up. When the fire reached my materials—all those gases and solvents placed adjacent to canvas and wood—it exploded, then seared so hot that the concrete floor cracked underneath. They think the paintings were simply blown apart. "Burning" was irrelevant, though my books, closest to the door, were sparked by a glowing box of drawing charcoal and they became the ashes that had floated into my hands like so many snowflakes.

Pieces of my paintings were found embedded inside the apartments across the street and permanently fused to the windshields of the trucks and cars parked down our block. The rocks and gravel rooted inside *Prudence* actually went through my skylights and broke a pair of French doors in a condo two stories up, though two of *Prudence*'s four panels landed unharmed on my neighbor's roof. *Temperance* was straight-up melted into the concrete cracks, a massive, blood-red pile of scorched rubies and carmine dust. *Obedience,* the first in the series, crated at the back of the stack, remained relatively intact—except for the part where the painting transferred itself to the crate in front and then the fiberglass substrate burned away and incinerated most of the paint, leaving the backside of a

mask. The uncrated *Humility*, *Modesty*, *Chastity*, and *Purity* all went
out my windows and into the street and onto cars and buildings
and lampposts and sewer grates and asphalt.

Someone gave me a debit card from the Red Cross with four
hundred dollars on it and a free bottle of water. I took as many
photos as I could of the building's exterior and the scattered pieces
of paintings, then hailed a cab. The cabbie asked how my day was.
I told him that my apartment burned down. He turned off the meter and drove uptown without saying another word. When we got
to 41st and Dyer I tried to give him a twenty, but he waved it away.

I don't remember getting upstairs, but somehow I did, collapsing
on the tweed sofa in Cady's studio. She held out a bottle of bourbon, and I fell into it, waiting to feel drunk. I never did, not even
when it was empty. I was exposed, pulled apart, a ragged bundle
of threads sailing through the air onto a condo balcony. Yet—no
matter how much I drank—I never felt anything.

The *New York Times* interviewed me about the explosion two
days later. "Abstraction has long felt like an afterthought," said
the image caption, "but paintings like *Tomato Tomato*, with their
feminine devotion to detail, are meticulous as a Vermeer. They
make evident the time spent on their creation, but it doesn't feel
like a chore." The reporter also described my previous work as
"wry," "spatially overwhelming," and "viscerally incursive." The
Times critic, when asked for a quote, helpfully noted that they
were impressed that a woman "could so successfully handle the XL
format," since it is "traditionally the domain of men." The accom-
panying photograph—in which I climbed, at the photographer's
urging, a scaffold to reach *Prudence*'s two unharmed panels—made
me look tough. Though it was meant to be flattering, I felt con-
descended to and boxed in. Overall it presented me as an imitation
of hypermasculine abstractionists—lady Pollock, lady Rothko, lady
de Kooning, my use of a bygone movement updated and validated
by my gender and youth—instead of a person unto myself.

Though I had renter's insurance, it turned out that they didn't have to pay if the apartment wasn't technically legal, which it was not. The building was zoned for commercial use only, which I violated by living there.

We weren't allowed in for a week. During that time the firefighters went back with a chemical bath and doused the entire space to dampen any possibility of further damage, so when I did get in, it was not what I expected. In the movies a domestic fire is always an ash pile, the end of a campfire, a ragged-edged photo of your wife clutching a golden retriever peeking out from the wreckage. But apartment fires don't actually burn that way — not if someone manages to put them out.

I walked into two soggy feet of swampy jetsam, made from the wall plaster and the more modern insulation in the ceiling, puffed up to a shredded marshmallow by the chemical tide. My scaffold and hydraulic lift were dented and bent into uselessness, their legs and posts buckled beneath them like an animal tumbling to the ground the moment after being shot. Beneath the jetsam lay everything else, including twenty or so unfinished paintings that were once stacked next to the sofa. Boiled into a seamless mass, the paintings resembled what you get when you heat crayons together on the stove. Even my laptop was melted into a silver disk.

I spent nine hours in there trying to piece together some semblance of who I had been, but it was ruined—all of it. Even the folder with my birth certificate, kept in an (unlocked) vintage safe by the door, had soaked in the chemical bath for so long that it was blank—the embossed STATE OF FLORIDA was intact but my name was wiped out. Same with my passport, bleached into emptiness. In the end I walked away with a bag of ghostly, rotten photographs, a strangely unharmed pink-and-green silk varsity jacket, my camera, notebook, cellphone, and the stone totem that my father's colleagues from the pipeline sent me when he died. My whole life fit in my backpack.

But the biggest problem was one of my own making. My new gallerist, that brass ring, Jacqueline Milot, called and asked if the paintings had exploded. *Because,* she said, *you're, forgive the expression, so hot. I've had dozens of calls. Everybody is so excited about the explosion. The article! I mean, you can't buy that press, I've tried many times. So, I am asking: Please tell me you had my* Rich Ugly Old Maids *in storage. I know we paid for some of them to be crated, the ones that already sold. That building was such a hazard . . . and you know, even if I want to, which I do* not—*I cannot sell hasty remakes. People would think that was sloppy, especially for an unproven young woman, no matter how talented you are. Female painters are the bargain of the century, I keep telling everyone, but a bargain is an Hermès scarf on sale, you know? It must not look like the price. I hope you had them in climate-controlled storage, like we discussed.* (We had not discussed this.) *Because this show looks like it is going to sell out. If it goes, I can sign you for life.*

Yes, I repeated obediently, staring at my notebook.

Yes, I had them in storage. (In a way, I did. At the Academy they taught us to keep detailed records of each and every project, and my notebook held the recipes for every *Rich Ugly Old Maid.*)

Only *Prudence* blew up.

The other six were fine.

Could I have an extra month or two?

No no no no no, she said, *we've already placed the ad buys. We went all out. We'll delay delivery for varnish if we have to. Can you remake* Prudence *in the next few months? That will have to be okay. We'll keep that our little secret. That's not in any of the ads, right? No. No. And nobody has bought that one yet. That's good. Because if I have to change the advertising you'll be on the hook for the marketing we've already done. You know that, I'm sure. It's in our agreement.*

Okay, I told her.

No problem.

And that is how I found myself committing fraud.

The day after my call with Jacqueline, I contacted every semi-reputable residency in America. Full of a manic certainty that I could make seven huge paintings in three months and that everything I'd worked for, everything I'd achieved, wouldn't be for nothing—*I hadn't submitted the wall text, no one knew what was supposed to be in the paintings, Jacqueline sold some already but only based on photographs, and it's not like she'd paid me yet, I only got paid on delivery, I didn't need to do anything other than copy myself, I was certainly allowed to sell whatever paintings I wanted, there was nothing wrong with it so long as I got paid in the end*—I dialed number after number and pleaded my case. The pinnacle of my creative career required pulling off an enormous, complex, physically laborious hoax, but I didn't question whether or not it was possible; I fixated only on getting it arranged. *All I needed was a space, and I could make everything right.*

But it didn't work. "We're full. Try us next summer!" they all proclaimed. Voice after voice shot me down with brightly colored arrows: *No, No, No, but next year we'd love to.*

"Your CV is *very* impressive. Just need to *follow those deadlines,*" the voices chirped.

I emailed almost every artist I'd ever met. They were either staying put for the summer—"DYING for the studio time"—or had already sublet their places while they traveled, and every response I got with a frowny face at the bottom made me want to throw Cady's computer out the window.

We called our closest friends over for an emergency meeting. (Mostly they were Cady's friends, and therefore my longtime, albeit warm, acquaintances.)

"We need a plan," Cady yelled over the din of box wine and records. Everyone knew I had to remake one painting. Nobody—not even Cady—knew it was seven.

"Why are you asking us?" Atticus said, the boyfriend and house in the Catskills long since forgotten. "I live in a shipping container in Corona Park. I can't solve your problems, baby."

"You know I still live with my parents," our friend Lola said. Everyone threw popcorn at her. "You can sleep in my sister's room if you want. But she has sleep apnea."

"Go back to the Academy and squat. Take a studio." Agnes was being sincere.

"Break into a warehouse in Trenton. There's a million." So was Jonny.

The room broke into an argumentative din. Our friends didn't know what to do. None of us had truly *made it* yet—I was the furthest along—and no one had the slightest room for variation along the tightrope of their financially precarious lives.

"We need to be talking to rich people," Jimmy Daltry yelled. "What the fuck is going on tonight? Who has a fancy invitation we can give to our favorite girl painter?"

"Brilliant idea," Cady said, pawing at a stack of mail. "There has to be something."

"HOLD ON," Agnes cried out, dumping her satchel upside down on the floor.

One hour later, wearing a blush-colored dress of Cady's with my pink hair in a tight ponytail and my feet strapped into a pair of her blocky wooden sandals, I was ushered out the door and put in a cab to Chelsea.

"I'll give you a hundred bucks if you cry *right now*," Cady said quietly, holding open the car door. "It's not healthy to keep all that inside. It's going to come out sooner or later."

"You'll give me a hundred bucks anyway," I said, and she smiled and rolled her eyes and handed me a roll of twenties, bound with a rubber band.

"Spend it on drugs," she insisted. "Do them with someone who can help you."

Fifteen minutes later, I was at a sit-down dinner for someone I'd never heard of. They were serving turtle soup, apparently some kind of social protest except there we were eating turtles, and nobody seemed to care that I was sitting at Agnes's embossed place card, because the people sitting next to me had read about my "situation" in the paper, which they mentioned loudly and frequently, though no one seemed to understand or care that it meant I was *actually* broke and *actually* homeless. Instead they seemed excited by it, in that disaster pornography way, the way their eyes gleamed when they said, HOW ARE YOU? YOU MUST BE *SO* UP-SET. And I knew in their eyes they would go home to their big bedrooms and whisper to each other, across the genteel wrinkles of their fine sheets, *We are so lucky.*

"What an *opportunity* for you, though," some drunk old crank in a shiny teal dress told me. "A real life change. *Cleansing.* I felt that way about my divorce. The Buddha teaches us to leave the past behind. Lucky that your old work is gone. You can be a new person."

"I don't want to be a new person," I told her.

"That's the stress talking," she said—and then she bought a fifty-thousand-dollar giant tortoise shell and all I could do was picture her wearing it. Before she could say anything else, a well-preserved man with perfectly round glasses and pale hair stepped into the inches between us, elbowing me out of the way until I got the hint and stepped backward.

"There's someone I want you to meet," he told Tortoise. "A phenomenal artist. You simply *must.*" Then he took her by the wrist and stepped back into me again, and I smacked into the nearest wall. When he turned again I ducked, narrowly avoiding a shoulder to the face.

The pale-haired man marched her across the room. Tortoise gave me a halfhearted, slightly embarrassed little wave goodbye.

He never even glanced in my direction.

I was used to it. Art has a way of putting everyone at their most transactional. I'm invisible until someone calculates my value. I drank heavily that night, primarily to cushion the anxiety generated by everyone's behavior, and also to force myself to stay at the party and talk to people in the hope that something would come of it.

It paid off.

At some point during drink number six, I found myself talking to Susan Bricklings-Young, wiry descendant of the Peabody sugar dynasty and one of my favorite elder exemplars in the human-being-category of "robust New England alcoholic rich person."

"You ought to go *upstate*," she drawled in her low voice—Katharine Hepburn on lithium. "What's that place? That place that used to be called Granger's—you know, it was one of those *terrific* places where you could come for the summer and *dawnce*—it was *restricted*, terrible, but true. What *is it called*?"

Something twitched in my brain, an errant spark trailing the metal tines of a plug from an unsafe wall outlet, but it didn't connect. I shrugged.

"This is going to kill me. Oh, what is it called? I should know. Mother and Father simply ah-dored it up there when I was a gurl. It was the *country*. Mostly *fahr-ms* and *fah-rests*. And—"

While she yammered away, waxing nostalgic about the time before black people could vote, I saw young Susan in Connecticut, petting a borzoi in a room full of peeling yellow silk wallpaper. Surrounded by Radcliffe tennis trophies and lace-sleeved ball gowns, she picked up the phone and accepted an invitation to a restricted hotel as though it were nothing. I wondered how many rifles she owned. *A lot*, I guessed.

"And then those *mahrvelous* artists bought it and gave it that boring name," she finished, effortlessly depositing her empty glass on a tray with her right hand while another ice-filled tumbler of vodka appeared in her left. "What is it *called*? I buy reams of Marlin's work every *yeahr* and I still can't remember. Dammit, I'm old."

Marlin. The plug slammed back into the outlet.

"Pine City," I told her. "They're called Pine City."

"*That's* it," she said, her bony fingers rising to her temples, a vein in her forehead gently deflating. "Thank you. I would have *died* if I'd forgotten."

"What do you know about the application process?" I heard myself asking, liquor burning in my esophagus, adrenaline shooting through my spine, stars in my eyes.

"There's no process, it's completely private," she said, shaking her head. "It's invitation only."

"Would you call for me? I'm dying, Susan. I need space, like, yesterday. Everywhere else is full."

"Hmm," she said, peering at me. "What do I get?"

"What do you want?" Anything—I would have given her anything.

"A painting," she said. "I want a discount on a painting." Though she'd never come to one of my shows, I wasn't surprised. Susan could turn around and sell it again in five years for twice the price; whether she liked my work or not, I made paintings, and paintings were things that you could stock and sell short.

"I'll ask. Hold on."

I pulled out my phone and texted Jacqueline. Four a.m. in Paris. She was out at a restaurant, still, and wrote back right away, and five minutes later we'd agreed that Susan Bricklings-Young would be the proud new owner of *Obedience*, the one on the poster for *Rich Ugly Old Maids*, for a 20 percent discount that would come directly out of my cut. (That hurt. My appetite for money at that point was monstrous. I was in voracious desire—not to keep—to *spend*. I wanted to melt emeralds into a plastic that covered all the walls and all the ceilings, so we could live inside them; I wanted to paint a twenty-foot-high waterfall in facets of hard-shine aluminum so that inches away you felt terribly afraid that the painting itself would cut you open. I wanted to drink every color so I could piss rainbows. I could never, ever go back to a different kind of life.) So I told Jacqueline it was worth it and when she said, in a blithe, indifferent way, *Whatever, c'est your vie, cherie*, I felt like even more of a fraud.

When I finished texting, Susan handed me a fresh drink and told me she'd get me to Pine City. We clinked glasses.

"You look like *her*, you know," Susan said, squinting drunkenly.

"Like who?"

Susan twitched. "You know—the one who drowned. The morbid one. There's something about your silhouette. It's rather uncanny."

"Where *did* she drown?" I asked.

"Up there." Her eyes darted from side to side, and then she leaned in. "She *filled her boots with cement* and walked into the lake." She waited for my reaction.

"By herself?"

"That's what they say. She was always moody. Nervous, if you know what I mean. Something behind the eyes. Anxious."

I nearly snapped that everyone raised without a safety net was nervous behind the eyes—that we did not have the room to be anything else—that people like Susan made us naturally nervous. "Why do you think she did it?" I asked instead.

"Oh, she was always strange...," Susan said, waving her arms dramatically. "Especially at the end. Those things she did were so...*unbecoming* of an *ahr-tist* of her stature. I'll never understand it. I have several of the sculptures, you know, in my collection. She used to be rational. But then—" The lines on her face deepened. Her liver-spotted hands, coated in gemstones and lacquered with polish, wrapped themselves atop my shoulders. She yanked me toward her. "*Something happened* to that girl," she insisted in a low voice. "Something...*bad.*"

"What do you mean?" I breathed. She gripped harder. One of her many rings cut into the skin of my neck, but I didn't care.

"She wouldn't listen to reason. She became so...difficult," Susan whispered. "I knew it was all wrong. And eventually, so did she." She nodded wisely.

"*What* was wrong?" I asked.

"The *performances*," Susan said. "That poor man," she whispered salaciously. "He was so very in love with her. It was all so upsetting."

"Tyler?"

Her eyes flickered. I couldn't tell if it was from alcohol or annoy-
ance that I actually knew something or both. "Mmm," she said. "Not
that *she* cared. Nervous *gu-hl* like that. Never saw what she had."

Before I could squeeze anything else out of the gin-dampened
sponge that was Susan's brain, the well-preserved man who had
shoved me into the wall earlier reappeared, a demon whispering in
her ear. "There's someone very important I want you to meet," he
said, loudly enough for me to hear. Then he guided Susan forward,
toward *my* body, as though it were an open space.

This time I stepped out of the way.

Thoughts of Pine City overwhelmed me on the walk home, my
brain obsessively running Susan's comments on a loop. *Nervous girl.*
Something bad. That poor man.

I imagined myself lying on the grass, bees crawling across my
skin, surrounded by Tyler, Jes, Marlin, and Jack as we discussed the
truth about ourselves and our work. I would talk about how hard
it was, sometimes, and how I never seemed to be able to predict
what would happen next. *Well*, one of them would say, *you know
what happened to Carey, right?*

No, I would say. *Tell me.* And then—then I would know how it
was all supposed to play out. I would learn what Carey did wrong,
and I would take care never to do the same.

By the time I stumbled into Cady's studio I was too worked up
to sleep. The feeling was one part the night before Christmas—
because I was nineteen again, Pine City was the most exclusive
party on earth, and I was about to be invited—and three parts nervous terror. As I lay on the futon, staring at the wires threading
across the ceiling, I had the sudden and very particular feeling that
everything was about to change. My stomach sank down to my
hips, my knuckles buzzed, and time paused. Everything was going
to change.

That's when I recalled what needed to be done. *I had to make seven paintings in three months in total secrecy.* All it would take was one phone call—or one photograph.

Time came right back, rushing past me so quickly I couldn't catch it. No—I said aloud—no. Yet—I had to do it. *It's simple*, I told myself: *Don't piss anyone off. You'll make your work, and maybe they'll notice you're making a lot of it, but nobody is going to bother you. It's an abandoned hotel, for Pete's sake. There's room enough for everyone.* If I could pull this off anywhere, Pine City was the place. *It'd be fine.*

The next morning, when the phone rang, my heart skipped a beat.

"You're in," Susan said simply. "Be there Monday. Someone will show you around. My boy will send directions."

She hung up.

I walked to a tire place in Chinatown known for their side business in used and abused automobiles, pulled out a credit card, bought a dented red Nissan pickup truck for seven hundred bucks, and went shopping.

Prudence

Chapter Three

Thirty-four, single, homeless, the pilot light of my talent flickering under pressure, I left Manhattan for good exactly three days later.

The truck bed was piled high with materials, lovingly tarped and bungeed. I was extra-careful with it, checking my mirrors over and over, taking turns slowly, missing lights. As I was about to coast onto the West Side Highway, a man in a windbreaker flagged me down. I eased to a stop behind his white van, collapsed inside the right-hand turn lane.

"I have a flat," he said, holding up a badge. I rolled down the window and stared at him, unsure of how I was supposed to help. I didn't have the courage to do anything other than scowl.

"My jack split. Everybody else is a gypsy cab." He gestured toward the glossy Lincolns cruising by. "They don't want to help."

It was then that I read the text on his windbreaker: CORONER. His van: NEW YORK STATE.

"You got a tire iron in there or what?"

Mr. Lin had thrown in a brand-new kit, just in case, and so I held up a finger and rooted around under the seat until I found it. While the man in the windbreaker shimmied under his van, spun the lugs, pulled the tire, and popped on a donut, I wondered if there was a body inside the van, whether the body was on ice or in a plastic bag or what. Bodies, plural, maybe. *Were they in a box freezer? Were they stacked on special body-size shelves? Were they strapped to gurneys in some kind of ambulance pantomime?* But I didn't ask, and he didn't tell; the man in the windbreaker simply thanked me, returned the kit, and drove off.

Finally: I hit the gas and lurched forward. I must have noticed other things as I drove, but my enduring memory of leaving Manhattan will always be that coroner's van and the bodies that I presumed were inside it.

I remember thinking at the time that I was lucky to get out alive.

The rushing current of the dawning traffic pushed me up the Henry Hudson and over the tiny bridge at Spuyten Duyvil, to the Bronx, the Saw Mill, and eventually onto the Taconic State Parkway, the gently sloping four-lane country highway that stretches along the state's borders with Connecticut and Massachusetts. I drove slowly, with the windows down, the breezes lifting my hair one way and another, under the stone bridges, switching on my hazards at the short merges, careful of my cargo.

The first part of the drive was not unfamiliar. My first years in the Northeast were spent seventy miles north of the city, at the Academy. There I learned the basics of painting—color studies, painting from life, materiality—and the building blocks of my own taste. The faculty encouraged us to despise figuration (for its mistaken glorification of the corporeal; for its bloodstained history as a colonialist relic; and finally, most important, for its intellectual limitations) and to worship the visceral joy of abstract expression; the clean pseudo-godliness of minimalism; the intellectual detachment of the early conceptualists; and the raw passion of performance art. I was an eager student, swallowing it all whole inside a perpetually empty stomach, and got a taste for color.

At the Academy, my earliest heroes—Joan Mitchell, Helen Frankenthaler, Robert Motherwell, Mark Rothko, and Grace Hartigan—were put on the shelf to make room for those they influenced: Morris Louis, Kenneth Noland, Ellsworth Kelly, Sam Francis, and Agnes Martin, whom I came to worship with a fever. By junior year, I could recite "The Untroubled Mind," her 1972 manifesto-slash-prose-poem, by heart, and I fantasized about making a pilgrimage to her adobe house in New Mexico. I longed to create work that lived as Martin's did—the manifested edge of an exhale, abstract expressionism light enough to be mistaken for minimalism. I thought that cusp was where I belonged. (I wasn't remotely like Martin, in the end, but that didn't stop me from trying.)

It began with *Ohne Titel*, my first postgraduate show. Ten untitled paintings. They were large-ish—six feet high, eight feet wide, each about the size of five doors set in a row—blank, unblemished, still pools of color, varnished with a dozen layers so that they shone with a lacquered gloss. When exhibited together, they were very clearly different shades of green. In fact they were an exact gradient shift from the green on the inside of a flower stem when you cut it, to the green of antique uranium glass, a green that is almost chartreuse, but not quite. However—alone? One by one? Nothing but large green rectangles—to any eye, the passé retreads of someone recently graduated from art school. Together, as I intended, they *were* something *new*—they were colossal—but in my youth and naïveté, I disregarded how easily and naturally they could, *would*, be broken, separated.

Those paintings, and my failure to maintain them as a unit, hurt me viciously. Even now—thinking about them—there's an ache. The two following shows had their own successes and heartbreaks, too, despite the fact that they sold, and each one brought up its own twinges of *something*. Yet during the past week, any time I tried to think about my *Rich Ugly Old Maids*, which were so beautiful, and of which I'd been so proud—I felt...nothing. It was so odd.

I told myself as I drove that it was shock, panic, and productivity at work: Maybe, if I took a second to feel anything about this loss, I wouldn't be able to finish their impostors. If I took the time to measure the distance of the fall, I'd never jump. I didn't have time to think. I had to *do*. Maybe my brain, against all odds, was protecting itself. That wasn't its historic strength—but maybe I'd grown smarter. Maybe I'd grown up—was that what this numbness meant?

I hoped so.

Pine City was not an actual city, but rather a derelict upstate summer resort turned private retreat by the charismatic young achievers who graduated from the Academy two years before my arrival as a freshman. Pine City (the group) founded Pine City (the place) when they were twenty-eight and I was twenty-two, moving upstate shortly after I arrived in the city, naming it after themselves and defining it as the last *real* artist-owned retreat. Pine City was meant as their personal antidote to the corporatization of patronage that had resulted in otherwise anti-capitalist mid-career artists competing without blinking to be the Swarovski or Louis Vuitton Fellow of the year, the Costco Resident, et cetera. They kept it small, inviting only one or two other artists each season, people who were already their friends, and the myth of the place grew alongside their own.

Though I'd never been there, I had seen dozens of photos of Pine City over the past decade—mostly of their dazzling annual parties, martini-soaked bacchanals set against a backdrop that was half *Dirty Dancing*, half *Twin Peaks*. The black lake with its armada of canoes; feather-haired young people sleeping on the beach, dried mud cracking on their skin; Tyler shooting fireworks into the sky with a grenade launcher; Jack reading Josef Albers in the lush grass of the lawns; Carey smashing a pyramid of empty Krug champagne bottles with a golf club. But those images were old. They all but dried up after Carey committed suicide. Over the last few years, the pictures of parties were replaced with portraits posed against gray curtains as the rest of Pine City marched past forty without her, their work becoming more serious, their attitudes more bourgeois, and their positions more establishment.

My interest in them was *more* than prurient. (It was fueled by prurience, but with selfishness, too.) I was genuinely hopeful that moving into Pine City would inflate my sails with the creative wind I needed in order to remake seven huge paintings. I told myself it was a strategic decision: I could live free of charge for four whole months with a handful of geniuses, walk the same paths that Carey Logan did, be animated by the same winds and leaves and sunlight. I would discover the secrets to her early success, and do exactly that, and I would find out, too, what pushed her to move into performance work—and then *never* do that. I would finish my paintings, and this time, *this time*, I would turn my show profits into something responsible, maybe a farm up here, *Ooh, look at that great farmhouse, maybe like that.* Sure—I was living on credit cards. But I felt certain that it would all work out. And each eighteenth-century manor that I drove past, with peeling columns and chestnut-laden gravel driveways, reminded me of how gracefully my professors at the Academy lived, and tempted me to consider myself their equal.

The perceived cheapness of upstate was, naturally, its defining feature and the ruler by which its opportunities seemed to be measured. Like everybody else in the city I'd had a million conversational daydreams about opening a bed-and-breakfast on a hobby farm ("like the Kaaterskill but closer and without sheep and less expensive but still with fireplaces") or a yoga studio in Beacon ("people are so *chill* up there, you know? And you can walk to stuff. It's like a *real town*"), restoring a Victorian in Hudson to its Depression-era glory ("I feel this . . . *instinctual need* for a clawfoot bathtub"), or even buying a warehouse in Albany with my friends and making a Little Detroit of our very own ("we could have a skate park *in* the building"). However, when the rubber met the road, as a childless, unmarried woman in her thirties, moving upstate on my own had previously appeared only to be a one-way trip to Crazytown: population, me. I'd long worried that artists who moved out of the city were ultimately destined to abandon their work in order to sell mosaic-topped garden tables to other alcoholic kooks, and I was terrified of *real* loneliness, of a life without the noise of the city, its bars, its parties, the comfort of its density and rancor.

But it turned out that when I really thought about it, I wouldn't miss the endless parade of dead-on-arrival relationships, or the hard edges that grew on me like a rash as other people got married and had babies and I stayed single, or how nobody in the city could ever commit to anything, or how easy it was to stay immature forever, or how I hadn't made a new friend in what felt like years, or any other of the same old boring piles of garbage I'd been circling like a vulture for the last decade. The facts on the ground were that the loft had been the only thing keeping me in the city. Without it, I would've been driven out long ago.

I'd missed the boat on New York real estate by at least two decades, if not more, which made this drive inevitable. Today, tomorrow, next year, five years, it didn't matter: Eventually, in every possible version of my life (except for the one where I died alone wrapped in rags on a subway platform), I was destined to get behind the wheel of a truck like this and head up the Taconic.

So—why fight it?

I felt myself detach, for the first time in twelve years, from the city I was leaving behind. Maybe that drunk old tortoise from the party was right, after all.

It was time to be a new person.

Susan's directions indicated I was to exit the Taconic shortly before the tollway to Boston and head north on Route 203, cutting through the rural area southeast of Albany and northeast of Hudson, then turn right on Route 7. After a wide spot in the road whose metal sign read UNION VALE, I was to drive two miles and look out for Granger Walk, the dirt road leading to Pine City.

The driveway was a two-mile gravel rut lined with tall, over-grown poplar trees, hemmed in by a thick, dark-green wall of forest and dotted with Granger's original billboards—DANCING! DINNER NIGHTLY! BOATING! AIR CONDITIONING—upbeat, scripted slogans whose promises were betrayed by their faded and peeling paint. Prickles of excitement, an electric current, raised all my body hair like the hackles of a dog. I let the truck slow to a stop and took it all in—the way the air tasted, the reddish color of the road, the yellowed light dappling the ground. I hoped to remember it forever.

I checked my teeth in the rearview mirror, brushed the crumbs from the SUNY Binghamton tennis t-shirt I'd borrowed from Cady, and flipped my hair to a fresh part.

A few minutes later, I was there. Someone waited at the end of the driveway, in front of a wooden multistory building with a cir-cular drive that had once been the main lodge. Metal posts stuck out from an overhang over the main doors, remnants of the let-ters GRANGER'S. There was no sign reading PINE CITY—no indication that this was anything more than an abandoned resort. They hadn't glossed it up. They hadn't made it for anyone but themselves.

The someone turned. Tyler Savage still looked almost exactly as he had that first time on Grand Street. Divine, untouchable, an athletic, tennis–player kind of body, under an inside-out t-shirt and faded chinos dotted with flecks of paint. He was smoking a cigarette and leaning against an old diesel Mercedes-Benz station wagon, and I thought for a second that I'd never seen anyone lean so perfectly against anything, ever. It was remarkably easy, in that moment, to slide from my independent grown-up identity right back into the body of that nineteen-year-old girl crossing the street, gaping self-consciously at the most beautiful people I'd ever seen in my life.

I pulled around, rolled down my window. A gallery girl sat in his passenger seat, tapping away on a BlackBerry behind a thick drape of hair and silver-dollar Lennon sunglasses.

Tyler was definitely older—his brown hair, dusted with gold from the sun, was clipped short on the sides to contain the encroaching gray and white. Still: *Wow*, I thought. *You're more handsome than ever.* Thankfully, nothing came out of my mouth.

"You're late," he said to me, grinding the cigarette beneath his heel.

"Sorry," I said, tucking my hair behind my ear like a teenager. "I'm—"

But before I could get my hand out the window to introduce myself, he got back into his car and drove down the paved service road, waving for me to follow. His coarseness stung, but I followed as requested, though I took my time, driving extra-slowly past the hard tennis courts, cracked and faded, their nets full of holes; grass ones choked to oblivion by tall, thin weeds; broken picnic tables and sun-battered wooden chairs; an upturned lifeboat roped to a fir tree; then the endless black lake with its huge, shabby restaurant on our right, and several slightly cleaner-looking outbuildings with metal signs that read ARTS AND CRAFTS, SPORTS, and THEATRE embedded into the hill—leftovers from the days when this resort was a kind of summer camp for rich WASPs. A few rusty single-speed bicycles were scattered here and there, and a metal rack near the beach held kayaks and canoes.

I didn't see people anywhere.

This place was supposed to be full of life.

The contrast between the photos I'd mentally hoarded over the years and this empty retreat was surreal.

Had I dreamed it?

We turned down yet another road, into a long cul-de-sac of

small, modernist cabins lining the lakeshore. There were twenty or so, about half an acre of yard around each one. The ones on my right were beachfront. The others nestled into the forest.

Every bungalow was impeccably restored, little sharp-angled modernist dreamscapes, a veritable Donald Judd Disneyland. Some had clean cedar siding, in varying ages and shades of gray. Others were painted exquisite shades of yellow—I spotted mustard seed, marigold, dandelion, pineapple, and ocher. All were trimmed with dark lines, blue-blacks like avocado peel and military navy. Their gutters were copper, and the fixtures on their doors and windows were brass.

Tyler parked on the beachfront side. As I pulled in behind him, the view of my soon-to-be house obstructed by a gigantic, overgrown honeysuckle shrub hanging off a chain-link fence, I felt a surge of happiness. I was certain that the beach houses were better than the forest houses, and I was flattered. Every morning, I could wake up and swim, if I wanted. I could sit on the beach and read every night.

Tyler hopped out and waved for me to follow him. Number nineteen, according to the enameled-metal number pinned to a stake at the edge of the lawn, was the last on the beachside row.

"Ty," the girl purred. "I need to take a call. We have to go."

He turned around and winked at her, then disappeared on the other side of the fence.

I followed, turning past the fence and into the carport, and at first—I was confused.

Dusty blue paint peeled off the rotted wood siding in sheets. There was a hole in the corrugated tin roof large enough to see from the road. The open windows had screens, but they were dotted with rips big enough for birds to fly through. It was a sad, rickety little thing that drooped and sighed. Nobody had taken care of it at all.

It looked exactly how I felt.

It did have a lovely set of bones beneath the scabs of worn-down sparkle linoleum and peeling marbled wallpaper. The front door opened into a small entryway, with hooks for coats and a built-in umbrella stand. To the left was a single-wall Pullman kitchen—the original, from the 1950s—made from a single set of metal cabinets connected to an ancient stovetop and refrigerator, the whole set stamped GENERAL ELECTRIC. The kitchen faced a large living room whose glass-fronted walls looked out upon the lake, and there was a small bedroom off to the left, with an adjacent screened-in sleeping porch.

Still—the toilet was so old that I was afraid the elevated tank would fall off the wall at a pull of the chain. The stall shower was teeny and smelled like rotten eggs. Piles of dirty leaves cluttered the corners; water stains bloomed from the ceiling; and there was absolutely zero furniture. A striped hammock swung limply on the deck, and a cracked brown plastic landline phone was fastened to the wall, but the bungalow was otherwise empty.

Tyler smacked a vintage push-button switch with the butt of his hand, and the two plain bulbs hanging from the ceiling buzzed alight. It was Depression-era depressing. *I must have done something wrong*, I thought to myself. A nagging voice in the back of my heart said, meanly, *It's because you're not as successful as everyone else. They don't think you deserve anything better, because you don't.*

"Thanks so much for hosting me," I said sincerely, my hands pressed against my heart. "It's so generous of you. I'm in a bind, and—"

"Well, Susan buys a lot of Marlin's work, so." He set his jaw and shrugged.

I was bitten by that—chastened—and couldn't imagine a reply. I leaned against the wall, suddenly dizzy, carsick from six hours behind the wheel, and closed my eyes.

"There's furniture in the main building, mattresses and things like that, if you need it."

I was stunned. Of course I needed furniture. *What the hell kind of question was that?*

"You can do whatever you want with your own space," he continued. "Obviously, you're Marlin's guest so you'll need to check with her about anything major." I had no idea what he was talking about, but I took it to understand that he was absolving himself of responsibility for me.

"All our phone numbers are on the map. Marlin should be here in a few days." He anchored a piece of paper, a hand-drawn map, with three spools of tape: one duct, one electrical, one masking. "You'll probably want these for the house, anyway. Put them on my doorstep when you're done."

"Which house is yours?" I asked.

"I'm in the black one," he said gruffly.

"And...where's the studio?"

"Uhhh...you can use the old barn. It's...picturesque. I'm sure you'll figure out how to make it work."

He took the map and scratched an X on it.

"There," he said, pointing to the X and lighting another cigarette. "That's the barn. Fill out the form if you need anything else and put it in the box. We only have one rule here: We never go in each other's studios. We don't interfere in each other's work. We won't go into your space, and you don't go into ours. Cool?"

"Cool," I said, too agreeably, shifting my weight back and forth from foot to foot, an active lie, because all I had fantasized for the past decade was hanging out in Tyler's studio while he lit things on fire.

"Um, is there wifi?"

Tyler frowned. "Never," he said. "There's no cellphone service, there's no internet and no TV. There's a VHS connected to a projector in the Mission, if you want to watch something, and a lot of books. Read whatever you want. Put it back when you're done, and don't dog-ear."

"Great," I said, trying to seem cool, like it wasn't a problem, like I wasn't disappointed by how gruff and rude he was, how empty this place was, how unwelcome I felt. I walked back out to my truck, pulled out the studio boombox and a huge paper bag of cassette tapes I picked up at the Goodwill, and brought them inside. A Neil Young tape fell to the floor by accident, and he picked it up and handed it back to me with a smile—not a lot, no teeth or anything, but it was enough.

"The landlines all work. The number is on the phone. There's packaged food in the restaurant. You're welcome to it if you haven't gone to the grocery store," he said as he reached for his car door. A fat beetle flew past his head, buzzing loudly. He didn't flinch. "Fix your meals there anytime. I have to get going."

I tried to keep the desperate panic from my voice. "You're not staying here tonight?" (I did not succeed.)

"No—" he said, squinting at me with suspicion. "It's the Biennale?"

"Oh, right," I said, embarrassed. *Venice.* "I'm not paying attention to anything right now," I tried to explain.

"Whatever," he said, one corner of his mouth pulling back, fingers waving dismissively. *He thought I was an amateur.* "Good luck."

With that, he drove off, gravel spitting out from behind the station wagon as he careened up the service road and around the bend. A cloud of dust swirled up as his bumper disappeared from view—and I was left all alone in the broken-down utopia that I'd spent so many years dreaming about.

Chapter Four

The first thing I did was open a seltzer. The second thing was to pick up the cracked brown plastic phone and call Cady.

"You made it!" she squealed. "WHAT IS IT LIKE?"

"It's completely empty and it's *super* shitty."

"Huh. Somehow I thought it would be, like, a resort, still. You get a welcome drink and your bed is already made."

"I know. It's the opposite. There's not even a bed. I'm sleeping in a hammock tonight."

"Who's there?"

"Nobody. Tyler showed me in, and then he left again."

"Is he still, like, the most gorgeous man?"

"He's a jerk."

"Do you think he's the reason?"

"Reason for what?"

"That Carey killed herself. That's what everybody says. That he broke up with her when she stopped making sculptures, and then did nothing while she slid into some massive depression."

"Oh God." I turned and looked through the windows at the black lake. Clean white crests rose again, and again, over the glittering onyx of the basin. "That's mean, Cady." I remembered how he treated Carey that night on Grand Street, with so much joyful tenderness. I stretched the phone cord over my finger, wrapping it around and around.

"You never know," Cady continued. "They had a crazy relation-ship. My old assistant Bennie said they were super manipulative, both of them, when she helped install that last sculpture show."

"Everybody's manipulative," I countered. "Bennie is twenty-six. She has the emotional range of a mynah bird."

Cady laughed. "People get depressed, you know. *I'm* depressed."

"No you're not," Atticus shouted. "You're hungover."

"I think—I think it has something to do with her switch to per-formance. I do," I said. "Susan Bricklings-Young said she thought *something happened to her* when she switched. Something *bad.*"

"Susan Bricklings-Young," Cady said piously, "thinks that any artist who doesn't want to make a salable object is *clinically insane*. She has told me that exact thing on multiple occasions. Susan was probably just complaining."

"Ugh, I know. I thought that too, when Susan said it," I admit-ted, unwrapping the cord from my finger. "But—still. There was no reason for Carey to stop making sculpture."

"Maybe she got sick of it." Cady sighed. "It looked like hard work."

"Who gets sick of the only thing they're good at?"

"Everybody but you, apparently. What's the studio like?"

"I have no idea," I said, peering at the map. "Apparently, an old barn."

"Go look!" she said. A horn honked, and Jonny called her name. Her show—it was installing today. "Eeek. I have to go. Call me later. Tell me everything. I need constant updates. Love you," she said.

"Love you bye," I replied automatically. Paper map in hand, I climbed into the limp brown hammock on the porch, hoping that it wouldn't break under my weight. Thankfully, it was dry and sturdy. I wished I'd stopped to get a blanket and pillows.

The map was a loose illustration of the colony, nowhere close to scale. All the bungalows were marked by artist (Tyler, Marlin, Jes, and Jack; Carey's name was notably absent) and the lake labeled as THE DARDANELLE. I traced the route from my bungalow—one of Marlin's—to my supposed studio with my finger.

There was no time to waste. *If I could unload everything, and get the house in order, then tomorrow could be a productive day. That was all that mattered.*

I packed up my hurt feelings, climbed back into the truck, and drove west, in the direction of a service road that stretched back into the woods. Summer air filled the cab, and as I entered the forest and paused to navigate around a particularly big pothole, the sounds came in, too, loudly enough to overpower the idling engine.

It was almost a shrieking—I heard it all so quickly. Wind battered the trees; birds screamed at each other. Cicadas rattled their exoskeletal cages like a jailed Christmas choir, and somewhere behind me, the vast, empty lake beat against its rocky shore. The outside world shrank and fell off the edges, like a twig going over a waterfall, and I had the sudden sensation of total solitude. These were the deafening sounds of human absence.

Next—the heat flew in, thick and choking with humidity. Sweat dripped down my sides in tiny tributaries, pooling against the sticky smack of my thighs on the old leather seats. Flies landed on my arms, crawling over my wrists while I turned the wheel this way and that as I drove for over a mile along that old dirt road.

It narrowed into a natural hallway. The ground was covered in foot-high weeds and gnarled tree roots, its sides walled closely with peeling birches and thickly needled conifers blanketed with cobwebs. The rare patches of meadow seen through the trees were tamped down flat, their clots of slender grasses depressed by the bodies of slumbering deer.

The farther I drove, the denser the forest grew. Soon I was in an older part of the resort, at least a hundred years neglected, a private, broken-down world that felt beyond time. I wondered if anyone burned witches here. When I passed a cluster of worn limestone gravestones that butted up against the road, I threw the truck in park and went to look.

The names were mostly dissolved from years of acid rain. On

one, 1742 was visible, sunk deep into the dirt and nestled in a pile of leaves, and letters poked out beneath. I reached down to brush the leaves away.

When my hand touched the pile, it was warm and soft—and then before I realized what it was, it moved beneath my palm. A big brown bat darted out, flapping and shrieking in confusion. Its tiny needle teeth flashed white as it emptied a high-pitched guttural noise directly into my face.

I screamed right back at it. Taut wings beat around my head as it circled once, then twice—and then, miraculously, it abandoned me.

The truck was still running. I scrambled in and pulled the door shut beside me, frantically rolling up the windows, shaking with adrenaline. My palm burned in the place where I'd contacted the soft fur.

"It was just a bat," I told myself, cradling my head over the steering wheel. "It was just a bat. It was just a bat. Just a bat." I looked around. No bat. *See?* I told myself. *No bat.*

I put the truck in gear and drove another mile, distracted and shaking. The only thing I passed was a damp, swollen barn whose boards zigged and zagged in opposing directions. The building strained and sagged, giving the impression that the slightest breeze could collapse it into a pile of soggy matchsticks.

I kept driving and driving but there was nothing. When the road stopped suddenly in a dead end, a wall of birches rising up in front of me like palace guards, I had to drive in reverse until the road widened enough for me to turn around.

The damp, swollen barn—*it was the X*. It was the only thing that could have been the X.

I should have driven back—I should have left—but instead I parked in front of the barn. A cardboard-looking door, with frayed edges, hung from a doorframe. At my touch, the handle came off in my hand, and the door itself fell and smashed onto the ground, breaking into pieces. I toed one of the soft, broken slabs, and it was so decayed that its fibers clung to the mesh of my sneakers.

Inside, it smelled like air after a storm—like a damp rag—and
when my eyes adjusted it became clear that the floors beneath my
feet were simply dirt, a brown expanse pierced by jagged shafts of
light and pitted with muddy potholes. Toward the back, over the
hayloft, the roof was partially caved in. To refer to this as a "barn"
was more than inaccurate. It was a moldering, oversize lean-to—a
total nightmare.

I touched the nearest wall. The wood came away easily, balling
up under my fingernail like a wet paper towel. Feeling bold, I
climbed the ancient ladder toward the loft, trying to reach a joist,
to see if anything in this building was solid. The first step was fine,
the second too, but halfway up, a rung fell away beneath me, exposing a cluster of nailheads that ripped a hunk of skin from my
calf as I tumbled to the ground.

Blood rushed from my leg and dripped wetly into the hollows
of my ankle. Stunned, I watched it run into my sock, over the edge
of my sneakers, mixing with the dirt of the floor in a tiny, glossy
puddle. My forearm was scraped raw too, blood seeping through
the dirt.

I took off my t-shirt, ripped off one sleeve, tied it around the
hole in my leg, and looked around the room one last time before
I admitted to myself that the whole building would need to be re-
built. It would take at least six months and a team of workers.

I was doomed.

It was rational to fear loneliness for all those years, I thought as I
limped back to my truck: This place, an abandoned hotel turned
abandoned retreat, had become in a single afternoon the physical
manifestation of my isolation. Yet there was nowhere else for me to
go. I had three thousand dollars in checking and forty-six thousand
available in credit, money that would barely cover my expenses to
remake my paintings, much less pay for shelter or studio space.

There was no plan C.

I sat behind the wheel of my truck for a long time. I thought
about renting a storage space and living in it. I thought about

squatting in Trenton. I thought about joining Atticus in his shipping container in Corona Park, and about going back to Cady's sofa. I thought about driving straight through the night and day and night again to Gainesville, the north Florida sinkhole of my birth, to sleep on my mother's sagging pullout couch, something that I had never considered before—not once, not ever. I thought about quitting.

But when I counted the days—roughly ninety—that I had to remake my paintings, I couldn't let go. They had to be finished; it was imperative; nothing had ever been more true. There was no plan C because giving up on my paintings was not an available future. Letting go of them felt equivalent to sticking a gun in my mouth and pulling the trigger.

Eventually I drove back to the bungalow and climbed out of the truck. Then I did what anyone in my position would have done: I picked up the cracked plastic brown landline and tattled to the money.

"Isn't it glorious?" Susan asked right away, after two short rings.

"No. Tyler left. Nobody's here. I can't use the barn they gave me. It's falling apart."

"It probably does need work. But that's how they do things, you know."

"*Susan*. We talked about this. It's an emergency. I agreed to seven paintings for my show. *This is number seven*. I don't turn in number seven, I don't get paid for numbers one through six. This could set me back financially for *actual years*. You said you understood. I *need* a usable space—a big one. How do I get into the other buildings?"

"All right." She sighed into the phone, sounding annoyed. "I suppose...my girl Friday, Julian, can bring you a key to another studio tomorrow. Meet him up front at...say, eight thirty. Don't be late."

She hung up before I could beg her to send him tonight.

Alone in the bungalow, I ripped into a bag of gas-station popcorn and unpacked. I had two bags of groceries, six pounds of coffee beans, a bottle of bourbon, a sixer of cheap beer, and three cases of seltzer. The metal cabinets in the kitchen thankfully revealed plates, cutlery, a coffeepot, and a smattering of pots and pans.

My clothes, destroyed in the fire, weren't great to begin with. They'd been easily replaced in one gin-soaked afternoon with Atticus. Given free rein in the Forest Hills Salvation Army a mile walk from his shipping container, he selected variations on one theme: Dennis the Menace. Out of the duffel Atticus packed came cutoff jean shorts, oversize secondhand t-shirts, overalls, and multipacks of underwear and socks from the drugstore. His idea of a joke. *Fine.* After I dumped out a bag of brand-new toiletries from Ricky's into the bathroom—soap, toothpaste, hair bleach, toner, and a purple lipstick it seemed I'd never have the occasion to wear—stacked four paperbacks from Goodwill into a pile, and duct-taped the hole in my leg, my hands were empty.

Unpacking my entire life had taken forty-five minutes.

I stood on my tiptoes to get the duffel onto the closet shelf. As I reached, pushing it to the back, I noticed one set of initials carved in the wood: MFC. I ran my fingers over the letters and wondered how long ago this house had welcomed a guest. I tried to imagine it before the leaves and cobwebs took over.

I stubbed my toe on a half-pulled nail. When I wiggled it out, a long nylon thread of avocado shag carpeting came with it, and I recalled the avocado carpet of my own childhood; pressing my face into it as the air conditioner wheezed out cold, wet puffs of barely filtered swamp air; the pernicious creep of fear that always came when the front door swung open, the screen door slammed shut, keys jangling unsteadily; and then I blinked, and the bunga-low came back as it was. Peeling linoleum, walls half papered in a marble swirl, a broken ceiling fan, dirty windows, broken screens, carpet long ripped away. I was not in Florida. This was not my childhood home. It was a new place—to me, at least.

I strolled onto the beach, where thick, pebbled sand dried out against the retreating waves, to watch the ruby sunset melt below the tree line. Tyler's black house was six houses down—number seven—and yet it wasn't a single black, not exactly. Rather, it was five shades of black. Lamp black on the roof; Mars black on the windows; a viridian-tinted-black on the door and porch trims; the siding almost navy, probably a blackened Prussian blue; the shutters in Payne's gray, a hard, matte black like charcoal. The screen door was locked. I tried the windows, and though they were bolted tight, I could see inside to where the walls and floor were black. The furniture was black. The lamps were black. The art on the walls was black.

In the photo shoot that was published after Carey's obituary, "Perpetual Persephone," the one where she wore a white dress dipped in flowers and smeared broken plums across Tyler's skin, they'd been in a house that was all white: the doors, the floors, the furniture, the lamps, the plates, the art that hung on the wall. The single black was a number painted on the side: 7.

This house.

This house—Tyler's house—*their* house—now painted black—every shade of grief. I shuddered and turned to watch the sun go down across the water.

The only black missing from Tyler's house was the glossy black of the lake.

Another hour passed as I carefully covered up the holes in all the screens, set buckets under the darkest spots in the ceiling, and chased down mosquitoes with a sneaker, all beneath the buzzing glare of the single electric bulb in the living room.

I tried switching it off—it was ugly and unpleasant—but under the slide-change of darkness, I was unsettled by every noise, every moving leaf. Immediately I wondered if there was a prison nearby.

I imagined men with biceps the size of bread loaves in orange polyester jumpsuits holding a knife to my throat, leering into me, expelling their rancid breath into my mouth. Like the subway but with fewer bystanders.

I flipped the light back on.

I thought about walking to the Mission, but I was afraid to go outside by myself. There were waves lapping, and branches breaking, and winds whistling restlessly through the trees. The moon insisted on staying hidden behind a cloud, and so the night loomed above me, the air thin as outer space and equally directionless. It felt like if I stepped outside, I'd float away into the night and nobody would ever find me again.

So: I drank, curled up in the hammock, with the light on. What else was there to do? I unscrewed the bourbon, made a t-shirt pillow and a t-shirt blanket, let the boombox play the A-side of a Carole King tape over and over, and thought about Carey. I wondered where her studio was—it wasn't on the map. I wondered if she'd been unhappy here, or lonely, or scared, like I was right now. I realized that if I ever wanted to find out what happened to Carey Logan, I would have to actually see, and speak, to the remaining members of Pine City. But it felt like none of them were ever coming back. *I'm going to be alone all summer,* I thought miserably.

I dreamed about the fire. I watched my paintings burn, flames wrapping around the edges of their framing, the paint itself boiling and bubbling and melting to the ground. My books lit up. The pages caught orange and turned to ash in my hands. The soggy birth certificate was in my palm again, the empty passport, too, with its blank pages. I screamed for help, but no sounds emerged from my throat. Silently I watched two years of work disappear into a wet black smoke, one that swirled around my face until I was gasping for air, awake and briefly possessed of the odd and unwelcome conviction that the paintings were *supposed* to burn.

In the morning, the shower ran hot, but brown. I hit my elbows and knees against the walls of the narrow, unfamiliar stall. In the kitchen, I reached for the wrong drawers and the wrong cabinets, but eventually, managed an egg and a cup of coffee: nearly normal. I put on the first t-shirt from the pile, an extra-wide, one-size-fits-all crop top with WHAT WOULD JESUS DO? positioned around a triangle. "Atticus, Jesus *would* wear a crop top," I agreed, rolling up the sleeves.

At eight twenty-five, I drove to the main lodge to wait for Julian. After half an hour passed, and Julian still hadn't appeared, I decided to look around.

Julian: Honk when you arrive, I wrote on a napkin from the glove compartment, tucking it under my windshield wiper.

The main entrance was locked. But the landscape banked steeply around the sides of the building, so I followed it up and around until a screen door appeared, banging in the wind, unlocked and naked.

Inside it was the fusty brownish dusty-dark of a hallway long neglected. I pressed along the walls on both sides of the door until a push-button switch rose beneath my fingertips. The yellowed bulbs turned on, one after the other, leading down a hallway to a half set of stairs that dropped behind the reception desk in the resort's main lobby.

It was a vast, double-story atrium—once a welcoming, airy check-in and lounge—the walls paneled in warm wood and modish squares of orange and green melamine. I stood behind the long reception desk, in a kind of faux-Mondrian design, where a rusty bell and an old ballpoint pen, draped in a soft pool of dust, were the only remaining office supplies. The keyholes were vacant, the shelves empty.

On the opposite wall, the main doors were padlocked with a thick bicycle chain. To my left, a wall of windows faced the restaurant and the lake; to the right, a wide staircase led to upper floors that must have once contained lower-priced, motel-style rooms for those who couldn't afford the expense of a separate bungalow. Dark rectangles haunted the walls at eye level, where pictures had once hung.

And in the middle, as Tyler had mentioned, there was a treasure trove of furniture. What had once been a breezy reception lounge was now a storage facility. Stacks of plastic and metal chairs rose between vinyl sofas and easy chairs, alongside metal bed frames, musty spring mattresses, ancient melamine side tables, and modernist lamps with torn, stained shades.

"Help yourself," I muttered, running my fingers through the quarter-inch layer of dust that coated everything. Nearly all the mattresses reeked of mildew, but one on the end had spent its recent exile in a sunbeam. The fabric was crispy to the touch and its once-floral pattern was now bleached a rancid yellow, but at least it didn't smell.

I dragged the mattress through the dust, wedging it behind the desk and up the narrow half stairs and out through the side door, then sorted through the bed frames until I found enough pieces to make something work. The vinyl sofas were too heavy to carry alone, but I was able to take two metal folding chairs, three side tables, a plastic-wrapped pile of linens—cheap, hospital quality—and four metal lamps too, and stack them out front.

Still—there was no Julian.

I went back into the lodge and crept up the wide staircase.

I expected more mildewed furniture, maybe some shag carpeting, but the upper two floors of the lodge had twenty-four empty motel rooms scraped down to the studs. Most didn't have flooring, only joists; the beginning of a renovation. In the room next to the stairs, I found a folded *NYT* crossword puzzle atop a three-gallon paint can. The date on the newspaper was three years old, shortly before Carey died. It seemed that no progress had been made since then.

I took the puzzle (it was only half filled in) outside with me and sat on the hill, watching the woods. Nothing happened—

wind shook the trees and some birds flew around, your basic forest action—and I mindlessly filled in the clues. When I was done, I paged through the remainder of the section, and found a review for a show by Carey Logan. According to the date, it was roughly six months before she'd died.

"I left asking myself two questions. One: Is 'Other People's Rules' a good work of art? Two: Is Ms. Logan a good artist? The answer to both is that Ms. Logan's electrifying personal presence, overwhelming as it may be, does not an artwork make. She may still be beautiful, but she is certainly no longer the daring youngster who asked us to look unflinchingly upon the bodies of murdered women; instead she asks us to regard her newfound privilege. Unlike her, I did not find it interesting."

It was so unkind and sexist and humiliating. Carey had certainly proved that she was a good artist—that she was newsworthy was the paper's own self-evident truth—and she did not deserve to be taken down so forcefully. I could not recall reading any review that assessed whether or not Chris Burden, who let himself be shot on-camera, or Vito Acconci, who masturbated under the floorboards of a gallery, were still attractive, or if any male artist was still attractive unless it was asserting that like Bruce Springsteen their butts were still worth grabbing. I'd never seen Richard Prince, Jeff Koons, or Chuck Close being admonished for showing us their privilege. The word *newfound* reminded us that she was uneducated and poor, that she was some kind of interloper into privilege, implying that she didn't deserve it or that she was a fool to be interested in it. And the byline enraged me most of all—it was been written by a woman, no less. The same woman, I realized, who so *generously* expressed her apparent shock that I "could so successfully handle the XL format," since it was "traditionally the domain of men."

"Judas," I hissed at the paper.

A brand-new Range Rover pulled up, emerging like a shiny black nightmare from the gentle scenery. When the driver's-side

window rolled down, I found myself looking at the smooth, ar-
tificially plumped face of an impeccably dressed man with dyed-
platinum hair and a permanent sneer.

"Hello?" the man whom I presumed was Julian snapped, though
he made no effort to introduce himself. "Ugh," he said, impatient
with disgust. "You're . . . bleeding."

I looked down. My tape bandage had worked itself free. "I cut
my leg in the barn," I tried to explain. "Thanks for bringing the
key."

He rolled his eyes unsympathetically, as though I had somehow
intentionally removed my own flesh in an attempt to skip the
nonexistent line of invisible people for usable studio space.

"You can use this for now," he said, passing me an orange-
capped key with PRINT STUDIO written on the label in tiny, impec-
cable handwriting. "It's for those doors." He pointed to the locked
lower doors of the lodge, the ones around the side. "Get to it. You
don't have a lot of time."

"Until what?" I asked, but he was already driving away.

Alone again—but now there was somewhere to go.

Chapter Five

I unlocked the doors and discovered a full basement-turned-printing-studio beneath the lobby. It had four huge tables, at least four feet wide by ten feet long; three slop sinks and a washout room; a full ventilation system; and long windows that looked down the sloping hill that led to the Mission and the lake. Along the walls, deep shelves were packed with bright jars of ink and yellow-skinned screens; a pegboard was hung with custom-cut squeegees of every size. The light was good.

One wall had no shelves at all. Instead, in hand-painted letters, it was covered in a quote I knew by heart:

> *The great and golden rule of art, as well as of life, is this: That the more distinct, sharp, and wiry the bounding line, the more perfect the work of art; and the less keen and sharp, the greater is the evidence of weak imitation, plagiarism, and bungling . . . Leave out this line and you leave out life itself; all is chaos again, and the line of the Almighty must be drawn out upon it before man or beast can exist.*

The passage, written by William Blake in a descriptive catalog to accompany one of his own exhibitions, was on the wall in the senior lounge at the Academy. Someone had typed it out in the 1940s and tacked it to the corkboard with a little metal pin, under the headline WE KNOW EACH OTHER BY OUR LINES—and nobody ever moved it. Generations of us ran our fingers over the lines and copied them down. Ask any Academy graduate how we are different from the others. *We know each other by our lines* is the answer. *We know the bounding line.*

Though the trend during my time was to avoid figuration, we nonetheless, as was tradition, entered the Academy with a natural hand and left with sharpened claws. Some of us were more talented than others. The gifted draftsman can use dime-store acrylic paint on a palette knife like David Hockney did in the '60s, rendering the subject flat-faced, buck-toothed, bug-eyed—and still the subject will feel as though they have been *seen* like never before. A line like that is the rarest of gifts. Blake had it, and Marlin Mayfield had it.

Below the painted quote, six of her prints lay on a drying rack. I examined them cautiously, flipping the wire shelves up with care. The dense paper, pressed flat, was handmade, edges raw and uneven. Marlin used more than ink—it looked like iron dust on magnetized paint—and so the prints were fuzzy, built up from the surface in a pattern of tiny hexagons. The images were of different anatomies: a hand, a leg, a torso. The edges were executed with such a specific, meaningful line that I found it hard to look away.

But they were not mine to look at. *I was here for myself.* I wheeled the rack of her prints carefully into the washout room, draped the whole thing with plastic, and looked at the studio. It would work—it would more than work. *We know each other by our lines.* I was, in one small way, home again.

I spent the morning unpacking my haul from Manhattan. There were power tools, sheets of plywood and copper, bags of powdered fiberglass, a thousand dollars' worth of powdered pigments, gallons of turpentine, then pints of linseed, safflower, and walnut oils, along with Liquin and Galkyd (chemical drying additives, *cheaters*, which I rarely used, but would be desperately relying on) and a host of other toxic mediums, resins, and plastics. When I found the superglue, I ripped off my makeshift bandage and squeezed the cold gel into the wound in my leg. *Not bad*, I thought, smoothing masking tape across the top. *There's always med school*, I joked to myself. *At least then I'd have health insurance.*

I refilled the truck with the borrowed pile of furniture, tarping it into place until there was time to unload it at the house, then locked myself in the studio. For the thousandth time, I said a silent prayer on behalf of Hayley Thomas, the professor who ran the Academy's freshman foundation course.

"There are no rules to this life," Hayley said, every year, "so you'd better write it all down or you'll never be able to remember. Write down your paints, the humidity, the time of day. Record everything about a piece—beyond your materials, I mean, who you spoke to about it, or how much it cost to ship it, and when you're having a hard day, you'll be able to look at your notebooks and remember how much work you did. When you have a success, you'll know how to repeat it. And when you make a mistake, you'll have a record of that, too."

Because of Hayley, the notebook that lived in my backpack, the one I brought with me the morning of the fire, contained records of every painting in *Rich Ugly Old Maids*. I planned to start with *Prudence*, getting into the rhythm with her two undamaged panels, and work my way backward as best I could, using the documentary photos in my camera and the notes in my notebook. Jacqueline had seen images, but she'd never seen the work in person. I told myself that I certainly had the right to make and deliver my paintings in whatever condition I saw fit. *Obedience* was on the posters and in the advertisements, but that one was basically all black. I could get pretty damn close, I told myself. Pretty close. *Close enough.*

I propped the two unharmed panels of *First Prudence* against the wall for guidance; since I couldn't afford to match her materials *and* remake all of my other paintings, she would remain half a painting forever.

The next hours were spent making new panels of *Prudence*. They would, when assembled, be a total of ten feet high and twelve feet wide. I cut and drilled, screwed and framed (the wood backing would be covered in fiberglass, so that they looked smooth in the back, effortless), over and over, four times, four panels. Once done, each panel took a table.

I was more than eager to remake her; I was desperate. As I spread a ready-made gesso over the wood in thin, even layers, the work hypnotic and soothing, I felt, for the first time since the fire, a sense of calm spreading through my body, warm, opiatic. It was a relief to discover that here, even in this strange place, cradling the ghost of a painting and bereft of my pricey tools, I could *work*, like I had for much of the past twelve years.

Painting had not left me.

Prudence would live.

I forgot about the loss of my home, about the loneliness that had swept me up the night before. I forgot about the emptiness of the resort in which I stood and I forgot about how afraid I was.

I was working again, and so my life was full.

Somewhere around 4 a.m., I curled up on the ink-stained sofa in the studio, pulled a moth-eaten blanket over my aching body, and forced myself to fall asleep.

This was my chance—no matter how strange—and I was determined to make it work.

One of my professors once told me that she started all of her paintings with a photocopied picture of her parents and the words FUCK YOU scrawled across their faces. The final compositions—abstract seas of color—show no traces of the beginning whatsoever, yet the paintings speak to you, screaming a version of FUCK YOU felt in the back of your throat weeks, months, or years later.

Whether we are pasting photos of our parents into the gesso or not, all artists are of course doing that same thing: We are burying our past selves within the work, pieces of which rise to the surface without our permission like bodies in a flood. I think oil painters are the worst—that we shovel the most shit onto the canvas. But—not everybody has a shovel. Watercolor painters, for example, aren't adding or shoveling but rather removing the occlusions of what we perceive as reality to expose what lies underneath, like wiping fog off a car window. Pencils burnish, create an impression, a frottage; ink is a violent stain; charcoal, a cloudy exhale; acrylic, a plastic advertisement; photography, a viewpoint. Sculpture is architecture. They're all different, these mediums of representation. I started working with oil because it takes the longest to dry—some of my paintings are so thick they won't be dry for a thousand years.

This was, strictly speaking, my biggest problem. In the morning, the air was so humid that the gesso looked like it was sweating, though I knew it was dry. Panic rose beneath my ribs: There was *no time* for this kind of humidity. Even Liquin couldn't stand up to this weather—not with the quantities of paint I was using. If the first layer was applied under these conditions, the rest would be affected, and the final product could be melted, unstable, even after months of drying—months I didn't have. That exact quality I was so attracted to—that heavy, damp shit-shoveling—it was a condition I could no longer afford.

I needed a solution. Today.

When in doubt, I always leave the studio and go for a walk. I'm not an exercise fanatic, but this is a solid, unwavering truth: Leaving the studio makes everything better. I locked up and walked down the driveway, past Arts and Crafts, the Theatre, and Sports, and onto the shore of the black lake.

It stretched ahead for a mile, maybe more. I stood on the only visible beach, which ran about half a mile, from the Mission to my bungalow. The licorice lake was lined around the soft curve to my left with pointed evergreens and thickets of shrubs, and a grassy hill rose opposite me, on the far shore. The water moved heavily, with windswept waves that were never placid. To my right it wrapped around the corner to the east, where a peninsula jutted out sharply and cut off the view.

I wondered where Carey had walked into the lake in her cement-filled boots. Was it here, close to the Mission? Was it in front of their house, number seven? Did she take one of the canoes and roll out of it?

I took off my shoes and let my feet touch the incoming swells.

It was cold—so cold that it made my bones ache from the inside out. I jumped back, then steeled myself and walked into the cold. I wanted to know how it felt, to be fully frozen and surrounded. My legs dragged back against the current, but I pressed on, gasping when it touched the back of my knees. I made it all the way up, past my waist, the ground silty and slippery beneath my feet, and then—I pinched my nose and dropped under.

The cold was a wallop to the chest, but it was tolerable. I dropped to the bottom and opened my eyes. Beneath the surface, the water wasn't black but *red*—pure Red Oxide, the color of iron—and it was dotted, quite beautifully, with little green caterpillars of algae whose fine fibers swung gently to and fro. I popped up, into the sun, considered swimming farther, into the deep—where there was nothing to hold on to. Yet the mere act of *thinking* about the open water made me step back involuntarily toward the shore.

It was impossible for someone to drown themselves here. It was too cold. It was too scary. I thought about all those pictures of the beach covered with people, feather-haired, mud cracking on their skin. Maybe in a crowd, it could be fun—lighthearted.

But not alone.

Alone, it was big as the ocean.

I returned to my bungalow to change into clean clothes and slam coffee—the beginnings of a routine. Rusty water streamed from my clothes the whole walk, turning my hair into wet ropes. Outside my porch, I paused, twisted the ends together, and squeezed out most of the water—and as it drained through my fists and into the sand, I had an idea.

Oil paint likes structure. Jay DeFeo, whose oil paintings weighed hundreds of pounds, was famous for using rope—rope like the wet ropes of my hair—to support the massive piles of paint. I didn't have time to learn how different ropes would behave, but I knew how raw wood acted. Raw wood drank oil.

In the studio I took two fresh pieces of plywood and carved holes, making organic, honeycomb-patterned lattices that roughly followed the contours of how *Prudence* had once looked, then secured the lattices flat atop the new backings. *Prudence* would be at least an inch thick above the substrate when she was complete, and this raw wood latticework interior would soak up much of the oil, hastening the drying time by months. I hoped that when covered the lattice would look and weigh much the same as actual oil paint would have. It wasn't a textbook solution, but it was something, and buoyed by the optimism of my own fresh ingenuity, I unscrewed fresh jars of powdered color and took out a clean palette knife.

The key to mixing paint is to let the pigments separate, to float them in the medium *just so*, so that the colors band in this distinct-but-merged way—like how you can see pink and orange and green winking all at once in an oil puddle at the gas station, or in the nacre lining the edge of an oyster shell. But to get this kind of separation, you have to know when to stop, to thin out, to pull back. Painting is about overestimating the time it takes to pull the trigger.

I tried to match the color of the red lake water that drained from my pink hair, reaching for something that wasn't totally pink or red, but held pieces of tangerine and sunlight too, with a smear or two of the softest, darkest algae, or the reflective blue of a fish scale somewhere in there. When I was satisfied, I made a lot of it.

I spackled the mix onto panel two and pushed it into the holes of
the lattice that I'd attached. I did this over and over, making pocket
after pocket of this nacreous blood red. And I was so involved with
my painting, headphones plugged in, my world reduced to *Prudence*'s four panels, that I didn't hear the studio door opening—or
someone walking up behind me.

"What are you doing?" a voice demanded angrily and directly into
my ear, cutting through the music. I jumped, almost tripping into
the painting. Marlin Mayfield stepped back. I watched her mouth
move as she gestured around the room and toward my paintings
and me. I yanked out my headphones.

"This is my studio," she was saying, hands on her hips, in white
overalls spattered with dark ink, narrow feet shoved into white
Birkenstocks, brown hair pulled into a knotted bun. "Hello? Are
you fucking listening?"

"I'm so sorry," I said quickly, sincerely, fingers splaying across my
chest, trying to diffuse the tension. "Ju–Julian gave me the key," I
said, the words coming out jumbled, too close together.

"We're already giving you a place to sleep," she said. "Now
you're taking my studio?"

"I completely understand," I said, raising my eyebrows, letting
my jaw fall open, my hands in the air, *don't shoot*. "Honestly, I'm in
a real bind here. I need the space. My studio *burned down*."

She squinted, stepped back, crossed her arms over her body, and
said nothing as she walked around the studio, looking at each panel
of *Prudence* carefully before she glanced back to my face.

"Huh," she said. "Well. I'm Marlin Mayfield."

"I—I know," I stammered, "I was at the Academy after you."

"I *know*," she threw back. "I read that article."

"That reporter wanted to fuck me," I said sheepishly. "It doesn't
count."

She laughed—an inroad.

"Listen, I'm *truly* sorry about trespassing in your studio," I said with what I hoped sounded like remorse. "I didn't know what to do. Tyler gave me the barn, but it's not usable. I respect that I'm a guest here. But I am completely at your mercy. I'm desperate."

"You know what...don't worry about it. These are good," she said, turning back to another panel, letting her palm hover over the wet, wavy surface of the oil. "How long again?"

"Three months."

"We'll find you another space. I need to be back in here"—she glanced at a calendar on the wall—"before June fifteenth." She turned and looked out the window, crossing her arms over her white overalls. "Rats," she continued. "That barn needs to be torn down. Tyler should have never given it to you. He can be combative. Don't take it personally."

"It's okay," I said. "I can't move these yet, though. I need another week or two. Is that okay?"

She nodded and scribbled her cellphone number on a piece of paper.

"Call me when you're ready. I'll let you get back to it," she said, turning on her heel and heading for the door. "We usually do sundowners at the Mission."

We. I wondered if Tyler was back. Not exactly an invitation, but close enough.

"Cool. See you," I replied, plugging in my headphones. Briefly, I let myself wear the slender thrill of inclusion before turning back to *Prudence*, and then I zeroed in and the day disappeared behind me. At some point the sun completed its arc across the lake and began to sink into the horizon. I stepped back, wrapped my palette knives in plastic, scrubbed my hands with a turpentine rag, and marched toward the restaurant.

I'd seen so many images of the Mission, of its scarred wooden floors and bedraggled red velvet curtains, of its massive round tables and the floor-to-ceiling windows that looked out over the lake, of its deck covered in a long line of wooden Adirondack chairs, that walking toward the real thing felt both jarringly surreal and slightly disappointing.

Images flashed through my mind of a wedding here, when the whole place was lit up by bottle-green votives and they'd sent brown-paper-bag luminarias off the end of the dock. According to the newspaper, the bride and groom, friends of Pine City, had climbed into an aluminum canoe bedecked with tiny silver bells and paddled off into the night while Yusuf Islam himself had played "If You Want to Sing Out." I thought about the video of Tyler throwing Jack off the deck, of the prints I'd seen at Johnson Reuchtig of naked male models lined up in the Adirondack chairs, of that hilarious photo of Karl Rove doing a keg stand, over there, near the hedge. Jes standing on a floating dock—which wasn't out there anymore—playing a theremin. Marlin and Carey laying thousands of rotten flowers along the beach.

Somehow it doesn't matter how old you grow, or how sophisticated you become. The people who impress themselves upon your consciousness at nineteen will never shrink or fade from memory. They will always be just a few steps ahead, and you'll both hate and worship them for it, because you cannot help but compare yourself.

The Mission had a big white metal sign done in enamel with a cartoon Jesus over the entryway. When I heaved open the wooden slab of a door, I don't know what I expected—I think probably for there to be a party inside—but what I got was a dark and empty room.

Marlin wasn't there, Tyler wasn't there, nobody was there. It was deserted. The only sound came from the refrigerator's compressor somewhere in the back of the kitchen.

The round tables were there, as were the bedraggled red velvet curtains. The walls were covered in hundreds of framed photographs arranged salon-style—but there were dozens of holes. I flipped on the light to see the pictures. They seemed to show every famous living artist in America, hanging out on the shores of the black lake, painting cabins in gym shorts and baking cakes in the kitchen and strapping sculptures to dollies, with the help of Tyler, Jes, Jack, and Marlin. Over and over, it was the four of them—Jes always standing closest to Tyler, Marlin and Jack their own pair—and there wasn't a single photograph that included Carey. That was, I realized, what the holes were. *Someone came through and took every photo of Carey from the wall.* As though they couldn't bear to be reminded. I put my palms in the empty squares, touching each star in the constellation left from bygone picture nails, and wondered what was supposed to replace her. *Nothing,* I thought, remembering the way she held the gallery at Grand Street in the palm of her hand. *Nothing could replace her.*

I imagined her in this room, leaning against the bottles, behind the bar. She would have smiled and welcomed me; she would have unlocked a different house; she would have given me a real place to work, right off the bat. Carey saw herself in me, I knew she did—and she would have treated me like a protégée instead of an interloper.

I sighed, walked around the bar to where she did not stand, where nobody stood, mixed two scoops of instant coffee with half a cup of cold water, choked it back, and returned to the printer's studio, where I worked until four before falling asleep on the sofa again.

In the morning, back at my bungalow for a shower and slice of toast, I found a note slipped under the door from Marlin:

jes n me went to hudson for the night, didn't want 2 disturb u, catch u soon, good luck

I experienced a cheek-warming flash of humiliation. In a moment of pity, Marlin tried to make me feel comfortable, then later regretted it. No matter whether or not I told myself that I had come here as their equal, the fact remained that I was clearly a very unwanted gatecrasher.

But I didn't have a choice. This was where I was. The work had to get made, and I was the only one who could do it. I pushed myself to repress my embarrassment—to keep going, to make breakfast, drink coffee, shower, get dressed, and return to the printmaking studio. After an hour of work my skin burned with the fever of my painting and I was myself again.

I don't need friends, I told myself. *Only work*.

The next nine days passed without interruption from Marlin, Jes, Tyler, or anybody at all. Each day was exactly the same: wake, shower, eat, paint, nap, paint, swim, sleep, repeat.

There's no other way to be. This is how the work happens—when there is nothing else to distract you. The bursts come for hours every day, and then between them, you sleep, because working takes everything out of you—opens a drain at the bottom of your stomach that lets the dishwater out. Then, later, some invisible hand refills you, and the cycle begins anew. It is the condition of my purpose. I am nothing else but this.

I ignored every part of myself that cried out for human companionship so that *Prudence*, my once-final, now first old maid, could grow shining and luminous.

And it worked.

On day ten, I went for twelve hours, nonstop, scraping a slab of oxidized copper with a razor blade dipped in vinegar. The scrapings went directly into a food processor borrowed from the Mission, where they were pulverized into nothingness. Eventually my labors generated nearly a pound of dust. I mixed a scoop of the green dust with some safflower oil, a daub of lead tin yellow, and a pinch of powdered gold leaf on a palette, using a long, flat knife. More yellow, more dust; more oil, more gold. When I was satisfied with the ratio, I mixed the remainder.

I was essentially making verdigris, a highly toxic and unstable pigment the same color as the Statue of Liberty. Seventeenth-century Renaissance painters, whose verdigris glazes and tints were initially a brilliant, minty-grassy green, lacked the chemical materials to prevent verdigris from degrading over time. No matter what kind of oil medium they used, as the varnish degraded and the oils dried out, the topmost layer of copper was inevitably exposed to oxygen and would turn a brackish brown. Essentially what they lacked was a material that could be mixed at room temperature and dry to a chemically impenetrable solid: They lacked *plastic*, that base petroleum by-product whose applications now intersect with almost every aspect of our economy. I like verdigris because it reminds us that everything is destructive. The Renaissance painters' lack of plastic destroyed their own work; my access to it is destroying the delicate ecosystems of our planet and so on. Everything that gets created destroys something else.

For *Prudence*, I needed a version of verdigris that was not only stable, but more yellow than blue and literally glowing. It was delicate, a chancy process the first time around, and I was nervous to repeat it. The color had been a light green, somewhere on the yellow-jade spectrum between pear and honeydew, a color that turns the lights on in the basement of your mind. Like before, I poured twelve ounces of casting resin into a bucket, folded in the verdigris with a paddle, and then added an ounce of hydrogen peroxide gel (dental bleach, essentially) to reach that glassy, milky quality, to make something that shone. After testing the color against a prep board in the corner and adding another half ounce of the peroxide, something clicked, and it was time.

I walked to a panel and began to pour.

Watching the glossy, virescent plastic flow out of my bucket and down onto the backing, seeing it expand across the painting's hole-ridden landscape, I felt *it*—the feeling that governed the last twenty years of my life—a rightness about the work, the material, the world. The green flowed for nearly a minute, a long, thin stream stretching out in front of me like a wire, before I stopped and tilted the bucket back up.

This wouldn't fully set for at least forty-eight hours. I took a breath, looked around, and felt myself close up, my skin thicken and expand. It was possible that it ruined the painting, this step a misstep, but I didn't think so. The click in my brain, the voice of the painting, my god, my north star, told me it would work.

Still—anything can be destroyed.

Chapter Six

The next morning, I found myself wanting to press something into the slowly curing surface, something organic. Something foreign and delicate. This hadn't been in original *Prudence* but it didn't matter. I was moving on, to something better.

I wanted tulips, orange ones, maybe. And—I was almost out of food. Time to find town.

The promises lining Granger's driveway were painted on the reverse with local attractions. Driving away from the retreat, I was presented first with a cluster of music notes dotting a cloudy painting of Tanglewood, the summer home of the Boston Symphony Orchestra; then a jockey perched astride a sprinting thoroughbred at the Saratoga Race Course; next, hikers adjusted their packs atop Jiminy Peak; then apple-cheeked families picking matching fruit from nearby orchards; and finally, renderings of the Colonial buildings at RPI and the Gothic ones at Emma Willard School were accompanied by "Parent's Weekend—Commencement—Book Early!"

I drove to Union Vale, the nearest town, where the only market was a Stewart's gas station. I bought boxes of cereal, a gallon of milk, and some frozen hamburgers, and as the cashier rang me up I asked for directions to the nearest farmers market. Speaking to another person after so many days of complete and total solitude sounded weird and I almost laughed at my own voice, so scratchy and halting.

"Uh..." She paused. "It's Sunday, so...it's the good one. New Lebanon, hon," she said. "North on 22. And—you got paint on your face."

"Oh," I said, raising my fingers to my cheek.

"No." She pointed, looking at me with unvarnished pity. "Your nose."

"Thanks," I told her, peeling off a strip of something whitish. She put out her hand like it was a piece of gum, threw it in the trash, and we both smiled. It was nice; she made me feel like a person.

I followed the two-lane road north, until a hand-painted sign announcing the market came into view. I parked in a dirt lot and wandered the dozen or so stalls, buying bread and cheese until I found someone selling wet bunches of tulips and freesias.

And as I was rummaging through the buckets of imported flowers, someone called my name.

"HIIIII!" the voice yelled, laughing. "OHMYGOD!"

A leggy woman in a silk minidress with dirt on her knees, a basket full of produce, and a filterless Lucky Strike clasped between her teeth was barking at me from across the parking lot. Huge sunglasses obscured her face, a faded Chicago Bulls baseball cap pinned her brown hair back, and gardening gloves covered her hand tattoos, but I'd have known Max de Lacy from behind a brick wall.

"You crazy fucking bitch," Max screamed. "I heard you came up here. But nobody, I mean *nobody* has seen you. I mean, you're a ghost. I cannot believe about your loft. That's so awful." She hugged me and I responded limply.

"I'm at Pine City," I said casually, as though I came up here all the time. "I've only been here a week or two."

"You're going to love it," she said. "It's magical."

"It's great so far," I agreed. A lie.

"Well, I'm glad we ran into each other. I've been calling. You don't answer emails anymore. You're *never* online."

"I've never *been* online," I told her.

"I keep thinking you're going to change your mind."

"Definitely not."

"Well. You can't hide. Not now that I've found you." Max was victorious.

"I guess so." I almost smiled. "Where are you staying?" I asked.

Max's eyes went wide. "We're right across the lake?" she said, a question, a reminder, but graciously, which is when I turned beet red.

"Oh, right," I said lamely. "I knew that."

Everyone knew where Eliot House was—at least, everybody who was anybody. Despite the gaffe, I did know quite a few things about the rust-and-concrete modernist behemoth cut into the hill seven years ago by Max's new husband, Charles Eliot, and his business partner and former spouse, Helen Sprain. Originally designed to showcase artwork from the vast holdings of their gallery, Eliot&Sprain, in a controlled environment, the "smart house" had been completely integrated with the first fully functional home-assist computer—and the interiors were designed by Carey Logan.

I'd never been invited there, either. The moment hung awkwardly between us—this special world, this famous country house she lived in, the hospitality that she had extended to everyone but me.

I looked at the limp bundle of tulips in my hand, which seemed so important earlier, and thought about the glassy corner of *Prudence* where I had longed to press their petals. Now it seemed suddenly pointless, almost dumb. Max had blown the urge right out the window of my mind.

I had to get away from her.

"I'm working. I have to get back," I said.

She handed me her phone, and I typed in the number from the

landline in my bungalow kitchen. Max wrapped her arms around me and hugged me again.

"I've missed you," she said. "I'm so glad you're finally here."

Her shiny hair smelled like the same shampoo she'd been using since we were teenagers, an expensive scent that had always made me feel self-conscious, and all I could do was look down, my face red and my ears burning. I got in my truck and drove off, trying to concentrate as I navigated the asphalt highway at seventy miles an hour. Though I rushed to Marlin's studio, tulips clutched in my hand, when I stood over *Prudence* their significance was gone. Whatever had propelled me to need them had disappeared. I wanted to throw the tulips on the ground.

Instead, I filled a jar with water, clipped the stems, and arranged the flowers on an empty table. They looked better there, I realized, and suddenly all I could see of my borrowed studio was what Max would see: the way the paint spattered on the floor, the meticulously spaced cups along the wide tables, the racks of hanging squeegees, and the poetic smears of printer's ink lurking on each door and frame. All I could see was a photo shoot, a glossy cover of my life, only the style and none of the substance. *#studiolife*. It made me crazy. It stopped me from seeing or feeling any of the things I needed to see or feel in order to make the work, because even at thirty-four, being around Max made me childishly desperate to be like her. A vein popped in my forehead.

As I looked at *Prudence* with new eyes—Max's eyes—I realized that she was complete: There was nothing left to do. A swirl of disappointment passed through me. I wanted to come to this realization on my own, not with Max's eyes in my head.

I looked around the studio. On to the next one—or ones. I needed to find the nearest hardware store as soon as possible, get more materials, to move to the next painting, but suddenly the stress of what lay ahead—eighty days of nonstop work—and what happened—my life falling apart, Max so safe with her husband and the home he gave her—hit me, and I told myself it was time for a break, that I'd earned it, that I needed to take a breath.

Five minutes later, clad in a tattered red bikini and sunglasses that were 60 percent duct tape, I pushed a rubber inner tube from someone else's porch into the water, the waves crashing gently over the round, matte-black surface.

One hand held the tube. The other, a bottle of bourbon from the Mission bar.

♠ ♠ ♠ ♠ ♠

If I'd ever been up here before, I would have known why Carey Logan had been hired, over all the famous artists that Eliot&Sprain represented, to design the interior of Charles Eliot's famous retreat: because Pine City was located across the water. She was talented—naturally—but she also knew the land. Eliot House wasn't visible from Pine City, but I was now certain that Charles and Max owned the other half of the shoreline.

I hoisted my butt into the middle of the tube and paddled with my free hand, spinning like a leaf, then committed to the undignified labor of emptying the bottle. I drank, lay back on the tube, and the lake shuttled me around its vast surface area as I tried to catch glimpses of what was now Max's house.

She'd been living up here for three years, I realized. We hadn't seen each other since my last opening. Max was someone who made me so viciously insecure that I went out of my way to avoid her—an impulsive, competitive reflex that I'd had since we were teenagers—even though I genuinely liked her. And of course, she could have provided an introduction to Pine City at any point, but she was the last person on earth that I would ever, ever ask for help.

Our friendship was an accident. When I was eleven years old, my parents sent me to see my grandmother on the cheapest flight available, one that had a five-hour layover in Atlanta. The airline was supposed to keep track of me. Not to worry, the travel agent told my mother. There was an entire lounge for unaccompanied minors with Super Nintendo and free gummy bears.

I'd been sitting in that lounge by myself for an hour when a stewardess walked in with the tidiest-looking kid I'd ever seen. She wore a crisp, starchy white collared shirt tucked into blue jeans, polished penny loafers, and a dark plaid blazer. Her glossy hair was pulled into a neat ponytail, and she spoke to the airline employees with precision and poise. By contrast I had jelly stains on my childish purple t-shirt, a large scab on my knee, visible knots in my hair, and no manners whatsoever.

"How do you do," she said to me politely. The stewardess smiled at us both and left.

"What's up, motherfucker!" she yelled as soon as we were alone. I laughed in shock at the worst word I had ever heard. "I'm Maxwell," she said. "My friends call me Max."

"Hi." We shook hands like adults. "Wanna play *Mario Kart*?" I asked.

"What's that?"

She'd never played before. I handed her a controller and explained. We spent the next four hours playing a dozen rounds of *Super Mario Kart*. We ate three bowls of gummy bears, sneaked out of the lounge, took the monorail to a different concourse, and stole copies of *Filly* and *Sassy* from a newsstand.

Max was flying from her dad's place in Los Angeles to summer camp in Maine, some ultra-preppy eight-week finishing school, with a gaggle of other rich girls to sail and play bridge. We exchanged our summer addresses and promised to write—a promise that we kept for years and years.

It felt special to have a pen pal, especially one as exciting as Max. Nobody else in my grade had one as good. Max lived in both a real New York brownstone and a real Beverly Hills mansion, and she sent photos giving me the peace sign in cool clothes from her vacations on sailboats on turquoise oceans, from limestone ruins in Rome, from a bridge in Paris. She sent dirty pictures that she stole from I'll never know where and soap opera gossip about her prep school that I cherished. The stuff I sent back—Polaroids of my pet snake, Randolph, "posing" in different locations in our local mall with horrified people in the background—was less glamorous, but she always said she looked forward to them most out of everything.

"You're the weirdest person in the whole world!" she always told me, and I believed that it was a compliment: She was so tidy and well groomed and good at tricking adults, and cosmopolitan, and I thought she knew everything there was to know about the world. She was my number one confidante and I assumed I was hers, and we made many plans for places we would live and businesses we would run and things we would do, together, when we were grown-ups. We carved out a whole world of mutual dreams.

Yet Max's dreams were steps from her brownstone, something I did not fully understand until we were older. Her babysitters became boldface names in the *Village Voice*; her mother was a fixture in Sunday Styles. Her father's family owned a whole town in Connecticut. He lived in Los Angeles half the year, producing movies. We spoke only once, on the phone, when I was fourteen. Her mother asked me questions with such disdain that I knew I would never be invited. Max came from privilege so elaborate it seems almost like an accident, but, of course, it is not.

· High school changed everything. In tenth grade she was cast in a supporting role in a downtown movie about graffiti culture, her pubescent body on display like Brooke Shields in *Pretty Baby*. She won an Independent Spirit Award. Then Max and her friends started appearing in magazines, like her exquisite mother: Her clique had a whole spread in *Sassy*. She began traveling to places that were so exotic I had never heard of them, places like the Maldives, Moorea, Soufrière, even Rangoon, which was a word I knew from the menu at the Chinese restaurant in the strip mall, but not a place I could find on a map. She picked up a camera. Two of her pictures ran in *Filly*, and all my friends could see the credit, right there, when it came in the mail: *Photo credit: Max de Lacy.*

She made being an artist look so possible—so *attainable*, the result of mere choice, of waking up and saying *I think I'll be an artist, that seems right*, though at the time I still didn't understand the gulf between my life in Gainesville and hers in Manhattan—that I scrapped my plans to go to the state university and focused on making a portfolio. Miraculously, I got a scholarship to the Academy, while Max got into an elite university, early decision. She wanted to be "well rounded," she said, didn't want to pick a medium, majored in poetry, minored in French, apprenticed with photographers like Ellen von Unwerth and Annie Leibovitz during the summers, and took up with a crowd of people like her, ones with Dutch last names and very expensive opinions.

I studied painting and only painting.

During that time we were only a few hours apart. My freshman year, her sophomore, I took the bus down to see her for the weekend. Max had a whole gang of people under her thumb, people who resented my closeness to her, and when she wasn't speaking directly to me, then I might as well not have existed. Everybody thought my major was stupid. "Isn't painting *dead*, though?" they asked, unable to hide their pity. "I mean, who cares?"

I wish I had replied that we don't all get to take counter jobs at galleries for minimum wage while still being expected to have a half-million-dollar education, a pert ass, a clothing allowance, a travel stipend, and multiple passports so we don't have to deal with pesky international labor laws. We don't all get to be dilettante jokesters who decide that our work doesn't need to make money, that institutions are the enemy of truth, and then wake up someday and miraculously discover that we have become the people in charge, but I didn't know that yet. I said nothing at all.

On my last night, Max abandoned me to hang out with people from a special club she wanted to get into, and I found myself sitting against the net on the tennis courts, smoking a joint in the dark with a group of her friends. I got stoned fast and told them that I thought time itself was a smokescreen, a construction designed solely to prevent us from discovering that the moment we were in was both the past *and* the future.

The handsomest of the group said dismissively, "You think about a lot of stupid shit." The others laughed.

I went back to Max's dorm, took a long hot shower, burrowed into my sleeping bag, and cried. In the morning, she came in as I was leaving, gave me a careless one-armed hug, and absentmindedly told me to stay in touch.

I didn't visit again. Our letters transformed into emails, which became infrequent and then simply annual obligations. After art school I moved straight to the city—first to that sublet in Brooklyn and then my loft on Dutch. Max was already living in a brownstone off the Bowery with her boyfriend, Petey Delano, the aggressively bearded, amateurly tattooed downtown artist whose Polaroids of her naked body wound up at the Guggenheim after he shot himself in the bathtub.

She got the brownstone.

One night, when I was twenty-three, in the days leading up to *Ohne Titel*, I saw one of Marlin's wheatpasted posters. FAMILY VALUES, it said. JES WINSOME. HIGH LINE. FRIDAY AT 8.

Cady and Atticus were out of town, so I called Max to see if she wanted to go.

"LOVE to," she said, with complete enthusiasm. "Absolutely. I keep hearing about Pine City. I want to see them up close."

We met at 34th Street, climbing over the chain-link fence and crawling through the holes in the wooden blockades all the way down the then-abandoned freight railway to the very end, where it abutted the meatpacking plant on Gansevoort Street. Over a hundred people were already there, a scrum of ripped denim and eyeliner, buzzing and crawling over the piles of trestles and pockets of wildflowers that burst through the gravel.

Jes had hauled full Marshall stacks, a projector, a twenty-foot screen, and six VCRs up there. Her film combined clips of Phyllis Schlafly protesting the ERA; Pat Nixon, rigidly sprayed into a

pantsuit atop a garden chair in Arizona to discuss her shopping
habits; Nancy Reagan on *60 Minutes*, wounded by "scathing" criticism of her White House redecoration; Tipper Gore in front of
Congress, gravely laying the blame for 1985's teen suicide rates at
the hands of popular musicians. Their comments were stacked and
clipped and looped until there was nothing left but the fragments
of their voices, edited to say, "We betrayed you. We will do it again
and again."

All the while Jes sang the lyrics to "Walking on Broken Glass,"
looping it louder and louder, over herself, over and over again and
again, until cops materialized in the street below us, lights flashing, torches beaming. We were forced to disperse. Max and I ran,
giggling hysterically, shrieking ravenously, the entire way. On 22nd
Street, we spied an unlocked roof door, held ajar with a cinder
block. We jumped five feet from the side of the High Line, skin-
ning our knees as we landed, tumbling down the stairwell and
bursting past the surprised doorman. We didn't stop running until
we got to the Half King on the next block.

I ordered us two beers at the bar while Max looked for a
table where she could smoke. When I came back outside, she was
leaning against the back window of someone's glossy chauffeured
Tahoe and giggling.

"Hey, sweetie, I'm grabbing a ride uptown," she said, running
into the patio area. "Kim and Thurston are having a last-minute
thing for Patti," she whispered. "You know how famous people can
be. I'll call if it's chill. Anyway—this was a blast." She kissed my
cheek and bolted.

I drank both beers at the bar, then went home and watched my
phone as it didn't ring.

After that I never asked Max to join me for anything ever again.

For the next decade we lived less than a mile apart but didn't
hang out much: She was busy with the drama of her life, acting,
photography, socializing with actors and photographers, and I was
busy with both my work and the surprisingly complicated process

of becoming a person who didn't think someone like Max had all the answers. We ran into each other occasionally, at parties both downtown and uptown, and she always pretended to be happy to see me, and I pretended back. She got herself invited to Pine City and went three summers in a row—a fact that made me so insanely jealous I swore never to acknowledge it to her face. She made an entire, thriving career out of the art of being herself, a self that, though it was given to her, though it was deposited via umbilical cord, is still its own medium, its own challenge. It's no small thing to be a lifestyle artist. It is a complex and difficult con.

When *Accounting for Taste*, my show at Parker Projects, became a reality, she acted like she was thrilled for me, and brought her friends to the opening, all those other people-*cum*-brands, and they took photos and oohed and aahed, and I felt embarrassed for myself that I'd become another piece of content for them to curate, and I was ashamed, too, that I couldn't get that kind of crowd on my own—they were here for her. I always felt like I was in competition with Max, even though there was no competition, none at all, because she would always win. But she made the gallery happy, and the paintings sold, so it didn't matter how I felt. Max tried to see me more after that—once I became *somebody*. She wanted me to appear on her wall—to be part of the photo stream of her existence.

But I wanted nothing more than to go back in time, to when we were young and I was nobody, and have her still want to be my friend, and there was no way to do that, so the gulf between us did not narrow. Still: She brought another crowd to *The Distance Between Our Moral Imaginations*, my second show at Parker, even though I didn't ask that time, and the crowd oohed and aahed again, and the work sold, and I got to switch to Milot and to make more paintings. Two years went by. Then my loft burned down, I drove upstate, and I ran into her on the day that I finished the first painting in my second, fraudulent set of *Rich Ugly Old Maids*.

♣ ♣ ♣ ♣ ♣

On that day, floating half drunk on the black lake above Pine City, I drank myself stupid, mourning the loss of my loft and my New York life, a loss thrown into relief by Max's appearance in the farmers market parking lot. I hadn't cried yet, but I was working my way up to it.

I was, in fact, wallowing, which is very close to crying. I wallowed *hard*, in all the self-pity I could muster, on an empty lake with a soon-to-be-empty bottle.

I wanted so badly to get in the truck and drive home, but since I didn't have a home, I settled for riding the currents. I lurked on the shoreline that I assumed belonged to Max, but the house wasn't visible; a sharp hill banked ahead, hiding their world from Pine City. Nothing as pedestrian as lakefront living for Max and Charlie.

The hill was round enough to be human-made and so steep it was nearly a cliff. A group of people appeared atop it, pointing left and right and all around, cameras in their hands. They wore the wide-strap linen fascist-minimalist garb of gallery flacks. Two black-suited arms waved behind them.

"Hey!" I slurred. "Yoo-hoo!"

Nobody heard me. I was too far below, the angle wrong, and then the arms were pointing and leading them away, down the hill, to the east, and they disappeared. I pressed a fingerprint onto my red-hot thigh and it came up goose-white. A bad sign. I wanted to talk to them, ask why nobody seemed to ever sleep at Pine City, and I wanted to see Max's house, and I wanted to get out of the sun.

My tube was rapidly approaching the shoals of the hill, covered in a dense carpet of poison ivy and stinging nettles. Paddling away from the shore was a no-go, as my motor skills were functioning in inverse proportion to the amount of bourbon I'd so diligently consumed. Lying there, weak, sunburned, and drunk, I wondered idly what it would feel like to drown, if it would feel *bad*—if it would hurt—or if the cold would knock out all your senses.

Moments later, in a pathetic attempt at standing upright, I lost my balance and found out.

I put down my legs and expected to find ground, but instead, I fell into nothingness—it was much deeper than I expected—and then the tube scooted away from me.

I've never been a strong swimmer.

I tried to get my feet on something solid, but there was nowhere to stand. The tube floated away; there was nothing to grab on to, but I kept trying, jabbing my feet downward, bobbing violently, searching with my toes for sand or rocks.

When I found one with the edge of my big toe, I put my weight on it. My mouth kissed the surface, with breath that was ragged and damp, but there was air. Toes balanced on the rock, I tried to calm down.

I shifted my weight.

Then the rock moved—and I moved with it.

My foot slipped, the algae greasy under my heel, and the rocks grabbed at my feet, catching my ankle and yanking me downward. I was jerked away from the surface.

NO, my body screamed. *NO.*

I tried to swim up.

The rocks held me back.

When my fingers touched air, my head stayed beneath. I reached down to my calf, to shake my leg free, but it didn't work.

I screamed. A mouthful of red water went down my throat.

I kicked and flailed and felt the skin of my ankle rip open, but the rock didn't budge. The water came quickly, in gulps, filling my throat, burning my nose. My arms pumped up and down, up and down, involuntarily, and I tried to reach the surface, but all I could inhale was more red water. Nothing worked. My head felt a rush of pressure, like it was going to explode. I tried to remember everything

I'd ever learned about drowning. I tried to stop swallowing water. My legs and feet began to kick, and kick, and I couldn't stop them.

I was a marionette jerking on a string.

And then, in a moment, a miraculous moment, I put my weight down on the other foot, and the rock moved. My ankle came free. I shot to the surface.

Air.

I gagged and gasped and vomited lake water in a stream. A coughing fit came over me; my arms were still pumping, and my legs were kicking, and a voice in the back of my mind told me to float on my back. *FLOAT*, it yelled. *FLOAT.* I managed to get my pelvis up, and then I was floating, still coughing, but floating. There was air on my skin, in my mouth, in my lungs.

I wasn't dead.

I didn't drown.

It took five minutes before I dared to lift my head—upend my balance—to look for the tube.

I made my way toward it, carefully, on my back. Adrenaline burned away the alcohol. Though I was trembling, cold inside, fizzy, destabilized, I had control of myself once more. I held on to the tube and kicked—and kicked—and kicked—for shore.

🌲 🌲 🌲 🌲 🌲

The first thing I did was throw up, heaving liters of bile-scented lake water into the vintage toilet, sunburned knees pressing tenderly into the peeling linoleum of the floor. Then I took a cold shower, staying under the needles of the spray for half an hour, until my skin stopped cooking itself. Afterward I crawled into bed and clung to the scratchy white sheets, shipwrecked until dawn.

The night was unbearable—rife with fever dreams and nightmares—and every time I heard the sound of the lake on the shoreline, it felt like I was still drowning, like the red water was still pouring from my nose and eyes and mouth.

I crawled out of bed at dawn, tried to put the near-drowning be-hind me and seize the day. Now that *Prudence* was done, there was plenty to do: Call Marlin and let her know that I was ready to move studios. Clean up my materials, box them, put them in the truck. Go out into the world to restock my supplies—set up for the next painting, and the next, and the next.

Yet—my chores happened on autopilot. All I could think about was the lake. I heard it, the waves and the wind, as I made my cof-fee, as I got dressed, as I walked to the studio past all the empty buildings. I saw it through the windows beyond my painting every time I raised my eyes. *No wonder Jack, and Jes, and Marlin, and Tyler were never here*, I realized. The lake was too loud. It would never let them forget.

Humility

Chapter Seven

On Friday morning, a tattooed courier stood in the carport, holding out a creamy white envelope with my name drawn in cursive across the front. I thanked her, still groggy. She nodded, climbed on a motorcycle, and sped away without another word.

It was an invitation, letter-pressed onto a card stock too thick to bend:

MAX DE LACY *and* CHARLES ELIOT
DEMAND the honor of your presence
at their annual SUMMER PARTY
JUNE 10 // 7 PM
ELIOT HOUSE // UNION VALE, NEW YORK
dinner // drinks // dancing!!!! BLACK TIE !!!!

The party was tonight.

I was a late inclusion—obviously—but it didn't matter. Max could have thrown an intimate dinner party with her mean friends from college and I *still* would have gone. That's how desperate I was to see other people.

The day was spent cleaning up after the hurricane that *Prudence* had left in Marlin's studio, working mechanically with the radio on, trying to sort and clean and scrape and sanitize, until the familiar chimes of *All Things Considered* came on at four o'clock.

I poured a drink and started picking the plastic and paint off my arms. My sunburned skin was sore to the touch, but the color, mercifully, had faded from tomato to peach. I did my nails, teased my curls into their fluffy champagne cloud, and put fresh masking tape over the glue bandage on my leg and injured ankle.

But I had nothing to bring, and nothing to wear. I hopped in my truck and drove the forty-five minutes into Hudson, intending to buy a bottle of wine and a dress. I parked, threw two quarters in the meter, and let myself stroll a few blocks of the sidewalks. At some point I passed a young couple pushing something I recognized from Tribeca: a four-thousand-dollar Silver Cross baby carriage. The dad had neck and face tattoos, wore a collared black cotton sweatshirt and matching drop-crotch sweatpants, and exuded an air of complete detachment; the mom, young enough to be in high school, wore a wispy, thrift-store dress, her arms covered in tattoos and cut scars, and a three-, maybe four-carat diamond ring.

I walked into a wine store and asked for a summer red. They came back to me with some wonderfully cold bottles in a clear, light-red color, a red Sancerre, they said, and I handed over my credit card.

I stopped in the vintage shop three doors down and picked out an armful of dresses—things in featherweight silk, the kind of things I never wore because of how impractical they were. As I stepped into a dressing room, the shop's bell rang, and two young women walked in. They browsed and chatted idly to each other while I stayed behind the curtain, trying on dress after dress until I fit into a long, sparkly purple gown.

When I had it halfway over my head, one of the women said a word so familiar that I stopped and listened.

"...Logan, but apparently she was so crazy that she would literally disassociate," said one of them, in a nasty, gossipy tone, dripping with delight. "My boss said that once she got so drunk they had to pump her stomach. Nobody was surprised when she did it, you know? I mean, look at her work. It was all one long prelude."

"Kind of brilliant, if you think about it. She's like a saint now," the other girl said. "She *owns* death." She sounded jealous, and slightly irritated, like Carey had taken control of an idea that should have rightly been up for grabs. A wave of rage swelled in me. They had no right to say those things about Carey. I wanted to jump out of the changing room and scream at them: *You don't know a thing about Carey Logan. Keep her name out of your thoughtless mouths.*

But I didn't get the chance. I was still pulling the dress from my naked shoulders when the bell rang again, and they walked out the door.

🌲 🌲 🌲 🌲 🌲

I drove back toward Pine City with the dress on a hanger, intending to pull over before the party to change so that it didn't wrinkle too much. I felt a current of electric fever as I drove: I was an artist, upstate, going to a party at Max and Charlie's.

Max and Charlie. My friends Max and Charlie. What a thing to say.

When I first met Charles Eliot—Charlie to me later—he'd looked exactly like every other insecure hetero middle-aged narcissist I'd ever met, a category of Manhattan man whose tastes are so insistent, so domineering and mediagenic, that we now have cortados in every coffee shop and hand-sharpened Blackwing pencils at every subway newsstand, lavender chewing gum and copies of *The Gentlewoman* side by side with herbal boner pills and magazines called *King* and *Side Bitch* to remind us that the world will sell us anything we want. Charlie was another product to me at first, a glossy paper cutout. Lean, tall, dark hair streaked here and there with gray, trendy eyeglasses, fine trousers and shoes, a black cash-mere sweater. A man concerned with appearances.

"This is my *husband*!" Max had shrieked at me when we ran into each other unexpectedly at a party, downtown, somewhere in Tribeca. "Can you believe it?"

I could, because he was rich.

"Congratulations," I said to him.

"We eloped." Max beamed.

Charlie stepped forward and held out his hand. A thin gold band circled his left ring finger.

"Nice to meet you. I'm Charlie," he said genially, in a genteel, upper-class British accent, and I replied, "We've already met."

He looked at me without recognition. "I'm so sorry," he said, shaking his head sincerely. The party raged on around us. A drunk woman barged into him and he guided her back into the hallway. "Nice to see you again."

I'd said it on impulse, to see what he would do. Behind him in the doorway Max rolled her eyes.

"She's messing with you. You've never met because she *never ever* goes out *ever*," Max had said decisively, exhaling and stubbing out a cigarette into the stairwell. (I did go out. All the time. But I was al-ways steps—blocks, even—behind her.) "Don't be mad—we didn't have a wedding. We eloped. Nobody even knew we were dating. It's only been six weeks."

"I'm not mad," I told her. "I hope it was fun."

"It was *so* much fun." She nodded. "Hold on. Let's get drinks," she demanded of him, before giving me a quick hug. "Stay right here," she insisted.

I nodded. "Sure thing," I said.

"Nice to meet you," Charlie said. I smiled at him and watched them walk away.

"Seriously, don't move!" Max yelled.

I waited until they were around the corner, and then I walked out the door and didn't come back.

I didn't see Charlie again until my next show, *The Distance Between Our Moral Imaginations*, where he stood dutifully by Max's side as she worked the room and I stood paralyzed in the corner.

"We met in the Atlanta airport when we were kids, can you believe that? But I mean, it was obvious even then. She's a total *genius*," Max squealed, over and over. "She's the last sincere artist in the whole goddamn world. Look at these things. Don't they make you want to burst into tears?"

At some point Charlie brought me a drink, a Campari and soda.

"You don't want that," he said conspiratorially, taking away my glass of cheap white wine. "It'll give you a headache. Drink this instead."

"I want to be drunk," I confessed. "This is terrifying. All these people."

"They don't see you, you know," he said. "You're wallpaper. Whether that makes you feel better or not, I don't know, but it's true."

It did make me feel better, actually, and we fell into an easy conversation, until Max decided it was time to go, and we all hugged goodbye, and they left. That was two years ago.

My dented pickup truck grumbled toward their road, turning at a large brass plate engraved with ELIOT HOUSE. Then I saw the cars; there must have been a hundred of them, expensive and shiny, already spilling out of the mile-long drive, and I felt very aware of every nick and dent on the truck as I rolled to a stop on the spongy brakes. I opened the passenger-side door and hid behind it, watching for passing cars and squeezing into my dress when there were none. Then I buckled Cady's wooden sandals onto my feet, used the side mirror to apply a swipe of purple lipstick, and got back behind the wheel.

At first glance, Eliot House was a kind of Mies-van-der-Hobbit-Hole, a plain door set into a grassy hillside with nothing else visible. From the sides it's barely a house—all you can see are rusted steel walls, commissioned from Richard Serra's studio—but the back is a gaping mouth, three stories of walls that lift like garage doors to open each level to the elements. Eliot House is basically shaped like three squashed donuts, stacked and shoved halfway into a pile of dirt. I've also heard it called the Carey House, a tribute to Carey Logan's interiors, though she died shortly after it was completed.

A twenty-something girl dressed like a lab tech, in a long white coat and spatter-guard glasses, took my keys and gave me a ticket in exchange. A second offered me a glass from a huge fountain of bourbon made out of a hundred coupe glasses stacked in a pyramid, and then I was past the fourth-floor foyer, walking down to the third floor, facing the covered interior courtyard.

What looked like a thousand people were milling around inside Eliot House, lining the courtyards that rimmed every floor, spilling in and out of doorways, openly snorting and licking fingerfuls of drugs from the little bowls of powder strategically placed at various intersections. Some of them I knew—familiar faces from the city—but most of them were strangers. It seemed, in those days, that the art world grew bigger with every passing minute.

Three pianists were positioned on the ground floor, playing the harmonies of a classical concerto. Max stood in the center of everyone wearing a backless gown of unlined organza, the fabric pleated over itself and wrapped tightly around her waist, holding a huge, full-frame Nikon D5 in one hand and a vintage Leica in the other. Her glossy hair was brushed out into big, round curls, like Diana Ross on the cover of *Mahogany*; her earlobes sagged under the weight of an enormous pair of ruby earrings. She was barefoot. I felt my chest cave in at the sight of her. No matter how many new dresses I bought, Max would always make me feel small and shabby.

I stood there on the third-floor balcony, with my wildly unnecessary bottle of wine in hand, and counted their money. There were smaller works, the coins of the realm: A Stella by Sturtevant. Francesca Woodman, her own face blurred out. An embroidery by Louise Bourgeois that read SO I THINK I LOVE YOU. Sarah

Lucas's *Chicken Knickers*. Ana Mendieta covered in blood. Then—
huge ones, the big bills: a fecund, fermenting mass of paint from
Wangechi Mutu. An architectural mass of scribbles and topography
by Julie Mehretu. Resin cylinders from Eva Hesse. A running
slide projection of *The Ballad of Sexual Dependency* by Nan Goldin.
Vines, green, real ones, grew from the ground-floor courtyard,
flowering clematis and morning glory and other varieties I didn't
recognize, and they trailed their way around the paintings and over
railings. I was shocked to see one of my own pieces, *7,067 (Tampons and Ruined Underwear Money)*, on the second floor facing the
courtyard. People hovered in drug-induced rapture in front of it,
holding their hands up to the glowing panels of plastic and oil.

It went on, millions of dollars' worth of artwork. Eliot&Sprain
famously only sold works made by women, though the conditions
of the market—buyers rarely paid top dollar for living female
artists—meant their most lucrative artists were long dead.

A group of people wearing fragile, nineteenth-century summer
whites entered and paused a few feet away. They gaped at the scene
in front of them and turned excitedly to each other.

"The *Carey* House," said one of the women in a singsong voice,
pulling and pushing against the balustrade.

"I can't believe Max lives here."

"She *did* buy new furniture. Still. There's not much you can do.
I mean, the design is the design is the design. You know—all the
hooks and knobs and stuff are *fingers*."

"Isn't this where Carey Logan died?" My skin went hot. I held
my breath and listened.

"Yes...she..." The voice went quiet. "Tyler pulled her out."

"I bet he did. I bet he took her organs." Someone laughed
meanly. I thought about his black house, and felt sorry for him,
suddenly, that nobody else seemed to be able to see his grief.

"Did you know her?" the singsong woman asked.

"No. I mean, I knew her work, obviously," one of the men answered. "It was spooky. All those dead bodies. All that...*rot*." I

felt anger rise up again. Carey's work wasn't "spooky"—it was—it was—I wanted to turn and tell him—*those are women's bodies—we are so afraid—we are so easy to hurt and nobody ever cares—it's not a joke*—but the sound of the party rushed into my hot ears and reminded me that this was not a place I could speak freely.

"Well," one of the women said, "lucky for Max, anyway."

"Not that she needs it," added another. I tried not to snort. That I could agree with.

They ambled down the steps and disappeared. I looked down at my hands, one of which had gripped the railing until the knuckles had lost all color.

Max was still mid-conversation, so, without anyone to speak to, I unclamped my hand, downed my cocktail, and stared down a large abstract painting to my right. It looked like a Rothko, but somehow . . . *better*, a door-size rectangle of blues and tans whose figures seemed to float over each other. The paint was applied *so thinly* that initially I thought part of it was made from layers of nylon stockings, and it wasn't until I examined the surface from multiple directions that it was clear how the work had been accomplished: by the talents of an extraordinarily skilled hand. I squinted at the corner, looking for a signature. Private collections rarely had wall text; the display wasn't for strangers. The point was to talk about it.

"Arcangelo Ianelli," a voice said. "Brazilian. He's dead."

It was Tyler, in a frayed and faded navy tuxedo, leaning against the wall, golden skin shining against the concrete, hands in his pockets.

"How do you know?" I asked, suspicious. I still didn't see a signature and I hated to be shown up about a painting.

"Mexico City. The Tamayo has Ianelli by the meter."

"I've never been," I said. "You mean—Rufino Tamayo."

"The one and only."

"Seems out of place. I didn't think they owned any works by men."

"It belongs to Max. Isn't it good? I think it's so good," he said, meaning it—then changed the subject. "Your painting looks nice."

I nodded, then turned very deliberately back to the painting in front of us. "Helen Frankenthaler was his student, you know—Tamayo, I mean." I was determined to regain my ground on my only subject of expertise. "She said in an interview that she made very good Tamayos. I once made very good Frankenthalers," I admitted. "But I would give my right arm to make a good version of this."

"You didn't tell me your name," he said, abruptly changing the subject again.

"I assumed Susan had."

"*Tomato Tomato*, at the Menil last year, right?" he said, referring to one of my biggest paintings, displayed in an exhibition at a privately owned museum in Houston.

I nodded.

"I'm madly in love with that painting," he said.

I didn't believe him. "*Tomato Tomato* has that effect on people," I deadpanned, swallowing the rest of my drink.

"So *that's* how you pronounce it," he said.

"Yes."

"I'm serious," he said. "I'm sorry for being so rude. Susan said 'my friend.' I thought you were some... dilettante. That's why I gave you the barn. I thought you would leave. She—Susan is old. She doesn't always communicate well."

"Do you haze everybody that way?"

"It's worked in the past," he admitted. "There's a socialite in Dallas with your rose-gold hair. She paints dogs. I honestly—I honestly thought you were her when you drove up."

"Because socialites drive dented twenty-year-old pickup trucks with counterfeit tabs."

"It could have been an affectation."

"It's not."

"Well, it wouldn't have been the first time."

"My friend Cady paints dogs." I was putting him through the wringer here.

"I'm sure your friend Cady paints the best dogs."

"She does, actually."

"Wait." He paused. "Did you say your truck has counterfeit tabs?"

"Did I?" I shook my head cluelessly. "Who can remember."

"I'm sorry. I'm sorry." He said it twice, leaning into me. His eyes were dark green, the rind of a cucumber. "I was late to the airport when I showed you in. I was distracted."

"Why do *you* do it?" I asked, to regain control of the conversation. "Your work, I mean." Savage's recent medium was the talk of the town: real human organs purchased on the black market. He dried them out to leather in the sun, coated them in bronze, and mounted them like trophies. *Slobodan Milošević's Liver* sold at auction the year before for over a million dollars.

"Everybody's trafficking in something," he quipped.

"Hah." I waited for a better answer.

"My gallery says the work is a commentary on commodities."

"What do you think?"

"Why does anybody do anything?" he replied. "What else am I going to do?"

I stifled a laugh. I was softening but didn't want to give him the satisfaction. He didn't know that I felt sorry for him; I wasn't going to absolve him of his bad manners after a few jokes, even if I wanted to. "So. Where's everybody else?"

"Over there. Jack, Marlin, and Jes are all here," he said, gesturing to a cluster nearby—Jack Wells, in an equally threadbare tuxedo, stood chatting idly with Marlin Mayfield, who wore an ocher-tinted cocoon; Jes Winsome, a navy shroud. The three of them were an impenetrable bubble that the party seemed to bob and weave around, a drop of olive oil in a glass of milk. "We were in the city, but we're back for June."

"I should say hi to Max," I said suddenly, the bottle of wine sweating in my hand.

"I'll go with you," he said.

"That's okay," I said, shaking my head. "I'll catch you later."

"Truly, I'm sorry," he said. "We do have a space for you. I'll give you the keys tomorrow. Tonight when we get back, if you want. It's huge, and it's watertight."

My mouth made a suspicious line. "Why?" I asked.

"We're not using it." He shrugged. "Everybody needs a solid sometimes, right?"

"Thank you," I said.

Marlin caught my eye from where she stood with Jes and Jack, and she waved, then pointed at Tyler and made the okay symbol with her fingers, raising her eyebrows as if asking a question: *Did he tell you about the space?*

I gave her a thumbs-up and sighed. "All right," I told him as Max caught my eye and waved. "I should say hi."

"I'll go with you," he repeated.

The stairs, a hard torrent of cement bars spiraling to the ground floor, were difficult to descend in Cady's wooden heels and I went slowly, clutching the bumpy tube of the brass banister. Tyler stayed a step or two behind. At the bottom, Max was waiting for me with her arms held open. I could count the ribs beneath her skin.

"Hello, sweet friend," she said to me, hugging me close. "Hello, Ty," she said to him.

"Hiya, Maxy." He kissed her on the cheek.

"You bought my painting," I said. "It looks nice."

"Good surprise or bad surprise?" Max bit her lip in childish anticipation.

"Good." I tried to smile. Whatever Max and Charlie had paid for it would never see the inside of my bank account.

She swiveled to Tyler. "Did I hear that you sold Idi Amin's lungs last week?"

"Maybe, maybe not."

"Let me know when you have another dictator," she said as she made eye contact with someone more important than either of us. She kissed us each on the cheek. "Try the ketamine," she said, pointing to a bowl. "Find me later. Let's talk, okay?"

I never got a chance to hand her the bottle. Flustered, I turned to walk upstairs, back to the food, but Tyler stopped me.

First he took the bottle and handed it to a server. "Put this in the cellar," he said. "It's through there." He pointed to the kitchen, then turned back to me. "You're sweet," he said. "Nobody else bothered."

"I noticed," I said, trying to swallow my pride. I hadn't realized that Max threw the kind of parties you didn't bring gifts to. I turned around in a circle, trying to find a way out.

"Don't split. You heard our hostess," he chided. "Try the ketamine!"

I smiled—barely.

"It's like a vitamin," he said, "except it's, you know, an animal tranquilizer."

That I laughed at. Still—I held out, trying not to let him see the warmth I felt. "You're going to let me borrow a studio?" I asked insistently. "Tomorrow? Because if not—I shouldn't even be here. I should be packing."

"Scout's honor." He held up three fingers.

"That's Girl Scout's honor."

"Isn't that better?"

He had me. I laughed and dipped my finger in the glowing green bowl he held out, a vintage jadeite saltcellar, piled high with flat, crystalline flakes that melted on my tongue and tasted like hair spray. I dipped again as we started chatting—and again—and again—until the world was a glassed-in ripple, warm as the tropics.

I plucked a section of vine from the wall. It vibrated with life. Tyler helped me circle the blossoming green rope of it into the cloud of my hair like a crown, and then we wandered into the backyard, an acre of clean-cut grass surrounded by stone walls overflowing with lilac and honeysuckle bushes. There was a huge bonfire in the center and the lawn was dotted with lounge furniture, most of it aggressive and modern looking, save for a huge vinyl blob covered in pillows. I took off my shoes to let the cold, soft grass grow between my toes, and it did, in long, silky tufts. Northern grass. Like everything up here, it was better, because it got to die and come back fresh. Everything in Florida is made out of knives, because there are no seasons and nothing and nobody ever leaves.

The garden wall was a pile of fieldstone, like an Andy Goldsworthy sculpture; it probably was one, I realized. When Tyler climbed on it I clapped my hand over my mouth in shock.

"Don't worry. It won't break."

I refused to follow, and, drawn instead to the vinyl blob and its nubby wool pillows, I sprawled across one end. The pianos played Haydn, and the notes scattered over us in bursts, like handfuls of birdseed falling on cobblestones.

I curled my mouth into a circle and took clean, cold breaths while the gentle hum of the party waved around me like a nest of seaweed. I remember feeling the way the embroidery of my dress scratched against the tops of my thighs, and the way the vinyl stuck to my skin, the woolly fur of the pillows in my arms. I was so grateful to be surrounded by people—by their noises and their sneezes and their footsteps in their jeweled slippers—that it almost didn't matter that it all belonged to Max.

Though it felt like days, I lingered on the blob for no more than fifteen minutes until Tyler lay down on the other end, our heads nearly touching, like a capital A. I became very aware of him, of the shape of him, though I didn't dare look in his eyes.

It was becoming clearer to me, on a personal level, *why* Tyler had done so well. Aside from being handsome, he was physically very charismatic; his jokes were delivered in the key of bittersweet; he said sincere things about what he liked and didn't like. He looked you straight in the eyes when he spoke to you and he didn't seem insecure. He was the kind of person you wanted to be around. And his artwork did something to the bottom of your stomach to make you simultaneously uncomfortable and afraid and curious, and that—I liked that. I think everybody did.

At some point a group of people nearby, three men and two women, started speaking loudly. I didn't know them, but they shimmered with the unmistakable patina of privilege. It emanated from them in waves. I rolled in their direction, away from Tyler, and made myself small against the blob, stacking pillows over myself, and poked my head out one end to eavesdrop.

"The gallery is so controlling about the estate," one of the men was saying, rolling his eyes. "I mean—she's one of his artists. That's his damn job. We need this work for the show. It cannot happen without it." The ketamine had dissolved, for the moment, all of the possessive anger I'd felt earlier. In its place stood naked, unbridled curiosity. I stopped breathing and listened.

"She was *the* rebel of our time," one of the women said, in a Southern lady's accent, all pearls and politeness. "So important. *Such* a powerful influence."

"I'll work on him," another of the women said. "We're having lunch next week. Ugh, Brits. You can punch them in the face and they say thank you. It's impossible to get straight talk out of them."

"Well—she left it all to *them*," one of the men said, nodding his head backward to the lake and Pine City. "They could've made millions since she died. Charlie's not the problem. He won't say it but—it's them. *They* are the problem."

Then—abruptly—I felt Tyler roll from the blob. The group hushed each other and fell silent. I twisted my head inside the pillow burrito and watched him, shoulders high and hands in his pockets, sit grumpily on an Adirondack chair in front of the fire.

"Oh my," pouted the Southern one, in faux-embarrassment. "Have we been...indiscreet?"

"Don't worry about it," another said reassuringly, though even I could tell he didn't mean it. "Let's get a drink."

After they retreated, I tunneled out of the pillows and headed over to Tyler, sitting in the grass at his side, digging in the dirt with my carefully polished fingernails. He didn't say anything and I wanted desperately to know how he felt.

"Are you okay?" I asked, wanting to put my hand over his mouth, feel his breath.

It took him an eternity to reply. "Are you one of them?"

"One of who?"

"The Carey Logan fans," he said flatly, rolling his eyes. He was angry—and tense, visibly tense; it was fluttering from him in little ragged pulses.

"I don't have to be," I said carefully. I was going to follow it up with something about how I thought *Yes, Carey was interesting, I mean, the work was technically very finished, and I'd been to several of her shows, and as another young woman artist who was compulsively prolific, she meant a lot to me,* but in the ketamine reverb I forgot to speak.

Relief flooded across his face. The pulsing stopped. He said, "Thank God."

"I liked some of the work, but not all of it," I said, which was true. "Sorry. I mean. The sculptures are extraordinary. The performance work was less compelling. I don't mean to be negative."

"No," he said. "I agree with you."

"So you *can* be agreeable!" Charlie said, appearing in front of us in an absolutely spotless shawl-collar tuxedo, the bow tie and top buttons of his shirt undone. His polished shoes were smeared with wet grass. Without thinking, I leaned down to his feet, plucked a blade of grass, and put it on my tongue; it was slippery and cold.

"*Hello,*" he said to me, his voice warm. "I saw your hair from across the yard. I was so sorry to hear about your apartment."

I put up a hand, and he pulled me upright. I blew the blade of grass at him and he stepped out of its way. Before he could kiss me hello, Tyler stood, and they were shaking hands.

"Nice to see you," Charlie said, his voice shallow. It was obvious that he didn't mean it.

"You too," Tyler replied blankly.

I shifted my weight from foot to foot impatiently. "Can I have a drink?"

"I'll get it," they both said at once.

"Allow me. I'm on duty," Charlie insisted. He managed to flag down a girl with a tray. I picked out a brown one in a round, silver-tipped glass.

"What are you doing with yourself?" I asked him, once we all had a drink in our hands.

"Managing an installation in an elevated park, rather like the High Line, in Macau. The artist is mainland Chinese—she's from a place that actually translates to 'Button City.' Lu Liu is her name."

"Oh." That wasn't what I meant. I meant more, *What do you feel? In your life?*

"You don't like it."

"You're decorating a floating casino?" I said, trying to keep up. "Why? Don't you have enough money?"

"We're devoting ourselves to public space. It's a first step."

"Macau is the least public space I can think of," I said slowly, trying to solve the puzzle.

"Nothing can *ever* be public," Tyler interjected. "Nothing belongs to everyone."

"If that's true, then it doesn't matter what anyone does ever," I snapped. Tyler smiled.

"It's a barter," Charlie explained. "If we finish this project in Macau, the Chinese government will allow us to build a four-kilometer walkway in Beijing, covered in two levels of air-filtering plant life. We predict that air quality within the Beijing Line will be improved by over fifty percent. It could see ninety thousand people a day—three times what they're hoping for with the High Line."

"You got me there," I told him. "Hooray for Beijing."

"Every woman in the world has an opinion on how I'm supposed to run my business." He laughed—but mildly. "Come on. I think we're doing quite well."

"You represent women. You shouldn't route the trafficking of our identity politics through some gaudy money dump that only exists as decoration for the world's richest people," I insisted.

"I heard Milot picked you up," Charlie replied. *Whoops. I'd gone too far.* "Congratulations. Do you want her to give your paintings away?" His tone was light; he was only teasing. No criticism from me could make Charles Eliot feel even the slightest bit of insecurity.

"Jacqueline says that women painters are the bargain of the century," I said. "Maybe she *is* giving them away."

"That's why Hen and I do what we do," he said, tucking a daisy in my hair. "Nothing's a bargain at Eliot&Sprain. We didn't even know you were on the market. You didn't give us a chance," he said, pretending to be hurt.

I rolled my eyes. "*Maybe* I'll be successful enough for Eliot&Sprain when I'm dead," I said, "and that's a big maybe."

Charlie smiled good-naturedly. "I'll have to console myself with the idea that you're too good a friend to do business with. Anyway—how's it going? I assume you're over there painting? I hope you didn't lose any of Jacqueline's beautiful paintings in the fire," he said. "She's been talking about them for two years."

"One. But I'm remaking it. The show is the eighth of September."

He looked at his watch, then back at my painting inside. "Jesus. Are you going to be on time?"

"Barely," I said, feeling shame pump into my cheeks—*it wasn't one painting, it was all seven, and no, I was probably not going to finish them, I was probably going to be even worse off in three months.* I pushed it down and tried to change the subject. "After that... I don't know. I'm looking forward to being between things. All those new ideas that I can't even think about, you know? I can fool around for a while."

"I like the betweens," Charlie said. "I haven't had one in years."

"Can't stand 'em," Tyler said. "I'm never not working."

A girl in a tuxedo leotard appeared and whispered something in Charlie's ear. He nodded.

"Me neither, I suppose." Charlie sighed, sticking out his hand again. "Pleasure to see you, Tyler." He leaned down and kissed me goodbye, the smooth surface of his clean-shaven cheek brushing hotly against mine. "Come over for supper. We miss you."

"I will," I promised.

Tyler watched him walk away. "How long have you known them?" he asked.

"Her? Twenty years, give or take. We were childhood pen pals. Friends, sort of."

"Him?"

"I've only met him a few times," I said, "but he's a nuclear flirt." I wandered into the grass and looked up at the stars. One broke free from the Milky Way and barreled across the sky; I looked around to see if anyone else had seen it, but the crowd around me was busy, talking and laughing, everyone except for a golden-blond woman on the other side of the yard, sitting on the Goldsworthy wall all alone. There was something familiar about her. Like so many other people at the party, she was a stranger who gave me the sense we'd been in the same room before. She caught me staring, pointed at the sky, and waved at me, as if to say, *I saw it too*. I waved back—a tiny little shake of my hand—pleased to have shared the moment with somebody.

When I turned around, Jes Winsome had draped her long arm over Tyler's shoulder, and they whispered urgently to each other. He shifted slightly under her weight, not uncomfortably, and my stomach fell.

"You're the summer girl?" Jes asked once we made eye contact,
her voice a razor's edge, a violent dog whistle, signaling ownership.
Her fingers rested on the lapel of Tyler's tuxedo, the skin dyed dark
blue up to her knuckles, matching the color of the fabric. Whether
it was ink or a tattoo, I couldn't tell. I suspected that was the point.
Tiny charms glittered from within the long ropes of her hair, and
gold sparked from the bottom of her mouth. Kohl rimmed her
eyes, inky pools of ash and hazel, and she drank me in.

This woman scared the living shit out of me.

"I suppose," I said quietly, automatically submissive, as she intended. When she narrowed her eyes, bored with my two-word
reply, I opened my mouth but—as in my dream about the fire—
nothing came out. *Ketamine*, I realized, feeling my heart drift
through the aquarium of my body. *Uh-oh*.

"This one doesn't even speak," she said, rolling her eyes.

I'm too high.

Tyler gave me an odd look. "Are you okay?" he asked.

"Excuse me," I managed to squeak. "I have to find a restroom.
I'll be right back." I grabbed my sandals from the lawn and started
walking toward the house, my cheeks hot, sweat running down my
sides, intending to flee. I didn't think I could drive. *Maybe I could
catch a ride home from somebody at the door, or even walk if necessary.*

On the second floor, I passed my painting. It was lovely as
ever. As my eyes ran over its contours, there were flashes of
making it. Though only six, maybe seven years had passed—*was
that possible?*—I felt much older than the twenty-seven-year-old girl
who had hauled its magenta acrylic up nine stories. That girl (and
she was a girl) kept pot in a little gold box and she loved a musician
who left her over and over again. She used to sit on the roof of 11
Dutch and look through binoculars at the buildings rising up over
her head and wonder if she was ever going to make it.

She could never have conceived of standing here, in this dress,
in front of this painting, in this house, in this context. I sighed
and ran my fingers along the edge. *That needed more beeswax*, I

thought, touching one section with the back of my index finger. *Oh, that's still so right, I remember feeling that rightness*, I thought, brushing another.

"You shouldn't touch the painting," someone said behind me. "It's completely disrespectful." They didn't specify to whom—to the artist—or the owners.

"I know," I said after a moment, withdrawing my little paw. "I couldn't help myself."

The scolding stranger stormed off, revealing an open door to the left of my painting glowing with warmth. I peeked in to find a spectacular library, a double-depth room extending down and lined with shelves, brass rails, and hanging ladders. There were thousands upon thousands of books—on every artist you could think of. *Oooh*, said my brain. *Picture books.* But as I was about to step through, a claw closed around my wrist.

"YOU," Max yelped, pulling me away from the doorway, dragging me to the third floor. The hard bars of cement felt dangerous beneath my bare feet, but soon they gripped a fine rug, and then we ducked through a doorway done in a pale-blond wood. The transom window was made from a smooth pink slab of semi-opaque rose quartz.

"Let's talk," Max cooed. "Welcome to my lair."

It was an extraordinary room. Under an enormous hexagonal skylight through which you could see the night sky, the walls of Max's office were painted with seventeenth-century florals—peonies and chrysanthemums, their petals shining and lush, giving one the overall impression of having tumbled into a Dutch still-life—and an egg-shaped chandelier hung in the corner, illuminating the room with a tender flush of golden light. The furniture was custom: a ruby-grapefruit velvet daybed, a bleached-cedar desk, two huge armchairs, a brass bookcase, and a small coffee table that was 90 percent ashtray. I perched on the edge of one of the chairs. She lit two cigarettes and offered me one; I took it. I don't smoke, but with Max, I always smoked and drank and snorted whatever she did. I couldn't help it. Nobody could.

"I'm so glad you live here now," she said, lying dramatically on the sofa. "I would die of loneliness if you didn't live here."

Max could have died of loneliness anywhere, though I didn't say that.

"What are you doing, Max?" I asked instead.

"Oh, well, I rented out the top of the brownstone because we decided to stay here for the whole summer. I kept the garden apartment open but I haven't been going back at all."

"With your time, I mean."

"I'm doing a book," she said excitedly. "I'm editing all of my photos from the last twenty years, starting with high school and writing about what happened in each one. They're calling it *Just Kids* meets *The Year of Magical Thinking*, but, you know, for our generation."

"That's a good idea." I took a drag of the unfiltered cigarette and picked tobacco out of my teeth.

"I have a *brilliant* writer. She does a ton of collabs. Fleur? Madrigal? Anyway, she's razor-sharp. She's around here somewhere. You should talk to her."

"What's it called?"

"The Art of Losing."

It took me a minute to realize what she was referring to. "... isn't hard to master," I said, recalling the line of an Elizabeth Bishop poem we'd loved as teenage girls.

"Exactly. Of course you would know that right away. Christ, we are so *old*. Look at us." She tapped her cigarette into the ashtray. "I mean, you don't look a day over twenty-five. But *I feel old as dirt*. All I do is get lasers pointed at my skin and needles injected into my arms. Thirty-five and they told me they were going to inflate my biceps 'like a tire' to get rid of the batwings. Can you believe that? And it *worked*."

Self-consciously I remembered the purple lipstick I'd put on ear-lier but never reapplied and reached up to wipe it away; I wondered if there was a purple ring around my lips, if I looked stupid and thoughtless.

"Don't worry, you're good," Max said nicely. "I bet you wiped it all off on Tyler Savage's face."

I snorted. "I absolutely did not. He's very clearly *with* Jes Win-some."

"Ah. *Jes.* She's starting to look like a wizard. But she's 'post-studio.' No competition."

We both laughed.

"He's up for it, though. Always some new summer girl," Max said melodically, looking out the window. Jes had used the same phrase—*summer girl*—and now I understood. "He's slept with half the women at this party."

"Since Carey died?"

"Since? More like during. They were like that, though. Anyway—he's a lover, not a fighter. Speaking of—how's George?" she asked. "Is he still around?"

"No," I replied, shaking my head. "He left me, what, a year ago? I retroactively support his decision. I was the worst."

"You're never the worst. You're the best."

"*We* were the worst, then. All we did was drink and have sex."

"What else is there to do?" She laughed, but I didn't think it was funny, because she was married to somebody who had a hell of a lot more to offer than drinking and fooling around.

"Do you get along with Charlie's ex?" I asked, suddenly curious. "Helen. It's impressive they still run the gallery together."

"Hen? Oh sure. She doesn't care about me—she treats me like a child, kind of, but not in a mean way. She's twenty years older than me. It doesn't bug me. I must seem very young to her. But...it's probably easier because they divorced before we got together.

When they finished the house. This house killed their marriage, they both say."

My skull felt heavy on my twig neck. *Ketamine.* I stared glassily at the spines of the heavy books that lined the brass shelves beyond her shining mass of hair, on artists whose work was only barely familiar to me. Their names lurked at the fringe of my mind: Bas Jan Ader, Hannah Wilke, Charlotte Posenenske.

There was a narrow volume on Lee Lozano, a painter I knew only from her *Wave* paintings—ten solid colors into which she had etched uniform striations in single sessions that ranged from eight hours to three days. The paintings were showstopping in their simplicity, radiating infinite space. I'd read once that there was an eleventh painting but she physically could not finish it and so it remained as a pencil outline, a broken window. She died somewhere tragically, I remembered, but could not recall how.

Max said something that I didn't hear.

"One more time?" I asked.

"I'm sorry you lost your home," she said sincerely, for the second time.

"I'm sorry too," I said, and then I missed my loft with a homesickness so acute that it seemed my bones might break from the pain of it. I missed the sounds, and the drafts, and the way that every nail revealed a dozen layers of paint, all in terrible colors, and the way you used to always have to stop on the seventh floor for a quick pause to catch your breath before the final two flights; everybody did it, that seventh-inning stretch. Nine flights is a lot, and the freight elevator that worked, it seemed, for one week a year, its cage doors held together with special brass tabs that I'd never seen anywhere else. I missed the pigeons that collected in the eaves each evening, turning the windowsills white and cooing me to sleep, and the hot plate and the minifridge and the plastic bathtub with its mystery stains. I would have given anything, in that moment, to go back in time and live the last six months all over again, to have put my paintings in climate-controlled storage like I was supposed to—to have a home of my own, to curl up anywhere the way that Max curled up in here.

Exhausted, and possibly on the verge of tears, I stubbed out my cigarette and stood up.

"I gotta go home, Max," I told her. "This is wild, though."

"No!" she cried, the ketamine melting her face into agony. "Please don't."

"I have to, Max," I said. "I'm overwhelmed."

She hugged me for the second time in the past two weeks and I realized we'd exchanged more words tonight than we had in years. "Make one of the staff drive you, okay?" she said. I nodded.

I let a freckle-faced teenager drive me home with the windows open, and told him to leave my truck at the end of Max's driveway, unlocked and with the keys tucked in the visor, then gave him a twenty. After locking the front door behind me, I shimmied out of my dress, poured myself another drink, and curled up in my new bed. Loneliness ran through me like poison, a jet-black stream of unhappiness that threatened to rip me open, to take the bones of my rib cage and break them in half. The room spun. I felt awful. *Why did I go to that party?* All it did was highlight everything I didn't and couldn't and wouldn't ever have.

I pulled the covers up over my head and shut my eyes until the world went dark.

Chapter Eight

The bright lemon light of the following morning—and the remembered promise of a new studio—blotted out any lingering sadness. I took the long walk back to my truck, taking in the leaves, the dappling light, and every new color of green. The trees shimmied and shook in the breeze, leaves flickering to the ground in bursts and rushes.

I kept thinking about Tyler's question as I walked, whether or not I was one of them. The Carey Logan fans.

I didn't like that phrase. I wasn't a fan. I was more like a disciple.

This is it. This is the end: This is late-stage capitalism. My generation does not get to consider the things that other artists did. The 1950s, '60s, '70s—those photos I used to fetishize of Helen Frankenthaler and Joan Mitchell in the Village—they're a cruel joke to me now. I can't imagine meeting with the Art Workers' Coalition, like Lucy Lippard and Faith Ringgold did, and having demands—not the meeting, that I can imagine. Rather, it is the *having* of demands that I cannot fathom. What would we ask for? And—from whom?

Because—now—nothing exists outside the market. Everything I could ever afford was designed by sub-sub-contracted freelancers, manufactured by modern-day slaves, and shipped through oceans lined with trash by seasonal hourly workers whose schedule is controlled by a computer, whose commute is two hours each way, who are longing for health insurance, who will die in debt. I cannot imagine what it was like to resist before every emotion I had, including resistance, was commodified. What it was like *before*— before we dug our own graves? Or, maybe more accurately, before someone else dug them and we woke up inside? Imagining resistance feels like a dream I cannot quite remember.

There's no avoiding it. We make work and it goes in the machine. If I don't make the profit on the first sale, then somebody else does the second time it sells, the third and fourth times, and whenever, say, the content aggregator "cultural brand" occupying the glass tower they built over the grave of 11 Dutch sees an art-related traffic spike on the horizon for whatever the upcoming art fair might be. "Eight Women Painters You Should Know," writes a penny-a-word freelancer working remotely for an anonymous advertising firm employed by the data contractor of the publicist of my gallery. Then it is reposted forever, until the end of time, accompanied by images of my paintings that don't belong to me because I didn't press the shutter, racking up money trees across the landscape of capital in which I am simply another thing to look at.

There are so many ways to exclude me from the profit margins.

What I loved about Carey's work was the pure, absolute, hard-edged *resistance* of it. Death—*actual death*—genuinely resists being called an artwork. The work of decay resists even being shown. It resists easy, clean, thoughtless profit by relating to our darkest fears. To re-create dead bodies and call them a work of art is to get people to ask what exactly they are paying for when they view an artwork.

Death doesn't resist the commodified conversation—it is perhaps the peak of such a conversation—but it nonetheless resists being replicated. A deliberately grotesque dead body is a work of visual art that (most) people will not take photographs of.

We can't alter the machine. We can, however, inject sites of con-

fusion, distance, forgetting. Even then—it is futile. It is. But still—
I try. I try to make paintings that reach inside people, open the refrigerator door of their chest, take out the eggs, one by one, and
throw them on the floor. The shells break, the yolk oozes into
the cracks of the hardwood—and they forget, if only momentarily,
about the machine they live in. It is true that few people can afford to own my paintings, but there is a sweet and sour satisfaction
in the twin facts that those very same people cannot afford to be
perceived as selfish, and that they will lend a work to any reputable
museum at the drop of a hat. Artworks might be commodities, but
unlike stocks, their value is almost completely derived from social
impact.

Carey knew all that. And she did it better. She had *really* tried.
And I wanted to know the whys and hows. I wanted to know
everything about her. I'd lied about the degree because it was
convenient in the moment; because I didn't want to make Tyler
uncomfortable; because I wanted him to like me—no, because I
needed him to like me. *I had my reasons*, I told myself. *Good ones.*

I wasn't the only one too spiral-eyed to drive myself home;
dozens of cars still littered Max's driveway. The caterers and a
cleaning van passed me; they'd almost certainly be taking dirty
plates directly from the arms of passed-out guests.

My truck was unlocked, keys tucked in the visor, as requested.
The road home was empty, the sun was shining, and with the
wind whipping through my hair and the hard plastic of the steering
wheel under my fingers, it all felt very free. After so long in the
prison of Manhattan, where you were never unlocked, where you
took your laptop to the café toilet with you, it was a rush to be in a
place where nobody wanted the meager things you owned. Sure, it
was because they already had something better, but still, it felt nice.

I returned to find Tyler sitting on my doorstep, knees up, arms
crossed, back in his casual black—sneakers, jeans, the inside-out
t-shirt.

"Heya," he said. "Ready?"

"I'm excited."

"You ran away last night." He rose up above me.

I stepped back a bit. "I was . . . tired, and overserved," I said—not a complete lie.

"No. You ran away from Jes," he said with a smile, stretching, leaning against the house. He was so at home here. "You shouldn't be afraid of her. She's extremely interesting, and incredibly kind."

"I didn't want . . ." I struggled to find the appropriate words. "To embarrass myself. I was saying whatever came into my head."

"I liked how you spoke to Charlie," he said.

"Well—it doesn't matter what someone like me says," I explained. "To him, I mean. I'm a little bug."

"Some bug." He laughed. "Do you need anything from inside?"

I shook my head. "I'm desperate to see the studio," I said. "Which building is it?"

"It's next door," he said, hopping up, walking down the driveway.

"You mean at Max's?"

"No. Between here and there. Want to walk? There's a walking route and a driving route. This way you can see both. Then we can come back and grab your stuff."

"Sure. I'm still starry from yesterday, anyway."

We crossed the resort, past the other bungalows, the Mission, and the lobby, and then we walked along the eastern edge of the forest and turned down a pathway so strangled by ivy and plant life that I wouldn't have dared set foot upon it without someone else leading the way. What had once been a proper road was now reduced to barely a footpath. Tyler marched down it confidently, scrambling easily over the fallen trees and hungry, grasping shrubs, and I did my best to keep up.

As we hiked, the lake making the occasional *shush* sound through the thickets of trees on our left, he launched into a history of the property like he'd done it a thousand times before, which, naturally, he had. Granger's Summer Resort, built in 1930, promised secluded lakeside hospitality equidistant between the Adirondack and Berkshire Mountains. As Susan had mentioned, it was once openly restricted, serving only white, married, hetero-sexual Christian couples. The Granger family allowed divorced couples and people of color after anti-discrimination laws were passed in 1961, but until they closed in 1975, they'd never, they proudly told their bank in a loan document, hosted a single homo-sexual.

"I think they probably hosted thousands of queer couples. In those days, you partnered up, got two adjoining rooms. It's fitting that we took it over," Tyler mused, holding a branch up so I could pass under. "Constance, the last surviving Granger, an eighty-five-year-old pain-in-the-ass, sent me a clipping that described the big bed we used to sleep in and begged me to burn the property down instead. Jes wrote back and told her we were renaming it *Queers*, like *Cheers*."

"No wonder they went out of business."

"No kidding."

I stumbled over a rock. He held his hand out like I might fall. I shook my head. "I'm okay," I said. "Keep talking."

Granger's closed in 1975, and the property sat empty until Pine City purchased it at auction over twenty years later. Waving his hands enthusiastically, beaming with the thrill of the memory, Tyler said they'd taken it on because of the youthful conviction that your own space gave you self-sufficiency and ownership but were ini-tially unprepared for the volume of work required to make the place habitable. It took years for them to fix up the cabins and their studio spaces. But you didn't quit, I pointed out. No. *We were stupid, and naive, and incredibly stubborn.* Influxes of money, he said matter-of-factly, disappeared instantaneously, dissolving tens of thousands at a time into the workaday banalities of roof shingles and updated sewage pipes and the money pit of studio equipment and materials.

I inquired about the studios. He told me that Jack's, the former

Arts and Crafts pavilion, was half textile factory, half woodshop. Jes filled the Theatre with computers, projectors, slides, film stills, and a darkroom, though she rarely used a studio anymore. Marlin's was the print shop, and he, in Sports, the former gymnasium, had installed a bronze foundry and a forge.

"Can I have a tour?" I asked.

"That we don't do," Tyler said, shaking his head, one hand running through the gray of his hair. "We rarely go in each other's spaces. We're together so much that we try to delineate our actual selves." His other hand fluttered with nerves, his index finger pushing back the cuticle of his thumb.

But they loved having guests, he said, or they used to, and most of the bungalows were set up as live/work spaces—the living rooms had the ceilings pulled out to reveal the rafters, so there was a fifteen-foot-high space in each one. Many of the bungalows had been renovated with the help of friends and guests, and in general, anyone who'd done the bulk of the work on a bungalow laid claim to the space in a long-term way. Tyler thought it was important for everyone who came through to see the creation of their work as something that was only in tandem with the reconstruction and resurrection of this aging, creaking, overgrown bygone paradise. He thought that it produced work that could only be specific to this place.

I asked if they were cataloging everything that came out of here, if all of this was a long-term real estate game—*buy the property where x, y, and z were made!* He shook his head. *It's not a game*, he told me. *This is our life. We built our own universe.* I asked if they'd ever worked on anything collectively, even though I knew the answer—they were, after all, the only collective in the world that had never once created a work of art together, only worked side by side—and he said, after a minute, no. Pine City was a way to stay together, to feel like they had a family. That they were a family.

♠ ♠ ♠ ♠ ♠

We popped out of the woods and came to a hill above the black lake. A narrow dock, sturdy and new, jutted from across the other side of the water, but I was certain it didn't come from Pine City; no, this was an aspect of the enormous lake I hadn't yet seen, a finger-shaped outlet that must have peeled away from the larger palm.

The hill sloped down to a grassy beach, where a rickety cedar dock stretched a dozen yards toward the newer dock on the other side. We bounded down a set of dirt stairs, risers made from chunks of four-by-four, and stepped carefully onto the planks. I was afraid that it would collapse under our weight. Tyler shook his head at my reticence.

"It's okay," he said. I nodded, but stayed behind him anyway. When we were halfway out, looking across the silent black lake, a cluster of storm clouds rolled in, bloated purple and gray specters, pregnant with rain.

The sky changed in an instant—from a bright, daffy blue to a sinister yellow-green, that sickly sweet color, like the edge of a bruise, that comes before a summer storm.

"I'm not looking to work en plein air," I said as a chilled gust of wind bit my bare skin.

"There's a barn through the woods. I'm showing you the rest of the lake. Pine City is over there," he said, pointing west. "That's Max's dock. Through that path is her yard, where the fire was last night."

"What's a Dardanelle?" I asked him, remembering the map.

"It's a Turkish strait," he said. "Marlin drew the map. It's some mythical thing." Then he was turning around, leaving the dock, squeezing past me without touching me. We returned to the woods, down another bedraggled path, thorns and weeds bending beneath our steps. Cobwebs dripped from the trees above us, their soft nets catching against my skin.

As promised, a barn appeared.

It was 60 feet across, 120 feet deep, and sturdy—the opposite of the moldering shack he'd given me on the first day—with a double-height loft and reinforced steel doors. I could barely believe it. It was more than a barn—it was a warehouse; it was a gift.

A paved road led away from it to the east.

"That driveway hits the main road just past Granger Walk, the Pine City driveway," Tyler explained. "We took the scenic route, so you could get your bearings," he continued, pulling a key off his ring and fussing with the padlock as the first raindrops fell. I helped him wrench the doors open. Lightning struck behind us as Tyler disappeared inside the barn, into the darkness. I was left alone as the rain came down, hard, the drops ricocheting off the ground and bouncing back up over my ankles. Moments later, the fluorescent beams hanging from the rafters lit up in rows, illuminating the interior all the way to the back, where an extra-wide staircase led to the hayloft.

It was a beautiful, completely professional studio. The concrete floors were level; the windows brand-new; the sinks stainless steel. A gorgeous cast-iron woodstove was installed in the center of the room. There were kilns, too—three electric, and one gas, the size of a walk-in closet. Huge sections of the roof were tiled in sheets of clear corrugated plastic to let in the light, and the side walls were bisected by a high stripe of windows. A small kitchen was partitioned in the back.

The rain started pelting the roof, the drops hitting hard. Tyler waited for my reaction. I couldn't help but stare back at him—at the golden skin running under the holes of his thin black shirt, at the curve of his collarbone and the long lines of his neck, at the raised burn marks on his forearms that I wanted to reach out and touch one by one. He waved at the studio and raised his eyebrows expectantly. I was supposed to speak.

"Why is this here?" I asked, incredulous. "This is—this is a dream." I wandered around the room, dragging my fingers over the empty shelves and racks that lined the walls, around the filigreed surface of the woodstove and the circle of its shiny steel chimney.

Lightning flashed above the clear plastic roof, exposing the space like a photograph.

"Do you like it?" he called.

"I love it," I said quietly, and it was easy to see exactly how to *be* here—to see myself working, to see my future. There was even a pegboard of paintbrushes—though, mostly narrow and ultra-fine, they were, to me, more decorative than useful.

"This was Carey's studio," he said slowly. "But it didn't get a lot of use, not after . . ." He trailed off, his face changing, going slack, then certain. "We want you to use it, for as long as you want."

"Why did she stop using this space?" I couldn't believe it. She'd made it so far that she, as Tyler said, built her own universe.

If I ever reached this level of success, I'd never stop—never.

His spine rose up, feet planted squarely on the ground, eyes boring into mine. "Does it matter? There's nothing wrong with it. It's a great space. It's pristine." Tyler didn't want me to ask about Carey; he simply wanted me to accept.

"Thank you." I continued walking around the room, feeling the space, looking at everything from the drains in the floor to the size of the sinks. The paintbrushes, which had sable tips, were shaped for the fine detail work required of her practice. CML was scratched into the thumb pads of their flattened wood handles.

As I wandered, Tyler stood against the wall, looking at the floor. He didn't notice me watching him. I saw him look at the cracks in the concrete and trace one with his foot, like it was his, like he owned it; I saw him touch the wall with his hand, run his fingers over the light switches, like he was trying to memorize them. His eyes trailed around the room, memory after memory clouding his face, and I wondered how often he'd been in here since she died. I couldn't imagine giving up my partner's studio— erasing them from the world so completely—but I tried to remember that it was *already* mostly empty, and Carey herself had emptied it. Carey wasn't on the map anymore. There were no photos of her anywhere. All of her things were gone. Pine City had already taken her away, for their own reasons, on their own timeline.

"Are you . . ." I ventured, and he snapped back to me, to our existence. "Are you, um, okay with it?"

"Sure." He sighed, nodding. "It's time." For a fleeting moment he looked so sad that I could hardly bear it, and then it passed, and he was his handsome, sunny self again.

"Why me?" I asked—a simple enough question.

"I told you. *Tomato Tomato* meant something to me," he said.

I looked at him with suspicion and he laughed. "Honestly," he said. "Fill this"—he spread out his arms—"full of that."

The piece that he kept mentioning, *Tomato Tomato*, was from my last show, *The Distance Between Our Moral Imaginations*. Each painting in that series was named with a word that conjured the differences between Americans and our long-lost colonial overlords, half named from the song "Let's Call the Whole Thing Off": *Potato Potato, Either Either, Neither Neither, Produce Produce, Privacy Privacy, Leisure Leisure, Patriot Patriot. Tomato Tomato* truly is a painting that everybody falls in love with. There is some quality of love that reaches out of it—love that is so big, and so real, you cannot remember what life was like before you felt it.

"And—because I know you'll appreciate it," he said.

He was right.

I was so engrossed that I didn't hear them pulling in through the rainstorm. Marlin in paint-spattered white jeans and a t-shirt; Jes in navy coveralls. Each carried a cardboard box.

"Whaddya think?" Marlin called out. They walked straight to a metal bookcase, halfway back, covered in tools and ephemera.

"It's an airplane hangar," I called back. "It's a miracle."

"Get your shit out of my studio, then!" she yelled.

"Right now?"

"No time like the present," Jes said, picking things off the bookshelf, boxing them up. "We came to move the rest of the Carey stuff."

"Oh my God, you don't need to move that," I said. "It's totally fine—please don't."

"We're not moving it for you," Tyler said, but nicely.

Marlin tossed him her keys.

"Let's go!"

He drove us back to Pine City in her brand-new Ford F-250, a black behemoth with a gleaming topper over the bed. I stole glances at him from the passenger seat.

When we got to the print studio, he had me open both doors so that he could back in and out of the rain, and by the time we got ourselves inside we were both soaking wet and depositing huge, muddy tracks across Marlin's studio floor.

"Whoops," I said, looking down.

"She won't care. She wants her studio back," he assured me, putting his hand on my arm. Startled by his touch, I tried not to blush. He let go, grabbed a box, and slid it down the truck bed. "We'll mop up later."

He started unlocking doors, revealing a staircase to the upper floors of the building. We draped *Prudence* in plastic and carefully moved her panels to the lobby, where she could lie flat for another month, undisturbed, then packed my boxes and materials into the truck's covered bed. We tracked more mud, this time all over the interior floor mats ("now we're *really* in trouble," he said, and laughed), and roared down the driveway again, zipping south to Granger Walk and then back up Carey's studio drive, a route now familiar on the second going, this time driving the truck directly into the barn itself, leaving huge tire tracks over the once-perfectly-spotless cement floor.

When we pulled in, Marlin and Jes were both leaning against the wall, seltzers in hand, and they helped unload without blinking. The three of them moved in concert, with a routine automation.

Minutes later, everything was unloaded and stacked against the wall.

"Where's the rest of your stuff, dude?" Marlin asked, running her hands through her waist-length hair.

"It burned down."

"Of course," she said, shaking her head, wrapping her hair into a knot. "Right. Sorry about that."

"It's okay?" I asked.

The three of them looked at each other.

"It's been empty since—for years," Marlin said. "We've been—well—miserly about it. It's dumb."

"Seriously?"

"Seriously," she said. "Welcome to Pine City."

Marlin tossed me a seltzer, and we touched the cans together.

"Where's Jack?" I asked.

"Home," the three of them said at once.

"He'll be back next week. Jack has kids," Tyler explained. "He doesn't sleep over anymore. It's only an hour back to his place."

"He has kids?" I was shocked. My long-standing impression of Jack Wells had been—well—Peter Pan, or maybe Robinson Crusoe: He lived on a boat. He spearfished the Hudson River. He carved wood and wove fabrics on looms and only did an exhibition once every five years or so. He was the absolute last person in Pine City whom I expected to be an adult.

"Oh yeah. Jack figured life out. He'll tell you about it, if you ask," Marlin said. She lifted a box, seltzer still in one hand, and then wrinkled her nose at her own armpit. "Ugh. I smell like a dumpster."

"Take a bath, Fish," Tyler said. He leaned over, tilting slowly, and then—before she could stop him—batted Marlin's seltzer to the ground in one swift movement. The can hit the concrete and bubbled over with foam.

She laughed right away.

"You're both idiots," Jes said flatly. I watched the seltzer travel in a rivulet across the floor, toward the drain.

"Let's swim," Tyler said suddenly, grabbing the boxes from their hands and putting them on the ground. "Come on. I'll race you."

He pulled off his sneakers and jogged into the rain. Marlin rolled her eyes but chased him anyway.

Jes turned her head slowly and looked right at me. Even in "regular" clothes—today she wore a runner's crop top and neon leggings with mesh panels on the sides—the ink on her fingers and the gold in her teeth made her look like a traveler from another dimension. Her eyes were cold and her nostrils flared with distaste. I stiffened beneath her gaze and dropped my eyes to the ground.

"He doesn't usually let his girls have studios," she said. "What's so special about you?"

"I'm not his—his . . . *girl*," I stuttered. "We only just met." I was still avoiding her eye.

"What are you even going to *do* with this much space?"

"My painting is big," I said lamely.

"Hey," she said, snapping her fingers.

I looked up right away. She'd moved closer to me, and I could smell cedarwood and sweat, could see the malice glinting in her pupils.

Then: "Boo," she cracked, inclining her chin toward me.

I flinched.

She rolled her eyes and jogged outside.

🌲 🌲 🌲 🌲 🌲

After a few minutes of pretending to use the studio bathroom, I followed. The drops came down, soaking my clothes, cold beads on hot skin, under the olive sky of the afternoon storm.

Tyler had jumped in, and Marlin and Jes followed, diving fearlessly into the lake. I walked out to the end of the dock and paused, tasting red water in my throat, panic on my tongue.

"Come on!" Tyler yelled as Marlin shoved him underwater.

Their bodies disappeared completely under the opaque tint of the surface.

You're not alone, I reminded myself. *Nothing bad is going to happen.*

I didn't jump, though. I couldn't bear it. Instead I scooted on my butt to the edge of the dock and dropped in gingerly, letting the water—it wasn't nearly as cold over here—rise up and over my shorts as I gripped the metal frame of the dock. I was pleased to discover it was shallow, only four, maybe five feet deep. I pushed my feet into the sand and stood still, holding my bearings. *Don't be afraid of the lake*, I told myself. *You have to look at it every day.*

That's when the rain stopped and the sun shone through, warm yellow beams dissolving the clouds.

Tyler was doing a backstroke and Marlin was towing Jes around, dragging her through reeds and into the sand. Jes actually smiled (not at me, and no teeth, but it was a smile) and then it was true summer.

We played around in the sun, floating on our backs, in the space that separated Carey's rotten cedar dock from the finished one on the other side. I swam over to it without thinking, climbing up the shiny aluminum ladder and scrambling across the polished maple of that finer Eliot dock, before I turned and looked back out at the three of them.

They'd stopped swimming and stared at me, hard, as though I'd done something wrong. Suddenly, I remembered Susan saying that I looked like Carey. Maybe she was right, from a distance, when my hair was plastered wet to my skull, maybe we were the same, two muscular little women with big eyes and big boobs, and what I thought was a shiver ran down my spine.

But it wasn't a shiver—it was a pair of hands that touched me. Warm, bony hands that wrapped around my waist and shoved me off the edge of the dock.

Chapter Nine

When I came up to the surface, someone was laughing, and the outline of a foot kicked water in my face. Max—smeared with dirt, still wearing her organza ball gown from the night before—sat on the edge of the dock. A thirty-five-millimeter camera, a Leica rangefinder with a wide-angle lens screwed onto the front, hung from her neck on a worn leather strap. Her long legs reached out toward me, water dripping from her polished toes, and the musical scales of her laughter bounced over the waves.

"You're still in your dress," I said, pointing to the muddy hem. Max looked down as though this was completely normal.

"I slept in it," she said, aiming the camera at me and hitting the shutter. "That's the privilege of being a *lady of the manor*. I sleep in my gowns. Plus, Charlie went to the city."

"Are you high?" I asked plainly.

"Not anymore," she said, pulling the camera away from her face and peering at me with one big blue eye. A strip of extra-long false lashes was only half glued to her eyelid. I squinted back at her.

"Cross my heart," she said lucidly. "I'm in control." She pointed the camera at the studio, capturing the truck's nose peeking out of the door. "What space were you in before?" she asked.

"My studio," Marlin said.

"This is better," Max stated decisively. Marlin glanced away. "For her," Max corrected quickly.

"Speaking of—" I pulled myself out of the channel, took off my t-shirt, and then my shorts, and squeezed the water out of each. "I have to get going. I gotta shop."

"No!" Max yelled. "You're abandoning me."

"Tick tock," I said, shaking my head, turning back to the studio. "Summer is short."

"See ya," Marlin called out. To my surprise, Tyler scrambled after me, grabbing Marlin's keys and holding open the door to her truck.

"I'll give you a ride," he said, checking the time. "You don't have time to walk back. The D-spot closes at ten, and it's a forty-five-minute drive."

"The D-spot?"

"Home Depot," he said. "I assume you need more plywood. Framing, too."

"Uh . . . maybe, I'm not sure," I lied, clipping my seat belt.

"Who do you think you're talking to?" He laughed, backing out.

"I don't know what you mean," I replied.

"That painting we moved into the lobby—it's done. I know it. You know it."

"Uh . . . maybe. Hard to tell, sometimes."

"If it's done, then what do you need this space for?"

"Um." I hadn't thought about what I was going to say. "Stuff?"

"You're a terrible liar."

"I'm a great liar. Not right now. I didn't have one ready."

"I called Susan to chew her out this morning and she said you were working on *one* piece. I didn't correct her, by the way."

"Thank you," I replied.

"How many were destroyed?"

"Two," I lied, smoothly this time. "They take a lot of time and space. I'll be out of here by August twenty-fourth. That's the ship date." I looked out the window, and the air collapsed silently between us.

I thought about Max's remark that he had a "new girl every summer," and Jes's repeated use of the phrase. I thought about Cady saying he was manipulative. I could sense that he was involved with somebody, though after forty everybody is probably emitting that same exact beacon, the one that comes from a lifetime of falling in love over and over and never choosing.

He dropped me at my truck, and I thanked him again for the ride.

"See you," he said genially.

"See you." I climbed in my truck and followed his taillights back down the driveway, where we turned our separate ways.

♣ ♣ ♣ ♣ ♣

I sat in the parking lot of Home Depot with a leaking Bic pen and a spiral-top notepad, doing arithmetic.

Six paintings, four panels each. Seventy-four days left, including thirty to dry (if I cut everything with Liquin, heavily), leaving me forty-four days to paint. *Prudence*—who went rather quickly—took thirteen days. Times six? I didn't have it.

Forty-four days. Forty-four days. *Forty-four days. Six weeks, two days. Seven hundred and sixty-eight square feet of paint.*

I lowered my head to the steering wheel and sighed, watching the condensation of my breath appear and disappear, over and over, on the textured plastic of the horn. The breath flashed in and out so fast, moving all at once, the world's fastest, smallest tide.

A tide. A body moving all at once. Swelling in unison.

A tide.

That was it: The only way to do it was like a tide—all at once.

Of course. Then—oh then, I could take my time. Everything would dry, no question. I could mess up and add a layer if I had to, scrape them back. *Oh—this was roomy, this was brilliant, this was the way to get it done.* I raised my head, climbed out of the truck, and skipped into the warm fluorescent embrace of the store.

Yet what seemed like a genius solution in the parking lot of a Home Depot on a ketamine hangover was significantly more distressing once I stood in the lumber aisle. I needed—shit—four panels per was a total of twenty-four sheets of five-eighth-inch plywood, at roughly eighty-three pounds per sheet was . . . nearly two thousand pounds.

Oh God. I sat down in the middle of the aisle and kept adding.

Plus two-ply lattices—one per panel; twenty-four sheets, twenty-three pounds per, another, what, five hundred, six hundred pounds? Each panel, backed with fiberglass, required twenty-four linear feet of wood to frame plus four feet to angle the corners, twenty-eight feet, times thirty-six, was . . . *oh God . . . a thousand? Ish?* Yes. One thousand and eight. Plus trash cans for mixing, foam to carve the molds, canvas drop cloths, four or five dehumidifiers, the big kind, however many they had, at least a dozen gallons of Elmer's, and four or five pounds of drywall compound.

I ordered from an associate at the counter, who promised they could deliver everything the following day. She rang me up, and then I remembered the sawhorses; I'd need . . . oh, two per panel, so . . . forty-eight of those, too.

"What kind of truck do you have?" she asked.

"Nissan," I said. "Six-foot bed."

"It'll be delicate but we can rope those in tonight if you want," she told me. "Tip the guys if that's okay," and I almost hugged her. The bill wasn't bad: five grand.

Five was only the beginning. I needed pigments, and dozens of gallons of medium, Liquin, Galkyd, and turp too—not to mention resin, silicone, bleach, rubber, beeswax—and so I sat with my notebook, adding it all up while they loaded the truck. When they finished and the tips were dispersed, I called Pearl once—no answer. I checked the time and called again: nothing.

On the third try, Jonah picked up.

He didn't sound happy. "You know we're closing right now," he said, annoyed, instead of the usual "Pearl."

"I have a big order," I said. "And I need it delivered ASAP."

"Where to?"

"Pine City."

He let out a long whistle. "You did it." He was impressed.

"How soon can you get a truck up here?"

"I can get Terry to do it, probably on Tuesday, maybe Wednesday."

Rattling off my list and confirming the quantities took another twenty-five minutes and cost over twenty-two thousand dollars, plus fifteen hundred for delivery. Jonah dutifully took it all down, and at the end, he said *Good for you*, and I could hear his smile.

"Hey, Jonah?" I asked, right before we hung up.

"Yeah?"

"Don't tell anybody, okay?"

He paused. My whole body tensed.

"Buy me a drink sometime," he said. "And we'll be even."

This time it was my smile you could hear through the phone.

He hung up. I called the Irish bar where Jonah often went after his shift and asked to charge a hundred-dollar tab to my card in his name, with a note that said, *Here's a dozen until I can buy you one in person.* The bartender asked, *Plus tip?* I said, *Sure*, high on charges. I'd spent twenty-eight thousand dollars in less than an hour, on top of the six I'd charged on my way out of Manhattan, *So yes, plus tip, thirty bucks, have a great night.* She said, *You too, dear,* and then I rested my forehead on the steering wheel and sighed.

I should have done this earlier. I should have sat down and talked it out with someone and made a legitimate, workable plan and not hightailed it up here and made one painting and gotten drunk and sunburned and fucked off for an entire night on animal tranquilizers like an asshole. I should take it all more seriously. I still had to pay for the crating, the shipping, and accidents; there would almost certainly be multiple mistakes to come, *I would screw up,* oh God, the whole thing was so complicated, what was I doing? *It was supposed to be fine art. These were supposed to be objects I'd spent two years on. Not forty-four days. This was fraud. This was wrong. I was a cheat. Above all else I was a liar. Someone would find out and nobody would buy the paintings and I would be thirty-four thousand dollars in debt with no job and no career and everything would be over forever. I'll be a warning sign, the cautionary tale professors tell their students, an apocryphal mistake.*

And then I did what I always do: shoved my feelings into the bottom of my body where I didn't have to look at them and went back to the studio.

Carey's studio. No—my studio.

Pine City took no interest in me until they knew who I was and saw for themselves what kind of paintings I made. This was exactly what I expected—what I'd grown to expect from everyone else—and it didn't bother me in the slightest.

For what is the point of a career, if not to legitimize yourself?

The point of a career as an artist, you might say, if you are lucky enough to have one, is to express yourself. Sure. *Of course.* Self-expression is the thrust of it. But it also becomes about identification; it becomes the bedrock of who you are as a person. I think there is something about accomplishment—where you become so embittered by the realities of how hard it is to make it, to get anywhere at all, even to a place where you're broke and living in a rotting shack in upstate New York and sleeping on a borrowed fifty-year-old mattress—that it is no longer possible to connect emotionally with anyone who had it easier than you or, more particularly, *differently* from you.

The struggle to be a working artist is its own special kind of challenge. It involves so many compromises and instabilities and trade-offs, you find yourself automatically discounting anybody who had it normal—anybody who had a five-year plan after college or, more likely, graduate school. Is it legitimately hard to get a decent corporate job and climb the ladder and go into a fluorescent-blinking-cubicle cage every day and make shapeless conversation with people you can't stand, to cash the indignity of such a paycheck every other week, to stick it out so you can feed your family, afford a home and a car and retirement? Yes. It is. It is *very* hard, but it is a different kind of hard from knowing that you ought to fly yourself to Venice and lie about a meeting with a collector so that you have an excuse to go to a party in a palazzo that you know will be photographed and thus place you on the party pages in the correct section of the intellectual department store, even though you don't speak a word of Italian, even though your bank account will subsequently be empty for weeks, which will eat you up inside until something comes of it, which it often does, often enough that you make those kinds of bets with unnerving frequency.

A five-year-plan kind of life is a different kind of hard than lying on the floor and waiting for paint to dry—than stuffing your brain with random information on blind faith that it may ferment and hatch and become something new—than putting all of yourself into something that eventually somebody will buy and take away from you.

I'm not saying a risk-heavy lifestyle of erratic creative production is better than any other way: only that what it is, is *mine*. It is what I know. Every shade and stripe of every possible variety of connection is about wanting, above all else, to be known; for someone else to see as much of you as possible. Shared experience is important. It's not everything, but it's *something*, because nobody wants to be explaining at forty to a hostile audience why they are the way they are, but you don't want to punch below your weight class, either, and wind up with somebody who only loves you because they don't know any better—because the day they do know better is the day they'll walk out the door.

What I mean is, if you're somebody like Tyler, or somebody like me, it's hard to form new friendships. I wasn't insulted by the way he'd come around after the first-quarter buzzer, and I took him at face value when he gave me Carey's studio because I truly did appreciate it. And—she was dead. She didn't need it.

But I *was* wary about the others. I had no idea what they meant to each other, or what Carey's studio meant to them. I couldn't see their allegiances, their hurts and scars, the depth of their love for each other. I knew it was there, like how you know the air is there, but I couldn't even begin to guess at the particular chemical makeup of the thing or how much oxygen was in it—or whether or not it would explode under pressure.

It took an eternity to physically unpack, assemble, and space forty-eight sawhorses, but I did it, and when it was finished it was the middle of the night and all I wanted to do was collapse. I considered sleeping in the truck bed, but double-checked the loft, though it looked empty from below.

Miraculously there was a long orange sofa, a vintage four-seater spackled with smears of paint, shoved all the way at the back. It faced the wall. I couldn't be bothered to move it, so I fell into it, pulling a stiff canvas drop cloth over myself as a blanket.

I lay there, picturing Carey doing the same, unwilling to sacrifice the minutes it took to return to her white bungalow, working as hard as I did—no, harder—but I could *not* picture her quitting, walking in here and saying no, no more, I don't need this, it's not for me. Painting was hard, but I knew what would happen if I stopped. It would be like the days after *Ohne Titel*, when I was lost and depressed and devastated. Carey was the same. Obviously. It killed her to stop. *There had to be a reason*, I thought. I worried that it was the nature of the labor itself—that eventually you had to quit or you'd die alone, become the rich, ugly old maid of my imagination. Working like this kept you estranged from people. I had an awful thought: *What if—what if, even with success, and travel, and friends, and lovers, and a beautiful home, all the things I want, all the things she had—what if, no matter what, it simply became too lonely?* Carey *worked*, alone in this room for months on end, *years* on end, while Jes and Tyler—what—fell in love? I thought about Jes's possessive meanness, performer Jes, who managed to be the center of attention by doing something extraordinary. *Was the temptation to perform because Carey wanted to be more like Jes? Was she afraid of losing Tyler? Had she lost him already—was it an attempt to get him back?*

These questions ran ragged in me, little hamsters on their wheels of doubt and anxiety, and I drifted alongside them until morning.

At dawn I rolled onto the floor, willing myself awake, face pressed to the cold concrete, trying to muster the energy to get up. When I turned from one side—*ugh studio, so much work*—to the other, facing the dirty orange tweed, I noticed the cardboard edges of shoe boxes poking out beneath the upholstered skirt. Seconds later I was on my feet, dragging the sofa aside to reveal a treasure trove of boxes beneath, and then I was wide awake, active, cutting open the tape that held the first box closed with the edge of my thumbnail. The nail broke. I bit it off, spat it to the side, and wrenched the box open.

It held a hundred or so small drawings on cheap penny sketch paper. They had a juvenile quality to them, a kind of childish, overly detailed look, like a Disney cartoon, too earnest. I didn't like them at all—they seemed very teenage, illustrated—and many of them were signed *Maria*. The next box held assorted photos of a young couple in the late 1970s, camping with two little toddlers, a boy and a girl; the same images that had been on the sketches, clearly drawn from these photographs. Halfway through the pile of photos, sliding them through my fingers like they were playing cards, I stopped and closed it back up. This stuff wasn't Carey's—

it looked like a Goodwill haul, the kind you'd pick up in bulk
for collage work—and still I'd gone through it like a hungry dog
rooting through the trash. I was bitterly disappointed. There was
nothing to get, not from this, and I was embarrassed on her behalf,
this Maria girl, for her terrible work. *Don't let this trash get into your
brain*, I told myself, and shoved the boxes against the wall and tried
to banish them from my consciousness.

The next five days were, as I expected, physically agonizing—
worse. The lumber, forklifted inside the barn doors, was shrink-
wrapped to the pallets in tall cubes, and I had to climb up the
ladder to get the top sheets down. Eighty-three pounds is difficult
enough when you're on solid ground, harder still when you're balanced on an aluminum staircase, so I broke two sheets in half—
dropping them and watching them bend in slow motion, snapping
and splintering—before getting the hang of it. Once they were
down from the pile, they needed to be dragged across the expanse
of the studio, which I did using one of the couch cushions and a
drop cloth (it turned black in about five minutes) before angling
them onto their sawhorses. I did this twenty-four times, and then
I spent the entire next day with a makeshift table saw (a circular
saw clamped to a sawhorse) making angled cuts on one-by-fours
for the framing. I screwed framing to each panel—performed eight
times per panel, twenty-four panels—192 repetitions of the same
action.

I didn't see anyone from Pine City because I returned to my
bungalow only twice in five days: once for a bag of groceries and
my toothbrush, and once to shower. I longed for someone to visit
me, to break apart the solitude, but I knew everyone would leave
me alone. If I wanted to see people, I'd have to go to the Mission, or Max's house, or, I guess, the nearest bar, which I still hadn't
found, but if I was going out, then my work wasn't getting done,
so I camped out at the studio, jumping in the lake to shower, using
the studio kitchen to make coffee and sandwiches, and passing out
every night on the orange sofa with a drop cloth for a blanket.

I was an animal.

Terry from Pearl showed up midway. We unloaded outside—I didn't want him to see what I was doing, because Terry delivered to *everybody*—and in the end I wound up giving him a hundred in cash and asking him directly to keep the delivery to himself. He agreed readily. It obviously wasn't the first time he'd been asked for a little discretion.

It took an hour for me to drag everything inside. As I grabbed the final boxes, I heard a splash in the channel. Jes sat there, in a red plastic kayak, tapping her fingers along the paddle, snickering loudly. Though we made eye contact, I kept unloading as though I hadn't seen her, as though everything I was unloading was a perfectly normal amount for one single painting. By the time I finished, she'd paddled away. I returned to the studio, panicked. *How much did she see?*

Jes did not like me. She had no reason to keep my secret—in fact I suspected that she would be delighted to see me fail. Still—Tyler liked me, I thought, and so did Marlin, and Jack—I could get Jack to like me, if I tried hard enough. If I appealed to the unit, I didn't think Jes would throw it out of balance. I resolved to stay out of her way.

Next: flip the panels onto their framing. After that: gesso, forty-eight coats, with sanding between, followed by lattices to cut out of two-ply. To keep track of what belonged where, I let myself paint a teensy, tiny bit, labeling the panels and the sawhorses: O1, O2, O3, O4, H1, H2, H3, H4, and so on.

Saran the paint bucket, Saran the brush. Stare down twenty-four sheets of two-ply and pencil in patterns you can barely recall.

That's when I broke—five days in—on the last step, only two lattices in, my arms so tired and my back throbbing and my quads burning and *I hate pencils, I hate them, only Agnes Martin made pencils tolerable, in my hands they are crude and worthless.* I cracked one in half, locked the doors, and left.

♣ ♣ ♣ ♣ ♣

When I returned to the resort, Jack Wells sat on the deck of the Mission, reading, so I threw the truck in park to say hello to the only member of Pine City I'd yet to meet.

He was alone, sprawled in an Adirondack chair, pajama pants and an Academy sweatshirt, nose in a book of short stories titled *Faces at the Bottom of the Well* by Derrick Bell.

"Hi," I said, introducing myself. "You must be Jack."

"The one and only," he said, smiling a genuinely nice smile. "Welcome to Pine City. I'm sorry we didn't get to meet at the party. Max said you weren't feeling well."

"Ketamine is not my strong suit."

"Totally fair." He pointed to the Mission. "I made a pot of coffee inside if you want some."

"I'd love that, actually," I said. "I haven't spoken to anyone in days. Refill?"

He nodded, drained his mug, and handed it to me. "Thank you," he said.

I ducked into the mess hall and behind the bar, filling the heavy, rounded ceramic mugs from an old Mr. Coffee flecked with orange paint. I stirred packets of sugar and powdered creamer into my own cup, and as the coffee swirled and mixed, I stared through the windows at the lake. In the corner of my eye, I saw a black-suited man, surrounded by people from the party, the ones who had spoken so carelessly in front of Tyler. *Charlie.* He was pointing at the lake, at the buildings, one by one, explaining something, and then he brought them over to the east again, toward the path that led to Carey's studio.

"Do you see Charles Eliot a lot?" I asked Jack as I settled into the Adirondack chair beside him.

He looked surprised. "No. Why?"

"Oh, he was there, on the hill, with some curators from the party."

"That's weird. What were they doing?"

"Pointing, taking pictures."

"Where'd they go?"

I pointed to the east. "Over toward their dock."

"The Carey Logan tour," he said, annoyed. "See where she lived! See where she died! Bathe in the water!"

"Oh, I'm sure that's not it," I said. I felt badly. "It's such an extraordinary property. I'm sure he likes to show you guys off. This place is crazy," I insisted. "I can't believe it, almost."

"It's nuts," he agreed. "It's such a liability. But it still works for me, even after all these years."

"Tyler filled me in a little, on the history. It must have been so much work."

"Oh. It was."

"Are you tempted to sell?"

"Never ever ever. Sunk cost fallacy." He laughed. "I think it was the wiring that pushed me over the edge. Tyler jokes that I'll be making my grandchildren do their homework under the lights in my studio, like—*you better appreciate the wattage, this is your inheritance!*"

I laughed. "I heard you have kids," I offered. "I didn't know anyone in Pine City had other responsibilities. I thought this place was a bacchanal."

"For everybody else, maybe, but I'm sober and married now, with, yeah, two kids," he said. "They're three and one, both girls," he added, in that proud-parent singsong, and I made a *gimme* motion with my hand. Soon he was showing me a video of a round-cheeked toddler in a Spider-Man costume helping her year-old baby sister walk in the grass, his wife chasing behind them in a pencil skirt and sweater, laughing, and I was in love with them immediately.

"Bell is three, and Audre is the baby, fourteen months, and Emmeline is my wife."

"That is a beautiful family," I told him. "You're so lucky."

"I know it. Thank you."

"What do you do during the year?"

"I'm the chair of fibers at the Academy." He said it like it was embarrassing.

"That's amazing," I replied.

"Yeah," he said, shrugging, "it's good. It's good to be back there. I was teaching at Yale some, but the commute didn't work with my wife."

"What does she do?"

"Em is a public defender," he explained. "She's extremely busy. And I don't have studio time during the semester anymore. Her mom comes and stays during the summer when she can," he said, making prayer hands and raising them to the sky, "so that I can be here during the week."

"Wow. Lucky."

"For now," he agreed, nodding. "I mean, my wife is on a roll. This time in our lives is about her. I never wanted to teach—hell, I never wanted to be sober either—but I couldn't continue to be unstable without making *her* unstable, you know what I mean?"

I laughed. "In theory. Definitely not in practice."

"You're young," he said. "You've got all the time in the world."

"It feels like I wasted it already."

"Oh, don't give me that," he said sincerely. "I must have heard your name twenty times this year."

"I'm freaking out, all the time," I confessed. "I feel like I'm holding on by a thread."

"What's next? I heard about your loft. I'm sorry, by the way. That's—unimaginable."

"Thank you. I don't know. Maybe—maybe I'll buy a place up here."

"You like it?"

"I like *space*. I don't have any feelings about the actual *place* place. I mean, what do I want?" I ticked off my wants on my fingers. "I want a studio and a nice bed and to not be a million miles away from everyone I've ever cared about. It's what everybody thinks about upstate, right? Like, it's the idea of the country, but the fact that it's outside the city is what counts. If we *genuinely* wanted to be rural and lonely and authentic, we'd move to Nebraska."

"Hudson looks like Greenpoint these days," he said. "White people with bad haircuts."

"On my way up here, I passed the nicest-looking union hall I'd ever seen. I asked somebody about it when I got gas and they said, Oh, Local 110 is a locavore restaurant."

"We're never on time, are we?" he said, laughing and shaking his head. "Baudelaire said we're supposed to have our fingers on the pulse—that's what makes us artists. But I'm late to everything."

"If I spent any time worrying about that I'd have to kill myself," I agreed, swatting at a mosquito on my thigh—before choking on my coffee with a cringe of regret. "I'm so sorry," I said immediately, wanting to claw it out of the air. "That was a terrible thing to say. Thank you, by the way, for letting me use Carey's studio."

"Don't stress," he said. "It's been a long time. It's not Carey's studio anymore."

"What was she like?" I heard myself asking.

"*She* was a trip," he said thoughtfully, looking out at the lake. His hands fiddled with his bookmark, pulling it out and lining it up with the bottom edge over and over. When he moved his thumb, I could see Eliot&Sprain engraved as the return address. "Did you like the work?"

"I—yes. I mean—there are not a lot of *us*. My work is sincere, to be honest, and I got the impression that hers was, too." He changed as I said this—closed up a bit—and I tried another tack. "Women are minimized so hard that when she was alive, I felt like I was in her wake, even if our work wasn't actually similar. Do you know what I mean?"

"I'm a Black man working in fiber, I'm sober, I'm a professor, I'm a dad. I've got about three role models and none of them are in my medium, even. Charles Gaines comes the closest. Jack Whitten, sort of, but he lived on an island. *Hell* yes, I know what you mean. I'm creatively lonely all the time."

"Right? It's so dissonant. I want to be an individual, I want my work to be so unique that everyone says there's nothing like it, but then, I'm always looking around, like, who's making tracks? Who can I follow? How am I supposed to do this?"

"Yeah. I think it's unavoidable."

"I met her once," I said. "Carey, I mean. She was the center of attention without doing anything."

Jack, looked at me intently. I couldn't quite put my finger on it—it wasn't quite suspicious, it was more than that—it was—*careful*. "That's the most accurate description of her I've ever heard," he said. "If there ever is a retrospective, I'm putting that in the wall text."

Or maybe—*friendly*. I breathed out. "Are you ever going to do one?"

"That's a hard topic around here. My personal feelings aside, I've had a hard time at shows where the person died only recently, you know? I *hate* seeing the bad work. I hate seeing the ephemera. It always strikes me as something that the artist wouldn't have consented to if they were alive."

"Isn't that true of all retrospectives? Isn't it rifling through a dead woman's purse, every time?"

He pursed his lips. "Well...not when it's a historical experience that is de facto presented out of context. I'd do it in fifty years, when everything is so different, and there's a lens, a conclusion about *this* time. But I personally don't have any interest in doing it now. We don't know what she would have consented to. And I don't know who it would serve—only the secondary market. And fuck those people."

I laughed. "I know what you mean." I looked across the lake, toward Max's house.

"Your painting looks great over there, for the record."

"That was a definite surprise."

"You should be flattered. They don't have any of our work over there," he noted. I was surprised that he didn't consider Carey's interior design—the concrete tomb—within that great big *our*.

"Ha. Well—it's good to know that everybody's burned by something," I said, "even you."

"You're welcome," he said, laughing in agreement. The stylish young man who once parked a convertible on the sidewalk in front of the Guggenheim—not the curb, the sidewalk itself—leashing it to the railings with a yarn woven from his own hair, had found middle age, sweatpants, and fatherhood, and I liked him so very much. Jack Wells made me feel, for a moment, like I finally had someone to look up to.

The conversation turned back to the other things we shared. We had a lot in common: He was from rural Georgia, a hundred or so miles from where I grew up; we went to the same school; we knew a lot of the same people, or rather, I knew *of* the people he knew, which I freely admitted, which he understood because once upon a time, he'd been my age, too, and so on and so forth.

"I'm tucking in," I announced, when the ache in my back screamed so loudly that I was reminded to go lie flat on my bed. "Thanks again for letting me use Carey's studio. It means a lot."

"Don't thank us. It's truly fine," he said. "She wouldn't have cared."

"Really?" I asked, incredulous.

To my surprise, he gave me a real answer. "No. Other people didn't matter to her. She was kind of a dangerous person, but she had a real aura to her, a sort of unreality that was kind of magically pervasive." The words poured out of him with a sudden rapidity. He didn't sound angry—but he didn't sound wistful, either. "Like you said, she was the center of attention without ever doing anything. You got the feeling that anything could happen when she was around," he continued. "And in retrospect, whatever happened, happened because she made it happen." Jack shrugged, turning his book over and over in his hands, staring out at the water. Then he shook his head and opened his book. "Anyway. Nice talking to you."

"You too," I said. "See you around."

I went home to my bungalow with his description of selfish, magic Carey Logan burning a little hole in the back of my brain, feeling, for the first time, jealousy curdling around the edges. Carey had all of this—and she walked away, onto a stage and then into the water, like it was nothing.

Chapter Ten

When the backings and their lattices were done, I'd made it to the starting block. It was time to *paint*. No more setup, no more fucking around. I was back in the art of my business.

The twenty-four panels were arranged adjacent to each other in long stripes: four panels across, six up, wide, roomy aisles between. Each stripe was its own row: *Humility* was first, closest to the door. Then *Chastity*, *Modesty*, *Temperance*, *Purity*, and finally *Obedience* lay blank and open below the steps to the hayloft. In a few weeks, I'd move *Prudence* in here, too, once she was firm enough to transport, and then they'd all be together again.

I planned to work from front to back, at first, to stagger and rotate the drying times, and I made a chart, of what to do on what day, how to move forward, how to take one step at a time, but I was nervous anyway. No—I was more than nervous. I was terrified.

The chart directed that I should start with the base layers of *Humility* and *Chastity*. Both required large quantities of beeswax, petroleum, and resin in the medium. I'd tested the proportions with Galkyd and it had come out clean. Everything would be fine.

There was no reason to be nervous. I knew exactly what to do.

Yet—when I went to heat the beeswax, my fingers on the wheel of the lighter, I was overcome. First my hands went slack, and the things they held fell to the ground. Pearls of wax rolled across the concrete. Immobilized, watching the beads run from me, a crack of pain formed in my right clavicle and my breath stopped. Then the studio became a collapsing balloon, its walls and floor turning to rubber, rushing at me, deflating fast, impervious, airless. It felt as though the air itself was a plastic bag over my mouth and I could not breathe.

I stared at the white ocean of gessoed wood in front of me. Carey had once filled this hangar, too, painting, glazing, and firing a veritable terra-cotta army into realistic facsimiles of dead bodies. My mind boggled to think about how much work that must have been: molding, casting, bisque firing, glaze firing, mistake after mistake, loss after loss. Yet: She wasn't afraid to work so hard.

I didn't need to be either.

I reminded myself that I had felt the weight of chastity, once. I had felt the forced perspective of humility, the delirium of purity, the rage of temperance, the blinding resentment of obedience, the shame of modesty, the regret of prudence. I had felt the burden of all those words *on* my body, *in* my body, through my brush; I could do it again. *I was thirty-four years old and I was going to get my work done, and I was going to keep forming the life that belonged only to me.*

I swept the beeswax into a corner—the fallen pearls were dirty now, and I could not use them—and poured a fresh batch. This time, my thumb pulled the wheel, and the flame took on the burner, and the wax melted, and the resin poured into a bucket, the Galkyd ran like honey from its bottle, the petroleum scraped down, the pigment swirled, the medium was made.

When it came out waxy and thick—translucent and matte, exactly as I wanted—I was ecstatic with relief.

And then I fell into my paintings again, and time was suspended, like always.

♠ ♠ ♠ ♠ ♠

No smear or flood or brushstroke held the exact same weight, the same body, as the originals. Regardless, I was delighted to see them, these newest versions, to work from a memory into a new place. I followed the notes in my notebook, worked against the photos in my camera, and let myself luxuriate in the freedom of those beginnings, where nothing has to come together yet— nothing is final.

In that rhythm, I felt, for the first time, genuinely comfortable at Pine City. It wasn't lonely. It was *alone*. We were alone with ourselves, living inside the universes we created, agreeing not to disturb each other's fantasies, only to meet in the spaces between them.

And we did meet—or rather, Marlin, Jack, Tyler, and I met, and Jes remained silent—nods and hellos and high fives, brief chats, meeting in the most literal sense as all of our timings, our patterns of behavior, seemed to be different. I woke up before dawn and painted until nightfall, showered, and passed out. Jes and Marlin were barely around in the evenings, going back and forth to the city and Hudson with relative frequency. I thought that Jack might be the person I saw most, but his daughters caught a summer flu; I ran into him as he was leaving, packing his minivan with a heavy sigh and matching frown.

"There goes this week," he said sadly.

"Catch you soon, I hope."

"Two weeks," he said. "See you then?"

"I'll be here."

That left Tyler and me alone on the massive property, and we soon fell—after several more days of *heys* and small smiles and waving with two fingers from behind the wheel after we passed on the road—into a nice familiarity.

Then, one night, when Tyler's windows were the only ones that glowed against the dusk, and his car the only one in the carports, he called to ask me over for dinner. It would only be the two of us, as Jes and Marlin had driven to Hudson for another opening, and Jack was home with his family. Did I eat meat?

Flattered—and nervous—I accepted.

On the inside of Tyler's all-black house, where he'd raised the ceiling to the angled rafters, the paint colors soaked up all the light so you could see the blues and greens of them, the browns and the grays. Lucinda Williams played on the stereo. His furniture was comfortable and uncomplicated. I leaned against the sofa with a beer, watching him cook, unsure of what to say.

He kicked it off. "How's it going over there?"

"Great," I said. "Everything's good."

He looked at me, long and hard, raising his eyebrows, mocking me. I looked away. The same envelope that had been Jack's bookmark, a piece of certified mail addressed to Pine City, LLC, from Eliot&Sprain, poked out of a stack of papers on his kitchen counter. I tried not to stare at it too obviously.

"Soooo . . . then tell me about the paintings you lost," he said casually, like it was nothing, flipping a hamburger.

I balked and offered a half-truth. "Um. *Prudence* was originally inset with a verdigris made from the copper gutters of St. Patrick's Cathedral—I, um, befriended the janitor there and he let me scrape them when they came down for cleaning—but I couldn't get that again. Obviously."

"Obviously." He shook his head and looked up, a grin on his face—a look that said, *Lady, don't bullshit a bullshitter.* "We can play this game if you want. But, look, I'm not going to rat you out. I swear."

I stared at him for a minute before I replied. He stared back. "Prove it," I said.

"Okay," he said, smiling, taking out his phone, and pulling up a photo. "Look at that."

It was a human brain, encased in a tall plastic take-out container.

The little microscopic pink lines of it; the squish against the walls of the jar—ugh—my mouth went dry, papery, and I had to grab the counter for support.

"It's so illegal," he said, taking back the phone, "and *so* delicate that I haven't been able to finish working with it. I can't get it to survive the electroforming bath. Thus far the legal arguments have hinged on the work as a form of public interest. But this is not a work yet—it's a stolen brain in a plastic Tupperware container that I bought in New Jersey for twenty thousand dollars in cash. That's why we don't throw big parties here anymore, by the way. Now: You have something on me."

"I still want to know why you do it."

"You already asked me that."

"Yeah, but I wasn't satisfied with your answer."

"Why do I acquire human organs on the black market, or why do I bronze them, or why do I sell them?"

"All of the above. Full enchilada."

"Uh—okay." He turned around and leaned against the counter, holding the spatula at a thoughtful angle. I did the same, aping his body language, and it seemed, for a second, like we were going to tell each other the truth.

"First... I guess I should say, I'm definitely taking organs from someone who is trying to bypass a list of some kind. My intervention stops the black market from being at its most efficient. But then—in some ways, I'm simply another variable. I'm probably raising the price of the organs by creating additional demand. I actually don't know if that's moral or not, and I guess that question is an interesting one to me." He thought for a second and then continued, ticking off his fingers as he spoke. "It is addictively dangerous. People die every day, but buying black-market organs is complicated. It's astonishingly remunerative, as art, more than it should be. But—and for me this is the most important thing—the finished work does something to people. It is objectively only an art object—the organs can't be used again."

"It's calculated."

"Of course," he agreed. "I mean, nothing is thoughtless. People assume it's insincere—it's not. It's a holy thing, to hold a person's kidney."

"I'm not in a position to criticize anyone for insincerity," I replied. He clearly knew what I was doing. I owned up to it. "I'm remaking work for the biggest show of my career. I'm terrified they're going to look like—like a bad face-lift. Jacqueline's been telling everyone that they took two years to make. She sold half of them already. It's fraud." It was a relief to say it out loud.

"It's not fraud," he corrected me. "It's your choice. In the end—nobody else gets to tell you who you are. That's the only thing we get, as artists. You're the only one who chooses it. The work you're making now is as real as what you made before."

"I hope that's true."

"You can't lean on the idea that there's some magic current animating you," he said, with a little bit of contempt in his voice. "Choice is what distinguishes us"—he meant fine artists—"from people who make houses out of bottle caps."

"I guess we'll find out."

"So how many?"

"Seven."

His eyebrows shot up. "That's a lot."

"I know. It was all of them."

"Does Jacqueline know?"

"No. They need to look exactly as they did."

"What are they called?"

"*Prudence*—you saw that one already—then there's *Chastity, Humility, Obedience, Modesty, Temperance,* and *Purity*."

"Prudence is a rich ugly old maid courted by incapacity," he said.

"How do you know that?" I asked, surprised. "You know Blake?"

"I looked it up after I saw the ad for your show." He winked. "Milot took out that billboard on Tenth."

"Oh, the billboard." I sighed, worry trickling down my forehead like sweat. "God, that billboard. How much do billboards cost?"

"She probably got a deal on it. Maybe fifty? It had five shows on it, one in every location. It's not your problem," he reassured me.

"No," I agreed, too embarrassed to reveal that *my* contract *made* it my problem, apparently, ten thousand dollars' worth of my problem.

"You know *your* Blake, though," he said.

"Yes. I *love* Blake. I love anyone who takes apart the church and tries to put you back together again."

"Your family's religious?"

"My mother is," I said. "She sins—and she prays—and she asks to be forgiven. Rinse and repeat." I trailed off, and felt him let me go, back behind my wall. "I'm living with more of a creative faith these days. It's the only thing I feel."

"Why are the paintings called what they're called?"

"Those words are women's words, if you know what I mean. Those aren't words used to police men's behavior. Only—only women's. I was raised to believe that being all of those things was important. More important than anything else. But I'm—I'm sick of them. It was time to grow up. For me, I mean."

"I don't know what that means."

"It means . . . the paintings are things that I love but I no longer need. Making a painting is a way to discard something. I put it in the painting, and then I'm over it. Or through it, maybe." Then I rolled my eyes at myself. "It doesn't always work. I'm still dyeing my hair pink, for example, even though I did a painting called *Hair Money*."

"Then—the names are very apt. Your paintings are transparent. It's like seeing your feelings. It's pretty unsettling, actually."

"Thank you. They didn't have names until, I don't know, five or six years ago," I explained.

"Why not?"

"I was too self-contained," I said. "I was making unconsciously. Even in art school I made unconsciously. Everybody treated me like I was Rain Man."

"What happened?" he asked.

"I don't know," I lied, downing my beer, hiding my face as I walked to the refrigerator and reached in for another. I didn't want to tell him—I didn't want to tell anybody. Not ever.

"So how long does it normally take?"

"To make a painting?"

"Yeah."

"Three, four months. I've never tried to go fast."

"How long do you have?"

"Uh—" I counted in my head. "Thirty-five days of painting. Thirty days to dry. That's when I have to build the frames and crates."

"Wow. Frames like the one at Max's house?"

"No, they're much better now. I know." I doubled over, and dropped my head between my knees. "It's too much."

"Why not wait? I mean, why not put off the show?"

"Because Jacqueline won't, for starters, and I'm flat fucking broke, and I'm homeless, and this—it's the biggest opportunity of my life. I can't waste it."

"It'll be okay," he said, reassuring me again. I wanted to believe him.

"I—can you please, *please* not tell Jes or Marlin or Jack or anyone about my paintings? Because you could ruin my life. If something goes wrong—I will be in huge debt, I will still be homeless, and I won't have a gallery."

"Of course." He looked insulted. "Of course I won't."

We ate dinner, seated cross-legged from each other on opposite ends of the sofa, plates in our laps, beers on the floor. He got up every now and then to change the record, but otherwise the evening was fluid; we talked about art, mostly, because it was easy, it was our lingua franca.

It was nice to be with him—to see him up close. It takes a lot of looking to see someone, to really see the shape of their nose or distinguish the shades of their laughter, even, or perhaps especially, if you've seen them from a distance a dozen times before. He began to come into real focus, separating from the mystery that had shrouded him, emerging as a real, independent person.

When he went to the restroom, I peeked at the letter on the counter. It was a demand letter for an artwork by Carey Logan filmed without permission on Eliot&Sprain property. It specified that the artwork contained two reels of film, which Pine City were to return to Eliot&Sprain upon receipt of the letter itself. The threat for noncompliance was a lawsuit to the gut-checking tune of $15 million. *A copy of this letter has been sent to Cartwright, Benson and Pendergast, LLC. Sincerely, Charles Eliot and Helen Sprain.*

An electric shock buzzed my spine, the vertebrae clacking against each other as my fingers pinched the paper. Two reels of film—that was all it requested. I nearly pocketed it before remembering that *I was not supposed to be looking at it.*

At the sound of the sink running in the bathroom, I eased the letter back into its envelope and took a beer from the fridge. When Tyler reappeared in the kitchen, I was tossing the bottle cap into the trash, my heart racing. *No wonder Charlie and Tyler had been so cold to each other at the party. They were in the middle of a war.*

"So you met the rest of Pine City at the Academy?" I asked the only question I could think of.

"Marlin and Jack. Jes and Carey we met after, in New York."

"How *did* you meet Carey?"

"I—" He stumbled and looked at his drink. The beacon, the connection to something, that lack of openness I'd sensed before, turned on behind his eyes, and I felt him move away from me. "Can we talk about Carey another time?"

There was so much misery radiating from his voice that I didn't think he could possibly contain it. I felt clumsy, beastly, even, for scratching such an obviously gaping wound. I didn't want to imagine him doing what the people at Max's party had implied—dismantling her body—or hurting her, like Cady had suggested—and inadvertently shook my head to dislodge the thought.

"Is that okay?" he asked.

"Oh, yes," I said, and diverted my gaze to the near-black planks of the floor. "I didn't mean to shake my head, I'm so tired, I'm—I'm doing the opposite of what I mean," I said, shifting my weight around, breaking the tension. As I moved, he caught sight of the still-healing scab on my calf. The glue had mostly peeled off.

"What happened there?" He grazed it with his fingertips, and a liquid blush traveled to and from the center of my body.

"I tried to climb the ladder in the barn, but it collapsed under my weight."

He looked confused for a second. "The old barn?"

"Yeah. It's okay."

Suddenly his hands were wrapping around my calf, thumbs on each side of the ragged pink and brown skin. He leaned forward, pressed his forehead to my calf, and apologized.

"I'm so sorry. It was thoughtless and cruel. I can be—I can be closed off," he said, breathing into the skin of my leg.

I could feel the tide of his breath forming and receding. It was so surprising—and instantaneously erotic, like completing a circuit—that I froze, closing my eyes, unsure of what to do, wanting desperately to remain completely still, to stay with it, with him, whatever he was.

But then he must have looked up. "Are you upset with me?" he asked.

"No," I breathed—and then I opened my eyes.

I wanted him, that night. Thinking about it even now makes me lovesick, stops me like a hand on my chest: the feeling of his skin on mine, of his breath moving across my leg.

Yet when my eyes flew open inside that black house, I saw only *how black* it was, and in a flash I was overcome by the physical act of repainting everything, of reupholstering all the furniture, of dyeing the lampshades and curtains. I saw only an act of grief that he was still inhabiting. My sense that he was spoken for was accurate—if not by a living person, then by a dead one.

A chill pooled beneath my skin, running every which way like a spilled glass of water. I took my leg back and stood up. Our eyes met—holding for a long second—until he did the same, pulling his hands back into his body, and then the moment was gone, absorbed into the blackness of his house.

"Thank you so much for dinner," I said. "But—my back is killing me. I should get some sleep"—and then I was out of there, running to my cabin, nearly slamming the door behind me.

Chapter Eleven

A dagger. Or a striper—or a sword. In any supply store, whatever the name, it's the same kind of brush. I like *dagger* best. The bristles of a dagger are four to five inches long (about the distance from your middle finger to your thumb), and when you dip them in liquid, they show you what a twirl looks like. Sign painters use them, as do custom automotive painters, because the dagger line is lyrical—wetly calligraphic, capable of becoming both delicately fat and softly thin. Not unlike a marker line, but with more . . . *puddle* to it.

They are ultimately not my aesthetic. Still, I sneak them, for compact baby swoops, for a little pizzazz on a rainy day, an orange slice kind of feeling. Then nine times out of ten they are squeegeed down later. Occasionally one of them stays—usually a little ombré gradient with a star on it, something that looks like part of an airbrushed t-shirt—a little hello from Florida no bigger than a square inch. I like to think they are messages to other painters through the vacuum of our collectors' living rooms: *I made this for you. I made this for me. I made this for us.*

Daggers are tricky to use. You've got to have a hand for them, because otherwise you're slopping all over the place, and the medium has to be the right kind of refrigerator-temperature olive oil. (You can't be working with Marmite-ish beeswax or watered-down gouache—not with a dagger. The paint needs to run heavy, like cold blood.) Gorky used them—then de Kooning—then Whitten—and now, me.

Five years ago, two years before she died, Carey Logan had a show at Eliot&Sprain titled *YOKEFELLOWS*, of bodies curled up together like cats. It was her last sculptural show before she moved to performance work. She was so astonishingly realist in most of the forms, despite (maybe because of?) the classical nature of the materials, that when I spotted a paint line—a long draggy river along a calf—I actually clapped my hand over my mouth in the gallery. *A dagger line.* It made me smile. Nobody can resist daggers. They are so musical.

Carey wasn't a painter, not exactly, though obviously it requires a very specific hand to realize glazes and paints and so on into sculpture. The most affecting parts of her sculptures were not the colors—they were necessary and very accurate and terrifying, but no—rather, it was the form, the way she took the mold of a living person's body and, later, imaginatively inflated the cast version to match the various degrees of decay. Skin puffed up or went hard or fell away, and that was the art. The paint was—it was a necessary afterthought. It was specific and accurate but not haunting. The shape was what mattered.

One single dagger hung on the wall of brushes. *Carey's draggy calf line from five years ago could have been made by this*, I thought, though it was hard to know. Brushes, made so patiently, so lovingly, were so easy to destroy. Leave them out too long and they sour.

Hers was in fine shape, if a little packed around the ferrule, the metal cylinder that held the squirrel-hair brushes in place, with remnants of old paint. I picked it up, gave it a solid wipeout with turp, then mixed a true neon yellow and painted the word YOKE-FELLOWS over and over across the panels of *Obedience*, where they could hide beneath the coming layers of blacks.

It's such an odd word, I thought, pushing and dragging and swooping the letters as artfully as I could. I laid the word down again and again, in twins and in stacks and loops and towers.

The only yokefellows I could think of were oxen. *Who else would share a yoke? When did people write about oxen? The Bible? The Middle Ages? Shakespeare?*

I made a mental note to ask Charlie what it had meant.

There's a video of Stevie Nicks getting her makeup done and singing her guts out on an early version of "Wild Heart." Cady used to play it on her computer. "I watch this every day and so do a third of American women," she told me. In the video, Stevie is sitting on a metal radiator in Annie Leibovitz's studio, so young, and so blond, eyes like dinner plates. You can't believe that she is ever going to be unhappy, or that she's already spent a million dollars on cocaine, or that her heart has ever been broken. She is a miracle in action. And you don't know why anyone would ever try to stop her.

I began to walk to and from the studio instead of driving, taking the weedy path along the lake before and after those long hours with a squeegee in one hand and a knife in the other. One night, when the air was cool and light, the double doors to the Theatre—Jes's studio—were thrown wide open. The unmistakable strains of Stevie, singing "Wild Heart" as she got her makeup done, were flowing out of the doors and into the grass.

I could not resist.

The music folded over itself, again and again. I tiptoed inside the foyer, where a kidney-shaped ticket counter sat altarlike atop a black-and-white-checkered floor. Behind it was a framed poster with two women's faces arranged like puzzle pieces—*Persona*, the Bergman film—and a wall painted silver. The doors were wedged open. The music blasted through them so loudly that I called it an invitation.

The aisles sloped downward, through rows of empty seats, upholstered in emerald corduroy and arranged in three wedges, semicircled around the stage. The walls and ceiling, with their peeling orangewood veneer, held parallelograms of acoustic paneling. In lieu of curtains, stacks of speakers framed the sides of the stage.

Jes sat alone on the stage at a folding gray plastic table covered in musical equipment and connected to earth by the umbilical cords of bright orange extension cables. Swaddled in yards of gauzy black linen, her dyed fingers pummeled the keys of a laptop, and her toes, encased in rubbery basketball sneakers, tapped away on the ground. She did not look up; she looked only at the screens in front of her.

Carey, with downy blond hair, caramel tan, feathers in her hair, sitting on the edge of a radiator in a window—exactly like Stevie—was projected on three screens around Jes, the refrain folding over and over again.

I slipped into the nearest seat and hid in the shadows. Jes began to play the electric piano at her side, manipulating the song, chopping it into pieces. On the screen behind her, Carey's faces merged—repeated—bubbled up, intercut by short clips of other women. I caught Nadia Comaneci winning her perfect 10 and Vanessa Williams being crowned Miss America, then Carey dressed like a gymnast, dressed like a beauty queen, dressed like a businesswoman.

Carey's faces went staccato, over and over again, shining back and forth. Stevie sang, and the words came out of Carey's mouth. To my surprise, Jes joined her, voice soaring, the gold at the bottom of her mouth shining, black dust rimming the amber pools of her eyes.

On the screen, she cut to Carey's mouth in close-up, like Beckett's *Not I*. Then little girls dressed up for beauty pageants appeared. A girl, four or five, with a mouthful of jumbled white teeth and a tacky bedazzled leotard in a dirt yard—little Carey.

The song became a prism of harmonies while all the Careys, a metronome of skin and teeth and hair, flashed in time. Something dark passed—something that hurt—but I didn't understand it. A feeling struck, like a church bell in the distance, and then it receded.

Then—Jes stopped abruptly, unfurling herself like a heron, stalking into the wings. The music was still playing, the song stuck on the refrain: *blame, blame, blame.* When I heard the rumble of a metal stairwell—she was climbing somewhere—I crept toward the door, planting my feet carefully, like there were land mines.

Please don't see me, I prayed silently, sneaking through the lobby and out to the driveway. Every time I saw Jes play, I knew more of who she was, and how precisely, cuttingly observant she could be. She taught me how to speak her language, even as I became more terrified of her. Terrified, genuinely, of what she would reveal about me. When I was twenty yards away, about to turn toward the bungalows, I disappeared around the bend and let out a long, low sigh of relief.

Then I heard her voice.

"HEY!" she yelled angrily. "Who's there?"

I reasoned that she had not seen me. Faced with the prospect of explaining myself, I could not. So—like a child, I turned on my heels and fled. I ran with all my speed back to my bungalow, turning at the hedge and fumbling with the door, locking it behind me, and crouching on the floor in case she came for me.

She never did.

Later, as I tried to recall the feeling, the church bell, that I'd had at the end of the film, I failed. Try to remember a sound. Try to hear it again, all the way through, without hearing it.

It's impossible.

Tyler flagged me down in the driveway after work a few nights later. I stopped. It seemed that he might lean into the window, but then he didn't—he held back and kept his distance, looking straight at me, like he always did.

"How's your back?" he asked.

"Aching, but"—I shrugged—"that's what it is."

He stood there with his hands in his pockets, shoulders hunched, nervous, and stared at me for a second before speaking.

"Um," he said. "Want to have a drink?"

Oh God. I didn't think I could stand to be alone with him. My eyes widened and he quickly course-corrected, raising his thumb toward the Mission. "Sundowners?"

"Sure," I agreed, throwing the truck into park and following him to the Adirondack chairs on the deck jutting out over the lake— and then we were sitting and talking and everything was simple.

Two drinks later, I went to bed.

Every night, for the next week, I found him waiting for me on the deck, in one of two chairs pointed out at the water. Mostly we drank beer, though sometimes we had tea. I would carefully take my seat and stare straight forward, and that was how we would talk. He didn't touch me again, and I never let the moments between us slow down, and never stayed on the deck for more than an hour, and so—we settled into a space of deliberate physical distance.

It made everything easier, that distance, pushing the tension away, over the horizon. I knew it was there but it wasn't in my face, and that was enough. We sat on the deck every night, looking out at the lake, talking about our work, our lives, the city, everything we had in common. Before the week was over, I caught myself thinking about him during the day—wondering what he was do- ing, what we would talk about that night—and looked forward to our evenings with a nervous pleasure.

I learned about two periods of his life: what I came to think of as before Carey and after Carey, but he never said her name—not once.

His early life was what I expected. Tyler was from Sharon, Connecticut—not far from Max's upscale hometown. His parents were both doctors: father, a surgeon, mother, an oncologist. His father died of cancer when he was in the fifth grade. Drowning in responsibility, his mother sent him to boarding school in nearby western Massachusetts from sixth through twelfth grades. He played tennis well enough for a D1 scholarship at UCLA. After a year he dropped out and attended the Academy against his mother's wishes.

"She wanted me to have a real job," he said, leaning back in his chair, wine in hand. "I don't blame her. But I wasn't going to be a professional tennis player or go into finance. I wanted to be a painter, believe it or not."

"Really?" I couldn't imagine him as anything other than what he was.

"Yeah. I wanted to be the next Gerhard Richter. But—I didn't have it."

"It's not entirely about talent," I said, though that wasn't true.

"You don't have to do that," he said, reaching over to me, forgetting our boundary—before remembering it and stopping midair. The physical distance remained, but our emotional proximity had grown like moss, lush and alive and nearly too detailed to measure.

"Gerhard Richter wanted to be Jack Whitten, anyway," I said.

"Yeah." He laughed. "It didn't matter, though. I wasn't talented enough. I ended up being overly influenced by Experimental Studies. I didn't realize at the time what a class-specific pyramid scheme it was—to make work that can't sell—and we completely bought into it. We graduated believing in making work that nobody would or could ever buy. Galleries pumped us full of drugs and sent us to parties, but we didn't make any money. They say one thing and do another. We were too young to understand the difference. We were marketing, so they could sell thirty-year-old paintings. I mean, eventually we figured it out. But the first few years out of school were hard. I had huge student loans."

"I remember that you were famous already," I told him.

"Famous at the Academy." He laughed. "I did these big installations of taxidermied animals. It was nonsense. Marlin was doing wheatpaste murals—everybody was so hot on, you know, graffiti, trespassing, fucking whatever, but you can't sell graffiti. Jes's films, I mean, that was the right place in the right time, but you don't make money on art films, only performances, and it's barely a living. She was more prepared for that, though. Did you know, she went to Juilliard? For cello. Anyway—Jack never wanted to make objects that went on a market. He wanted to intervene differently."

"But Carey was *so* successful, right from the start," I blurted out. "Wildly."

"She was built that way." His eyes flicked to and away from the water. I felt something, then, in the air—the tender charge of his anxiety about everything Carey—and he turned to say something—I could see it on his face—but then he discarded it. Disappointment gathered in the back of my mouth. I swallowed it down.

"Lucky that you met her."

"It wasn't luck," he responded argumentatively—and he stopped himself again, and changed the subject.

"May I ask a question about your work?" he said instead. I nodded, and he continued: "I saw *you* in *Tomato Tomato*, I mean, really saw *you* in the painting, clearer than I've ever seen anybody in my life. And then I met you and you were so exactly that," he said.

"What's the question?"

"How do you do that?"

I didn't know what to say.

The real answer was that none of it was on purpose. My work was not the result of any artistic choice or intellectual legacy; instead it was the result of my inability to make any choices at all. Painting was a compulsion that I could barely control. I was no better than, as he'd said, the people who built houses out of bottle caps or covered their yards in cement garden gnomes, and if I'm being honest, the only threads that separated me from a life among the bottle-cap people were woven into the borrowed suit jacket of class distinction. Like Carey, I was a compulsive fanatic who found success purely by chance. I was nothing like Tyler—I had no journey. I had no critical growth. I didn't deserve to be successful.

"I don't exactly know," I ventured, telling the only part of the truth I could bear to admit. "When I'm making a painting, the rest of me is defenseless. And . . . it is hard on me. Sometimes I feel the moods and pulses of other people's feelings so strongly that it makes me physically sick. My skin gets so thin you could slice it open with your fingernail. It's . . . I'm absorbent." I trailed off. "I don't know how to be different."

"That sounds terrible."

"I'm a saint," I offered, in a self-effacing deadpan, "bleeding from my eyes."

"You're a something," he said, and then I could see he wanted to say something. Instead he paused, his eyes caught by someone behind me.

Jes walked down the beach in a black bikini, her long hair wound atop her head and her skin gleaming with drops of lake water. As she passed the Mission, she didn't turn to acknowledge us, though we were plainly visible. At first I assumed she hadn't seen me, but when she crossed through a bungalow three doors down, her head turned our way—stamped with a look of unadulterated malice—and a chill ran through me. *Trespasser*, an imagined voice whispered. *Pretender. Fraud. You don't belong here. You don't belong with us.*

I said my usual good night and goodbye after that, and so did he.

And then—the next night, he was gone, a note tacked to "my" chair on the deck that said *Went to Vilnius early to install, back next week, good luck.*

The note hurt much more than I wanted it to.

Chapter Twelve

The hours I'd been filling with Tyler's company now, in his absence, felt like days. I'd grown used to having something to *do* after the workday was done, something to stave off the loneliness.

I decided to keep myself busy. The first night, I bleached my roots; then did a conditioning mask; then toned. Still, the clock stretched out ahead of me and my eyes refused to close, listening to the sound, as always, of the opaque little ocean beside me, glittering like polished obsidian in the moonlight and beating a sullen melody across the rocks.

One night I tried all the doors on the property. But everything was locked up tight.

I did need to be alone in the studio, to keep at it—to work, and work, until there was no work left. Though I was productive, I started to feel deeply lonely. When I got a late-night call from Cady, Atticus, and Jonny (the boy—now man—whose room I'd once taken over at 11 Dutch), tanked on a Lithuanian honey liqueur called Virtya, huddled inside a raccoon-fur-lined Humvee they insisted was "a horrible joke" as they waited for the sun to come up outside Vilnius, I felt achingly left out. They'd also arrived early to help assemble Jonny's sculpture for one of the competitions, and they were buzzed on the joy of it all—of sharing baroque mansions with each other before the crowd arrived, of having the kind of experience you could only earn and never buy.

I tried to party, but sipping bourbon and reading paperbacks alone, while enjoyable, does not a party make, at least not when you've been doing it for days and days in a row. I worked in the studio every day until my back was screaming in pain, and whenever I was done feeling lonely, I felt anxious and scared.

The more I thought about it, the more it seemed reasonable that Carey had stopped making sculpture because she could not bear to spend the rest of her life alone in a studio, watching everyone else get married and have children and build lives. I was working, for the first time, at the same pace she had, after spending years of wondering how she was so successful, how she made so many objects, how she managed it all. Her pace was hard on the body, but it was much harder, I was beginning to realize, on the mind.

I felt a sudden longing for the 42nd Street library, where they kept the Wallach Division, the collection of everything that has ever been written on art. I used to walk up there, sit in the great big reading room, and read *Art Talk* by Cindy Nemser, a book of interviews with fifteen women artists, over and over. The closest thing to the library, I reasoned, would be Max's house—that extraordinary collection I'd spied so briefly at the party. I called her cellphone as soon as I thought of it.

"Hi!" she said brightly. "How's everything?"

"Aces. It's going really, really well," I told her. "I have a favor to ask you."

"Shoot."

"Do you have that book on Anselm Kiefer that came out recently? Or anything on Jay DeFeo? That big article on *The Rose*?"

"Actually, I think we do, the Kiefer at least. DeFeo, uh...we might have that last catalog. How have you not committed the *Rose* essay to memory?"

"Well, I had it in hard copy and PDF'd on my computer."

"Fuck. Right. Well—everything's in the library—go on in any time. The door code is my birthday. It's in a panel to the left of the front door. Then to set it before you go, keep the door closed and type it on the inside panel."

"Star? Pound?" I wrapped my hair in a t-shirt, holding myself and the phone upside down.

"Enter."

"Okay. I'll drive over now, if that's okay."

"It's totally fine, but I'm not there. Fleur and I drove to the city this morning. Klaus is hosting a dinner tonight on a barge across from Hart Island."

"That's disgusting." Hart Island was a potter's field—a mass grave of unmarked bodies.

"I know. I'm going to try and get ashore."

"Don't fall in."

"I might. If anyone's going to fall in, though, it'll be Tyler." My heart fell at the mention of his attendance. "Eat and drink anything you want, okay? Gotta run. Talk soon. I'll be back next week."

I was horribly, hideously crushed after that phone call. He was already back. Tyler had no reason to invite me to that party in the city, and even if he'd wanted to, I was working: All I could do was work. I couldn't leave. We both knew it. There was no rational reason for me to be upset, but I was, and I sat there feeling stunned and miserable and left out. Then I combed my freshly pink hair out, violently, yanking at the knots with enough force to pull them from my scalp in little clusters, hard enough that I had to physically stop myself.

At Max's, I could be distracted. I grabbed the nearest clean t-shirt, another Atticus choice that had a smiley face on the front and the words HAVE A NICE DAY: FUCK SOMEONE on the back.

The drive to Eliot House took another ten minutes, and I parked directly in front of the Mies-van-der-Hobbit-Hole door, finding the access panel easily and gaining entry in thirty seconds.

The house was completely silent; I was alone in the concrete spectacle.

Now that it was free of living people, I could see all the details. The doorknobs were indeed all hands—shaped in fists and handshakes and open palms and every other permutation—each one different from the next. The brass banister, at the top, was the crook of an elbow, as if you were taking someone's arm on a slippery sidewalk. I realized that the tube of it was bumpy because it was a series of different biceps cast in one long, undulating line.

The light fixtures, hanging in clusters from the ceiling, looked like the bulbs were made of grapes. I peered at one and saw that it was an eyeball, with a pale iris and an opaque white pupil, held to its cloth-covered cord of ivory silk, braided with tiny, irregular veins of red and blue, with a grommet made from a golden coin.

The transoms above each door, to let in light from the atrium, were, like Max's office, smooth slabs of semiprecious stones. The edges where the stone met the wood were ever so slightly beveled, like they were gigantic pieces of jewelry in the setting of a door. Max's office was rose quartz, and the other doors on the third floor (which I didn't dare open) glowed, backlit by their own glass ceilings. There was rusty carnelian, Caribbean-blue apatite, chartreuse brazilianite; the second floor had transoms of paper-thin jade, pear-tinted heliodor, and crystalline Egyptian faience. One door—the one next to my painting, for the library—had a cage transom, laser-cut brass patterned in tiny hexagons, same as the ones on Marlin's fuzzy prints.

My palm fit seamlessly into the outstretched brass hand of the knob. When it turned, in a handshake, I found the library exactly as it had been before.

The catalog appeared to be alphabetical by movement. Each shelf was sleek and full to the brim, though here and there a book had been removed. At each hole in the collection, I tried to figure out who or what was missing, if it was only the books I'd seen in

Max's office, but my knowledge simply wasn't complete enough to guess the names that had been taken out.

I started browsing. I wasn't exactly sure what I was looking for— I was enjoying the search, waiting for something to catch my eye, for something to jump out and tell me, *This is what to do!*

On impulse I took out catalogs from recent exhibitions on the early abstract painter Clyfford Still, the Bauhaus professor László Moholy-Nagy, and the medieval painter Giotto di Bondone, a fourteenth-century muralist who worked at the beginning of the Renaissance and was mentioned in Dante's *Divine Comedy*.

I tried to read. Instead my mind wandered and my eyes kept lifting to stare at the room. The library was massive: Two stories, it had stacks on both floors, a narrow central courtyard, and walls lined with books, brass rails, and ladders. The only shelves I couldn't read were at the very top of the room. They looked full.

I scaled the first ladder. The top shelves held files on Eliot&Sprain artists: catalogs, binders, file boxes, stacks of paper that I didn't dare touch. I rolled the ladder awkwardly to its neighbor and climbed over; the next shelves were the same, full of privacies I wouldn't dream of violating.

Yet on ladder number three, at the very top, I found myself looking at a series of black notebooks that took up an entire shelf, labeled with white paint marker on the spine with different project names. They looked exactly like my own.

The spines read:

HOLD ME
CAREY 2
FORGIVE/FORGET
THE BURIAL PROJECT
72 HOURS
TOMBSTONE PIZZA
CHOKE ON IT
SLEEP DISORDER

ELIOT&SPRAIN HOUSE
OTHER PEOPLE'S RULES
DROP OUT
YOKEFELLOWS
LOVE THAT MIRACLE
SIDE EFFECTS (MODAFINIL)

Next to the notebooks, museum and gallery catalogs, along with a tatty binder full of clippings, occupied the remainder of the shelf.

It took me a moment to understand what I was seeing.

It was Eliot&Sprain's entire Carey Logan collection—the archive of her, the locus of her memory—the only place she still lived.

I let out a tiny gasp. Here was the exact thing I wanted.

It made me feel good simply to touch them. Finding evidence that Carey had existed at all put a cork in my loneliness. *It is completely natural*, I told myself—*accepted, even—to be posthumously interested in dead artists. Everybody does it. You're exactly like me*, Carey told me that night on Grand Street. *You're exactly like me.* I was already using her studio. *What difference would reading her notebooks make? Was it any less intimate than what I was already doing?* I wasn't sure, and negotiating with myself didn't matter because I couldn't stop. I grabbed the closest notebook in the row, which said *HOLD ME*, and opened it to the first page.

HOLD ME: I WILL INVITE PEOPLE TO A GALLERY AND WRAP ALL THE VISITORS IN A NET AND HOLD THEM FOR AS LONG AS THEY ALLOW ME TO. THIS PIECE IS SHORT IN BOTH DURATION AND DIFFICULTY.

It was her first performance piece, set up almost exactly two years before she died. There was no explanation as to why she'd changed course so abruptly. The rest of the notebook was filled with detailed notes related to the piece, things like:

10.2: MET WITH JOAN J. FOR COFFEE ON LES IN THE AFTERNOON, SPENT ONE DOLLAR SIXTY-FIVE CENTS. SMOKED ONE CIGARETTE. JOAN IS SUPPORTIVE.

10.05: SENT LETTER TO CURATOR AT MASS-MOCA. NO REPLY YET.

11.06: PHONE CALL WITH JORDAN ABOUT MS. GALLERY

11.07. EMAIL WITH JORDAN AND KIM ABOUT MS. GALLERY. SEE USB.

11.07. EMAIL WITH JORDAN AND KIM ABOUT MS. GALLERY. SEE USB.

11.07. EMAIL WITH JORDAN AND KIM ABOUT MS. GALLERY. SEE USB.

11.07. EMAIL WITH JORDAN AND KIM ABOUT MS. GALLERY. SEE USB.

11.07. EMAIL WITH JORDAN AND KIM ABOUT MS. GALLERY. SEE USB.

11.08. EMAIL WITH JORDAN AND KIM ABOUT MS. GALLERY. SEE USB.

11.09. EMAIL WITH JORDAN AND KIM ABOUT MS. GALLERY. SEE USB.

11.21. TOOK NET TO MS. GALLERY ON MTA SUB-WAY.

11.22. MS. GALLERY SHOW. I HELD A YOUNG MAN
IN BLUE WHO SMELLED LIKE SOUR TOBACCO. I
HELD AN OLDER MAN IN RED WHO TRIED TO
FEEL ME UP. I WASN'T SURE WHETHER OR NOT
TO LET HIM? AM I SUPPOSED TO RESIST? I THINK
IT MADE ME UNCOMFORTABLE. AM I SUPPOSED
TO BE UNCOMFORTABLE? IS THERE A BOUND-
ARY?

Interesting questions, in theory, but there was nothing to explain why she needed to ask those questions in the first place.
The notebooks were not diaries, exactly; they were deliberate,
businesslike records. The details went well beyond what we'd
been instructed to do at school, though she'd clearly learned
the exact Academy process from Tyler, Marlin, and Jack. I
slid *HOLD ME* back on the shelf and grabbed the next one,
FORGIVE/FORGET:

FORGIVE/FORGET: Cast bodies into a slow dance, like
a high school dance. This piece is short in duration, high in
difficulty.

11.17: ROBERT called today to say he thinks my material
process is lacking and that I need to work harder at bridging
the realist gap. He wants me to call RON and get some
tips. I am scared to because I am afraid RON won't think I
am talented enough. I'm scared he'll make me demo talent.
Drank three beers, ate a turkey sandwich for dinner.

The process of her practice—paint shades, glaze recipes, firing
temperatures, mold forms, shipping costs, phone numbers—were
all there, a patchwork of block print in different inks. The notes
contained exactly the same luxurious banalities as the last—the sort
of information that would be interesting to a curator, or an art

historian, or me. I wished I had the time to read them all, but it was terrifying, up here on the ladder, and I was hit with a sudden wave of guilt. I was genuinely trespassing. I quickly returned it and opened the next one, *THE BURIAL PROJECT*, the show I'd seen my sophomore year of art school:

THE BURIAL PROJECT: I will cast and paint body parts in different stages of decay and bury them, one by one. When one is found I will bury another one. I will catalog their discovery over the years and the confusions that result. This piece is extra-long in duration, medium in difficulty.

7.15: SHOULDER from BODY 32 discovered outside of Albany. Police called. Crime scene erected. Sculpture revealed when coroner arrived, who is now v. familiar with my work. He says the county is going to sue for wasting their resources. I told him to go ahead and that he would be embarrassed to learn how many more parts are waiting undiscovered.

8.30: LEFT FOOT from BODY 12 discovered in Taghkanic farmhouse by elderly widow. She knew immediately that it was fake. I'm not sure how. Age, I guess. She drove it over here and dropped it off. Kind of a letdown.

9.11: FINGER from BODY 38 found at bottom of dumpster at Montessori farm school by janitor. Very satisfying: school shut down for a day. Coroner called again, extremely angry, I taped our conversation, so much authority and rage in his voice. Upsetting. I tried to explain about the Calusa— the Native Americans in Florida who buried their dead wherever they fell down—but he wasn't interested in discussing anthropology.

It became clear to me that her notes were intended to be read by the other members of Pine City, especially when it came to her feelings on a critic, curator, gallery, or museum; like everyone else, she was keeping score—except she had four people to leverage in any given situation.

"E&S are hesitating, I can hear it in their voices," she wrote. "I think they need to be encouraged—Tyler and Jack, can you say something to JR about a studio visit, Marlin and Jes, can you say something to Donna, too, and let it slip to people?"

On another occasion, over a formal dinner that Eliot&Sprain wanted her to host in Miami:

> Charles is asking me to host a dinner. I'll insist we commission Jack for the table and Jes for the sound.

I reached for *YOKEFELLOWS*, nearly falling off the ladder as I did. For a dazzling instant my guilt gave way to a wild freedom, a sisterhood, a sense of being in the right place at the right time.

YOKEFELLOWS:

TO YOKE ME AS HIS YOKEFELLOW, OUR CRIMES OUR COMMON CAUSE

YOKEFELLOWS BODIES WILL BE PINE CITY'S BODIES: TYLER, JES, JACK, MARLIN, AND CAREY, TANGLED TOGETHER, IN PROGRESSIVE STAGES OF DECAY.

The bodies weren't identified when I saw the show—in any of the text or any of the materials. I went cold, thinking about it, that I had seen what Tyler's body would look like when it died. That I knew already what it would look like. And worse—that he had seen Carey's fake dead body in the show—and then Carey's real dead body, later.

What followed the initial idea were notations: on molds, casts, temperatures, firings, glazings, the usual. I read and read until I got to a page that only read

6.01: There's a dagger line across T6 calf

The same line I'd noticed in the exhibition at Eliot&Sprain, ten years ago, when I was twenty-four and lost in the depressive years between *Ohne Titel* and *Accounting for Taste*. And then, in Carey's blocky handwriting, adjacent and in a different color—

Decided to leave it

Nothing more. It seemed that she had done it by accident and later changed her mind. It had been her last sculptural show; after this, she transitioned entirely to performance. *One last painterly gesture*, I thought. There were probably myriad mistakes in her other sculptures, the kinds that nobody sees except the artist. Yet this was the only one I'd ever noticed. I liked that, intentional or not, she'd left a big one for the road.

After *YOKEFELLOWS*, I went back in time, paging through *CAREY 2* and *TOMBSTONE PIZZA*. I felt immeasurably calmed by the details, by the evidence of how much *work* her work required. Mine was overtaking me. Hers did too. I was not alone.

Frequently she was personal and emotional. After a turbulent phone call with a curator, she wrote, "Dan from [redacted] called me an ungrateful bitch today, making me out to be less than nothing. I cried when I hung up. When things like this happen, I see that my role requires me to undertake more emotional and spiritual abuse than everyone else. I don't think any of us should work with him again and I resent having been put in this position."

In my own notebooks, I only wrote about people to record my impressions in the moment so I could make the best of a situation, like, "Phone call with Jacqueline Milot. She asked me to pitch her a show and I agreed to send something in the next month. She speaks very quickly, so I think it will be better to exchange over email." My notebooks were written only for me, and it was fascinating to read through narratives so clearly intended for public consumption. Pine City, I realized, taught Carey how to record her work in the way we did at the Academy, and naturally—she put her own spin on it. I thought too about Jack Wells, and our conversation about the retrospective. He'd insisted there was no way to know what Carey would have consented to, but the notebooks seemed so deliberate to me— they were more than consent. They were very nearly instructions. I thought about Jack's eye-rolling about his job at the Academy—how secure he was, how successful he'd been, how he graduated from college into a literal boat that kept him above the waterline. Jack might have known Carey, but he couldn't understand her.

The pages trembled in front of my eyes—my hands were shaking. I was desperate to whisk these away. It felt like I was meant to find these—like I was meant to have them. *Like they had been written just for me.* There was something here—I knew, I knew it in my bones. There had to be. There would be an explanation, a rationale, a reason for changing her work, for killing herself. Maybe— maybe it was in the details of that mysterious final work, the film that Charles and Pine City were fighting over.

I looked around and assessed their location. It was impossible to see these two particular shelves from below. They were located to the left and five feet above the doorway, so you didn't face them walking in, and then the vantage point from the floor was so far down that the only thing you could see was the bottom side of the shelf, not the contents. Still—if someone got on the ladder and looked—they would know the books were gone.

Yet—I could take pictures without anyone knowing, I reasoned, so I left Carey's work on the shelf, slid to the bottom of the ladder, ran outside, and grabbed my camera from the truck. I darted back inside and jumped down the stairs two by two, intending to document as much as I could before anyone came home—only to find Charlie standing in the middle of the room.

Chapter Thirteen

Some cat burglar you'd make," Charlie said, looking up and smiling at me. "I heard you the second I closed the garage door."

"Hi!" I sputtered, trying not to look up at the shelf above the doors. "I thought the house was empty."

"You decided to break in and read all my books?"

I stared up, willing him to keep his eyes in one place. I waved my camera. "Research. Max gave me the code."

"What are you looking for?

"I can't say...," I told him truthfully. "There's something about verbalizing what I'm doing that renders it irrelevant, do you know what I mean? As if, when I say it out loud, that's what it will be and I won't want it anymore...I was sort of hoping for some library magic. For something to call out to me."

"I understand."

"The gist is that I'm looking for alternative methods of attaching pigment."

"Isn't that your entire milieu?"

"It's an infinite question," I said, smiling. "A lifelong question."

"Well, I'll leave you to it," he said. My stomach growled. "Would you like dinner?"

"Is it that obvious?" I chuckled. "That would be amazing. If it's not too much trouble."

"It's no trouble. It's already cooked, I only need to heat it up—it's the Fourth of July, after all. We should celebrate. Half an hour okay?"

"Sure. I won't be long."

"You're welcome to borrow these, if you want."

"That's okay," I said. "They're heavy, and my fingers are always covered in paint. Pictures and notes will do for now."

"Sure thing. I'll knock again in a bit."

The moment he closed the door, I snapped my eyes up to the Carey shelf, where, thankfully, nothing poked out. Then I wondered, far too late, if there were any cameras in here. I moved my head slowly, trying to seem casual, and found the security-pod bumps dotting the ceiling. Once I saw their encasements—opaque white lenses—I breathed a sigh of relief. *Motion detectors. Not cameras.*

Still—I didn't quite dare climb the ladder again, not all the way to the top, anyway. I took one picture of the spines before shame washed over me in a choking wave: *This wasn't my property, and this wasn't my house.* If I was caught trespassing like this, it would ruin an important professional relationship. I didn't want Charlie to perceive me negatively.

I assured myself that Charlie hadn't seen anything amiss, that if he had, he certainly wouldn't have invited me to dinner. I returned to work, distracting myself with the Still, di Bondone, and Moholy-Nagy books, taking photos and notes whenever I found a passage that described a material process that intrigued me: Still's original rabbit's-foot glue recipe, an elaboration on the chemical properties of lime as a binding agent when painting a fresco on wet plaster, what the original material used in the development of *cliché-verre*—a cameraless, hand-applied early variant of photography—had been (smoke from a kerosene lantern). I tried not to think about what I'd been doing up on the ladder; it brought

up an equal measure of curiosity and disgrace that made my stomach roil. By the time Charlie knocked, I was officially starving.

"Finished!" I called out.

"Dinner's on the second-floor balcony," he said, and I nodded
before returning the books to their correct positions on the shelf
and cleaning up the table I'd been using. My feet practically floated
up the steps to find that Charlie—sweet, good Charlie—had set
a beautiful table for two on the balcony outside his office, with a
decanted bottle of wine, roast duck, heaps of steaming vegetables,
even a fresh bunch of tulips in a pale green ceramic vase. On the
edge of the deck, a red plastic sugar feeder hanging from a thick
brown sailor's rope was crowded with hummingbirds, buzzing in
the air like oversize wasps.

I sat down and pulled the heavy canvas napkin over my lap, feeling very briefly ashamed of myself as he filled my glass with a 1990
Bordeaux, a wine I knew from my days at the restaurant. It was
too good for me under any circumstance, especially this one. He
was clean-shaven as always, hair jet black, shirt white and untucked,
dark-gray trousers slim and pressed. But tonight there were bags
under his eyes, and a slight hunch to his shoulders. I glanced into
the area of his studio visible beyond his narrow figure and realized
it contained a whirlwind of drawings, practically hundreds, stacked
on every surface, plans for shows from a decade ago, along with
new ideas. I loved the thin paper he used, all that white and blue,
and how it seemed so delicate and specific and intentional, how
everything was a plan. Helen, his ex-wife, was the booming, enthusiastic personality of Eliot&Sprain who made all the deals and
did all the publicity. Charlie stayed in the background, more or less,
to deal with the artists and the visions for the work.

"Long day?" I asked, pointing to his studio.

"You've no idea," he said, raising his glass. "Cheers." He downed
a swallow immediately. "The Beijing project I was telling you
about at the party?" I nodded. " . . . is turning bad. They now want
to put a high-speed monorail on the bottom, which means the air

around it will be filled with fumes and the artist would need thirty times the weight capacity. They're asking her to become, or hire, I suppose, an architect. It's a disaster."

"Why don't you delegate all this stuff?" I asked him. "I mean, you don't need to be dealing with these details. Isn't that the artist's job?"

"That's the difference between us and the others," he said. "We only have about forty artists. Hen and I handle everything on our own. This way everything always gets done right the first time. We've never lost an artist, you know. Nobody has left Eliot&Sprain. Not ever." His eyelid, pale and greasy, twitched. His hand flew up to hold it still.

"Sorry." He chuckled. "I'm falling apart."

"That sounds very stressful."

"It's mostly *boring*," he said, tilting his head. "I'm the only one paid to be bored; it won't do to pass the burden. Let's talk about something else. Or my eye will jump off my face."

"It's not boring. It sounds hard," I said. "I don't think I've ever done anything that hard in my life."

"You spontaneously create monumental objects of desire," he offered. "No big deal."

"Yeah—then it's over. Everything for me is about giving birth, I think," I said. "Somehow I get pregnant, and then eventually a painting comes out, but I don't have to maintain it or nurture it beyond the moment it is 'finished.'" I made exaggerated air quotes with my hands.

"What about if your paintings fall apart? Don't you preserve them?"

"For a hundred years of hanging on the wall, maybe, but I don't use varnish anymore sooooo...uh. No. And they fall apart anyway—*Leisure Leisure* lost its pound of real gold last year. Fifteen thousand dollars fell on the floor because I hadn't properly attached it. I told the curator to put it back on with a blowtorch and she told me to call her back when I was sober."

"Did you?"

"I *was* sober! I even sent her a *telegram* saying the same thing but she's ignoring me. So now it has a big patchy hole in it and they left the gold exactly where it fell, and there's a guard standing watch all the time. They framed the telegram and put it next to the painting. So. Win some, lose some."

He laughed, an easy sound. Sipping the wine, I was once again astonished at how too good for me it was: The taste was broad, like a field, and loamy with dirt, sharp with minerals.

"Wow," I exclaimed—like a little girl. *I sound like such a clod.*

"A case of this was a gift when I got divorced. Well, when Hen left me. I'm drinking it down."

"Nice gift."

"It was," he said. "It should have been. It was *from Hen.*"

"That's . . . exquisite." I shook my head in disbelief. "I've never left a relationship on a high note. Only low ones."

"Hen's the most socially adept person on earth," he said, looking out across the yard, over the Goldsworthy wall and toward the lake. "She has no enemies."

"Whose idea was it to have Carey do the house?" I asked, lightly—casually—as though it were an afterthought, like I was merely curious in the way that normal people were curious.

"Both of us. We thought she'd do a wonderful job. And she went bonkers for the idea—she literally accepted on the spot, which was very un-Carey. She usually deliberated over everything for weeks— then took years longer than she was supposed to."

"Were you here when she died?" I heard myself asking the rudest question in the world.

"Yes. It was terrible. Tyler found her, you know."

My arms, folded in front of me, went rigid. I glanced down— yet they hadn't moved. They were the same old arms—the same old legs—crossed in the most unpremeditated kind of way. I felt rooted to my chair, the sensation of it suddenly overwhelming.

"I've heard that. He hasn't mentioned it."

"He wouldn't," Charlie said. "I don't imagine it's a thing one discusses."

"How can you still live here?" I heard myself asking the second-rudest question in the world. "She's—she's everywhere."

"I don't know," he admitted. "It's been—well, I don't mean to put you in the middle of anything, but Carey assigned us the management of the estate. She shipped us most of her work before she died, with very deliberate instructions, which was awful but also, you know, *it was what she wanted.*"

Instructions. *He means the notebooks.* I turned my face toward the long grass, watching it bend in the breeze, so that Charlie couldn't see the ravenous interest shooting from my eyes.

"And we appreciated that," he continued. "We have a responsibility to raise the profile of the estate. She left the profits of the estate to Pine City, which makes it all very complicated. Hen and I—we've been *trying* to do what Carey wanted. But they won't sell a single thing, even though it's all worth five times what it was when she was alive. And Carey would have known that. She had no problem selling any of her work. But there's one *particular* work that could upgrade the market for her previous works quite significantly—and they won't give it up, so . . . it's been several years of limbo. It's a delicate course. I genuinely don't understand why they won't let us put it on the market."

"What is it?"

"Well—that's not entirely clear. We haven't actually seen it," he said.

"What would they get out of it?" I dared to ask.

He rubbed his fingers together and then opened them to the air in a way that suggested it was an extremely appealing amount of money, enough to, say, buy the planet. "I think, what I would call real money. We can't seem to come to an agreement. I've been trying to encourage them, but I'm getting a bit frustrated. I've always found them very hard to deal with, frankly. They close ranks like the military."

His eyes flicked up at me, and I sensed he wanted me to give him something in return. But I had barely any information.

"I'm working in her studio," I offered. "It was empty when I moved in." I realized once it was out of my mouth that this was not strictly true, but I didn't think he'd be interested in a box of terrible drawings that belonged to someone else—they were genuinely, not merely comparatively, worthless. "Do you—do you know why she stopped using it?"

"No idea," he said, widening his eyes and shaking his head. "She came over one day, said she was done, and that all future work would be performance. That was that. I was nervous for her. Everybody was. Tyler especially. We thought it might damage her career. But in the end—it was too brief to make a difference. They were livid, though."

"Pine City?"

"Yes. They cared about money while she was alive, they were always inserting themselves in everything, pushing on her behalf, but now that she's dead they seem to want the whole thing to go away. It's—"

My face had lost all pretense of innocence. I was rapt, nearly drooling. I was too much. The second Charlie noticed, he backtracked.

"I—I shouldn't be talking about it," he said. "I'm so sorry. I don't want to sour your relationships over there. They're good artists. They mean well. It was all very tragic, and I think if we could resolve everything in a way that was satisfactory to everyone, then yes, Max and I would like to do something new."

"Time for a new house, maybe," I said, after a beat.

"Perhaps," he agreed. "I've been thinking of doing something big. A museum."

"For the write-off?" Savvy collectors who turned their collections into legal nonprofit entities needed only to "show" the works a few times per year in order to save hundreds of thousands (millions?) of dollars in taxes.

"No, an actual museum." He laughed. "Open every day, cheap to access, nice bathrooms." It was my turn to laugh. "The work, and us above. Like the old English country houses, you know, bygone, genteel aristocrats living upstairs with their dogs in one heated room while the public clomps around for 2p downstairs."

"Won't that cost like a billion dollars?" I laughed at myself. "I'm sorry again. I cannot stop asking you the rudest questions. I don't know what's wrong with me."

"It's okay. Yes. We opened a gallery in Dubai. Literally ten times what we make anywhere else. It only sells prints. No—it's that, we have so much artwork, more than we can display, far more than I know what to do with. I like to see people looking at it. It gives me joy. And Max needs...not to be alone so much," he said lovingly, shaking his head. "I worry about her. Do you worry?"

"About Max?" I was incredulous. "Never," I told him, with certainty. "Max, out of anyone I've ever met, knows what she needs and how to get it." I'd never thought of Max as being fragile or confused or in danger of anything at all, but then again—I realized that we barely knew each other anymore. Max could be one big performance, and I would never know the difference. "Why do you ask? I mean...besides the fact that she's physically isolated and you're always out of town. She seems happy to be working on that book."

"I guess I don't have a reason. A feeling...I don't mean to be paranoid." He trailed off. "It's probably down to the house. I love this house. But it's not hers."

We sat in silence as I poured us both fresh glasses of wine.

"I think the impulse to make a home that belongs to you both is probably a good one," I said, as sincerely as I could. He nodded and began eating, scooping up huge forkfuls of duck and potatoes while I stared out at the yard. Orange rays sliced across the green grass from the west, shadows pooling under the trees. We drank a second glass, then a third. The wine flowed through me, hot like blood, and the whole world transformed from a drab gray outline into full-scale Kodachrome color. I felt everything: the dusk in the air, Charlie's smile across the table, the glass between my fingers, the wine on my tongue, the clean smell of the evening dew, so faint that were dew a color it would be the water in the jar where you rinse your watercolor brush.

After that we returned to small talk, enjoying the night air, trading war stories about expensive professional mistakes we'd made. I got the sense that he didn't know many people with whom he could discuss the real details of his life; and whether I had earned it or not, my history with Max placed me in a family-like proximity that genuinely meant something to him. It made me feel terrible, how easily he trusted me, because I didn't deserve it. At last— when we were halfway through a second bottle, glasses four and five—I confessed something I'd been holding on to for years, the fingers of my brain too drunk and guilty to hold their secrets any longer. Courage grew from the base of my spine and bubbled out my mouth.

"Do you remember when we met?" I asked.

"At that party, downtown. The one with the elderly, nudist acrobats. Who could forget."

"That's not where we met," I said, grimacing. "I've been meaning to ask for so long if you remembered. I would have said at the party but Max was being..."

"...so very *Max*," he said, laughing. "Yes. I understand. So where was it? How could I possibly forget?"

"It was a while ago. Six, seven years. It was October. I was coming out of Canal Plastics with huge sheets of neon acrylic, and I couldn't get a cab, and I was trying to get them home, and I kept slipping, and I actually hit you with one and knocked your briefcase in the street. And instead of being mad, you took an end and walked with me—"

"All the way to some alley in the Financial District! Up nine flights of stairs!" His face opened up, and Charlie stared at me with an expression of total disbelief. "I *can't believe it*. I can't believe I didn't remember you, with your hair and everything."

"I had a scarf over it," I said faintly, wondering what he would recall.

"Yes," he remembered immediately. "A floral thing. And sunglasses, even though it was sunset. And a janitor's uniform, with some kind of turtleneck underneath. And socks with sandals." He laughed. "Now I get it. You didn't have heat."

"Eleven Dutch Street had many fine qualities. Heat was not one of them."

"Oh, I'm such an arsehole." He groaned, reaching for my hand across the table with his left and putting his forehead in his right. "You know...I looked for you at Carey's funeral. A year later. I don't know why. I thought you might know her. Out of all the events we attend, that was where I thought of you. It's funny, now, to remember that."

"We didn't trade names."

"No. Because you *berated* me the whole way back. I thought you were going to kill me."

"You dropped six hundred dollars of magenta acrylic on the sidewalk!"

"Because you were walking too fast," he said, still laughing, still holding my hand in his long fingers, the knuckles on his left hand stained from the ink of the extra-fine-tip markers he used. I felt self-conscious and drew my hand back, leaned away in my chair. Charlie didn't let me make any space, though; he immediately put my hand to his face, a gesture that shocked and delighted me, and I wondered if he remembered doing that same thing six years ago, before kissing me in the stairwell of my building—that sweet kiss we shared before he walked down the stairs and into the night without another word.

"I *did* know you," he said. "I'm sorry. I should have known you this whole time. Oh...please don't stop being my friend. Please don't be angry."

"It's New York. Nobody remembers anything," I said lightly, blushing. I felt a magnet hold my hand to his jaw—a magnet so strong I broke the connection in shock—and he returned to his own space, leaning back again, telling me what he'd been doing that day, who he'd been that year, reminiscing in a rush, the words and memories coming as fast as the beating wings of the humming-birds who still gathered around their sugar feeder.

I listened, and that was where my confession ended, that I had known him, after all.

I did *not* confess that I dreamed of running into him for years after that day, pictured him at all sorts of moments, mostly lonely ones. On some days, every tall, dark-haired, clean-shaven man wearing an expensive suit had been a potential Charlie to me, and I would see them in the subway or on the street and wait for them to turn—

—and then it would always be someone else.

Until that party downtown.

There he was, at long last, and married to my friend.

Chapter Fourteen

The next day was horrible, backward. The notebooks interrupted time and time again. I kept looking at the digital camera's tiny picture display of the spines, spinning the wheel to zoom in. *CAREY 2, FORGIVE/FORGET, THE BURIAL PROJECT, 72 HOURS, TOMBSTONE PIZZA, YOKEFELLOWS, ELIOT&SPRAIN HOUSE*: Those were all sculptures. *HOLD ME, CHOKE ON IT, SLEEP DISORDER, OTHER PEOPLE'S RULES, DROP OUT, LOVE THAT MIRACLE, SIDE EFFECTS (MODAFINIL)*: Those were the performances. Two rolls of film, the letter said. Pine City had possession of two rolls of film. A work that, in Charlie's words, "could upgrade the market for her previous works quite significantly." Something that would make everybody money. Money that Pine City didn't want. What could it be? A film, but of what? Which one was the film? *SIDE EFFECTS (MODAFINIL)* was the one where she stayed awake for days. *SLEEP DISORDER* was when she slept in a box, with the aid of constant supplements of sedatives. *CHOKE ON IT* was the hot dog–eating competition. *OTHER PEOPLE'S RULES* was the one with the awful review. But *LOVE THAT MIRACLE* and *DROP OUT*—I had no idea what those were. One of them had to be the film.

I would drift off like that, then blink back to discover paint pooling onto the canvas from where I'd paused mid-stroke. My daydreams became impossible to avoid.

Eventually I stopped working and scoured the studio, looking at every forgotten tool, in the kilns, in every cabinet, but there was nothing: no film canisters, no CDs or DVDs, no USB drives, nothing. I even checked the shoe boxes of terrible drawings again, going through all of them this time instead of just two. All I found in the three remaining boxes were more drawings and two pieces of clothing.

There was a vintage white dress, an embroidered white sheath with a low neck and fitted drape, wrapped carefully in tissue paper and encased in a plastic bag. It was the kind of thing that Carey would have worn. It looked to be about my size, and I tried it on, wiggling out of my shorts in the middle of the hayloft. It fit *almost* perfectly, though it was a little tight under the arms and long at the knee. Folded beneath it was a rolled cloth coat, printed with a leopard pattern and lined in peach silk. It slid over the dress like they were made for each other, the hemlines matching exactly.

The other boxes held more of Maria's cartoonish, juvenile drawings—some signed Maria Clarke, some signed Maria Frances Clarke—and when I found an unlabeled portrait of Carey, drawn from life, recognizable but still repulsively terrible, it occurred to me that Maria Frances Clarke was probably the MFC who had once carved her initials over the shelf in my closet.

There were scenes of small-town life, with WAPPINGERS FALLS, Carey's hometown, written on the back, and a house with CLARKE written on the mailbox. The house was a one-story rathole with vinyl siding and a rusted-out Toyota Camry parked in the driveway. My mother's house often looked the same way. It made me shiver, the similarity of it all, the repetitive nature of small-town alcoholic poverty. I pawed through them, and after a while had to put them down. The drawings grew worse, revolting, even, with each page, and I boxed them back up. They reminded me of Portfolio Day, the alumni duty where we gathered in a high school gym and examined the work of would-be Academy hopefuls, which I thought of as the saddest day of the year.

I tried to situate Maria in Carey's life. Same town, so...Maria was probably a friend of Carey's from high school, someone to whom Carey wouldn't have been able to say no.

I pictured the toddler from the family in the photographs, all grown up, twentyish, maybe, beautiful, arriving at Pine City, maybe nervous, maybe jealous, maybe thrilled. Then I saw her getting dumped, like I did, in the worst house, and working quietly on these awful drawings while Carey realistically reproduced a human corpse like a magician. I pictured Carey helping her pick out this dress for the summer party.

Someone who made work like this would have found it impossible to talk to any member of Pine City about anything except the weather and traffic. She must have felt so lonely—and unwanted. I pictured her carving her name into the wall before she left, still the outsider, the two of them—Carey and Maria—split at the seams, enough to leave her drawings behind, to fold the dress up in tissue paper so politely that Carey couldn't bear to look at it. I felt sudden, tremendous pity.

And—dread.

I didn't want to be a Maria.

I was a Carey.

No—I was *better* than Carey. I wasn't going to give up.

I took the dress and the jacket, tossed them in my truck, shoved the boxes to the side, and returned to my paintings.

The next night, when I returned to my bungalow for dinner, the phone rang.

"Hello?"

"Hey." It was Tyler. His voice wavered slightly.

"Oh. Hi," I said nervously, curling the cord around my fingers. "What's up?"

"I'm—I'm sorry I left so abruptly," he said right away. "Things got crazy with the install. I had to catch a ride over on somebody's plane because of some customs bullshit, which meant I had to go to the city earlier, then I had to come back with her, blah blah, anyway, you were working and I didn't want to disrupt you."

"That's fine," I said, in a way that I hoped could be described as blithe. I'd been to art fairs overseas, too—back when I had money for hotels and travel, when I had a mailbox where invitations rendered in invisible ink or disguised as prescription pill bottles could be delivered. *When I had a passport that wasn't blank.* "I'm working, anyway."

"Fifty days, right?"

"Nearly. Nineteen to paint."

"Can I bring you anything?"

"When?"

"Tomorrow, maybe Friday night."

"I'm fine. I'll see you when you get back," I said noncommittally.

"You sound like you're in it. Are you done for the day?"

"No. I was only home for dinner. I have to go back, though."

"All right. See you soon. If I'm in the studio, knock, okay?" An invitation. He was trying to close the gap between us.

"Okay," I agreed. "See you soon."

Two nights later, Tyler's station wagon was parked in his carport. His house was dark. Down the road, narrow lines of light burst through the taped-up edges of his studio windows. My stomach dropped with anticipation. Nervously, I washed my face, carefully brushed my curls out into a big '70s halo, tied my t-shirt into a knot at my waist—this one had Opus T. Penguin on it—then marched over to Sports and knocked loudly.

"Two minutes," he yelled. I leaned up against the wall and bent one heel to it, staring out at the sunset on the water while I waited, and there in those high wooden heels I felt young again. Then, a stab of panic. With a mere seventeen days left to paint, I shouldn't have left the studio for anything. But I was vibrating with stress—for good reason. I *was* making progress. The days were long. *I need to take care of myself,* I told the panic. *I need to have some fun.*

I heard the hiss of hot metal colliding with cold water, of steel clattering against concrete, and then the lock turned and Tyler poked his head out of the studio. He wore a heavy waxed apron and thick leather gloves that went up past his elbows.

"You look like summertime," he said, raising his face shield, grinning. "Come on in." He didn't hug me hello, though for a moment it seemed like we should, but then he lowered his eyes to the ground and turned abruptly.

The studio was exactly as he'd described it, a gymnasium-turned-brass-foundry, the wooden floor ripped away to leave a concrete surface, mostly covered in metalworking grids, different sizes of autoclaves (small round ovens used to heat metal), and an electroforming bath. There was a walk-in refrigerator, humming away, and several chest freezers. The back wall was lined with an enormous forge; the sides were lined with machines. I could identify a CNC router, a 3-D printer, and a table saw. A row of lockers to the right were all heavily padlocked.

"Is that where you store all the body parts?" I teased.

"I'll never tell." He winked and pulled his faceplate up and off, the halo of it moving his sweaty hair over and back. "Yes. And in here." He yanked open the door of the walk-in refrigerator and motioned for me to look inside.

There were shiny, blood-red torsos, lungs, hearts, kidneys, livers, stomachs, intestines; feet, hands, heads, and legs. At first—they nearly looked like bodies with the skin ripped off—until I reached out and touched one. It was smooth and solid.

"They're extra wax positives," he clarified. "Outside, they'd melt."

I picked up a man's head and held it in my hands. "Who's this?" I asked.

"It's me," he said, letting his face go slack. "Can't you see?"

"It doesn't look like you at all," I marveled. Only the shape of his nose was obvious. The rest looked like it belonged to a stranger.

"I know. It never does," he said. One of the hands on the top shelf stretched toward me in a handshake, and I realized that it was the hand from the Eliot House library door.

"These were Carey's," I said without thinking, reaching for it. But it was too high for me to grasp. I glanced around, checking for film canisters. There were only shining red bodies.

"Uh . . . yeah," he said, surprised. "How'd you, uh, know that?"

"They're the hands in Max's house."

"Oh—of course. Yes. Only the organs are mine." He turned abruptly and ushered me back into the studio. I brushed past him. Our shoulders touched, and once again I felt a liquid blush travel from the center of my body to the ends of my fingers and toes.

"I thought you sold the real organs, covered in metal—not copies."

"I do. I still make a mold first. They don't all survive the process."

He moved a propane torch to the side and set his gloves in front of an empty ceramic crucible.

"Careful. It's still hot," he said, gesturing to the crucible.

"It's empty," I noticed. "What did you make?"

He pointed to a long sand mold, running the whole back of the table where molten aluminum shimmered like mercury in a long, skinny line, five or six feet of it. I peered at it but didn't understand.

"What is it?"

"It's a brush. Well, it's a brush-holder, like a cigarette holder. When I was in Vilnius, we visited a studio outside of town where they were painting the sets for an opera at Bregenz. They stood above the fabric and used these long sticks with brushes on the end. I don't know if you'll use it, but I wanted to make it. It's a rod, essentially. Lightweight. And I put your name on the end."

"Thank—thank you." I stammered. "That—that's incredibly kind of you."

He leaned, pointing at the end of it, grazing the edge of my arm.

"It's on the bottom side of the mold. It should be okay to take out tomorrow."

"Thank you," I said, one more time. He glanced at me over his shoulder, and I smiled, wondering, in the back of my mind, if he had done this for Carey.

"It's nothing. I like to make stuff," he said with a shrug. Nervously, he cleared a stack of metal scraps from a chair and gestured for me to sit. I looked down at it and frowned, then hopped up onto a clear spot on the opposite workbench. Sitting like this I was tall, almost even with him.

"What have you been doing with yourself?" he asked. Sweat beaded on his forehead.

"Work," I replied. "Only work."

"I felt badly, leaving you." He looked at me—and I looked back. The air grew thick between us, humid and dense in the way that a car window fogs up if you sit and talk for too long after killing the engine.

"You missed me," I tried to joke, my words tripping over each other again.

"I missed you," he admitted after a moment.

The drop of sweat rolled down the side of his temple, down his jaw, and without planning it—I reached for it. When my fingertip hit his jaw, he held still against my hand.

He wanted to touch me, and I wanted the same—I wanted to give him something of myself—and so neither of us looked away or broke the spell, and then—we kissed—I kissed him—he kissed me back—that round pout of his mouth landing on mine. I pulled him to me, collapsed into him, felt my body wrap inevitably around his, and I didn't wonder for a single second whether or not it was a good idea, because we were really kissing, *kissing*, the endless kind of kissing. Long, searching kisses, kisses that exist as an end unto themselves, kisses that are as alive and as intimate as anything else you could do with two bodies, kisses that are as real a conversation as the first time you stay up all night talking.

He ran his hand up my bare leg, all the way to the ragged hem of my shorts. Then he flattened his palm, wrapped his fingers around me, and squeezed. His nails left half-moon dents in the fat of my thigh, white bites haloed in red that bloomed and faded.

I never wanted that feeling to end—not then and not ever.

Chapter Fifteen

Someone honked. Once, twice, I don't know how many times. Soon they were laying into the horn, and the sound separated us. Tyler wrenched open the studio door. I remained on the bench, out of sight of whoever was behind the wheel.

"Shark. I'm in the middle of something," he snapped.

"SO AM I!" she snapped back, insistent. "You promised!"

"Oh. Right. Five minutes," he said, tilting his head, raising one hand in apology. "I'll see you in the studio." He shut the door and returned to my embrace, his mouth back on mine. "Sorry," he murmured. "I promised Marlin I'd help her tonight. We have to fix her monotype machine."

"That's okay," I said, palm flying to my chin. I could tell it was turning red and raw already. "We should probably take a break. I don't have a callus for you," I said, tracing the edges of his stubble.

"Don't worry." He laughed, pushing his cheek against mine, burying his face in my neck. "You'll grow one." He put a finger on my chin. I opened my mouth and bit it.

"You're going to ruin me," he said, and then we were wrapped up again, for thirty long seconds, before he extricated himself.

"Ahem," he said, taking both my hands and helping me down from the bench. "To be continued."

"I need my shirt." It had flown somewhere, but in the piles of metal and debris it was totally camouflaged. Tyler found it snagged on the edge of the table saw, a ragged hole cut into the shoulder. I pulled it on, inside out like he always did, and he grabbed my hand.

"Come on," he said. "It'll be fun."

Marlin stood over an ancient monotype machine, greasy rods and screws in hand. The heaviest parts lay on the floor, alongside wooden trays of type and neat piles of grommets and bolts.

"I think I'm breaking it," she said, frowning.

"We'll fix it," Tyler assured her. "We always fix it. We always fix everything."

"I think... *that* one," I said, pulling a short rod from her hand, "goes here." I slid it into a narrow hole and screwed it into place.

We spent the next hour passing pieces back and forth, trying to reassemble the mechanisms that would hold its heavy weight, swearing and laughing at our constant failures until everything was where it was supposed to be. When we were finished, Marlin arranged a series of letters into a block, poured liquid gold into a sponge, and smeared the surface. Then she inserted a heavy black card stock and pulled the lever.

The machine pumped and pressed, forcing the letters into the paper. In carefully spaced sections, it printed TYLER SAVAGE, MARLIN MAYFIELD, JES WINSOME, JACK WELLS, CAREY LOGAN, TOM HEALY, ANELE MUIR, KERRY BEE, JEANNE PETIT, LENA ADDARIO, RACHAEL KRIEGER, MAX DE LACY, and DAVID BIRD.

She took the paper and sliced it on a cutter, the long knife raising and lowering, raising and lowering, until there were thirteen cards with a name on one side, the other blank. She folded them into place cards.

"There," she said, stacking them into a V-shaped mountain. "For tomorrow."

When she folded the one with Carey's name, Tyler plucked it from her hands.

"You printed the wrong name." His voice was low—affectless.

Marlin turned a peculiar shade of gray.

The paper turned over in his hands. It was so quiet that you could hear the rasp of his fingers across the fibers of it as he smeared the ink with his thumb. Then he set the paper carefully on the table and looked at Marlin like she had deliberately broken something precious: hurt, anger, betrayal.

"Oh—" she replied unsteadily, soggy with guilt. "I—old habits." She took the place card from the table and threw it in the trash. "I'm sorry. I'll make a fresh one." She turned to the machine and I could see that she was about to cry.

Tyler turned on his heels and walked to the door.

"I'm beat," he said, in that same low voice. "See you tomorrow."

And with that, he left Marlin and me alone with each other in the studio.

♠ ♠ ♠ ♠ ♠

Marlin's shoulders trembled and twitched as she arranged the letters for my name. I poured the gold on the sponge and handed it to her, along with a fresh piece of black card stock.

"Thank you," she said, falling to a whisper. "I keep forgetting she's not here."

"That's probably . . . normal."

"I want to," she said delicately. "I—I can't." A tear rolled over her freckles and plopped on the machine. I nearly reached out and hugged her. She breathed in, sucking the air to the bottom of her chest, and pulled the lever—and in doing so, pulled herself back together. Then she wiped her hands against her white overalls, cut and stamped my place card, and stacked it atop the others. "There," she said. "Count these done."

"What are they for?" I asked.

"Oh. It's the summer dinner tomorrow," she said. "Didn't anyone tell you?"

"No."

"Everyone's coming," she said, eyes angling downward, becoming commas. "It was supposed to be fun this time. I'm completely
messing it up. Carey used to take care of everything. We did what
we were told."

"It'll still be fun," I said, trying to console her.

"It's never been fun," she muttered. "Why start now?"

"What do you mean?" I pressed.

"Sometimes I don't think we even like each other anymore," she
said, stacking paper restlessly, moving it across the room for no reason. "He's still so *angry* about it all," she finished desperately, the
sound coming out in a pressured rush, like she was a bellows—and
then she clapped her hands over her mouth. From the look on her
face, she wanted to claw the words out of the air and take them back.

"That's okay," I tried. "People can be angry. He's allowed to be
angry." I looked up at her freckled face.

She sniffled and squeezed my arm. "I know," she said. "Thank
you." She wiped her eyes and laughed at herself. "I'm such a mess,"
she said. "You must think I'm such a mess."

"I don't think that," I said to her. "I think you're all still recovering from a tragedy."

She nodded, collecting herself again, and this time, it stuck. "By
the way—everyone is going to be walking around," she said point-
edly, eyes lingering on the hole in my inside-out shirt. "We'll open
our studios. You don't have to, but you might want to move your
painting from upstairs."

She was clearly aware that I was remaking more than one painting. Yet—it didn't feel like a threat, coming from Marlin. It felt like
a warning.

"Thank you," I said. "I'll move it tomorrow."

♣ ♣ ♣ ♣ ♣

I called Tyler the next morning, in case people arrived in the afternoon, to ask if he could help me move *Prudence* from her station in the lobby over to the studio so that she could be framed and crated along with the rest. He agreed readily and arrived ten minutes later without apologizing or acknowledging his disappearance from the night before. I let it go. When we were finished, we clicked her panels together and set her upright in the back, against the wall, overlooking the other six.

He asked what I wanted to do with the two older panels of *First Prudence.*

"Burn them," I said.

"Can I keep them?"

I laughed. "Why?"

"Because they're a piece of you."

"They're only a fragment," I said, shaking my head.

"I'll settle for fragments," he told me.

As we kissed, I wondered how fragments could ever be enough—for him, or for anybody.

Chapter Sixteen

I sent Tyler away so I could work, but it didn't go well. I was distracted and nervous. Everything felt like a mistake even though I was following my own instructions exactly. I worried, all day, that the feeling had gone out of them—that the feeling is the thing that made them real and not knockoffs. I felt extremely lost and under a great deal of pressure.

But I pushed through and did what I was supposed to. At the end of the day, I used two rocks to grind stray ribbons of aluminum into a sparkling dust. When I struck handfuls of it over *Humility*, she was finished.

Or at least, I think she was—I wanted her to be—and so it was true.

Tyler knocked while I had one leg in the kitchen sink, half covered in soap, a razor in my hand and rollers in my hair.

"Come on in," I said, running the razor under the water. "I need five more minutes."

He carried the silver brush-holder, weighted at one end and nicely balanced. "I meant to bring this earlier."

"I can't wait to use it." He leaned against the wall. "You want to watch?" I teased, waving my razor at him.

"Absolutely," he said, and then we kissed again. I wrapped one wet soapy leg around him, bubbles disappearing into his shirt, and it wasn't until I felt the tenderness of my chin that I pulled back.

"I'm not going to dinner looking like"—I waved my hand at my mouth—"a teenager."

"Fair enough," he said, backing off. When I finished shaving, I unclipped the rollers and brushed out my curls. He watched me curiously as I added mascara and my purple lipstick.

"It's funny to see you in makeup," he said. "I don't think of you as someone who wears makeup. You're so natural."

I pulled one pink curl and let it spring back. "Real natural," I said with a smile, ducking into my room.

"Your hair seems as though it grows that color."

"I'm *trying* to dress up," I said, pulling my purple dress on. "See?"

"Nice." Tyler smiled. "There's a stain from Max's party, though."

I frowned, picking at a spot of grass and dirt caked to my hip. "*Atticus*," I muttered, spinning on my heel and marching to the closet. "My friend bought all my clothes and they're all insane. I look like a teenage runaway." Piles of dirty clothes coated the floors and shelves. I hadn't done laundry for weeks. The only clean thing I found, a knee-length t-shirt with a male bodybuilder's be-Speedoed beach body printed on the front and back, was both ugly and wildly inappropriate. Then I remembered the white dress from Maria's boxes. *Maybe that's a better idea.*

"One second," I yelled. The zipper got stuck halfway up, and I backed out of the closet, tapping it. "Could you?" I asked.

His fingers touched the skin of my back and the fabric of my dress. I heard the sharp buzz of the zipper rise and rise and rise, but then it paused an inch or so before the top. I turned around, confused, and he glared at the dress. He looked slightly horrified. I patted the sides—*had I ripped it? Didn't it fit?*

"Where'd you get this?" he asked.

"Maria's boxes?" I said, a slow question. *Uh-oh*. "The boxes in the studio?"

"Maria." He said her name quietly, like he was trying to recall who she was.

"Carey's friend from home? She left behind her drawings in the studio. They were horrible."

Startled, he ran a hand through his hair, twice in a row. "Oh. That's what you meant."

"She stayed in this house, I think," I said, gesturing toward the closet. "Her initials are in there." He didn't look at the closet, or at me. He only looked at the ground.

"This was Carey's dress," he finally said, pulling the zipper back down, in ragged little yanks. I hated it—I *hated* how he tugged— but I was too stunned to move. *Carey's dress. Not Maria's. I was such—I was such a creep*. "I don't think you should wear it." *Of course not*. By the time I took over the zipper from his shaking hands, his cheeks were olive green, and sweat mobbed his hairline.

"Oh my God," I mumbled, clutching my chest. *Maria wasn't even sophisticated enough buy her own dress. Of course Carey lent it to her. I should have known. It's exactly my size*. "I'm so sorry." I retreated into the closet and yanked it over my head. Too tight, my breathing too heavy, it stuck somewhere around my bra, pinning both arms above my head. "I'm so sorry," I called out, my voice muffled by the fabric, as I twisted and wiggled, anxiously trying not to rip it. "I didn't even think about that. I thought that because it was in the same boxes ... I just assumed." I sucked in my stomach, gave a hard yank, and it flew to the ground.

"It's fine. Carey probably gave it away," he mumbled.

He sounded so upset. I hated what I'd done.

I reappeared in the purple dress, one hand on my hip to cover the grass stain. "This is all I have."

"It doesn't matter what you wear," he said, and he was far away, shaken up, lost. I was so mortified that my cheeks burned neon red all the way to the Mission, and I kept apologizing over and over.

"Let's forget about it," he said, taking my hand. "Please?"

His fingers were wrapped so strongly around mine that I had to wrench one hand away and pry them off. When he noticed the strength of his grip, he jumped. "Oh no," he said, taking his hands back. "I'm so sorry, I didn't mean to—"

"It's okay," I told him. "I know the difference. I know when it's on purpose."

Then he fell into me, burying his face in my neck, smelling my hair, whispering apologies that I didn't need. I kissed him, there in the shadows of the trees that sighed and fluttered above the driveway. The lights draped across the deck grew brighter with each passing second; I saw the bonfire flickering, heard bluegrass music in the air, and everything was as I'd imagined. The summer heat, the fireflies, the streaks of orange light—the colors of golden peaches and ripe grapefruits, shades so bright you could taste them—that signaled the beginning of sunset.

We let go of each other and made our way to the party. One of the enormous round tables had been moved outside to the deck, overlooking the water, and set with the gold-and-black place cards. Candlewicks burned in erratic, sculpted lumps of wax, pooled in a delicate, oddly shaped ceramic dish. Someone had placed fresh wildflowers bound with clear fishing line at each setting of striped napkins and mismatched, tarnished silverware. I found my place card next to Tyler's. Max was on my other side.

"No Charlie?" I asked.

Tyler, fully composed, shook his head. "Artists only," he said, as though that was the only reason.

Tom Healy, a sculptor who worked mostly in foam and plywood, was sitting in an Adirondack chair and playing an old acoustic guitar. He nodded at us gently and kept on singing a country version of "Stardust." A group of people were inside at the bar.

Marlin burst out of the restaurant with a cartful of glass pitchers filled to the brim and garnished with different fruits. She poured us each something clear, basil leaves floating to the top.

"Thank you," I said softly.

"It's tradition," she said, kissing me on the cheek, an unexpected burst of affection, before turning around and running back to the kitchen. "Ty, we need your help!"

He squeezed my hand and ran to follow—and left me alone on the deck. In that moment, Jes walked out and climbed atop the railing, like a cat. She turned and looked at me with narrowed eyes, dissatisfaction slicing through the air.

"Was that you the other day?" she snapped.

"I—I don't know what you mean."

"Really?" She tilted her head back in contempt.

"I don't know what you're talking about."

"It was you. You sneaked into my studio and then ran away. I saw your hair."

"I'm—I'm so sorry," I stuttered.

"Did you seriously *run away*?"

"I . . . I panicked."

"I was at your studio the other day, and you acted like I wasn't even there."

"I was . . ." I looked at her skeptically. "I looked at you. You didn't say anything."

"I smiled at you," she insisted, her face equally dubious. I knew she'd sneered at me. She knew it, too. *She was trying to knock me off-balance.*

"You had a lot of stuff," she observed. *Damn.*

"Well, I'm very sorry," I said to her, trying to sound like I meant it. "I'm not . . . I'm not like Max. I'm . . ." I shook my head, trying to figure out what to say. "I'm shy."

"Whatever," she muttered, rolling her eyes. "Grow up." She spat that one at me, the words stinging like a hard slap, then swung from the railing and walked inside to the group, all smiles.

I looked over at Tom Healy, singing happily to himself, and he nodded, as though nothing had happened at all.

A laugh went up from the group inside. I didn't dare go introduce myself—not while Jes was standing there talking to them. Cheeks burning, I stood frozen, watching the peach of the sky turn to apricot and then cherry, across the half mile of glassy black lake that stretched in front of us. I thought about Carey walking into it and wondered if Jes was the one who had pushed her to do it.

Eventually Tyler came up behind me, putting his arms around my waist.

I unwrapped them. "Not here," I whispered.

"You're embarrassed of me?" He smiled.

"No." I shook my head. "I don't want people to think I'm only a summer girl."

Tyler tilted his head in confusion, like he'd never heard the term, but before he could reply, Max appeared, and we were hugging hello, and then a group of famous artists stood in front of me, shaking my hand. Anele Muir, the sculptor who carved boat-size pods, was there. So was Kerry Bee, who made enormous installations of electrified fabric. Filmmaker Jeanne Petit, photographer Lena Addario, performance artist Rachael Krieger, and conceptual sculptor David Bird rounded out our dozen. They had all been guests here. Tonight, they would stay over, and linger through the weekend.

"Oh these plates, Marlin! I forgot about these," Jeanne said, in her beautiful accent. She sounded like Isabella Rossellini.

"Me too. I made them for the Yokefellows dinner," Jack said. "Now, *that* was a million years ago."

"What does that mean?" I asked.

"Oh, he threw them," Marlin explained. "Jack is magic on the wheel." She rolled her eyes. "He has a three-D brain. Some people have all the luck."

"Before your babies," Jeanne said, and Jack was already pulling out his phone. "Oh, these fat babies, I want to be as fat as this baby," she cooed. "A little butterball of baby."

"No," I said, haltingly. "I mean, Yokefellows." I nearly recited the line from the notebook: *to yoke me as his yokefellow, our crimes our common cause.*

"Oh—it's James Joyce," Marlin said quietly, leaning in and putting her hand on my arm. "Do you mind if we—if we don't right now?" She flicked her eyes at Tyler, the electric fence around everything Carey.

I nodded, chastened, and then I walked over to Max and clung to her skirts like a lost little girl.

It took forever to sit down to dinner. Everyone had to get cocktails first, and then they were smoking cigarettes and catching up. When Marlin and Tyler were back in the kitchen, still cooking, I found myself on the edge of a conversation with Tom and Lena and David and Max about the party they'd all been at, the one on the barge floating in front of Hart Island.

"Did you meet Suna? The woman from Pakistan who only creates forgeries?"

"I heard her telling the Browns that they should pay her to replicate everything in their collection and then they could sell the originals and keep the copies, and nobody would ever know the difference."

"I love lesbians who wear hijab. It hits so many buttons."

"Oh, Suna's equal opportunity. She's married to Spark Suleman."

"For the passport?"

"No, I think they have a baby."

"Did you eat those bananas he brought? They taste like oranges, apparently. I was too grossed out to try one."

"Starting a farm of genetically modified fruit is a massive-scale project. At a certain point, aren't you just a farmer?"

"He exports the fruits into other nations. The customs paperwork *is* the artwork."

"He must have a gig."

"I think he's at RISD."

I stood there quietly, nodding occasionally. The conversation continued in the same vein for an hour, until we all sat down to eat, and then during dinner it got even worse. Every artwork they discussed was an idea, a piece of an idea, a joke, a commentary, a repositioning of a theoretical argument from twenty-five years ago, a reaction, an indictment, an impeachment of something else. It was like someone had taken the last two hundred years of culture, put it in a blender, pureed it into a sauce, and eaten it, only for this semiotic mash of ironic purposelessness to be then expelled back out again. I nodded along, laughing when I was supposed to laugh and shaking my head when I was supposed to be outraged, at the money someone had been paid for a joke that wasn't that funny, or at how they hadn't been hailed as geniuses, and we might as well have been discussing television, or politics, because all of it centered on our reactions, the infinite hall of mirrors echoing our responses to and over each other, to the arts that had become our entertainment.

Eventually, someone asked me a question. "...political purpose?"

"I'm sorry?" I said.

"Does your work have a political purpose," Lena said slowly, deliberately, and Tom and Anele turned to listen. Jes raised one perfect eyebrow and waited for my inevitable stumble.

"I'm not sure what you mean," I replied.

"Well, in this day and age almost nobody is *just making paintings*," she said, and then everybody turned to listen, and anxiety surged through me as I tried to think about how to respond. I'd never found a way to cleverly encapsulate what I was doing. I mean, I'd thought plenty about bullshit. Part of the beauty of abstraction is that in theory, you can bullshit your way out of anything. "It's a meditation on discourse," you could say about a big blue square. "It's an indictment of a post-formalist universe whose lenses are viewed solely through a Rawlsian utility-dependence." "It's about Ana Mendieta falling out a window." "It's about the impermeability of dirt." Really—you can say anything and get away with it, if you're bold enough. And yet I was not a person of theory. I was a person of practice; my paintings were the exact things I meant for them to be. They were not bullshit. But I couldn't defiantly tell her, *Well, I am*, because it could only sound angry and defensive. I settled on deflection. And first, I wanted to acknowledge the hostility of putting me on the spot like that.

"*Hold on*," I said, trying to keep my tone light. "Can a girl get a drink first?"

It worked. Everybody laughed. Tom reached over and poured me one. Tyler handed me a lit cigarette.

"Here, take this too," he joked, and I took a long puff and rolled my shoulders, like a boxer, and everybody smiled, though Jes's was predatory. Then all of a sudden I was talking.

"I make enormous oil paintings," I told them, a quiver in my voice at first, "because they are the pinnacle of labor. They are expensive, delicate, unwieldy. They take more work than anything else I could imagine—work and investment and time and space— and that work, that labor, takes me outside of myself. The paintings are not a criticism—or an indictment—or a commentary." The quiver stopped, and I heard myself speaking in another woman's voice, one that was confident and sure. "They are objects that exist unto themselves, moving and beautiful, worthy of the space they take up in the world, political because they do not crouch in a corner, because their labor is obvious. Their weight is obvious. Their heft cannot be ignored or dismissed. They are the only part of me that is big," I said, and then everyone, even Jes, silently stared at me as though I had said something radical, and I could not believe what I said about my own work. It sounded so vain.

"I know that I'm not supposed to be vain," I heard myself saying, "that I'm supposed to be humble. But my work is huge and loud and important even if they are, as you said, *just paintings*. I know that's outré—everyone else is playing some hundred-year-old game where they make fun of the gallery, and the collectors, and the people who are taking selfies, and find a clever new way to sell immateriality and throw gold in the river, to be wink-wink know-it-alls, repurposing the archive to destroy the institution from the inside...but I'm not ironic. I make things that are emotional," I confessed, and in that moment, with the candles flickering and the lake splashing against the pillars beneath us, it was true. "And it's all that I am."

For a split second, everyone looked at me with these funny little smiles, and I thought it was all ruined. I thought about Maria Clarke's terrible drawings and wondered if I was the latest version—if I'd be leaving here humiliated and alone. But then Tom slapped Lena on the back and said, "In Italian I think she said *vaffanculo*," and then the others were throwing their napkins at me, and Lena was laughing, with her hands up in defeat, and Jes turned away to light a cigarette, and Tyler wrapped his pinkie around mine under the table, and Max pointed at my wine and said, "I'll have a glass of *that*," and it felt like I'd held, if only for a moment, my own.

♦ ♦ ♦ ♦ ♦

After dinner everyone took cocktails to go for a studio walk. Someone asked if we could go to mine, but before I could answer, Tyler spoke.

"She's running the dehumidifier. Everything's sealed for another few days," Tyler lied, so smoothly, and as he said it I realized that I probably should do that. He winked at me and I smiled gratefully.

We walked up to Marlin's first, where she gave everyone a small framed print: three stripes of iron-dust ink that looked like the fur of a metal caterpillar. There was even one for me.

"Thank you," I said.

"Of course," she said, but before I could say any more, someone

was opening a flat file and demanding her attention. For ten minutes, her friends rifled through everything in her studio, oohing
and aahing over recent works and reminiscing over older ones.

"I *love* this one," Jeanne said. It was an old wheatpaste, brick dust
still clinging to the back, peppered with holes and fragile as a ghost.
A drawing of Carey.

Marlin looked at it sadly. "Me too," she said, patting Jeanne's
hand. They hugged briefly, and a tear rolled down Jeanne's cheek.
Jack, meanwhile, had his arm around Tyler's waist and was pivoting
him toward Tom, who was telling an elaborate anecdote about
falling down a well. Jes was nowhere to be seen.

Our next stop was Jack's studio. The former Arts and Crafts
pavilion was a soaring, peaked cabin filled to the brim with rolls
of fabric, three vintage looms, and a scaffold. A large net was
in progress, made from different colors of monofilament—fishing
line—and swaths of parachute silk riddled with fabric flowers, woven leaves, yarn-wrapped ceramic objects, and glazed porcelain
feathers. It was breathtaking—nearly religious in its delicacy and
scope.

Jack swept in, shoving things from side to side, but the rest of
us stepped lightly and carefully. When we were on the far side of
the net, a waterfall of silk and plastic separating us from the rest
of the group, Max clutched my arm and pointed to a little glass
globe suspended from a golden coin, suspended so seamlessly
within his aesthetic that I hadn't even noticed it. "That's exactly
like the light Carey made for my house," she said. I couldn't tell if
she was being derisive or not.

"I think they're all doing that," I whispered back. "I think she's
in all of their work."

"You better watch out," she said playfully.

Then Tyler's arm brushed my waist, and my focus shifted so ar-
dently that I have no idea what Max said after that.

Before our next stop, we fixed a fresh batch of drinks. Tyler
caught my eye while I was mid-conversation with David Bird.

"You have to follow the work," David was saying. "The work is the only thing that tells you who to be."

"Absolutely." I tried to keep a straight face. In principle I agreed, but over his shoulder, Tyler was biting his lip and smiling at me in a way that made it impossible for me to pay attention to anything. A plum blush lit my neck and worked its way to my cheeks.

"Let's . . . get you a drink," David said genially, glancing at Tyler.

"Danger Beach," Tyler said. "Don't tell her anything about me. I want her to think I'm a good person."

David laughed. "It's too late for that."

From there we headed to the Theatre and piled into the green corduroy seats. I tried to sit next to Tyler, but got stuck between Kerry and Anele instead, who were gossiping over me about the extramarital affair of a famous downtown artist.

"This grad student was crying about it to one of her friends at the bar in Philmont," Kerry whispered. "I was sitting right there. I almost leaned over and said, Honey where do you think you are, the Port Authority? Everyone in here has an asymmetrical haircut. We all know exactly who you're talking about. Anyway—I texted him to stop being so indiscreet."

"What an idiot," Anele agreed. "His wife is on the Biennale committee."

The gray plastic table swarming with mixing boards and orange extension cords was still there, as were the screens and the stacks of speakers, but Jes didn't touch any of it. Instead, she dragged a folding chair into the middle of the stage, then disappeared into the wings, returning with her cello.

She set it between her legs and held the bow aloft.

"I've been trying to remember who I was before Pine City," she said. "Not that I don't love you." The group laughed. "But I want to get back to basics. So—I'm a little rusty, but here we go. This is from the Philip Glass score for *Dracula*."

She played for twenty minutes, the bow rising and falling as the notes climbed over each other, her dyed fingers plucking the strings, kohl-smeared eyes squeezed closed between occasional glances at a grid of sheet music on the floor. She did not use a looping pedal or an amplifier; that night she used only the sound of rosined horsehair on catgut strings and their deep echoes in a belly of bent maple. Her foot smacked against the floor between the occasional releases of held-in breath.

The piece, with its tenuous creeps, its plaintive, deathly romance, surrounded us; we were dizzy with it. Every now and then the bow would go all the way across the strings, from one end to another, and the full sound would be drawn out in a throaty scratch. Jes visibly strained to hold the notes. What had once been automatic, the result of hours of daily practice, was no longer. Yet there was a depth to the struggle that shaded her sound into a dreamy intensity, and I could not have imagined it any other way.

At the end, she let the bow fall to her side and her head drop.

I was the first to clap, overcompensating for the tension between us, and was soon drowned out by the others. After a moment she raised her head to reveal a face that was blood red and drenched in sweat. She looked to Tyler for approval. For the first time I saw Jes herself as vulnerable and fragile.

Superb, he mouthed to her across the crowd—and then he went to her and took her hand, helping her down from the stage. They walked together out into the night, her head upon his shoulder, his arm around her waist.

In Tyler's studio, the last stop, everyone got rowdy and decided to light the forge. He was the center of attention, the orbit around which each conversation anchored itself. Jes hung at his elbow like a girlfriend, and everyone treated her that way. They were intimately connected to each other. As they leaned against the workbench where he and I had shared our first kiss, I had the awful realization that we would never share anything the way he shared Pine City, and all his memories of Carey, with Marlin, Jes, and Jack. Even if he did want to tell me, someday, it would never be the same as having lived it in the first place.

As I stood near the door, marinating in jealousy, Max gripped my wrist and pulled me, quickly, into the walk-in refrigerator. When the door slammed shut in the chilly darkness, I yelped. Max ignored me.

I waited for an annoyed Jack, Jes, Tyler, or Marlin to pull us out of there, but nothing happened. Concerned, as always, that I might alienate them, I reached for the handle, intending to leave, but Max swatted my hand away. I yelped again. She switched on her phone, waving it at the waxy red hands lining the top shelves.

"Look. The hands from *my house*."

Her hair was flat, but her eyes were enormous. Max was drunk. Not the drunkest I'd ever seen her...but compounded with the fact that she was not currently the center of attention, I suspected I was in for one of Max's patented baby tantrums.

"It's a refrigerator, Max. They'd melt anywhere else," I said reasonably, then relaxed into the cool air, delicious after the heat of the forge, and waited for her to spin it all out.

"These hands shouldn't be here," she said indignantly. "They should be archived in a museum. A curator should have these." *Huh. So—Max thought it should all be shown, too. Of course she did. She was married to Charlie.* I wondered if he'd told her about the film.

"Probably," I replied, baiting her.

"Don't you get it?" she said, her tongue a little thick. "The coin? *Dracula*? The hands?"

"No." I leaned in.

"They're not making work *about* Carey," she said. "They're *stealing* from her. They're vampires." Her eyes were wild, the fake lashes hanging heavy, and she gripped my wrist again, the edges of her diamonds threatening my thin skin, and for a moment—our breaths clouding the air between us—for a moment I believed her. "My house is supposed to be special. What if they make another one? They're *not supposed to do that*," she said sullenly.

Someone leaned against the door, and I saw the rubber gaskets

smoosh in. *We had to get out of here.* "Nobody is going to replicate
your house, Max," I said sternly, putting my ear to the door. I
couldn't tell who it was, but they were laughing, the bass of it vibrating through the metal. "That's ridiculous."

"Is it?"

"Yes," I said, hard, like the strike of a gavel. "It is." I pried her
from my wrist.

"All I want is to be special," she said, her tone very serious.

I laughed. "You're plenty special, Max." She curtsied, then
blinked up at me, expecting another compliment. The weight
came off the door, and the rubber gaskets narrowed again.

"Listen," I told her sternly. "We can't be caught in here. This
is totally—" I searched for a word that Max would understand.
"—RUDE."

She nodded. "For sure." She clicked off her phone.

I tested the door handle, pushing it inch by inch, quiet as a
mouse, then peeked into the studio. Everyone was gathered around
the forge, burning something, facing away from us.

"Let's go." I pulled her out in one quick motion and leaned
against the door as it shut, covering its movement with my body,
like we'd been standing here the entire time.

"Jes IS a vampire, though," she said, and I looked over to
see Jes resting her head on Tyler's shoulder. "SHE DRINKS
BLOOOOOOOD."

Seeing them together made me feel like I was running a race
I'd already lost. My whole body went slack, a loser, giving up.
Max saw, and poked me, hard, with the edge of her orange
fingernail.

"He is NOT in love with her," she whispered. "You're so wor-
ried. It's silly. He never liked Jes. Carey liked Jes. But Tyler is only
Jes's friend." She laughed and repeated herself, changing the order.
"Tyler is Jes's *only* friend."

I watched Tyler and Jes, at the way they looked at each other,
and wondered what Carey would have done in this moment. Prob-

ably walked over there—taken his drink—or *her* drink—anchored herself in front of him—then turned on her light, so that he couldn't look anywhere else. She would have blinded them.

I leaned against the refrigerator, with the petulant jades of jealousy and the insistent reds of frustration coating my insides—and did nothing at all.

Chastity

Chapter Seventeen

Falling in love is a fever, a disease, euphoric and despairing, a rush through the body that warms everything. Suddenly you have twice as much blood as you did before—you are bursting with it. You make enough blood to dissolve the hardened internal plaque of your loneliness. With each new cell you grow ever more swollen and tender and fragile, your skin stretches thinner and thinner, enough for other people to see your heartbeat from the outside. When it is thin enough for someone to take in all of you—your bones, your nervous system, your deepest internal self—then you're a goner, with someone else's breath inscribed so deeply on your heart that nothing could erase it.

The next morning when the sun came up, I went directly to the studio, refusing to look in Tyler's windows as I drove past his house, wanting to keep him from my mind. I spent a heroic amount of energy trying to drain my body and quiet my heart, but it was too late—I was already sick with him, feeling the illness of him settle in my stomach, heating the back of my rib cage, shadowing my every thought.

The moment the clock hit eight, I was out the door, speeding to the Mission, where—sure enough—Tyler waited for me, sitting in "his" chair, and I flew into his arms for more of those endless kisses, this time not so endless.

We went into the Mission, pulled the curtains shut, locked the door. I climbed onto the bar top and soon my clothes were the only thing between us, and then those were gone, then I was pulling him inside me, holding him against me and looking into his eyes.

Is this what it is to fall in love in the modern era? To find yourself having sex without a condom, to give in to what that means, to look the other person in the eye at the exact moment you are doing it, to let go, without thinking about it in advance? To let them come inside your body—to say, Do it, I want to feel it—and for them to look at you with shock and delight, just before both of you push into each other until there is no looking back?

That night, we cooked dinner naked and fucked on the floor of his screen porch. In the morning he brought me coffee. We wove our bodies together. I watched the dust motes swirling over his skin in the sunlight coming through the window, like every lover in the history of time. He drove me to the studio. He picked me up at sunset when the day was done but pulled over two minutes later and fucked me in the back of the station wagon halfway through the driveway because we couldn't wait another second. That night we played gin rummy naked and I told him about my adolescence. The next morning we kissed for an hour, my chin turning raw and red by the time I forced myself to go.

After work on the fifth day, we took a long shower and touched each other with so much enthusiastic tenderness you would have thought we were teenagers doing it for the first time. Later we cooked dinner and split a bottle of wine, and slept wrapped around each other. We spent an entire week this way, not apart for more than a few minutes once the workday ended. I went to the studio every day with skin like tissue paper, overflowed into buckets of paint, and then at night I went to his house and filled back up again.

I became more infatuated with him after every single reckless encounter, and I was open to him in every way that it seems possible to be open to someone. But he was not open to me.

On the eighth evening in a row that I slept at Tyler's house, he told me about his father's illness while we were lying in bed, the sounds of the lake and the wind in the trees drifting through his open windows. It was an awful story and he told it with clean concision, the sort that comes from having thought, if not told, the same story over and over in your mind for twenty-five years. I wondered if he would follow it with more stories about death—about Carey—but it was as though she'd never existed at all.

I simmered with unease as we fell asleep that night. I wanted desperately to interrogate him about her, but I worried that confessing the depths of my interest would jeopardize whatever was growing between us. I had spent too many years alone, or with the wrong people, trying to love them even when I knew that I didn't, and that half-living-half-loving made me unprepared for the real thing.

And so I kept all my questions about Carey to myself.

I was perched on a ladder, tapping loose pigment from above onto a panel of *Chastity* coated in white paint and grease, when the rolling sound of tires on gravel came through the nearest open window. I glanced toward the locks; I'd flipped them.

"Hold on," I yelled out. "Out in a minute." Whoever it was, I'd squeeze through the door and talk to them outside.

But it didn't matter what I wanted. Max skipped right on into the studio, unlocking the door with her very own key, from a bundle ringed on a silver leather fob. Though she wore baggy jeans and a plain white shirt, hair piled messily atop her head, she still managed to sparkle, bright like an opal, eclipsing me even in my own space.

"Nice key," I said angrily, frozen to the ladder.

"I have keys to everything," she said, laughing. "I know we're not supposed to crash people's studios, but I barely talked to you at the dinner. Uh—" She paused and gazed out at the room, seeing the twenty-eight panels and their 896 square feet. "Holy shit— what are you doing? What do you have, like, a hundred paintings going on?"

"Max—you are not supposed to come in here."

"Oh my God," she said, in a drawl that was half awe, half disbelief. "*You're remaking them*," she said, looking out at the paintings. "They *did* burn. Holy shit." I wanted to grab her, shake her, throw her out. She was an endless poison, Max. "They're beautiful," she said in wonderment, walking the aisles of my work.

"You cannot tell anyone," I insisted, paralyzed atop my ladder, gripping the metal so hard my knuckles were white, then colorless. "This—this is bad, Max. You cannot tell anyone at all."

"Lockbox," she said, crossing her heart with an X. She looked back at me to gauge my response. I didn't bother to hide my anger, but kept working, tapping away with my jar of pigment. Ocher dust rained down into a spotted pattern that quickly dissolved, leaving a dense stain.

She lit one of her unfiltered Lucky Strikes. "This is *gooooood*, though," she said after a drag, nodding and looking around. "These are good, honey. I mean, I didn't see the first ones up close. But maybe it was meant to be."

"I—I don't know. I hope so. Thank you."

"How you feeling?" she asked.

"Tired," I told her, "but—I don't know. I mean. I love them."

"They're more than good...God, it feels *so* different in here. Less dismal. That's a real change."

"Did you hang out in here a lot before?" I asked.

"Not really." She shook her head, smoke coming out her nose.

"Were you close with her?" I couldn't help myself but ask, even as I wanted to pull the words out of the air and stuff them back in my mouth.

"Ugh. I *don't* want to talk about Carey," she said, screwing up

her face. I tried not to roll my eyes, but goddammit, I was getting sick of this. Carey was everywhere, in everything, but nobody
wanted to talk about her. "I'm actually here for me—"

I interrupted her. "Max, I have one question."

"Fine."

"Why did Carey stop making sculptures?"

"I have no clue. Tyler knows, for sure. You should ask him." She
looked annoyed.

"Fine. What is it?"

"I have a favor to ask. Fleur, my writer, who was at the party, I
don't think you met her, anyway, she's coming to live up here in a
little bit and then we're gonna work on the book for a month. You
have to tell her everything. About me, I mean. And I'm going to
need your help with all my photos."

I climbed down from the ladder, grabbed another jar, and
climbed back up. "I don't think you want me to do that." I tapped
the jar, and a shower of blue powder rained down onto *Humility*.

"I'm a straight shooter." She winked. "I've got nothing to hide."

"Okay. What about the year you had cornrows?"

"Hilarious. Go ahead."

"The dad you fucked in the coatroom at Helen what's-her-
name's bat mitzvah."

"Finger fucked. But yes, sure. That guy was such a pro," she said
wistfully.

"What's he doing now?"

"He's in prison for tax evasion."

"And Petey?"

"Absolutely," she said happily. "There's a whole chapter on
Petey."

"Charlie?"

"Well. *No.* Ha. I mean, the, like, *adult* part of *my* life isn't even a
good story."

I exhaled heavily. "I have so much to do," I told her. "I need
to keep going. I don't have time for your stuff, to be honest. I'm

sorry—until these are ready to sit and dry, I'm busy all day all the time. I have less than a week to paint, but then I'm around."

"Then let's get you an assistant," she said, pulling out her phone and texting rapidly. "Pine City can always put up more people."

"No. Max, don't worry about it. My last assistant got a way better job. Goat Group started giving health insurance."

"Are you sure? It's no big deal."

"Nobody can know about this."

"That's what NDAs are for. I want you to feel supported."

"I do," I told her. "You can make me feel supported by keeping this to yourself," I demanded, waving my arm over the room. She zipped her mouth and crossed her heart again, then reached into the canvas tote bag she'd brought with her and pulled out two cans of ice-cold seltzer.

"Want?" she asked, pulling the tab, cracking it open, handing it off to me before I could even reply. I took a long sip and belched ten seconds later, loudly.

Max laughed and we were both suddenly ten years old again. "Let's have a beer," she said.

"I can't drink and work."

"You cannot possibly do any more work today," she insisted. "Come on. Let me feed you. It's the actual least I can do."

I looked at *Chastity* from above, at the four greasy eggshell-and-pearl panels scattered with bombs of color, and mentally assembled it.

"Lady...this is *done*," she said approvingly, and I knew Max was right. This time, I didn't feel the need to fight her; I didn't feel the need to compete with her about my own work. I accepted what she saw, and she climbed up on the ladder, to be certain, and then we both looked at it from the stairs to the loft, then minutes later I'd locked up the studio and was seated in the passenger side of Max's open-top vintage army jeep, seltzers in our hands. She drove us back to her house, taking the east exit and going left on the main road and left again, counterclockwise around the lake, a route I hadn't yet taken. It felt quicker than going the other way.

At the end of her driveway she turned down a hidden road to the left of the front door—that plain metal doorway set into the hill—and we careened toward a glass wall that parted just in time. Max pulled into a huge garage and threw the car into park. I ran my fingers over the spotless enameled bodies of the three other vehicles lining the space: one green vintage convertible, one shiny new electric SUV, and a jet-black motorcycle, its edges hard and matte. Max pushed open the nine-foot-high bleached-cedar door into the house and ushered me through it.

"DANNY, make dinner!" Max yelled once we walked in, popping out somewhere on the third floor. I was taken aback at her rudeness. The Max I knew was privileged, sure, but she would never yell at anyone, certainly not her help. I stopped short and looked around for the person she was screaming at, but Max laughed at me.

"I'm talking to the house," she said, and right on cue the vocal stylings of a smooth California lady robot bubbled from a speaker in the ceiling.

"Duck or pork?" asked the house's disembodied voice.

"Pork," she said definitively. "You had the duck already, right? When Charlie made you dinner?"

I nodded, squirming inside at the memory. "It was delicious."

"Forty minutes," the house told her.

"That's the DANNI: the Digital Atmosphere Neural Net Infrared. It's the 'smart house' thing," Max said as she led me down the concrete waterfall that made up the central staircase. "It was designed after these 'future houses' that Charlie was obsessed with as a boy—those things they had at world's fairs, you know, the ones that would show you how future people lived. He wanted to make one. The floors and walls contain the heating elements; the plumbing is a gray-water system that comes from the same stream that feeds the lake. It gets filtered, used, and eventually irrigates the property . . . this house is like a bunker, in its own way. It has a kind of self-sufficiency."

The ground-floor courtyard was filled with a handful of extra-long velvet sofas and an enormous round dining table. When we got to the kitchen—a room paneled seamlessly in bias-cut bleached cedar, same as the doors throughout the house—she pressed her hand into the wall. It moved away to reveal a hidden wine cellar the size of a standard living room, with walls made from a packed, damp chalk, like a real champagne cave in France. Max strolled through the racks, turning over bottle after bottle until she came across something that met her standards. I pulled angled red wine glasses off a shelf near the door. She popped the bottle open easily and splashed some into the glasses.

"Did you see the house at the party?" she asked. "Or did Charlie show you around?"

"The courtyard, the library, your office, and the deck," I told her. "Is there more?"

"Let's walk," Max insisted. She took me through each room in the house, through its seven bedrooms on the second and ground levels, where the beds hung on chains from the ceiling, floated on hidden platforms, were cast deep into the floor, or, in the case of the master, dug into the hill itself. Their bed was cocooned halfway inside a glass bay, stretching back five feet into the dirt of the hill. Tree roots, ants, rocks, and layers of soil were the only things visible through its windows, a layered, sedimentary view, a unique variation on the wide picture window. The walls were painted a glowing, velvety blue, and a ten-by-ten painting, a wild abstract made in the early 1960s by Joan Mitchell, was positioned opposite their bed. I stood in front of it for several minutes and let her colors pass through me. I felt them all: dandelion white, Kool-Aid pink, Italian teal, shining medieval goldenrod, the cold blue of the bottom of a rain cloud.

"Someone told me you were her aesthetic granddaughter at the party," Max said as I stared. "I completely agreed with them."

"Milot is trying that one on. They're calling me the 'daughter of post-post-modern painting.' It's this whole riff on the idea that painting 'died' and it's being 'resurrected.' "

"Are you?"

"Well...No. I don't think painting is dead. Despite the fact that ninety percent of famous living painters are men, painting still is and has always been an essential element in the art market, the hydrogen in their ocean of money. And secondly, no, I'm nobody's daughter, that's for sure," I said, rolling my eyes. "I hate that we're supposed to have these matrilineal bonds of motherhood and sisterhood. Like everything for women is about this kind of physical connection. But—men get to be themselves."

Max nodded, and we continued the tour. Plant life bloomed everywhere in the house, through living walls—vertical gardens integrated into the building itself—and she told me about many of the plants, moonflowers that bloomed only at night. She told me, too, about each painting and work of art we passed, and had a funny, loving, or kind anecdote about the artist who had created it, positive stories that built on whatever myths were already associated with each particular person.

On the second floor, she took me into Charlie's home office, the one I'd seen from the deck. The white-walled and white-floored room was filled with drafting tables and shiny red enamel stools. Slender drafts of installation plans, labeled with handwriting that was blocky and even, hung from clips on the walls. The air in the room was so still that the delicate papers fluttered from the breezes made by my body as we passed them by, and I felt that I was disturbing not just the drawings but Charlie's own aura—the room rang with presence and particular, deliberate energy.

We returned to the third floor, where the garage, Max's office, and her darkroom took up most of the space, though there was a small box by the front door. "Where is that messenger," Max muttered. "He was supposed to pick this up an hour ago. The lawyers called this morning and *insisted* that I box up the original design plans for the house *immediately*. But the messenger still hasn't bothered to show."

"Why? What do they want them for?" I had to put one hand over the other to stop myself from reaching for the box. I was desperate to know how she did it—how someone so untrained, from nothing, from a backwater like me, learned how to translate her ideas into the magic of this house.

"She didn't tell me," Max said flatly. "When it comes to Carey, we're all supposed to go along with *whatever*." Anger radiated from her, echoing against the cold walls that surrounded us, and I didn't dare press any further. By the time we got to her darkroom, the feeling had disappeared, and Max was all smiles once again. She punched a code into the door to unlock it.

"Eighteen thirty-nine?" I asked.

"The year that commercial photography became available to the masses," she said, the door clicking open. "There are so many people who come through this house for Charlie's business that I'd rather they didn't mess around in here."

She walked me slowly around the darkroom, a thousand-square-foot studio with a wall of purple-tinted windows, blocking out the UV. A framed black-and-white portrait of her as a teenager by Ellen von Unwerth hung on one wall. She started animatedly describing the works in process that hung from clips around the room and the differences between the vintage film stocks she was using, but I barely listened; I was thinking about Carey. It was impossible not to, in this house that reeked of the essence of her work—work that defined the place where life met death, where cold and hard met soft and yielding—despite the firm architecture Charlie had commissioned to contain it, or the décor Max had chosen to try to erase her. Max rifled through a flat file, wine still in hand, while I stared at the cement wall.

"Look, here's the one of you." Max was holding up a photo. I snapped to attention.

The picture was of me at sixteen years old, wearing a too-tight thrift-store halter dress and standing underneath the metal halo of an inner-city basketball hoop, its net long gone, deflated basketball in my hands, taken during her first and only visit to Gainesville. Max had surprised me by flying in for the weekend, so she could tell me all about filming her first movie.

It was a complete disaster. My mother was particularly awful, trying the first night to get Max to go with her to the bar (without me), then eventually coming home so drunk that she passed out parked halfway inside the garage.

Everything about my childhood that had previously seemed utterly normal to me—TV trays, Lucky Charms, bologna sandwiches with mayo and pickles on Wonder Bread, microwaved meat loaf, store-brand Kool-Aid, hanging out with boys who skateboarded in the parking lot at Walmart, getting our makeup done by my friend Jolie's mother, Lea, who was a topless dancer and part-time hairdresser—all these things were suddenly unforgivably terrible once Max came to stay because she had literally never seen anything like it before. She was polite but asked so many sincere questions (Max didn't know what mac and cheese was, even) that I knew my whole life was a garbage pit. It was like hosting an exchange student from Planet Money. Everything was a strange and curious wonder to her, which could only mean that every single thing in my life was something that Max and her friends, the glamorous girls who appeared in magazines, wouldn't touch with a ten-foot pole.

The Saturday night of her visit, we walked along the highway after smoking a joint with two boys on the basketball court where she'd taken my photo. Straining for another cool thing to do, I suggested that we stop by the Sally Beauty in the Sun Towers strip mall and look at makeup. Max perked up right away. That was how we first bleached my hair and toned it with the wrong bottle, accidentally tinting it the palest of pinks, like the inside of a seashell, a color I had never seen before on a human person, only cartoons.

Yet Max pronounced it beautiful and chic, and she meant it. That was the only moment of the weekend that she looked at me with awe instead of confusion.

I remember thinking that Max would never want to be my friend after that trip, a prediction that came true once we got to college and she could brush me away without feeling badly—chip the barnacle of hideous me from the smooth, painted surface of the luxury yacht that was her life. I realize now that the experience of visiting Gainesville must have been agonizing for her, to witness the strange, manufactured, standardized poverty in which we lived. It must have been a waking nightmare, to see every sad contour of my life.

My mother, to this day, keeps a green square of clean AstroTurf in front of the screen door because she thinks it looks "classy." That Saturday night, when Max and I were walking home from the strip mall, Max stepped in a puddle and got dirt all over her boots. She wiped the mud on the AstroTurf mat, thinking she was being polite. But when my mother came home from the bar the next morning and saw the dirty mat, she slapped me hard across the face for making such a mess in front of a guest. I don't think I even blinked—I was so used to it. It didn't hurt. What I felt was *humiliation*—that she'd done that in front of my most important friend. And I think that I wanted Max to be shocked for me. But Max didn't say anything at all.

Then, to make it worse, my mother, who by that time of day was too drunk to drive, made us take the bus to the airport. Max and I barely spoke as the bus lumbered down the freeway; I mostly stared out the window. When I got home I discovered that Max had accidentally left a bottle of her expensive salon shampoo behind, and I used it on special occasions for the next two years until it ran out.

We'd never discussed that weekend. Not ever.

I held up the photo—that photo that has been in three museums, that photo I never look at, that photo she put in the ICP show years ago. This was the thing that prompted me to start painting again after the lost years, to make *31,492 (Hair Money)*.

I looked at it and couldn't believe how young I had been once, or how beautiful. My face was defiant, sneering, angry; I saw myself so clearly, a little girl smarter than her circumstances who was yearning to follow Max onto the airplane, back to the exquisite cocoon of her life so that I too could one day emerge as something gleaming and precious.

"I *hated* Florida," I muttered. What I hated was that Max showed everybody where I came from, when I only wanted to be known for where I'd gone. I wanted to make more of my life than what I'd been given. Every time I pictured that photograph, I worked harder—even now I wanted to run to my studio, to overcompensate for it, for the image and the underlying fact that the photo was probably the reason that Parker Projects knew my name. But most of all, I hated that it still pumped gas into the oven of my being, that it could still motivate me, that competing with Max still mattered.

"I don't know how you did it," Max said.

"I read a lot of books." I shrugged. "The schools weren't *so* bad."

"You know what else I have," she said, turning and darting toward a bookshelf in the back, covered in white banker's boxes, labeled by project. She pulled a bottom one out, labeled MOST UNIQUE, and came back with a puffy photo album, the kind with plastic sleeves that you could once buy at the drugstore.

"Look!" she said, and it was all the Polaroids I had sent her during our years of letter-writing. There was Randolph, my pet corn snake, at the car wash, pretending to be a hose; there he and I were at the movies, sharing a bucket of popcorn when we saw *Before Sunrise*. We were in the library reading a stack of plastic-bound books; we were at a college football game, Randolph wearing a tube sock with GO GATORS written on it in marker. There were nearly thirty pictures in all. I marveled that she had kept them for so long.

"These are some of my favorite things in this whole stupid world," she said.

"He was such a companionable snake," I said. "He was social. It was so funny."

"How long did he live?" she asked.

"I don't know, actually," I told her. "My mom drove him to the swamp and let him out when I was at school. If he learned how to hunt, he maybe could have lived for a while longer. He was ten already."

"You're kidding."

"No," I said, shaking my head. "I was seventeen, I think? It was right after I got accepted to the Academy. I mean, she didn't want to take care of him. They wouldn't let me have him in the dorm, anyway."

"Jesus . . . You know, I have always wanted to say this. On that visit your mother hit you because I wiped my feet on the mat. And I never told her it was my fault. Or you. I didn't say *anything*. I was a coward. I'm sorry," Max admitted suddenly, a tear falling down her cheek.

"*I'm* sorry you had to see that," I said, feeling an embarrassment so acute it knocked the wind from my chest.

"No. *I'm sorry*," she insisted. "I've felt bad about that our entire lives. I'm *so sorry* that I got you in trouble like that. I didn't know."

"Oh, Max," I said to her, my voice breaking. "There's nothing to be sorry for. If it hadn't been the mat, it would've been dyeing my hair, or the way I folded the sheets, or anything else."

"I can't believe that," she said softly.

"It's true," I snapped, surprised. "I'm *not lying*."

"No, I mean, I can't believe you've never told me that," she said.

"I don't tell anybody that," I said. "My mom had a hard life. She was damaged, and she damaged me. I have a better life. I try not to think about it."

I set the photo down, but Max picked it back up.

"Does this picture make you feel like shit?" she asked sincerely.

I hesitated—I didn't know if she was making fun of me or not—and then, overwhelmed by trust, nodded. Max ripped the photo in half, then quarters, then eighths, and kept ripping until there was a pile of shredded confetti in front of her on the floor. Next, she scanned a wall, pulled out a binder, paged through its plastic sheets until she found the negative, pulled a lighter from her pocket, and lit it on fire. The celluloid collapsed into her fingers and she dropped it on the floor into the pile of confetti, letting it burn down to ashes.

"There," she said, as the house rang three loud notes out of the nearest speaker. "Let's eat dinner and get drunk and forget about it."

🌲 🌲 🌲 🌲 🌲

Two hours later, I was on Max's phone, calling Tyler.

"Hey." He was casual, warm.

"Heyyyyyyy yourself," I said, full of beans.

"You're alive," he said, and I could hear him smiling. "Where you been?"

"I'm at Max's house. She kidnapped me. My truck is still at the studio. Can you come and get me? I don't want to walk in the dark."

"Uh—sure. I'll be there in ten minutes," he said. I ran to the front door, pulled it open, and left it ajar for him.

"Is Tyler coming?" Max screeched from the bottom of the courtyard, where she was swaying to the music, wine glass in hand, a baby-rose ball gown zipped up over her t-shirt and jeans.

"Yes!" I called out, lifting the enormous blue tulle skirt that she'd buttoned over my romper and descending the steps one by one.

"Yay!" she squealed. "I told you, he's crazy about you. They *never* come over." Then Max brushed out my curls. "This color still looks so fresh," she said approvingly. "You've mastered the formula. It's like . . . the inner peel of a peach."

"I halved the quantities," I told her. "The shades are the same—royal blond, rose gold, nectarine."

She turned up the music as I poured more wine and we jumped around.

"'Motownphilly' is the greatest pop song of all time," she announced.

"It's so good. But it can't be the queen. You can't choose the queen and not make a list."

"Hit me then."

"'Faith,' George Michael."

"Ooh, that's maybe a burn. But it's so dramatic."

"'You Make My Dreams Come True,' Hall and Oates."

"Too yachty."

"'I Wanna Dance with Somebody,' Whitney Houston."

"I'll give you that. That's a jam," she agreed. "But is it *the one true jam*."

"Prince, 'Kiss.' Beyoncé, 'Single Ladies.' Jackson Five, 'Want You Back.'"

"These are all very good songs, but I don't hear anything to compete with 'Motownphilly' coming out of your mouth," she yelled, and with that, the house played the song for us and we went berserk.

By the time Tyler walked in, I was dancing on top of the grand piano, pouring a bottle of Ruinart directly into my mouth. Max was hopping up and down next to the window and hitting all the high notes. We'd opened the lower-level glass garage wall out into the yard, and fireflies were streaming in, electric yellows and greens.

That's when it became a blur.

Here is exactly what I remember.

Laughing, Tyler grabs me off the piano and holds me in his arms, and I dump champagne into his mouth, and he kisses me with a mouth full of foam, and it drips down onto Max's beautiful skirt. He slides one hand inside my top and we keep making out, momentarily oblivious to Max's presence.

"Hey!" she yells, popping open another bottle of champagne. "Get a room!"

"Don't tempt me," Tyler says.

"You are just the same," I say to him, running my fingers down his ageless face. "Are you a vampire?"

"The same as what?" he asks.

"The first time I saw you," I tell him, and he looks confused. Then I let go of him, grab the new bottle of champagne, and run outside. Max follows me and we race down the grass, chasing an invisible finish line, until I trip and fall face first into the soft green carpet, and I wipe my face and a chunk of dirt comes away but my skin isn't hurt, so we laugh and laugh, and the world spins around us, and Tyler is watching us from the house, and then I am suddenly very, very sad. Max takes a pack of cigarettes from her dress and lights one and hands it to me.

"Do you think he's still in love with her?" The words come out but I don't remember why I thought it was okay to ask them.

"You're so much better than her." Max sighs, collapsing into a bubblegum pouf in the grass. "I'm so glad she's gone," she says, her eyes big and wide. "It was terrible when she was here. She was the unhappiest person I have ever met. Nobody got anything they wanted when she was around."

"What do you mean?"

"It's better now. She was crazy," Max says insistently, not answering my question. "Everybody is happier now."

"Everybody loved her," I tell Max, confused.

"Everybody *hated* her," Max whispers, and then Tyler is grabbing me by the hand, and he is whisking us both back inside, giving us water and playing more music, and we dance some more and I don't get another chance to ask Max what she's talking about, and the rest of the night is dark, gone from my memories.

Modesty
&
Temperance

Chapter Eighteen

I blinked awake on a king-size bed covered in gauzy linens, surrounded by the paper fingers of a hundred ferns. Sunbeams shone through the windows and landed on my skin. Plants crept up the walls, so dense and green that I could practically feel them growing: Waxy, heart-shaped leaves brushed my shoulders, and porcelain fingers protruded from the walls, holding up ropes of vines like a surrealist gift. The sounds of a tropical hothouse—misters, birdsong, a gentle waterfall—played through invisible speakers recessed somewhere in the concrete room. I didn't remember going to sleep, and at first, I wasn't sure where we were.

Tyler lay next to me with a pillow over his head. I still wore the romper. The blue tulle skirt made a soft mountain on the floor. My head thrummed unhappily, pushing up against the dry hollows of my skull.

Max's house. Champagne. Ugh.

I stumbled toward what I hoped was a bathroom, brushing through ferns like a dinosaur with every thundering step, hoping Tyler wouldn't open his eyes before I could clean myself up. I eased the door open, pushing the hand—this one made an *okay* sign—to find an elaborate en suite on the other side.

More strings of ivy wrapped their way into a walk-in shower

so huge that it didn't need a door. I let myself luxuriate in there, soap foaming over my skin, water hot and blissful, the shampoo that same expensive bottle that Max had once left behind—except this time I wasn't in a molding tile bath in Florida, wishing I were anywhere else. This time I was a guest. Max herself burned the evidence. She took me into her home, showed me her life, made me part of the club. She finally gave me permission to move on from that girl from the wrong side of town.

Tyler was still sleeping, so, wrapped in a bath towel the size of a blanket, I hunted for coffee. I didn't have to look far; a tray waited on a console table outside our room, set with two porcelain mugs, a camp thermos, and a gold-edged notepad. Max's familiar scribble was on the top page:

> *getting fleur from train in Hudson, maybe catch you, maybe not. call me later!! let's all hang out!! & please set the alarm when you go—you know the code—xmax*

Once again—I was alone in Max's house. Almost—and that was close enough.

Wet hair slicked back, wrapped in an oversize towel that stretched to my ankles, my feet left damp blotches on the concrete as I scurried up the stairs. Three steps from the top, I could see that the box of Carey's plans for the house was already gone.

I was about to swivel and make a beeline for the library when I heard Tyler's voice.

"Whatcha doin', gorgeous?" He was across the courtyard, pouring himself a cup of coffee outside our room and watching me run for the top floor.

"You're awake!" I squeaked.

"Barely." He frowned and blew on the coffee. "What's on three?"

"I was going to check my email on Max's computer," I lied, pan-icking. "She went to pick that writer up from the train."

"How's the shower?"

"Extraordinary."

"I'll try it out. Go take advantage," he said.

"Wh—what?" I stuttered.

"Of the internet?"

"Right." I nodded, clutching at my towel. "The internet."

"I'll be out in five minutes. Want me to bring your clothes up?"

"That's okay. I'll come back for them," I said, taking one long look at the library door and dragging myself into Max's office instead. *Dammit.*

I didn't give two shits about my email. It could have been deleted for all I cared. I exhaled and looked around.

Inside the floral cabinet of her work space, Max's bleached-cedar desk held an enormous laptop and a glossy electric-blue folder from the Young Museum, but not much else. The ashtrays were empty, the coffee table bare. The bookshelf, however, still held the volumes I'd noticed at the party, and I laid them across the pink velvet and ran my fingers through their glossy pages.

All of them were artists who had somehow disappeared.

Dutch conceptualist Bas Jan Ader vanished in 1975 while attempting to cross the Atlantic Ocean in a one-man yacht, the *Ocean Wave*. The act of crossing was an art piece he titled *In Search of the Miraculous*, after a series of photographs. He managed to keep radio contact for three short weeks. His boat was found empty ten months later.

Hannah Wilke documented the changes in her body during the months preceding her death from lymphoma in a series of devastating photographs titled *Intra-Venus*, revealing the rampant destruction wrought by her chemotherapy and radiation treatments.

Charlotte Posenenske, a German minimalist, resigned from artistic practice in 1968 with a formal manifesto, the last lines of

which read "I find it difficult to come to terms with the fact
that art can contribute nothing to the solution of pressing social
problems."

By the time I opened the slim black volume, titled *Lee Lozano: Dropout Piece*, my heart was working overtime. Lozano, who made
the paintings I loved, the *Wave* series—disappeared soon after they
were done. Someone had told me once she did it on purpose,
the leaving. The book asserted that Lozano had indeed left the art
world in 1971 with a performance titled *Dropout Piece* that ended
with her burial in an unmarked grave outside Dallas in 1999. "I
will give up my search for identity as a deadend investigation... I
want to believe that I have power & complete my own fate," she
wrote in her notebooks.

The title echoed across the empty canyon of my struggling brain:
Dropout. Dropout. *DROP OUT*. That was one of Carey's three
notebooks in the library that I could not identify.

I made it six steps before he said my name. Tyler was in the doorway to our room, pulling on his inside-out t-shirt in the doorway.

"Want to get breakfast?" he asked.

My eyes flicked to the library. "Sure." I sighed.

As I descended the rest of the steps, Tyler ran his hands over the
railing to where it angled into an elbow on the banister. He was
lost in a dream. It was the same look as the first night we had dinner in his cabin, when he looked so devastated that I could barely
stand it.

"Can we stop at Pine City first?" I asked. "I'd love to brush my
teeth and change. And I need to go to the studio right after. I can't
lose today."

"Tell you what." He inclined his head to the side. "I'll make
breakfast at home."

"Are you sure?"

"You're right. We should both get the day started. We'll get day drunk in town some other time."

I changed back into my clothes, and we climbed the stairs to leave. As I reached for the front door, he held out an arm and stopped me.

"Alarm," he reminded me.

"Oh—right." I typed Max's birthday into the keypad, realizing that she hadn't written it on the note. She didn't want Tyler to know it. I supposed that made sense, given his conflict with Charlie, but it was nonetheless surprising, given that she had keys to all of Pine City.

Tyler held open the passenger-side door of the station wagon for me, and closed it when I was buckled in. He lit a cigarette, rolling down the window with one hand and driving with the other. He was a good driver, sticking to the middle on those narrow country roads, and as we made our way back to Pine City, my mind wandered back and forth and over the lines in the book on Lozano. Lozano, Lozano. Carey named a project after her. Max was researching her and other artists who had disappeared.

Then—it was as though an avalanche had been triggered in my mind. Facts tumbled down the slopes in a rush:

Marlin's, Jack's, Jes's, and Tyler's studios were littered with pieces of Carey—the hexagons, the eyeballs, the film, the wax positives. Yet it seemed they could barely tolerate the mention of her name.

"There's one work," Charlie had said, "that could upgrade the market for her previous works quite significantly. They simply won't give it up."

"Everybody hated her," Max whispered.

"It's never been fun," Marlin cried in her studio. "Why start now?"

"Other people didn't matter to her," Jack was saying, book in hand, that day on the lake. "She was kind of a dangerous person . . . anything could happen when she was around."

I thought about Tyler's face whenever her name came up, and Jes—possessive, angry Jes, needy with Tyler and nobody else. Her film that showed Carey as a sad, empty copy, and the way she snapped at me every time we spoke. Jes didn't want me around. I wondered if she hadn't wanted Carey around, either.

My next thoughts were like boulders, smashing against the floor of my chest. *What if—what if Jes had something to do with Carey's suicide? And what—what if all of this was about protecting her? Or what— what if Carey was still alive?*

Then the car was pulling to a stop. Tyler's arm reached over me, the hard meat of his biceps and forearm pressing against my chest—

Whatever happened, Tyler knew exactly what it was. I imagined he'd guessed my thoughts, and my face opened up in wide-eyed panic—

Until—

His hand hit the plastic handle. He unlocked the door and pushed it open.

"Home sweet home," he said—and then he kissed my cheek.

I had one hand on my clavicle, like I always did when panic took over for reality, and then—as soon as I realized it—my lens changed. I ticked off a mental list: I was hungover, hungry, tired. I was obsessive; I was jealous; I was stressed. I was acting, as my ex-boyfriend George used to say, like a paranoid, insane person. I took a step back and tried to think it through a second time.

Jes was gruff, but people like us didn't kill other people. Tyler was sad. Marlin was sensitive. Jack was preoccupied. None of them wanted to keep thinking or talking about Carey, and that was their right. The more I rationalized their behavior, the more my own thoughts seemed silly and irrational—as foolish and superficial and crassly speculative as the people at Max's party.

Five minutes later I was at Tyler's. Water boiling for coffee, eggs and bacon frying in a pan. I sat at his burnished black dining table, folding his black linen napkins into tiny swans.

"Where'd you learn how to do that?"

I hesitated before replying. "I was a maid in a motel, the summer between high school and college."

"In Florida?"

"Yeah. Horseshoe Beach, Florida. It's on the Gulf. It's *very* Gulf," I said. "Everybody had tribal tattoos. That was the summer I worked with my mother."

She was fired six weeks in for drinking on the job. After that I drove to work in her car every day alone, and returned to find the house empty. She would be out somewhere, with someone. The day I left for the Academy, I worked my shift and came back with my last paycheck. She wasn't home. I signed the reverse, tucked it under a lamp, shouldered my duffel bag, and took the bus to the airport.

But I didn't tell Tyler that.

He finished making our breakfast. I sat there, roiling in confusion, unsure of what to say. I was dying to ask about everything, to find out whether I was rational or irrational. I wanted to know about the lawsuit, the notebook, the film, the connection to Lee Lozano, but it had been made very clear that pressing him on Carey would only cause a rift between us, like when Marlin had accidentally printed her name. Every ounce of my curiosity about Carey was tempered by my dependence on him.

Still—it went that way after all. I read once about the noises our throats make when we are rehearsing a thought; we speak without speaking, and those around us hear us without doing so. It's how, sometimes, you know exactly what someone is going to say— because they have already told you, with their eyes and their posture and the inaudible speech they've been rehearsing in their heads and passing imperceptibly through their vocal cords.

He handed me a mug of coffee. My fingers spread flat across the surface of it. He paused and peered at my fingertips.

"Have we met before?" he asked.

"Do you know who the president is?" I replied, holding my hand to his forehead.

"No, I mean, like, before this summer." He held my hand and stared at it. "Last night you said I look the same."

"Ohhh—I was dru-unk." I grimaced. But—determined, against my better judgment, to pick away at Carey—I said it. "Well—I *was* in one of Carey's shows."

"What?" He turned to stone.

"My hand was, anyway." I held out my left hand. "She cast my hand in a show at a gallery, while I was still in school, and I saw it, years later, in Paris. The show was called *72 HOURS*. I was, like, hour forty-two or something. The skin was falling off, but I recognized my fingernails," I said, rubbing my fingertips against each other to make a hard, rattled noise. "See? They have ridges. My mom has them, too."

"Why didn't you tell me that before?"

"Uh...because you're in mourning?" I offered. He looked incredibly confused.

"What do you mean?"

"You—I mean, wasn't she your partner?"

"Y—yes."

"She died two—almost three—years ago. You painted the house black. You wear all black," I said. "You're visibly upset whenever her name comes up, and you've never talked about her, or even what your life was like when she was alive."

"I'm not still mourning Carey," he snapped.

"Well—then what the fuck is wrong with you?" I asked, but nicely.

He laughed. "Nothing," he said. "Can you believe that I'd rather talk about you?"

"No. I have a ton of questions. For starters—" I was about to ask about the lawsuit, but he cut me off.

"That *doesn't* mean I can talk about her."

"Weren't you together for a decade?"

"On and off for fifteen years. But it was not a perfect relationship by any stretch of the imagination."

"You can't omit fifteen years of your life."

"I know that," he said. "I—I *cannot* talk about it. I cannot discuss Carey, or my life with Carey."

"Why?" I could not help myself. "Why on earth not?"

"I—I can't. There's things you don't talk about either. You don't talk about your mother. That's the first time I've ever heard you say anything about her other than she lives in Florida and you don't go home."

"That's different."

"Is it?"

"My mother is only sad."

"Well, for me, Carey is only sad."

"But I'm asking you to. If I told you about my mother, would you tell me about Carey?"

"No," he said plainly. "I can't."

"You mean you won't," I said, shoving my chair back from the table. "That's different."

"No—I would, but I can't. You shouldn't *care*. It doesn't have anything to do with you."

"Is this because of what's happening with Charlie, and the work you're holding hostage?" I asked, the words landing before I could take them back. He looked at me the way he'd looked at Marlin— angry, hurt, betrayed—but I didn't stop. "Because—I'm not going to run and tell Max everything you say."

"Apparently you are, because she's telling you all about our business," he snapped, and then we were two dogs fighting, circling each other.

"She didn't tell me that," I said, exasperated. "Max never talks about you. At all. She has her own things going on. *Charlie* did. He says you're holding Carey's work hostage and that it's all over money."

At that Tyler turned almost purple. "Why the fuck is Charles Eliot talking to some random painter about our business? God, that guy is such an asshole."

That's when my brain melted, neurons firing in every direction, heart beating through my teeth while anger flooded my bloodstream.

"*Some random painter.*" I screamed the only words I'd heard him say. "SOME RANDOM PAINTER? *You* are the asshole!" And then I was out the door, running through the narrow path in the woods, over branches and leaves that swatted and scratched at my skin, all the way to my studio—the only reason that I was here.

I don't remember working, though I know that I did—long enough for my t-shirt to soak through with sweat; for my hair to float up into a nest, then plaster itself back to my forehead. Long enough for my bare feet to turn black with dirt and my shoulders to hunch in pain. A pile of empty beer cans rose up in the corner, evidence of a fresh inability to abstain during working hours, a failure of my own personal temperance; coffee grounds and Pop-Tart wrappers filled the trash. I worked for—what—a day? two?—but don't remember any of it.

I only remember being devastated.

I knew it. I knew that I didn't matter to him. I was, of course, *some random painter.* I didn't have a name or a place in his consciousness. I was simply another young woman in a long line of young women who came here to make beautiful things with our beautiful bodies. We each stood in for Carey until the summer ended and he could send us away. I felt foolish—and blind—and humiliated. I would never see Tyler's inside—not really. And though it was the closest I'd ever been to Carey Logan, I'd never know her either, and the loneliness of it all nearly killed me.

Something was happening with *DROP OUT*—that had to be

the film—but I was torn right down the middle. The more I dug up about Carey, the more I jeopardized my own future. All Pine City had to do was ask me to leave before my paintings were finished, or call Jacqueline, or Susan, and rat me out—and then I'd be finished, too.

I had to complete my work. By my count, I was almost out of time: four more days to paint.

Sometime in the middle of the night, Tyler drove up and asked if he could come in and talk.

"I'm fine," I told him through the door, without opening it. "I need to work."

"I hate that I hurt you," he said.

"I'll be out of here soon, and you'll have Carey's studio back for the next one. The next random *whatever*."

"That's not how it is," he said sharply. "That's never been how it is."

"I don't care," I told him, and then I walked away from the door and turned up the stereo as loud as it would go.

Ten minutes later I heard him drive off.

As I collapsed onto the orange sofa—Carey's sofa—I wondered if this had all happened to her once, if she had slept here with a broken heart, surrounded by the only thing that mattered, that was always there for her: work.

The next morning, I moved with a fury I hadn't known for years. I was a burning, licking flame that passed over each panel in a focused heat, transforming every scrap of the virtues that had so consumed me for the past two years, passing them once again from my brain to the brush as if some empowered ghost were animating my body.

I had worried that it would be impossible to remake my own work, and yet, now I think, *Could it have ever been any other way?*

Did I believe that a single effort could rip these words out of my body for good? No; it seemed they had only grown back bigger and stronger. This time, I let the palette knife scrape the cavities of my soul right down to the bone.

SOME RANDOM FUCKING PAINTER. I finished *Modesty* before the day was out. Not only was *Modesty* identical, but she was better than before—she was lurid and crude and hypersexual. I realize it sounds weird to say that about a pile of paint, but that's what she was.

Four down; three to go, the final layers. I doubled the concentration of Galkyd, stuffed a towel under the door, and ran the dehumidifiers on high.

I slept on the sofa again, waking with cracked lips and dry skin. Three days left—but I wasn't ready to call them done. The next task, building the frames, was a labor so complex I hesitated to even think about it. I tried to motivate myself with the knowledge that once I built the frames, a truck would take them away and I would never ever have to see anyone from Pine City ever again. *These will sell, and I'll be flush again, and I won't buy a house up here, I'll get a new passport and move to Berlin, or maybe Warsaw, they say that's the new Berlin, right? Somewhere in the former Eastern Bloc.* I would cash my checks and buy all new clothes, start a brand-new life somewhere all over again. I would finally dye my hair a different color, and then I'd be a brand-new person, for real this time.

Yet—my body wanted to stop. It didn't matter how little time remained. I was very nearly broken.

Yuck, I thought, smelling my armpits, which had spent days sweating through my shirt, recoiling as my stomach howled with emptiness. *I don't have any clothes. I don't have any food. I need a shower.*

Back at Pine City, everyone could be there—Jack and Marlin, Jes and Tyler. Maybe even Jack's beautiful family, maybe even their friends. I didn't want to see them. *Some random painter.* I couldn't bear the humiliation of it all.

Dizzy, I climbed in my truck and drove to the Stewart's in Union

Vale for snacks. The clerk, the same woman who had kindly told me about the paint on my nose the day I'd first run into Max, stared at me with open confusion as I walked around the store, ripping hungrily into a bag of chips as I filled my arms with a case of seltzer, assorted snacks, cheap toiletries, and a promotional t-shirt three sizes too big that read ROOT BEER FOR LIFE. I smiled at her sunnily, ambling around the aisles on my blackened bare feet, dirty fingernails and paint-covered arms shoving a credit card into the reader while she bagged up my purchases.

It failed. She turned the machine around and punched in a code. "I have to cut this up," she said.

I nodded agreeably and rooted through my pockets until I found another, handed it to her, and crossed my fingers behind my back.

"You okay, honey?" she asked as the machine dialed. Concern shading her face, she handed me a pair of flip-flops. "Take these. On the house."

"I'm fudging great," I said, popping a potato chip into my mouth and stepping into the sandals. "Everything is great." The machine blinked APPROVED. I signed the credit slip with a flourish and skipped back to the truck. She watched me through the window, biting her lip, hand on her cheek.

At the studio I showered with the hose in the driveway and washed my clothes with a bar of soap, painting in the root beer t-shirt until they were dry.

I took a break to brush my teeth and stared at myself in the mirror. My eyes were bloodshot—raw wounds in a pallid face. My hair was limp and laid flat against the bones of my skull. The veins of my skin pulsed below the surface; the edges of me were starting to wear away, to disappear completely. I was a floating bundle of nerves. I wondered if I would survive this, if I *was* surviving it, if there was another me who had already died somewhere along the way, if I was only half a person, if I wasn't supposed to be here. I wondered if Carey had stood here, in this spot, facing this mirror, and felt this same way. I reminded myself that she was fine as long as she made sculpture, and that she killed herself when she let go of it. *It's okay to work this hard*, I told myself. *It's necessary. If you let go you might float away.* It felt for a second like I was flashing in and out of existence, but it was only the flickering of the fluorescent lights above my head.

The declined credit card was troubling. My three credit accounts were set to automatically withdraw the minimum from my checking account every month, so it was either maxed out—a distinct possibility given the interest charges on the approximately thirty-nine thousand dollars I'd spent so far this summer—or I'd failed what would now be a hefty minimum payment. Or both.

There was only one way to pay it off. I went back to work.

By the dawn of the next morning, I was almost done with *Temperance*, the carmine red of her surface better than before, deeper and sadder, even without the rubies. I took a break to catch a few hours of sleep on the sofa, but before I knew it, it was late afternoon, and someone was banging on the door.

"You cannot hide in here," Tyler was telling me through the door. "I don't accept it."

"Too bad," I yelled. "I'm not hiding, I'm working. Isn't that the point of all this? How else am I going to stop being *some random painter*?"

"That's not fair," he said.

"It is completely fair and accurate," I told him.

"I'm coming in," he said, and then he was unlocking the door and walking inside. He was wearing a hooded sweatshirt covered in burn holes, and clean black jeans in place of his paint-spattered black chinos, and he had three days' worth of beard growing over that angle of a jawline. The humidity forced his hair into loose curls, and large purple swipes of exhaustion cut his cheeks. Unmoved, I glared at him from behind a sea of paintings.

"I know you're upset with me, but I'm *worried* about you," he said. "Look at you. You look like an insane person."

I ignored him. "Does *everybody* have keys to this place?" I snapped. "Give it to me."

He looked alarmed but rolled it off the ring and set it on the hook next to the door. "It's my property, so yes, I have keys, but no, no one else has keys to this studio," he said flatly.

"Max has keys," I said.

"Max is not supposed to have keys," he said, putting his head in one hand and closing his eyes. "That's not good."

"Max knows everything and I'm not even allowed to say Carey's name," I told him, saying what I shouldn't have said, the anger in my voice so sharp that Tyler flinched.

"Max does *not* know everything," he said. "I—look. I am not trying to keep secrets from you. I—we are sorting something out, delicately, and it's not my place to discuss it."

"It is crazy to keep such a wall between me and them. You don't talk about any part of your Pine City life. You have these big 'we' statements and then, like, I don't know, change the subject. And what's worse is you don't *want* me to know."

"What exactly do you want to know?"

"Seriously? Everything. I want you to tell me about yourself."

"Be specific." He was daring me to ask something, but I couldn't tell what it was.

"Okay, for starters, my hand was in Carey's show, and I tell you about it, and I know you were there, I mean—you looked horrified. But most people would be interested that we, *you and I*, shared something like that. And I want to know the hows of it. The whys of it. It's—it's our shared creative life. But you close up like nothing matters between us at all."

"I—I know," he stammered. "I know it. You're right."

"And—then—the other thing—is that she's everywhere here." I waved my fingers in the air. "She's in everything—the artwork, the missing photographs, every part of Max's house. And—she *mattered* to me. Haven't you figured that out? It is so...it is SO lonely to be me. You don't understand. You make this work that...it has a brain. It's experimental. It's ideological. My work, like her work—it only has heart. She was an unsophisticated girl from a bad family and so am I. You will never understand what it means to be a young woman in this business. Or to be—someone who *makes things* all the time and they don't even know why and they can't stop. She did that too. And so, what I am trying to say, is that she is someone that I *need*. I need footsteps, Tyler. I need to know how she did it."

"She didn't." He said this very firmly.

"Oh—her successes don't count, because she killed herself? That's completely unfair. We all die, Tyler. *I want to know how she lived.*"

"I realize that. You've begun to make that very, very clear." He sounded furious.

I didn't care. "But you won't say anything."

"I can't tell you. It's not that I won't. It's that I *can't*. Don't you understand the difference?"

"You're telling me that the allegiance you have with your friends is more important than sharing her with me."

"I wouldn't put it like that."

"But it's like that."

"What do you want from me?" He sounded so pained. "My career—my life—my friends—those things are *mine*. I made them." He pointed at himself. "I won't *give them away* because you don't have any heroes."

"You have been given so much. You had a blue-chip gallery at twenty-four. You've had sixteen years of a career that I'm *thisclose* to never starting. You have friends, property, legacy. You're right: I don't have any of that. I don't have that many friends. I don't have any money. I don't have any family. I don't own anything except these paintings. I *don't* have *anything* at all."

"You have me," he yelled.

"No!" I yelled back. "No. I don't."

It was so sharp that everything deflated immediately. He took a step back.

I did the same, then looked away, at *Temperance*.

It became clear to me, in that exact moment, that she was complete; there was nothing else to do. In the horrible silence between us, I took a breath and motioned to Tyler to help me shift her panels closer to each other, and when they were properly assembled we walked up to the loft to stare down at her.

"Oh my God," he said, and his voice broke a little bit, and he was folding himself around me, pulling me into his body, and then we were kissing, those endless kisses, and I tasted a tear in my mouth.

"How can you be the person that you are?" he asked me. "How do you walk around full of that?"

"I don't know," I said, pushing my face into his shirt, realizing the tear was mine, it had leaked out of me somehow, and then I made myself let go of him, and held open the door to the studio and forced him to walk through it.

"Goodbye, Tyler," I said, shutting the door in his face. I reached for my eyes, expecting to feel another tear, but nothing came out.

Purity
&
Obedience

Chapter Nineteen

Max answered the door with an unlit cigarette in one hand and a glass of wine in the other, mid-laugh. It took less than a second for her smile to fall and her long arms to wrap me in a hug.

"Oh honey," she said. "Come in." She didn't flinch at my baked-in body odor.

"I don't want to go back there," I mumbled, my face pressed into her shoulder.

"That's okay. You don't have to. You can stay here as long as you want." She squeezed me again and led me inside, holding my hand tightly, like a sister would, and for the first time since we were children I was certain that she loved me.

"What do you need?" she asked.

"I don't know . . . a shower, clean clothes. A good night's sleep." I looked down at my feet; they were caked in dirt. My legs were covered in flecks of paint, my shirt was stained with linseed oil, and my hair was held up with an oversize rubber band.

"I can do that," she said, taking me to the second floor and depositing me in the guest room where the bed hung from the ceiling on chains. "There's an attached bath in there. Hop in, and I'll bring you some stuff to try on. Sorry—I'm taller than you." She mumbled to herself, "Whatever, you know that. I'll figure something out." She slipped a hair tie off her wrist and snapped it around mine. "There's a toothbrush under the sink and all that stuff."

"Max?" I asked. "One more thing."

"Anything."

"If Tyler calls, tell him I'm okay, but please don't let him come over. Is that all right?"

"Sure, honey," she said, nodding and closing the door to my room. "Anything you need."

Fleur turned out to be the sweet, familiar-looking blonde who had perched alone on the Goldsworthy wall at the party, the one who waved at me. She sat below me, on one of the sofas, and from my perch on the balcony I could see the small fingers of her manicured hands, the top of her bony skull, the part in her hair, and the collar of her printed dress as she typed away on a gold laptop. In one of Max's old shirts and a rolled-up pair of Charlie's jeans, I walked down the stairs, twisting my hair up as I called out to her.

"Hi," I said, wrapping Max's hair tie around my bun and wiping my hands on my jeans. I held one straight out. "You must be Fleur."

Fleur set the laptop to the side and grinned, then bounded up and shook my hand strongly, with a confident grip.

"Shooting star," she said right away, and I smiled.

"Yes. Hi. Nice to see you," I said.

"I don't think we've ever officially met," she said, head tilting to the side. "But I'm delighted to know you. I hope you'll let me interview you. I'm a big fan. I've seen a lot of your work."

"I'm—thank you. Uh . . . today is not a good day. I'll have some downtime soon," I assured her politely. "In a few weeks."

"Max said you're hanging with us for a while," she said. Max popped out of the kitchen, squeezed me from behind, and placed a wine glass in my hand. I nodded.

"Drink up, honey," Max said, grabbing another bottle and walking toward the glass doors of the garden. "I think we should build a fire."

Twenty minutes later we had a roaring flame going in the fire pit, and the three of us stood around it, watching the orange glow and shifting against the plumes of smoke in a little circular dance.

"Where's Charlie?" I remembered to ask.

"The city," they said in unison. Fleur's face was blank while Max rolled her eyes.

"Whatever," Max said, blowing out a sigh. "He'll be home this weekend. Until then: ladies, ladies, ladies."

"I do have to go back to the studio," I said. "I'm not done."

"Want to talk about it?"

"I mean . . . yes, but no? I don't know. I'm in love with him," I said, telling Max the truth for the first time in years. "I'm in love with him and he's not in love with me. And he is so successful and it's so easy for him. And he doesn't—he doesn't understand what it is for me to be, I don't know, *myself*. He doesn't understand how lonely it is."

I wanted to say, *Carey is between us*. But I didn't.

"I hate men," Fleur said, nodding with understanding. "Like, I really *hate* men." I appreciated her brevity.

"Yes." I laughed. "I hate men too."

"To hating men," Max said, and we raised our glasses.

"What can you tell me about the book?" I asked. "I want to know everything."

"Oh my God, it's sooooo good," Max said.

Fleur smiled bashfully. "Max has a lot to say about a specific time, so it's easy to write," she said. "I'm the coauthor. It's *her* voice. It's her everything."

"But you make my voice sound *not insane*," Max said. "Without you I'm basically some bananas magpie with a pile of photographs and a billion intersecting stories that read like the drunkest cocktail party of all time."

"What's your favorite part so far?" I asked.

"Uh—" They looked at each other in cahoots, with one of those secret friendship faces, and then back at me.

"We can't say yet," Max said excitedly. "But I'm dying for you to read it. DYING."

"What's your second favorite part?"

"It's the part about you, actually," Fleur said. "I realize that's probably terrifying."

"I hadn't realized that I merited inclusion." I was genuinely surprised.

"There is nothing better than that photograph of you," Fleur said. "You're the teenage dreamer. It's a classic American photograph. I think it's the cover."

"But—I mean, Max, you—Max burned it."

"I did," Max assured me, blue eyes wide as teacups, hand pressed to her heart. "I'll never reprint it as a fine art photograph. Never. That's my promise. I won't break it. But the best chapter *is* about you, that photograph, and my friendship with you."

"That's not what I thought you meant."

"We don't *have* to use it, if it bothers you," Max said, her voice now softer than a cat's paw—and twice as quick. "It's the publisher... *they* think that it's the one. I'm open... to anything."

"I mean, what's so bad about having your face on next year's bestselling memoir?" Fleur asked, flattering me now. "You're the Mapplethorpe. It's so honest."

I turned pink and stared into my wine. "What is there to say?"

"It's about what it meant to capture someone's vulnerabilities and profit from them. And what it means, now, to be friends with an actual magician."

I was shocked by that answer.

"Don't act confused," Max said, drinking her wine. "I know who we are to each other. I'm not afraid of it."

"I am," I said, not kidding, and they both laughed.

"Don't be," Fleur said. "It's such an extraordinary book."

"Are you asking?" This ambush was making me nervous.

"*I'm* asking," said Fleur, sitting down next to me, cross-legged, her whole being tuned into mine. Max was suddenly at the fire, moving the logs around, on the other side of the column. "Max loves you. Max wants to protect you. I *like* you, but I *love* this book, and I want to protect it. That picture—it is *everything*."

"That's ridiculous," I said, overwhelmed by frustration. "I'm sorry but—no. I don't want that. I don't."

"I know," said Max, pressing her hands to the ground like she was trying to calm a screaming child. I looked around; nobody was screaming. "I know, and I won't do anything that you're not comfortable with."

"I mean, think about it, right?" Fleur asked.

"No," I said, and it snapped off my tongue so cleanly that we looked over each other's shoulders without speaking for the next thirty seconds, all of us stunned.

Ultimately, Max broke it. "I totally get it. I'm so sorry for asking," she said, pulling one of my curls affectionately. "Let's fucking *get drunk* and forget this whole thing. Fleur, you have to tell her about your apartment. It's crazy. Fleur bought the world's cutest apartment. It's like half skylight. It's so charming."

"It's half skylight because it's seven hundred square feet but yes, thank you, Max, it is charming. I'm fully redoing it except for the skylight. Actually—would you mind looking at photos and tell me what you think? I want to paint every wall gold but Max says it's crazy."

"It's not crazy, it's genius," I said, faking girlish camaraderie while my insides boiled over with hurt. Fleur winked, then scampered inside to get her laptop.

"Isn't she the best?" Max said, watching her go with a dreamy look on her face—one I hadn't seen in years. Max was always at her best when she felt seen. I smiled benevolently at her.

"Yes, Max, she's very lovely," I lied. "It seems like she under-stands you." That one was true.

The rest of the evening passed quickly as we drank wine and went through pictures of Fleur's new apartment until suddenly they were aware of being tipsy, and tired, and they tottered back inside to make tea. Then we were hugging good night, dispersing to our bedrooms, and I was all alone with my wounded heart.

Even Max's patented brand of calculated manipulation wasn't enough to keep Tyler from my thoughts. I thought about him all night. About the shape of his face and the smell of his armpit, and the feeling of him, that destabilizing unfolding that took place whenever we reached for each other. I tried to tell myself that I would never feel those things again, so I might as well get over it tonight. The sooner the better. But then the other half of my brain would wish for him to open the door and tell me that he was sorry. That's the real cruelty of a broken heart. The only person you want to discuss it with is the person who did the breaking.

I ricocheted like that, between regret and desire, for hours and hours. Each time I began to fall asleep, I would think something—a want of him or the burn of rejection—and jolt awake again. It felt like waking up in the bathtub at the exact moment the water has entered your mouth: It's not clear which way is up. In that state I relived every single one of our conversations, seeing them from a new perspective—the one where I was a dumb girl from a small town, buzzing around his chest because he was the center of the universe and I was a fly. All us flies look the same.

"I'm a saint, bleeding from my eyes," I remembered telling him, something I meant at the time even though I made it sound like a joke. Now I hated it. "My skin gets so thin you could break it with a fingernail." Absurd. I wished that I could take it all back and do none of it over again. This time I would not reach for him in his studio. I would not look him in the eyes. I would not let myself want.

It is so awful to want. I have let myself want so few things, because—the tension of it—I can barely stand it. I let myself want my paintings, when I am making them, and then I force myself to push them away, and that's—I can barely handle that.

If God is real, then *Don't Let Yourself Want* should be the first commandment. Don't let yourself want anything. Be happy with the life you've got. It's all she's going to give you.

Purity—and then *Obedience*—and then frames—and then crates. The closer I got to the end, the more work seemed to appear. As the paintings cured, I would build their frames: custom semi-opaque fiberglass encasements, rather like giant cellphone cases, ones that I liked to ring in bands of brightly colored, rubberized silicone because I preferred the texture of how rubber sits against a wall over the hard gnash of almost any other material.

I couldn't move any of the paintings myself. The panels, yes—they were only 100 to 150 pounds each—but the whole assembly weighed somewhere between 600 and 700 pounds. Because of their heft, I would need to build a lightweight dummy painting, carve a foam inverse of the frame shape that I wanted, and create a mold from that. Then I'd need to cast seven frames, or more likely eight since I always managed to break one. (This is why you have assistants.) Each of these actions—building the dummy, carving the foam, creating the mold, casting one frame—would take a day or longer. I'd need to rent a hydraulic lift to fit them onto their corresponding paintings. Then—I'd have to build their crates for shipping.

That work, the work I needed to do once I was done painting, should have taken all summer. The realization of this hit me the moment that I woke up at Max's house—and then I was filled with the desire to lie in bed all day. I didn't want to go to work. I wanted to do anything but work. *But I can't*, I reminded myself. *I need to finish, as soon as possible, or there will be no more money to send my mother, no more money for shelter, or food, or for more paintings. It's not negotiable. There's no time to take off—no boss to call—nobody to cover my shift.* I told myself that this was the last time they would be mine. As I held the knob of the door in my hand, I heard Carey's words echoing inside my head: *The work comes first. Always.*

I drove the long way back to the studio, clockwise, so that I didn't pass the entrance to Pine City, and then I worked. I was now an entire week behind schedule.

But when I saw my paintings—those long, winking stripes of color, innocent and helpless—I was their mother again and nobody else mattered. They needed me. I had so much work to do, and so little time to do it in.

I spent the day with *Purity*, using a V-shaped tool to carve a little series of trenches. Then I took a propane torch and fired a smelting bucket full of tiny lead ingots until it turned red. When the molten metal splashed down—first, burning the paint, then that black-silver pewter color pouring down the trenches in mercurial runnels—it was so delicious that I nearly touched it.

It would have cleaved the skin right from my fingers.

At sunset, I sat on the rickety dock and watched the sun go down over the far side of the black lake. Tyler would be doing the same, somewhere around the bend, with his real friends.

The ones he would do absolutely anything for.

In those moments, so close to the end, I wanted to quit. Perhaps I could have.

Back at Max's, there was a note on the kitchen counter. *At opening tonite in Hudson!! If you want to come it's the Bright Gallery 7–9 and the dinner after is at Wazo. If not back later xmax*

I had the house all to myself for the third time.

That profanely beautiful house.

I wonder if it happened like it did because of Max's house. In some ways, all I ever wanted was to know what the rules were. I wanted to be like Max, who could look at her mother and grandmother to learn how to be beautiful and poised and decorative in a way that gave her hard economic security. I wanted to be like Charlie, who could look at every man who had ever lived to learn how to be the man who got to decide which women were the most important.

Even though I knew there were no rules to this life, I wanted to know what they were. I wanted there to be someone like me who could tell me that yes, work was hard and sometimes your heart gets broken, and here is how you finish something. I wanted to know what the signpost was between *keep going* and *give up*. I needed to know the difference between *move on* and *drop out*.

I went straight to the library.

Chapter Twenty

A pit formed in the bottom of my stomach as I examined its coffee-stained first page. The handwriting was ragged, but it was unmistakably Carey's.

DROP OUT PIECE:

I WILL REMOVE MYSELF FORCIBLY FROM THE WORLD IN AN INTENTIONALLY POSTHUMOUS WORK. I WILL FILL A PAIR OF LARGE RAIN BOOTS WITH QUICK-DRY CEMENT (VOLUME OVER MY FEET IS 1.6 GALLONS PER FOOT, AP-PROXIMATELY 30 POUNDS PER FOOT) AND WALK INTO THE LAKE. *DROP OUT* WILL BE FILMED FROM TWO ANGLES. THE FOOTAGE SHOULD BE EDITED INTO A CONTINUOUS, LIN-EAR NARRATIVE AND DISPLAYED AS A FILM. IT MUST NOT BE REFERRED TO AS A SUICIDE: RATHER, IT IS MY FINAL WORK. I AM OF SOUND MIND. I KNOW THIS LIFE IS OVER. I CHOOSE TO DOCUMENT THE END.

The rest of the notebook was empty, but this single page, covered in fingerprints, had clearly been read over and over and over. I stared at it, reading the words, amazed by what I saw, sick to my stomach at first but then angry that it had been a secret for so long, that it had never been validated, or framed, or hung on a wall, or even talked about, because I felt, suddenly, and so strongly, that it deserved to be. If Bas Jan Ader could sail into the Atlantic on a one-way trip and call it a romantic artwork; if Hannah Wilke could photograph her own fatal disease; if Lee Lozano could call quitting itself a performance piece; then Carey Logan deserved to have these explicit final words made public.

Regardless of medium, I believe absolutely that any work of art *needs to make you feel something*. It needs to draw you in, to create and manage desires that you weren't aware of. It needs to kick you in the stomach like a donkey. We look at death all the time—films and paintings and Christ—obituaries and biographies—memorials and televised funerals of celebrities. How many dramatizations of that last breath have I seen? Hundreds. Thousands? We desire representations of death, but we do not televise murders, or footage of school shootings, or the bodies falling from the towers. We do not want to look at *actual* death. It is sacred. But what is the difference? What is the difference when we are being explicitly asked to observe?

What kind of museum would buy it? What kind of collector? Who would show it? Who would buy tickets? Carey always made me feel that I was skirting the fault lines of what I was supposed to want to look at, and this was the pinnacle: I'd never seen anything like it. It was terrifying and sad—and it was a conscious, rational choice, written out the same way as all her other artworks, methodical and planned, a decision.

That's what struck me the hardest: how deliberate it was.

I wondered if the film truly existed. It didn't have to, not necessarily. She could have written this page and never filmed a thing.
But either way, Carey did not get what she wanted, because everyone referred to her death in the same exact way: as the suicide of a
woman suffering from a long-term mental illness.

I read it again. *It will be filmed from two angles.* Two reels and a
notebook; this was almost certainly the work that Eliot&Sprain was
suing Pine City over. Oh—holy cow—this was it. To be certain,
I grabbed the other two notebooks that I could not identify. They
both contained many pages of notes. I was surprised to find that
they were both written in the same color ink, whereas the sculpture ones were written in such a patchwork of color, but I reasoned
that she did a lot less moving around on these—there was probably
a single pen that never got lost, as opposed to studio work, where
you're always getting dirty and losing things.

LOVE THAT MIRACLE turned out to be a tribute to Carolee
Schneemann's *Interior Scroll*, the piece where Schneemann pulled a
poem from her vagina and read it in front of an audience. *OTHER
PEOPLE'S RULES* used a quote attributed to Lee Lozano's
notebooks—"artist, critic and dealer friends, I can still smell on
your breath those other people's rules you swallowed so long
ago"—to justify its performance of smelling people's breath from
across a table. The notebook was filled with descriptions of the
breaths. According to the date, it was her last performance. It made
me feel something. It wasn't quite as . . . expected . . . as the others.
Weird, in a good way. It seemed like she was starting to get somewhere.

I pulled down the white binder of her clippings and paged
through it, looking at the dozens of reviews Eliot&Sprain had collected on her behalf over the years, until I got to her obituary. A
sentence toward the end caught my attention:

**"Carey became incredibly depressed following the
unnecessarily cruel reviews for** *Other People's*

Rules," Mr. Eliot told The Times this week, referring to a performance series in April of this year where she smelled the breaths of strangers. "She retreated entirely into her own world."

I remembered the nasty review I'd seen on the back of the crossword, my first morning here, how it admonished her for her confidence. "She is certainly no longer the daring youngster who asked us to look unflinchingly upon the bodies of murdered women; instead she asks us to regard her privilege," it said.

It was cruel, I thought, agreeing with Charlie. *DROP OUT* was her response: a fresh request for us to look unflinchingly upon the body of a dead woman.

♣ ♣ ♣ ♣ ♣

Tyler found her body. If there was a film, he would have found it too, so if the film existed, then Pine City had it, and they—or perhaps Tyler alone—were holding it hostage against Carey's explicit wishes.

There were a million reasons not to give the film to Charlie. My first thought was that it was likely grotesque and difficult to watch. My second thought was that if Charlie was right about the potential value of the work, then once it hit the marketplace, Pine City could very well find themselves in a position to do nothing but discuss, support, disseminate, and manage the work of Carey Logan for years. They could be completely eclipsed by her—spend the rest of their lives living in her shadow, even more than they already did. Everyone would be curious. Everyone would want to know the truth. Everyone would be like me, scratching at their private lives, demanding to know their thoughts and feelings.

Like me and—like Max. I thought of her secret smile the night before and the books in her office. *Of course—the research was for her*

book. Nothing was off-limits. Not to Max—even when she had absolutely no right at all.

Telling this story would make her more than a lifestyle photographer from a rich family; more than a rich man's daughter;
more than a rich man's wife. She didn't even need the film. All she
needed was a picture of the first and only page in the *DROP OUT*
notebook, and if she couldn't get permission, she could simply de-
scribe what she'd read. Maybe it was gimmicky—but *nothing* is a
gimmick when the artist is already famous. And especially when
the artist is already dead.

Then—it's history.

Max was right. I was dying to read it. Without hesitating, I
left the library, ran to her office, and wrenched open her computer.

Max foldered by project name, not year. I clicked through
them impatiently. There was the project where she circled global
industrial sites in a helicopter and blew up the photographs to
billboards all around Los Angeles, titled *There Is So Much Money
in the World and None of It Is Yours.* There was *I'm So Authentic*, the project where she'd tried on other people's clothes, how
the photos all looked awkward, like she was wearing someone
else's skin. There was *Connect-I-Cut-Myself*, where she took photographs of street corners in her hometown. *First Kiss*, one of
them was called; *First Time Someone Called Me a Whore*. In the
photos, the houses were tidy, the skies blue, the whole thing ro-
botically sinister. I'd forgotten about that. I'd forgotten that she
was a good photographer.

But I couldn't find a folder with *The Art of Losing* written on it,
or one called TAOL, or Book, or Memoir, or anything that looked
like it. I tried opening Word and recalling recent documents, but
they were about shows—edits on press releases for her gallery and
drafts of emails and random notes—not book files.

One email, sent this morning, appeared when I searched *TAOL*.

To: Anneke Bice
Cc: Fleur Madrigal

Hi Anneke! We talked to the subject and she's still hesitant, but ofc I have the original release so we're clear to do what we want. Still, I would LOVE her support on this, so I'll keep working on her and we'll get there by pub day! Fleur is right—it's still one of my best pictures. Talk soon—xmax

There was an attachment. I clicked it open: It was a full PDF of the mocked-up cover. On the front, Carey Logan stood on the shores of the black lake, wearing the cartoon-dipped white dress she'd worn in the "Perpetual Persephone" photo shoot. THE ART OF LOSING, it said, in beautiful gold letters below her feet. On the back cover, another photograph took up all the space—of me, standing in front of a basketball hoop, gazing into the camera with desperation in my eyes.

The back cover. Not even—like Fleur had implied—the front.

There, in the luxurious reliquary of Max's office, sitting at her beautiful desk, smudging the keyboard of her golden computer with my oily fingers, in my shabby clothes and tangled hair, a dirty little ball of rage penned inside this concrete kennel—I figured it out.

Max didn't love me like a sister.

She loved me like a pet.

Max didn't have the manuscript, I realized. Fleur would probably have it. She was the writer.

I was asleep by the time Max and Fleur came home, or at least I was pretending to be, door shut, my lights out. They giggled and talked a hair too loudly and smoked a cigarette somewhere—I smelled the edges of the smoke curling under the door—and then they were calling good-nights to each other, and bathrooms and bedrooms were slamming shut, and Eliot House was quiet again.

Everything was back in its place, I was certain. Still: I lay there for another hour, waiting for either woman to burst out of her room and march over to mine and demand to know what I'd been doing in her underwear drawer.

Yes. Underwear drawers, bedside tables, mattresses, closet shelves, under sofas. For three manic hours, I pried and peeked and snooped and climbed on chairs, in every room except Charlie's office, which was locked up tight.

In Fleur's room there was an empty suitcase under the bed and an assortment of minimalist silk clothing draped from the hangers. Her underwear was folded neatly and she only had two pairs of shoes. There was a phone charger, but no phone, and no gold computer; those were almost certainly in her handbag.

The other guest rooms turned up nothing. Max and Charlie's bedroom revealed a lot of expensive clothes and accessories, which I was tempted to take, or destroy, like a bad dog, but didn't. When I typed 1839 into the keypad on Max's darkroom, the door sprang open.

The room was exactly as I'd last seen it. Red lights glowed in the ceiling and hundreds of negatives hung from clips around the room. The little pile of scorched ash from where she'd burned my portrait was still on the floor; it had been scattered, stepped on, maybe, but not cleaned up.

I pulled open Max's flat files, went through all four of the huge storage units, and found nothing. I peered under tables, sweeping my hand across their undersides, and even looked in the trash, underneath the plastic bag, before I remembered about the box she'd kept my Randolph pictures in: MOST UNIQUE.

I ran to the back, opening the box to find the puffy photo album—and a huge ring of keys on a silver leather fob.

The keys were in my hand when I heard the garage door opening. It was too late to leave. I fled to the guest bedroom, locked the door, and turned out the lights as they came chattering inside.

🌲 🌲 🌲 🌲 🌲

I spent the entire night fighting with myself in a hallucinatory half sleep. I stared at the ceiling and wondered what would happen to me when I died. Would someone put my notebooks on display? If I managed the career that I wanted, then yes, almost certainly. Would I want them to put my unfinished paintings on display? Would I want to be contextualized by the Maxes, the Fleurs, the Charlies, people who could not ever begin to understand me? Would I want my life to be summarized and commodified—every detail of it interpreted without me?

No—especially when it came to Max—but I would want the chosen work, anything I'd put in a show, to *be* shown. I would want all of *Ohne Titel* reunited, all of *Accounting for Taste*, all of *The Distance Between Our Moral Imaginations*, all of my *Rich Ugly Old Maids* and whatever else was to come, to be together again. I loved them. I wanted them to survive. I wanted someone, someday, to see the passage of my life as it had truly been.

To see what my hands had done every good day of my life.

Chapter Twenty-One

I left Eliot House well before dawn, stripping the bed and leaving a note on top of the bare mattress. *So much to do. Thank you for the hospitality. I'll be in touch when I'm free.*

The woods were quiet as I drove, for them, anyway; the breezes still ruffled the trees but this time it felt like they wanted me to be there. Climbing out of the truck, I felt the dirt and the roots gathering around me in a swirling carpet. As though I were the only person the earth loved that night and she was folding me into her path, her trees watching me go, her lake doing the same.

I walked to the edge of the water, letting my feet absorb the cold, touch the sand, touch the algae. It furred between my toes. I reached down and pulled it up, and it stretched, long and wet, its caterpillar magic evaporated by the air. When it went back into the water it was itself again.

Some things are like that—themselves only in one single context.

The studio was dark, save for the moonlight reflecting off the white-tinted panels of *Purity*. The black rectangles of *Obedience* seemed to suck all the light out of the world, and as my vision adjusted to the gloom, a crack sounded, loud and terribly close.

At first, I held still in the darkness, watching the moon inch across the sky through the ribbing of the plastic-paneled skylights, waiting for something, anything to happen—but nothing happened at all. There were no more noises from anywhere, except for the rhythmic rise and fall of my own lungs. I switched on the lights and told myself sternly to be brave. The fluorescent bars above revealed that the only things in the studio were me and my paintings. All twenty-eight panels of my seven enormous *Rich Ugly Old Maids*—my precious, impossible livelihood—took up nearly every square foot of space.

At last, I went hard on *Obedience*.

The only taste in my mouth was blackness and murk, colors that bruised every part of Tyler's house. Lake stones and pieces of the crumbling dock outside Carey's studio rolled across my tongue; chewed-up pieces of the neon-green lichen that grew on the end of the Eliot House dock across the water stuck to my lips. I coughed out the air of their house, tasting the cement walls, so hard they made your teeth hurt just looking at them, the vines they let run wild through it, the dirt they slept in every night like a tomb. I pulled handfuls of the beautiful Dutch-style peonies painted on the black walls of Max's office from my throat and tried to choke back the lush, strawberry velvet of her chaise. My teeth and jawbones became the red enamel of Charlie's stools and the matte-black tailpipe of his Ducati motorcycle, all these consummately designed objects intersecting with nature, in a futuristic, self-sufficient house that would one day sink beneath vegetation, for not even concrete and rebar can withstand the power of roots and earthquakes. I felt Carey Logan walk into the lake in her cement-filled boots, I drank the fear in her skin, and, so possessed, I worked in a trance until the sun sank again.

By two in the morning, I felt it—it was time to stop. The ocean of oily slabs gleamed, each one a tiny universe unto itself, and it became obvious to me that they were done, each of them complete, not a one in need of a single drop of anything.

They weren't yet dry, but they were, at long last, complete. They had to be.

I was out of time.

I returned to my bungalow along the weed-choked path that Tyler first guided me down, flashlight in hand, trying to be as liminal as I had once felt. I wondered what Tyler had told the others about my sudden absence. That I was crazy, probably, that I was temperamental, that I could not control myself. Or perhaps nothing at all. Perhaps no one had anything to say about a woman they barely knew.

But they were gone. The houses were empty, the studios were locked up tight, except for Tyler's. His station wagon was still parked in his carport.

As I crept into my bungalow, Tyler's lights turned on. I saw him through the window, stretching, making coffee. I wanted to reach for him—and then I was washed over in heartbreak. *He doesn't love me, and he never will*, I thought, suddenly, knowing that it was true, and with that one thought, the hurt turned to rot and worked its way into my muscles and tendons. *He doesn't love me, and he never will. Nobody does.* A rancid fungus blossomed over the ventricles of my heart. *He doesn't love me, and he never will. Nobody does.* Each repetition washed the thought into a fresh cell of my being, the thought souring one capillary at a time, until they were all ruined.

When Tyler left later that morning, there was no note tacked to my door, or "my" chair on the deck of the Mission. As I walked to his house, I reminded myself that he could very well come right back; he could be at the hardware store, or the grocery store, or at a friend's house, but when I opened his door with one of Max's forty keys, the trash under the sink was empty. The bed was made; the dishes washed.

He wouldn't be back for days.

My plan was to snoop with a kind of reckless joy—toss the place—but I didn't need to open a single drawer. Certified mail addressed to Pine City, LLC, from Cartwright, Benson and Pendergast, LLC, lay open on the counter.

Dear Messrs. Savage, Winsome, Wells and Mayfield,

In the class-action civil lawsuit of Eliot&Sprain, LLC, Eliot, Sprain, Bricklings-Young, et al., vs. Pine City, LLC, *the court requested on Friday, July 22, to examine the artwork in question. Judge Elaine Rafferty has issued a subpoena for the "DROP OUT" artwork. She requests that it be delivered to her chambers by Thursday, July 28. All parties are to bring any associated material, including but not limited to notebooks, film negatives, film reels, reproductions of film negatives or reels, writings, letters, images, digital or electronic files or any manner of documentation that may be pursuant to the decision at hand. All documentation is to be submitted to the court in perpetuity, and as such must be made accessible to the court. The court has requested prompt compliance and Judge Rafferty has made strong assurances that a lack of compliance will result in search of the Pine City property, immediate charges of contempt of court and possible jail time.*

Please advise us of your decision. Copies of this letter have been sent to all voting partners of Pine City, LLC.

Sincerely,
Jeffrey Cartwright, Esq.
Cartwright, Benson and Pendergast, LLC

I looked at the calendar on his wall. Today was Monday, July 25. Everything was in motion.

♠ ♠ ♠ ♠ ♠

The row of metal lockers, padlocked one after another, were easy
enough to open, steel doors clanging as I flipped their latches.

Mostly they contained the paperwork of his own practice. He
documented the acquisition of every organ in those same black
Academy notebooks, his handwriting always tidy, if small and a bit
hard to read. Everything was anonymous. Names were truncated to
initials; meeting places were coded; hospitals were all simply called
"hospital."

Many of the organs seemed to come from donors who had been
in accidents, people whose organs were pulled but not used for one
medical reason or another. Tyler managed to inject himself along
the black-market chain to intercept these lesser, second-rate body
parts as they moved from unscrupulous hospital orderly to foam
cooler to someone's car trunk to hopeful line-cutter.

Met Orderly K at a Sunoco for a cup of coffee, he wrote. *He makes
8/hour and doesn't have healthcare. He's been at the hospital for two
years. F told him about outside opportunities. He wants in. I have to
think about it. He seems desperate. Too—too interested.*

I read through a handful, then kept looking.

Box, after box, after box. I rifled through them carefully but
found nothing that belonged to Carey. One plastic container was
filled with hard drives, and I set it by the door so that when I found
a computer, I could connect them.

When I was done I set a piece of masking tape on the locker that
the hard drives had come from, and carefully locked the rest, wiping my fingerprints away from the steel with a rag. Then I turned
to the chest freezer.

As I expected, it contained body parts, lots of them, shrink-
wrapped in plastic inside little aquariums of preservative chemicals.
I was nervous to touch them, but they had been placed carefully
in clean metal trays that stacked neatly together. The freezer was
spotless—no buildup of freezer burn anywhere. All of the packages

were labeled by hospital staff, all of them downgraded for one reason or another: too much fatty tissue; not oxygenated enough; a
lesion; a growth of unidentified cells. The date of retrieval was on
each, some as old as five years, all of them marked with the cause
of death.

In the first few layers, there were two blood-colored kidneys,
three purple-brown livers, and one bubblegum-pink stomach.
There was a creamy pair of lungs; there was a severed foot; there
was the brain. I moved them quickly, worried that they would lose
temperature, though I wasn't sure if it mattered since they wouldn't
be going in another body.

On the lowest level, all on its own, was a human heart.

Cause of death: asphyxiation, the label said. NOT VIABLE was
stamped in red. The date of retrieval was the day that Carey Logan
died.

🌲 🌲 🌲 🌲 🌲

I felt the meat of it—that hardest, firmest, always laboring
muscle—pushing against the flat of my palm. I pressed it with the
tips of my fingers, watching the chemicals around it squish up and
around like any grocery store package of meat, and was surprised
at how dense it still felt, after three years—how resistant.

White fat ringed the ventricles and lined the seams of muscle
in lacy little squiggles. The exterior of the heart was mostly a
dark purple-red-blue—the inside of the thickest rare steak you've
ever eaten—that faded to a brownish peach as it approached the
fat. The ventricles themselves, thick, chewy tubes, were a true
pink.

It weighed less than a pound, but more than I expected it to.

Drops of condensation began to form on the lid of the freezer.
When one of them fell, splashing against the clean bottom of it, I
panicked. I wiped out the freezer and set the heart back in its place,
then stacked the metal shelves atop each other again and loaded the

organs back in, wiping each one clean, hoping that I had not damaged them.

I locked the freezer and stared at it for a long time. It had a puck-
ered white surface, a kind of textured ripple, an aluminum band
around the top, and it was where Tyler kept Carey's heart.

I heard his voice, asking if I was a fan. The guilt that spilled out
of his eyes whenever her name came up. I saw the look on his face
when I asked about Carey directly, all that misery, and it shook
me right down the spine, the vertebrae clicking like ice cubes, like
Carey's frozen heart.

That's when I noticed the coolers: brand-new, vacuum-sealed,
five of them, piled up next to the freezer. It didn't matter, for Tyler,
if there were police on the property. He was planning to move
everything.

♠ ♠ ♠ ♠ ♠

I let myself into Marlin's studio. She was in progress on
something—another series of bodies. The lines were unruly,
printed over and over, the registration deliberately off. She didn't
have any locked doors or locked freezers or anything. There were
banker's boxes filled with paperwork, but it was all hers. No film.

Jack's studio was nearly completely overtaken by his net—it had
almost doubled in size in the past two weeks. There was so much
stuff everywhere, detritus, and I couldn't imagine rooting through
it or that he would be the one to keep such a thing. Simply looking
at the room made me feel overwhelmed. I told myself that I would
come back only if there was nothing anywhere else.

I locked the door and walked the path to the Theatre, Jes's studio. My stomach clenched tighter with each step. After trying six
different keys I landed on the correct one.

The double doors opened into the musty foyer with the ticket
counter and the *Persona* poster. The heavy wooden doors on either
side were no longer propped open, but they weren't locked.

I followed the beam of my flashlight down the aisle, toward the stage, to where the orange extension cords stretched away and to the left. They snaked through the side curtains of the wings, the flashlight illuminating the dirty wooden floors beneath, until plugging into a wall. Next to the outlet, a small spiral staircase led to the upper level.

Up here a small walkway, the brass railings smooth and shiny from decades of touch, led to a closed door, where I fumbled again with the keys, nearly dropping them, the hard plastic of the flashlight between my teeth, until I found the right one.

A library waited for me on the other side: racks of plastic film reels in different widths, a dozen different kinds of cameras, rolls and rolls of vintage film stock, and reels labeled with marker and masking tape along the seams.

The next room was the projectionist's suite. Two manual projectors were pushed to the side and a digital projector was wired to the aperture, facing the stage, with a metal folding chair placed behind it.

The third room had a light switch outside the door. I flicked it, and after fumbling for another key, cracked it open. The unmistakable sour chemical smell of fix and developer hit my nostrils. It was a darkroom, recently used, though the plastic basins were empty and the dry lines were clean, their clothespins vacant.

Two metal canisters sat next to the enlarger, their blank, unlabeled tape cut right down the middle. They were empty.

I returned to the racks in the library, searching through the canisters until I found the reel labeled WILD HEART(S). I wound it onto the 35mm projector, inserting the end into a slot and carefully winding the center of the reels like a cassette. The celluloid, silky between hard bites of clear plastic tape, loaded easily, and the image appeared, out of focus, on the wall. I followed the reel from splice to splice, stopping with every mark. Carey as Stevie, Little Carey, over and over. Miss America, Little Carey, Carey, Carey, Carey.

And then I found it. A single set of frames, only six, no—seven. I cranked the reel by hand, and as I adjusted the lens, I knew—I knew what I would see.

They were murky stills of a woman in a plain white dress, standing at the bottom of a lake, head tilted in a way that suggested she was unconscious. Her arms waved in motion with the current. Her rubber boots were perfectly still. And she was Carey Logan.

I ripped through Jes's library, opening canister after canister, holding them up to the light at every splice, but it was no use. I couldn't find another frame anywhere, not after twenty-five canisters. As I sat on the ground, winding up the reels and replacing them on the shelves, I realized that the film could be hidden anywhere; it could be taped behind a rafter in any of the buildings, it could be set beneath floorboards, it could be buried in the ground. It would be impossible to find the rest of the film without knowing its location.

I cut the seven frames from *Wild Heart(s)*, folded a piece of scrap paper, taped them inside, and slipped them in my back pocket. I returned to Marlin's studio and looked again at her anatomical prints, this time holding the frames to my eye, and what I saw was that the arms were Carey's arms; the legs were Carey's legs. In Jack's studio I saw that his net, woven in mostly white silk, had a yellow beam down the center that mimicked the light streaming through the water above Carey's head.

And in Tyler's studio lay Carey's heart, waiting to be bronzed.

Pine City were all making work about her death. They could not help themselves. And yet they refused to give up the film—a refusal that could result, in a few short days, in a search of the studio where my paintings lay.

I saw the policemen swarming the studio, touching my paintings, photographing them, making a list, sending it to Charles

Eliot's attorney. I knew exactly what Charles would want in exchange. If he didn't get it—he would call Jacqueline, she'd feign surprise, Susan Bricklings-Young would confirm that the police photo of *Obedience* was not the same as the one she had committed to buy—and so would all of Jacqueline's other buyers. The show would be canceled, my name destroyed, the only one I'd ever had. I wouldn't be a painter anymore. I'd be the warning sign: the girl from Florida who conned the blue-chip gallery.

I'd be homeless. I'd be $39,000 in debt. I'd have thirty-five hundred pounds of paintings that nobody wanted except me.

Someone will film Carey's story. At the end they will put the actress in a waifish white dress, which will pool and billow in highest contrast to the muddy red water of the black lake. The actress's eyes will be purple and the teeth in her mouth will be so white and big. The texture of her skin will be velvety and the line of her breasts will be pert. Her muscles will be taut from Pilates, but the implication of the camera will be that stress and suicidal thoughts and the artistic temperament have made her so enchantingly thin. She will be Ophelia, clothes spread wide, floating in the brook atop garlands of sweet flowers, and she will look absolutely nothing like Carey Logan.

The camera will hold steady. Ankles taped with bubble wrap, she plunges her toes into the wet cement pools of her rubber boots. A single air pocket might release under the pressure and belch against her calf. She will stand there for five minutes, maybe ten, in the water, and wait for them to dry. Then she will start walking.

Maybe they'll cut to Tyler in his studio: a razor blade pressing down as a glass slide catches a very neat, carpaccio slice of brain. Maybe they'll show Jack playing with his kids. Maybe they'll show Jes playing cello and Marlin pulling a print. Maybe they'll go back to that night on Grand Street and show the five of them sharing a cigarette and laughing, or some other scene, one I haven't witnessed, the first time they all met. Or maybe they won't do any of that and it'll be a long shot: She walks, she shudders at the cold, she hesitates, she walks again. Cut to underwater: flailing and eventual stillness. Above again: water slapping against the beach like nothing was ever there to disturb it.

It will be a documentary or a Lifetime movie or a multipart series on HBO. It doesn't matter what they do or how they would do it or who the "they" in question would be; whatever they do would make her body into their commodity, like Tyler was going to do with her heart, and Carey didn't want that. She wanted to own that commodity on her own terms.

And she had labored for so long.

She deserved to have what she wanted.

So did I.

Chapter Twenty-Two

The next morning, it was very easy to strip the pink from my hair—six or seven washes with baby shampoo took it right out—and the Sally Beauty in the strip mall had everything else. A Savers down the block was an easy place to find a little turban-like hat, a pair of black heels, and cat's-eye sunglasses, and after a stop at Home Depot, I was done. My hair took the toner right away—and then I was an ashy-gray dirty blonde, just like her.

She had freckles. They were very easy to replicate with a little brown pencil.

After an hour in the bathroom with the shower on hot, the white dress and leopard coat from her studio steamed out very nicely. I painted my fingernails bright red—lips too—and zipped up the cream-colored sheath. I slid my arms into the silk lining of the leopard-print coat, set the sunglasses on my nose, pinned the little turban firmly to my hair, slid my feet into the heels, and it was—it was eerie.

Setting up the cameras took a lot longer. I had no clue what I was doing, and was exhausted from the sleepless night spent at Jes's computer, hardwired to the internet, googling *how to load a 35mm camera* and *how to connect reels* and *how to tell one vintage film stock from another.*

Fake concrete was impossible, so I filled a quick-dry concrete bag with silver grout. It wouldn't harden but would still look realistic going in the boot.

I wrestled with the tripods in the water but they refused to be stable, so I set them up on the grass, one angled in each direction so that there would be a very wide shot.

It was ninety-eight degrees that afternoon with 90 percent humidity.

First I had to bring the manual shutters to where the boots and cement bag were, exactly between the sight lines of the two cameras and right at the edge of the water, and then I had to stand still and hit one with each hand. I moved very stiffly—what I hoped was deliberately—trying not to betray anything so that I didn't betray the wrong thing.

I was already sweating when I dumped the grout into the rubber boots, carefully mixing in lake water that I scooped up with a green glass jar from Carey's studio kitchen. The sunglasses dared to fall down my nose, but I pushed them back up, over and over, with a single finger. Once the grout was the right consistency—I used a wooden paint stirrer—I carefully put one foot, ankles taped with bubble wrap, into one boot, and then the other, the grout sucking between my toes. The volume rose up inches below the tops of the boots, but the cameras couldn't see how it dried. They were too far away.

Ten minutes is a long time to stand still and look at a lake. I cycled through a lot of feelings—fear and trepidation, but mostly regret—and wondered how on earth Carey managed to maintain her composure. After three minutes, it was so hot that I slid the leopard coat from my shoulders and let it crumple to the wet sand. My dress was eclipsed by moons of sweat: a sweet crescent on my low back, wide ellipses beneath my arms, dripping down my thighs and into the boots.

By the time I walked into the water, I was burning up, ready for the cold, and it took a great deal of self-control not to dive—

to walk forward, ramrod-straight—until I disappeared under the surface.

♠ ♠ ♠ ♠ ♠

I'm still not a strong swimmer. I had to move quite far underwater to get out of the shot, and I had to do it in a dress and rubber boots without disturbing the surface. Every step was fraught with a biological urge to swim to save myself. The grout in the boots weighed me down, but I could have kicked out of it if I wanted to. I kept telling myself that it was a game, over and over, hoping that I could convince myself. My arms trembled, preparing themselves to move, to pump up and down involuntarily, like they'd done on that first day I floated drunk on the lake. Sooner or later, my body was going to take over.

Had I calculated correctly?

The sky above me became only a faint pink light. Water crept into my nose, through my sinuses, dripped down the back of my throat, and I began to panic—but then I pushed forward, staying on the bottom of the lake for ten more feet, until I reached the bicycle tube weighted on a neon yellow rope to a seventy-nine-cent brick. The check valve barely opened in my shaking grip; I had to bite my hand to hold it down, but when it opened—when it did, I could breathe. As I sucked in, greedily, the sunglasses tipped off my nose and sank to the bottom.

I pulled myself along the neon rope, making it to the next bicycle tube, and afterward, finally, to the far side of the water, the end of the neon line, and the anchored silver canoe. Somewhere along the way, the boots kicked off and they receded into the red-black water, the weight of the grout pulling them down.

When my hands found the boat, I was dying for air, lungs near to exploding.

My nails clawed at the gunnels, black-red water streamed out of my lipsticked mouth, and I gasped once—and then quietly, little

choking ones, like when you are crying but trying to hide it.
Though they were fifty feet away, at least, there were still small mi-
crophones on the cameras—nothing much—and they would run
to the end of the reels, only a few more minutes. Enough time for
a person to drown.

Once the reels ran out, I moved. It took a great deal of negotiating
to get my body into the boat itself without capsizing it, as the narrow cut of the dress held me back. But once I hiked the skirt up
and over my waist, I managed to get atop the stern, arms out flat,
my weight almost even.

I lay in the bottom of the boat for some time, breathing evenly,
trying to calm down as the sun descended over the horizon. I took
the pins from the turban and dropped them over the side, hearing
them disappear into the water with a sound so tiny, such a fragile,
narrow plop, that I wanted to record it all on its own.

When the moon rose in the sky against the coming night—I was
ready to move again.

The canoe shook as I hauled in the neon line and its three bricks.
Covered in threads of silt and drowned algae, they coiled in a pile on
the bottom of the boat, like the catch of the day. I paddled carefully,
unsure of myself, changing sides over and over to guide the boat to
where it was supposed to go. At the beach beneath the deck of the
Mission, I climbed out, stubbing my toe on a brick as I stepped,
then grabbed it by the nose and yanked it up the sand as far as it
could go, beaching it. I hurled a sandy, silty armful of bricks and
rope around the nearest support pole of the deck, and then, sand between my toes, walked down the beach to unpack the cameras.

That part was harder. I'm not a filmmaker, and so I was shaking
and nervous as I unscrewed them from the tripods and carried
them back—over my head and away from the soaking, muddied
damp of my dress—to Jes's studio.

I closed the darkroom door and turned on the red light like we had done in class. Repeated to myself, over and over, the instructions from her computer. Lift the lever. Wind the reel. Wait for the click or feel the tension. Then—pop it out.

The reels were sealed, as they'd been before they went in the camera, and in theory, whatever I'd done wrong would have likely already ruined them, but I wrapped them with another strap of light-tight tape anyway, and placed Jes's cameras back carefully on her shelf. I collapsed the skeletons of her tripods back into their rolls of carbon fiber and wound the power cords from my fingers to my elbows, closing them with tabs of blue tape. I hung the manual shutters back in their place on her pegboard, and then I realized— it was time for dinner.

First I selected a record—*Roy Orbison's Greatest Hits*—and threw a Mission apron on over my dress. It was old white cotton, the kind that has been washed a million times, that you see among your grandmother's dish towels, and the mud from the lake soaked right through it. I pressed my hands to the top, where my bra was, and the last rivulets of red water ran down my legs and formed a puddle on the linoleum floor.

I stepped over it with satisfaction, then put the biggest pot I could find to boil. In the cabinets and fridge I found venison, canned tomatoes, jarred garlic, olive oil, dried pasta, and spices. After an hour of chopping, slicing, sautéing, and simmering, the sauce was delicious. Another pot went on to boil for the pasta, and I turned my attention to the nearest big round table.

I laid place settings for five, with water and wine glasses, cloth napkins, and nice plates. I stacked my new film canisters, taped shut, undeveloped, in the middle like a centerpiece, for what was almost certainly going to be the world's worst dinner party, and as I did, the front doors of the Mission swung open.

It happened quickly: Their eyes adjusted to the darkness, they walked two or three feet, and then they stopped. I felt their horror, and gave them a deranged smile in return, wiping my hands on my apron.

I was bedraggled—yes—my white dress covered in mud and the apron soaked through with it—yes—my legs and arms scraped up from the bricks. I was barefoot and blond, the leopard coat hanging from a peg behind me, and I was standing next to a dinner table, looking like the very picture of the dead and drowned Carey Magnolia Logan.

Chapter Twenty-Three

Tyler was the first to move. He ran to me. Ignoring the mud, he wrapped his arms around my waist, moved his head to look into my eyes. I peeled his arms off me and handed them back to him.

"What's happened to you?" he asked, searching me—for damage, for insanity, for something. So kind, so worried.

I regarded him with clarity. "Like I said on the phone: I made dinner. I have something for all of you. It's about your lawsuit. It's like"—I rolled my eyes—"a whole long conversation." I pointed to the table. "Sit! Food is almost ready."

Jack, Jes, and Marlin hung back, glancing at each other with wild eyes, alarm bells rattling their faces. I saw Jack pointing to me with the edge of his thumb, a kind of incredulous gesture, and I waved at him aggressively.

"Hello, Jack! Yes! We can see each other. Is it the dress? If it's bothering you, I can take it off," I said, reaching up, clasping the teardrop-shaped zip between my fingers. It refused to budge, immovable against the wet fabric, and I reached my other hand to hold the neckline in place. Tyler took my hands and stopped me.

"Don't do that," he said, fingers on my wrist, feeling the pulse.

Tyler was afraid that something was wrong with me—the way something was wrong with her. "You don't have to do that."

"Okay," I said, shrugging, and then I was in the kitchen, picking up a piece of pasta and throwing it at the wall. It bounced right off.

Tyler stood in the doorway, watching me. Beyond him, Jes, Jack, and Marlin took their seats at the table, and Jes was examining the centerpiece of canisters.

"Those aren't developed," I said. "Not yet. Can you wait a minute?"

I checked the clock, then threw another piece of pasta at the wall. It, too, bounced to the ground.

"What is going on?" Tyler asked.

"I know. I know what you did." I put my fingers in the boiling water, letting it scald me as I grabbed a third noodle.

It sailed past Tyler's head and stuck on the wall.

"Now we're in business," I cried out, ladling the pasta into a colander and shaking it dry. "Can you get five bowls, please?"

Tyler complied, ceramic ringing in his arms. I ladled pasta, then the sauce. It ran to the edges, red and bright from meaty chunks of tomato flesh. He watched me from the doorway with terrified sweetness—as though he were watching a nervous breakdown. At some point, I felt my hands pulling my hair back and knotting it atop my head, securing it with one twist of a pen from the bar top, and then I felt more like myself.

I served them, one by one, from the left. I grated Parmesan and cracked pepper from the mill, and then I filled their wine glasses with bourbon, holding it from the base like we did in the restaurant, wiping the drips with a folded triangle of napkin. For Jack I grabbed a can of Coke from the bar and poured it with the glass angled to the side, managing the brown foam.

Nobody spoke. Everyone stared at me with agonized regard. They couldn't figure out if I was more of a danger to myself or to them.

At last I sat. My heart beat overtime, the thump of it in my jaw, in my fingers. Washed through with nervousness, I could barely look at them.

"Um," I said, twirling the wine stem in my fingers, the golden thick of the bourbon swirling in circles. "Whew! This is a lot more difficult than I thought it would be."

Jack leaned back in his chair defensively; Jes and Marlin grew stiff; and Tyler turned his body into mine.

"I don't even know where to start. I guess, with gratitude. Thank you, for having me here. I know that I'm your guest. I know that you gave me access to the world that you made. And I don't want to break that world. I want to help. But—I do know, now. *I know what you did."*

Not a single one of them moved—they didn't look at each other, they didn't let their faces betray shock—nothing. I was on the right track. I took a huge bite of pasta. The sauce ran down my chin. I wiped it away with the back of my hand, then continued.

"You have explicitly refused to give Carey what she wanted. And I get it. I would not want to watch a film of anyone I know dying. I wouldn't want anyone else to watch it either. I couldn't bear it, probably. It's horrible."

Nobody responded. They were waiting me out.

"Maybe it's not even that. Maybe there's something else on the film? I don't know. I've only seen part of it."

"I thought you took care of it," Jack said to Jes.

"Not quite." She frowned.

Tyler shook his head at them, the tiniest bit. I used my fork to point at the canisters in the middle.

"Well, I made you something to give to the judge. Instead of— instead of whatever you have. And even if in the long run, it doesn't work, it'll buy you a *lot* of time." I pointed to the canisters again. "We all have the same problem. You don't want to give up the film; I can't have anyone in my studio. So. Go on. Take it." As I shoveled the pasta in my mouth, I realized it was the only thing I'd eaten that day. I kept going—I was starving.

"What's on it?" Jes asked, leaning back in her chair ever so slightly. All eight of their eyes flew to the canisters.

I explained between bites. "It is a film of a woman who looks exactly like Carey Logan walking into a lake and disappearing under the water for over ten minutes. It is filmed from two angles, wide shots, at the lake, with the Eliot property in the background. She does not resurface." I released the pen from my hair and pushed the turban over it, then reached over and took Tyler's sunglasses from the V of his neck. "I bought cat's-eyes, but they sank. I had freckles earlier too, and lipstick, but most of it washed out. Anyway. See?"

"That's not—" Jes stopped herself from speaking. She reached for a canister, but Marlin's arm shot out and stopped her.

"Don't touch that," Marlin said.

"It's not right?" I asked, still eating, though everyone else's plates remained untouched. "I know, the original was underwater. But— it's exactly what the notebook says. I used vintage thirty-five millimeter film stock from Jes's studio on a double reel, which makes it about twenty-two minutes long. I don't know where you found her body. Possibly the angles will be off? But does it matter?"

"It's fraud," Marlin said immediately. The woman I'd known thus far as a soft freckled smile was suddenly all angles. "How are we supposed to resolve that? It's first-degree fraud."

"What do you mean?"

"I mean it is explicitly fraud. It is a course of a conduct with intent to defraud ten or more persons by false or fraudulent pretenses to so obtain property with a value in excess of a thousand dollars. And for you personally it is criminal impersonation in the second degree."

"So then..." I drummed my fingernails against the table. "...don't give it value in excess of a thousand dollars. Don't let Eliot&Sprain sell it," I said. "Let them have it, to display, or loan, but...explicitly state that it does not have a value. I mean. It shouldn't have one, anyway. I don't even know how you would calculate that. Are there... what are they called, actuarial tables for this? What's the going rate for watching someone die?"

"I—that's not a bad idea," Marlin said, her frown dissolving. She eyed the others.

"I'll ask Jeff," Tyler said to her. He turned back to me, looking carefully into my eyes. "And—it's undeveloped. You want us to give undeveloped film to the judge."

"Sure. Why not? I didn't develop it. I'm not a filmmaker. It's as it would have been when it came out of the lake. I mean: Do whatever you want with it. But I think you need it."

They looked at each other, exchanging information without speaking, and then when one of them nodded, so did the rest. Tyler walked to the bar, pulled a number from his phone, and dialed.

"Jeff, hi, it's Tyler. Yeah... I know it's late. I'm sorry. We have— we have a better solution. We're willing to hand the film to the judge, but it's not been developed..." There was a long pause. "She would order it to be developed. Are we supposed to?... No. The plaintiff will? Okay. That's fine. No. Can we ask them to sub- mit a proposal for the development? Can we approve it? Okay. Let's draw that out as long as we can. Okay... And the other thing is that—it cannot be valued. That's right. It does not have a value. No, it can't be sold... Uh, sure, it can be loaned. But right, yes, exactly... it has *no value*... That has to be the condition... You're the lawyer... Good... We don't—okay."

He came back and sat at the table. "She bought us ten months. Maybe a year. What do you want to do?"

"That doesn't change anything—" Jes wasn't finishing any of her sentences.

"I know," Tyler said, throwing his hands in the air. "I know."

"We're still split," Jack said. "I won't change my mind. I'll lose my job. I'll lose my family."

"I *know*," Tyler said, wearily. From the look on his face, they'd had this discussion one or two million times. "I know we are."

"Jack, it's going to come out. You have to see that by now," Jes said.

"Shut *up*, Jes," Marlin growled, and she was that different Marlin again, someone angry, someone new.

"What did you guys *do*?" I asked.

Nobody answered.

Tyler shook his head and turned to me, genuine concern sunk in every fine line of his face. "Why did you do this? Why did you make this for us?"

"Me?"

"You."

"Well . . ." I drummed my nails on the table again, their rounded ovals of bright-red paint now slightly chipped and packed with dirt. "I think that *DROP OUT* deserves to exist. As an idea, at least. Carey wanted it to, so in that way, it's not even up to you, though obviously one of the problems is that she *did* leave it up to you. However—I think that it doesn't necessarily matter if the film is real or if it's fake. I don't believe you have a moral obligation to disseminate the real film, because the only people for whom the real film has a specific meaning is you. And you've watched it. A public audience needs only to believe that whatever they're seeing is real in order for it to serve the point. And even then—they can wonder if it's fake. The wondering itself is part of the work. The genuine article is completely unnecessary. And like I said, because I really need there to not be a police search of my studio right now. But most of all, it's because of Max."

"What about Max?" Tyler asked.

"Max is going to write about Carey and *DROP OUT* in her book because, you know, *Carey's notebooks have been sitting in her library for three years* and memoirs need news hooks."

Shock rippled across their faces, from Tyler to Marlin and back again; they hadn't known about Max. "Max has a lot of things, but she can't have everything. I don't think it's quite fair for a woman who is going to inherit an entire town in Connecticut to profit from the literal dying body of a working-class hero. This is my way of interrupting that. She won't know the difference, but I will."

Jes snorted with laughter. She didn't like Max either.

"What exactly did Max write?" Tyler asked.

"I haven't read it. My guess is that it's probably a description of the work itself, followed by Max's personal narrative about Carey. She's citing Lee Lozano"—I raised my fingers, one for each point—"that guy who sailed his boat into the Atlantic and died; the German woman who wrote that manifesto; and Hannah Wilke. Fleur, her collaborator, is probably the only person who's read it, but they'll send it to an editor, soon, I would think. Oh, and Max thinks you all hated her. Carey, that is."

I was looking down when Jack hurled something across the room. By the time my eyes found it, there was a long crack in the window, the thin brown soda already pooling with the curlicues of broken glass across the floor. The violence sucked all the air out of the room.

"This is not how this goes," he said, pushing away from the table. "We worked *so hard*. You know, I lied to my wife. I lied to my sponsor. Where's Max? Let's—" He started going through Marlin's pockets, looking for her keys.

"Stop it." She grabbed both of his hands and stood up. "Jack, you have to stop. There's nothing we can do." Jack ripped himself away from her and began to pace back and forth.

"We knew this would happen," Tyler told him calmly. "We've talked about this. A or B."

"I don't want A or B," Jack shouted. Anger—ugly, a slur—transformed his face. He no longer resembled the man I'd met that summer. He didn't look like a man at all. He looked like a scared, suburban teenage boy.

"There's nothing else to do, Jack," Marlin said soothingly. "We'll all figure it out."

"This is going to ruin my life," he snarled at her. "You don't understand."

"I'm on your side, Jack. I have *always* been on your side. You *and* Bell *and* Audre."

"You remind me every single day. But my children are not your problem." He spat the words at her with surprising venom. Yet— Marlin didn't flinch.

"That's—you know what—that's cruel," she admonished him. "You know why they're not mine, Jack? Because I was so stressed out, over all of this, that I didn't have my period for most of my thirties. You wouldn't lift the pressure. And then—you found somebody else."

"You did this for yourself as much as anybody else."

"No," Marlin said. "I did it for you."

"We all did it, okay?" Jes shrieked, pounding the table. The three of them looked at her, stunned. "Pick A or pick B. I don't care anymore."

Silence descended over the room. Marlin swallowed her wine glass full of bourbon in a series of long gulps, refusing to look at Jack. Tyler put his head in his hands. Jes stared at Jack. Jack stared out the window. They seemed to have completely forgotten that I was there.

"What *did you do*?" I asked them.

When nobody responded, I turned to Tyler. "What did you do?" I asked again. He didn't look up.

"This is it, Ty," Marlin said. "You've been voting A for three years. Pay up."

"No," he said. "We have to agree."

"You're kidding," I asked. "Right? After all of this? You won't tell me?"

Tyler raised his head, those green eyes looking right through me. "No," he said, shaking his head. "No. I won't."

I'd never heard a no that held such clarity. It broke me right down the middle.

By contrast, Tyler's ardent refusal seemed to change something in Jack—as if he had been yanked from a reverie with the snap of someone's fingers. Jack took his seat at the table, patted Tyler on the back, then turned to me.

"What do you need?" Jack asked me, in this explicit way, like we were making a deal—like I was a man he was paying to stay away from his daughter.

Tyler wouldn't look at me.

"I don't want anything from you," I said. "All I want is to be left alone to finish my paintings. No police, no Charles Eliot, no trouble. I'll be gone soon."

I pushed back from the table and walked to the door.

Chapter Twenty-Four

In the morning, all of their cars were gone. I stopped in the Mission to find sunlight bleaching the naked wooden circle of the table we'd sat at the night before. The canisters were gone, too.

I drove to the studio with a rock in my stomach.

Fifty feet away, I spotted the edge of Marlin's black truck, parked in front of my studio, where the front door was wide open. I slammed on the brakes, jammed it in park, and ran full-speed toward the studio. *Were they touching my paintings? Were they ruining my life?*

Panic pushed me forward, filling my lungs, pumping my legs up and down. I gripped my keys so hard they drew blood. I don't know if I've ever been as terrified as I was during those fifteen steps to the door, and I burst through it like a bomb, the scream already forming in the bottom of my throat.

All four of them—Tyler, Jes, Jack, and Marlin—were sitting patiently on the hayloft steps in the back, coffee mugs in hand. Jes was reading my notebook. I ran, scanning my paintings, out of breath, sweat running down my inner arm. *Nothing—they hadn't moved anything. That I could see.*

"What are you doing in here?" I shrieked.

"You slept in," Tyler said. I felt his eyes on me, but I couldn't even look at him.

I turned in a circle, tears ready to leak from my eyes as I looked for any sign of damage, but there was nothing, and it made me even more suspicious. *What had they done?*

"What are you doing in here?" I shrieked, again, borderline hysterical. "Don't touch anything." My hands flew to my collarbone and I worried it, over and over. "I thought I had the only key."

"Chill," Marlin said, brows up, hands pressing the air in a calming motion. "We're here to help."

"Why are you reading my notebook?" I barked.

Jes turned another page. "You go through our stuff, we go through yours," she said with a shrug.

"We have some time, and we can help you." Jack stood up. He had no patience for my panic. "I don't have to be home this weekend. Jes canceled a gig in the city. Marlin pushed her meetings. Ty—whatever, Ty's at your disposal. But if you don't want us here, we're happy to leave."

"No," I said, shaking my head, clutching my stomach. "No—don't go. Stay. Just—just give me a minute," I muttered, gesturing to them to stay seated. "Finish your coffee." Marlin took a sip. Jes turned another page.

Scowling furiously, I dragged lumber, blocks of foam, tools, and adhesives into the middle of the studio. When I was ready to speak, my voice trembled with adrenaline.

"I need help making frames." The words pushed into each other. I paused, shook my head to clear the anxiety, and searched for reference photos on my camera. When I found an old one I passed it to them on the steps and tried to explain.

"I like it when the frames look like Fruit Roll-Ups made in outer space by very sentient aliens," I heard myself saying. "They should have a gritty-translucent-fruit-leather depth...and sometimes they should sparkle. I mean, like a lot, *a lot* of sparkle. Like a disco."

"So?" Jack sounded annoyed.

"Uh, so—we have to make them. The frames, I mean. From scratch. First we make two dummy paintings. One is to make the mold, the other is to cast the frames. We stick the foam to one of them, and I'll carve it. Then we coat the foam in layers of latex—that'll make the mold—and then we have to make seven casts, one for each painting. They're all different colors. There's a chart in there. And, um, we also have to make silicone nubs for the back part. That's for the wall."

They blinked at me dispassionately.

"That's it?" Marlin asked. They seemed unimpressed.

"Well, I mean, then I need to put the frames *on* the paintings and build the crates."

"I think we should make two, maybe three molds," Jack said. "It'll go faster."

"Won't they look different?"

"No. We'll make one, then the other, from the same positive. It'll be exactly the same."

"Trust him," Tyler said. "All those objects in his nets—he makes them, as you say, from scratch."

After that—it was like I didn't even need to be there. The four of them worked in the smoothest, easiest concert I've ever seen; they had a rhythm and a pace all their own. They didn't reach for the same tools, or the same lumber, or step in the same place—not once. I was the one in the way, and soon backed off.

"Call out the measurements," Tyler ordered.

"What?"

"For the dummies. Call out the measurements as we cut."

"Oh—uh—I guess I could do it that way," I assented. "Hold on." I paged through the notebook and felt only marginally useful as I called the measurements. Jes ran the table saw, Marlin positioned the lumber, and Jack screwed it into place.

Tyler stood off to the side. He'd given me his job, only to be polite.

"You guys are very good at working together," I observed as they glued the foam to the frame with absolute precision, without a smudge, without a drip, without a single mistake.

"No kidding." Jes snickered. She looked at Tyler with an expression that said, *I cannot wait to be free of this stupid idiot.*

I used two very fine hot knives to cut the foam: both curved, one like a scythe, the other a shallow crescent. The foam sloughed off in sheets, falling away in buttery peels as I formed the long, rounded lines of the frame. I felt them watching me—and I didn't imagine it—there were waves of approval as I cut the support wedges in the back, the ones that would become the notches upon which the paintings hung. They murmured something to each other, and I imagined that it was kind.

When it was time to apply the latex, I tried to speak to Jes, Jack, Marlin, and Tyler with the voice that I used for assistants. I did not bring my hand back when we reached for the same tool or move out of the way when we stepped in the same direction, and I bit my cheeks every time the word *sorry* threatened to bubble up from the back of my throat.

After a few hours, a new hierarchy settled into place: When I moved, they stepped aside to let me pass. When I reached for something, they handed it to me. They waited for me to speak before speaking. And at the end of the day, there were three molds—something that would have taken me a week on my own.

"This—this looks like *years* of work," Marlin said to me as I locked up, pointing to my paintings. "You did this alone? In three months?"

"It was more like two. Yes, I did."

She shook her head. "It's enough to break someone."

"Carey did it," I said to her. "Carey did it a thousand times."

"I guess so," Marlin said, turning away. "I guess Carey did."

The next morning, I tacked a chart to the wall.

painting	color	frame
Prudence	interior pink and Verdi green	unripe peach
Humility	4 a.m. night sky navy	metallic silver w/ 2% acid green
Chastity	eggshell and pearl, rainbow	dun gray (the darkest feather on a pigeon)
Temperance	the bloodiest red	rothko chapel purple
Modesty	grease yellow	fuchsia (disco)
Purity	almost white	absolutely crystal clear, carbonated
Obedience	every black	absolutely crystal clear, carbonated

Tyler arrived first. I pointed at the chart without making eye contact.

"Will you speak to me today?" he asked.

"No."

"I'll mix *Humility*, then."

"Fine." I turned my back on him.

"Have you eaten anything?" he asked. I didn't reply.

When Jes arrived, she took my camera, photographed the model frame, and plugged into her laptop. "Hey—" I tried, but she held up her hand.

"I'll rig up a model in CAD. It'll help us calculate the exact quantities of resin to mix," she said.

"Oh." It wasn't a bad idea. "Thank you."

Jes was mixing the second test batch of translucent silver and acid-green resin while I asked for more and more glitter until she rolled her eyes and dumped half a cup into the sample bucket. We poured it into the mold with buckets, spreading it with wooden panels, brushing it up the sides and checking the levels, the Kermit disco pond settling exactly as it ought to.

Marlin walked over with my silver brush-holder. "This is rad," she said, affixing one of Carey's old brushes to it—the dagger, the one with the long bristles. "Look at how much distance."

"I know," Tyler said, smiling. She handed it to him and he dipped the brush in the glitter, then swept it across the floor, six feet away. A long, draggy line appeared—exactly the same as the one on the body that had been in *YOKEFELLOWS*—and then I saw it.

I finally saw everything with the right pair of eyes.

Tyler painted.

Jack made molds.

Marlin shaped bodies.

Jes calculated materials.

"*We know each other by our lines,*" I whispered. "*We know each other by our lines.*" I went over to the line of glitter on the floor and ran my finger through it. Tyler stopped and watched me, struck silent.

"We know each other by our lines," I said again, this time nice and loud. Marlin looked over, and then Jes—and then Jack. I said it again. "We know each other by our lines."

They stared at me like I had lost my mind. I'd never been so clear about anything.

"We know each other by our lines," I enunciated, pointing to one of them with each word. "I was so impressed. What a crock," I spat.

"What are you talking about?" Jes asked—what a faker—in a voice so feeble I didn't know why she bothered. Tyler stood on the other side of *Purity*, petrified with dread. I took my fingertip of glitter and wiped it across his cheek. His green eyes looked into my clear ones, fear pulsing from his pupils, and then—I knew that I was right.

"You did it," I said. "You made Carey's work."

They looked at each other—one to another and back again—and transformed from a solid, impenetrable foursome to a pile of broken glass. They fell apart in front of my eyes. What had once been a great wall was now a group of ragged people.

"You did it," I said again, my voice low now, commanding them, angry with them.

"You *all* did it!" I said, shaking my head. "What a pack of liars. I—worked so hard." I paced, frustrated with the fountain of rage that was exploding beneath my feet. "I worked so hard this whole time because...I thought Carey worked so hard. I thought she was this practical artist like me and you were these, like, intellectual, experimental geniuses who never got your hands dirty, not ever. I thought, oh God, I thought that she was this model of, like, a compulsive person who was fine as long as she made things, that she lost her mind when she stopped. I thought it was, like, this signpost. *Be like her.* But none of it was real. You did all of it. *YOKEFELLOWS*. To yoke me as his yokefellow, right? That's what she wrote...Or you wrote. *You* wrote it, in the notebooks. All the different colors of ink. And when you stopped helping her, she killed herself."

As I'd stared them down, pacing back and forth in front of them like an angry general, the four of them had moved next to each other. They stood in a row, hands at their sides, mouths agape.

"And this is bad, but—to keep it a secret for so long," I said accusingly. "Oh my God. Susan was right all along. What's eating you? What'd you do? What did you do to her?"

Tyler looked at the rest of them in slow motion.

"Are we agreed?" he asked.

"Why do you care about agreeing with each other?" I snapped. Anyone could see that their bond was broken. Why the charade?

Still—he waited, and one by one, they nodded.

"The last time we disagreed, Maria Clarke killed herself."

"Maria Clarke? What does she have to do with anything?"

"Maria Clarke was the actress who played Carey. Carey Logan was not a real person," Tyler said. "*She was not a real person.* She was our project. It was all of us. Always."

♠ ♠ ♠ ♠ ♠

They told me everything. From the beginning, when they made the first sculpture, to meeting Maria and inventing Carey Logan. It was the biggest fraud imaginable, and they told it with their heads in their hands, crying, arguing, offering justifications, half-truths, selfish righteousness, absolute shame, and unabated sorrow. Sometimes they were the heroes, Maria, the villain; sometimes Maria was a martyr and they were her sacrifice. Sometimes they were simply people locked into a problem. It held all the prisms of who they were, and all of their truths and projected wants mixed up together, and I saw what a mess it all was among them.

It boiled down to a few simple facts: Maria Frances Clarke was an actress they hired to play the part of Carey Magnolia Logan. When they wanted to stop—when they had made enough money—they told Maria it was over. But she was not ready to do anything else; she'd never done anything else. They tried to stop her. They couldn't.

She wanted to be Carey.

She could not live up to it.

It destroyed her.

♠ ♠ ♠ ♠ ♠

I walked outside, closed the door behind me, leaned against the wall, and cried. The person that I looked up to most in the world was a lie. The man I thought I was in love with kept his boot on her neck for fifteen years, and lifted it when he was finished, and left her alone by the side of the road.

"These people," Carey told me, that night on Grand Street, "will make not only your work, but *you yourself* into a commodity. They'll buy you and sell you. Let them. But make sure you always do it on your own terms." She meant Pine City. They bought her, sold her, controlled her. "She was built that way," Tyler told me, one of those nights on the deck, when I commented on Carey's success. "She was the center of attention without doing anything," I'd said to Jack. His careful reply: "That's the most accurate description of her I've ever heard." Jes and Marlin kept their language in check—but not their work. Jes's film presented Carey as an imitation, while Marlin refused to change her hand, continuing to make the same hexagons, the same anatomies, the same lines.

The notebooks, the multiple colors, the blocky handwriting disguising actual handwriting. *Dagger line, T6 calf—decided to leave it.* Tyler, Marlin, Jes, or Jack speaking to each other. A directive, not a notation. There'd been something about spiritual abuse. Someone called her an ungrateful bitch, I remembered, seeing the pointed scratch on the page. *"I cried when I hung up . . . my role requires me to undertake more emotional and spiritual abuse than everyone else."* That was Carey—Maria—documenting how people treated her. *"I'm scared he'll make me demo talent,"* she'd written on another page. A real fear. Not an insecurity.

"I want to express myself," she told the *Times*, when she "switched" to performance—no—reduced—*distilled*. She was telling the truth. She wanted to express herself.

I'd misunderstood all along.

I leaned against the wall outside my studio—her studio—their studio—and kept crying. I felt so sad, and so foolish, and so alone. It was the first time I'd cried since my apartment burned down. I thought it would make me feel better.

It didn't.

I returned to the studio, threading my way through my paintings, sitting on the steps. I did not speak. After a moment they gathered at my feet like guilty little children, looking up to me as though I was supposed to mete out their punishment and forgive their sins.

"What is the A/B vote?" I asked, my voice steady.

"A is, we tell," Jes said. She was the strongest. "We go ahead and tell; we tell the gallery, we tell collectors, we tell anyone who will listen. B is, we wait and see how long it takes to come out, and we take that chance that it never will. Tyler and I have been on the A side. Marlin and Jack are B."

"The problem with A," Marlin interrupted, "is that we're talking about at least a hundred counts of fraud in the first degree. The artworks themselves are products of a fraud, subject to state and federal charges, based on the transaction. We didn't commit tax fraud—we took all the money through a company called Carey Magnolia Logan and paid her out through that—but we did take in over three and a half million dollars from Carey Logan. We filed a fake birth record and death certificate with the county; that's a federal crime. Criminal charges would put us in jail, and civil lawsuits could come from any collector. All it takes is for one single piece to decline in value, and then we're getting sued. This lawsuit alone has cost us thirty thousand dollars to defend and we haven't even met with the judge yet. Plan A is asking to lose everything in exchange for peace of mind."

"The problem with B," Tyler responded, "is that if we simply wait, someone will unravel this. *DROP OUT* will undeniably raise the price of the other work. With B, we are raising the price of our own eventual suffering."

"With B, there's a good chance that nobody ever figures anything out," Jack reminded him. "They haven't so far. Why would they?"

"She did," Tyler and Marlin and Jes said in unison, looking at me.

"What would Carey have wanted?" I asked.

"Carey's not real," the four of them said in chorus. I wondered how many times they'd repeated that to each other.

"Sorry. I'm still getting used to it. Maria, I mean. What would Maria have wanted?"

"Maria was *not* an artist," Jack said harshly. "She was only a performer."

"I know," I said. "I saw her drawings. But—nonetheless, I think you owe her a vote." I set my hand on Tyler's. He took it, gratefully, and it surprised me, how easy it was to make him feel something, now that I would never feel anything again. "*DROP OUT*, and all those last performances. I don't care if you think they're bad. They're hers. She was a part of this. She should get to vote at least once."

"She didn't vote. That wasn't her role."

"That's completely unfair," I said. "Her notebooks are crystal clear. She wanted people to see that film."

"She ruined our lives," Marlin said, looking up at me. "She put her dead body in our hands. She asked us to validate something that we can't validate."

"No, she didn't," I told them. "She didn't ask. She *told*. She did exactly what she wanted. It's not yours to hold hostage. You don't get to choose for her. I don't care if you think it's bad. It's hers."

Eight eyes, pained and sharp, snapped onto mine. They knew I was right.

"A," Tyler said before I was even done speaking.

"A," Jes followed.

"A...A," Marlin stammered. They all looked at Jack.

"A," he said. "Absolutely A. She wanted to be her own person so badly." He sat down and put his head between his knees. "This is going to ruin my life," he said. "Goodbye job. Goodbye to my wife and children. Hello bankruptcy. Hello prison."

"I don't even know who we would call," Marlin said. "I don't know where to start."

"I do," I told them. "I know exactly what to do."

Three weeks later, the completed frames were affixed to the dry paintings, like big plates of melted candy, or panels from a spaceship. They were flawless. We sealed my seven old maids in crates like wooden coffins and the preparators came. I hovered, buzzing like a fly, every muscle tense, as they loaded my paintings into the truck and drove away.

Tyler stood behind me as the white square of the sea container disappeared through the trees.

"I don't want to give it up," he said, looking around at Pine City.

"I know."

"I would have done anything to keep this from you."

"I know that too."

I kissed him, to see what it would feel like, if there would be anything. It was a good kiss, one that had my back up against the truck and threw my judgment to the wind. For a split second, I wanted to bury myself in him, to run my fingers through his hair, to curl up in his bed with tea and bourbon and his body and mine. And then I remembered, and I stopped feeling anything at all.

When I let go, I got in the truck and drove, and drove, and drove.

I drove all the way to northern Florida, where I checked into a motel and slept through an entire day.

My mother's house looked better than I expected. The rotting siding had been lifted and patched; the screen door hung neatly on its hinges. The spiky grass of the lawn was mowed evenly, and her car, a newer Civic, was washed and parked straight in the driveway. It was as though someone had lifted it up and set it back on track.

The bell rang loud and clear; she'd had it repaired. Through the screen, the house looked neater and tidier than I'd ever seen it; the carpet was vacuumed, the furniture was aligned, not askew. An elderly woman came to the door. At first, I didn't recognize her. Her hair was short, curls brushed. She wore almost no makeup and walked with a bit of a shuffle, the hesitancy of age. But behind the sun spots and the wrinkles, she was still my mother.

"Honey!" she cried, almost jumping through the screen. "Honey. You came home. You know, when I didn't get a check from you this month, I started to worry."

"Sorry, Mom," I said, hugging her tighter and tighter, burying my face in the sagging skin of her neck, relishing her smell: menthol cigarettes and coffee and sunscreen. "Things have been a little erratic. I can't stay long. I can send more money soon."

"That's okay, that's okay," she said, keeping me in the hug, rocking me back and forth. "Things have been real good down here," she said. "I got my sixty-day chip. It's better than last time. I got a new sponsor."

"That's good, Mom." We'd had this conversation before. "I'm proud of you." I'd said that before too.

"I'm proud of *you*," she said, crying too, and then she was backing away from me, holding my hands, looking me up and down. She looked like a mother—a grandmother, perhaps—in pressed Bermuda shorts and a teal tank top with big wide straps over Teva sandals. The bloat had melted away at long last, taking with it the glassy sheen of her once-vacant eyes. Her mascara was tidy, unsmudged.

Still—her fingers trembled as she lit a cigarette. "How long can you stay, baby?"

"About a week. I have to go, um, I have to go to Paris, actually."

"Paris? Paris, France?"

"Yes, Mom. Paris, France."

"Whatever for?"

"For work, Mom. My paintings are being shown in a really nice gallery there."

"Oh my gosh, that is so exciting," she said, buzzing around and around. "Oh my. Okay. We need Arnold Palmers. Not Laura Palmers like I used to do, 'course. Come in, honey, come in."

She pulled me in through the screen door and told me all about her new friends, her sponsor, her job, what was going on with the house. She asked about my paintings, and I tried to explain. She wanted to know the names of the paintings, but I could see in her eyes right away that she didn't understand.

"Jesus loves you, baby," she said, loving, condescending, dismissive. "I'm sure God is in the details. I'm sure those paintings will make people feel the things that you call them. I taught you how to be those things. Isn't it good to be reminded how to be? To remind others?"

I didn't know how to tell her that those words taught me only how to follow, and never to lead. It wasn't that they were fundamentally bad. They weren't *enough*.

I didn't want to fight with my mother. I wanted to be close with her for a while, while her eyes were open, and her breath smelled like coffee, and her recycling was empty, while she was, for this moment, alive.

When, later, she told me that she was sorry—she didn't say what for and I didn't ask—I said thank you, and I meant it. At one point when she went to fix dinner, I thought, *Even if this try at sobriety fails, I'll still have this day.*

I stayed in the motel for a week, not wanting to disrupt her space or the tenuous peace between us. I met her sponsor and some of her new friends. I helped her clean out the kitchen and the garage, and then it was time to go. I sold the truck to a used-car dealership, took a taxi to the airport, and went to Paris to install my *Rich Ugly Old Maids*.

One Year Later

Chapter Twenty-Five

The last time I saw Pine City, I was thirty-five years old. They were standing on the sidewalk in front of the Young Museum, and they were huddled in a circle, sharing cigarettes and talking quietly.

It seems in my memory that everyone turned to look—that diamond-collared collectors craned their necks, that the young men in front of me whispered and stepped aside, that businessmen looked up from their phones—and that even Pine City stopped talking—as I crossed through the party, head held high, and made my way through.

I was almost an hour late. I wore a long black gown over sneakers. My hair was pink again, and bigger than ever. Everyone moved out of my way. I could have turned—I could have gone in any direction—but I made a beeline for the window that separated the courtyard from the party, the shortest path to his location. With my feet on black granite, his on white travertine, I held my hand to the window. Tyler spread his fingers to match mine. Marlin, Jes, and Jack gave a small wave. They were pallid, worn through with anxiety.

"Hold on," I mouthed through the window. *"I'll come find you."* I

picked up my dress and turned—which was when the crowd swept
me up, and I was pushed away from Pine City in a wave to the
museum's formal theater. Though the whole museum was devoted
to *BODY OF WORK*, the Carey Logan retrospective, it would be
closed off until after the screening. The heat from a hundred pairs
of eyes licked my skin as I found an empty seat and lowered myself
into it, but I was safe in the knowledge that nobody actually saw
me at all; I had finally become comfortable in my own skin—and
separate from it too.

Max took the empty seat beside me as the lights went
down. The room hissed with whispered rumors.

"Hi," she said carefully.

"Hi."

"I didn't know you were coming."

"I decided at the last minute."

"I want—" When Max said *want* I turned away, because I didn't
care what she wanted, and she paused. "You haven't answered any
of my emails," she tried. "Are we okay?"

"We're the same," I told her.

"The same as what?"

"The same as always," I said evenly.

"I'm sorry," she said. "I want you to know how hard I fought to
keep that photo off the cover."

"The *back* cover," I said snidely, and couldn't help but laugh.

"I did," she pleaded. "I want you to know that."

"It's fine."

"How's Berlin?" she tried.

"It's good."

"Everything changed after you left. I mean—well, you'll find
out about all of it tonight." She pointed to the program. "Open
it." How quickly she cast off her sorry demeanor and began fizzing
with excitement instead, and I thought, *Max, you will never, ever
change.*

The program was nicely made; a keepsake. An article. Thick paper—tactile letterpress—a rich emerald ink. I didn't pretend to be shocked.

BODY OF WORK

a film by Pine City

NOTE TO VISITORS: This film shows a graphic death by drowning. It is not suitable for children.

This film contains footage from:

DROP OUT PIECE

35mm film

Clarke, Maria

Born: 1971, USA

This film is the final work of Maria Frances Clarke, a performance artist and filmmaker previously known for her role as Carey Logan. Carey Logan was the fictive persona of Pine City, the collective of Tyler Savage, Jes Winsome, Marlin Mayfield, and Jack Wells.

DROP OUT PIECE is the last of Clarke's seven known works.

Max took in my blank face with confusion, then—a funny kind of understanding.

"Well, it makes sense that he told *you*," she whispered, disappointed. "I guess it doesn't matter now." As other people around us began to read, a murmur went through the crowd, and then people were talking loudly. The lights went down. I don't know if Pine City took their seats. People were talking right up to the opening credits.

BODY OF WORK

A film by Pine City

The first page of the *DROP OUT* notebook was projected. People audibly gasped. Then—twenty-two minutes passed as we watched a woman who looked exactly like Carey Logan on the shores of the black lake. Sweating through her leopard coat, her white dress, she mixed cement and poured it into her boots. Then she walked into the water and she did not come back.

The atmosphere of the room was like a solar eclipse. One second, everything was normal—and the next, it was inside out, shadows dripping from every ceiling tile, spreading from beneath every seat, filling our throats, our chests. "She swam out of view," someone said. "There's nowhere for her to go," someone else pointed out. "That was fake, right?" another asked. "I hope so," their companion replied. Agitation shuddered through the room, the wooden armrests shaking, the velvet seats suddenly scratchy and too small.

The film cut to Tyler in his studio, a close-up, in front of an unlit forge. He looked tired. "We were twenty-one," he said. "Me, and Marlin, and Jack. A mortician visited Senior Thesis and taught us how to sculpt a human ear. We were impressed. We made ears, as instructed. We got inspired, and stayed late in the studio, after the mortician had left. We made noses, and later that week, a head, a torso. It was soothing, a welcome distraction, from the pressure of our own thesis projects."

Cut to Marlin, in her own studio, light streaming in from the window onto her lovely soft face, the Blake quote on the wall behind her: "We decided to try our hands at a whole body. The process was initially difficult, but we found a way to work that combined our preferred mediums: paint, ceramics, fiber. We could all draw—that great and bounding line—we all had the hand."

Cut to Jack, in his studio, sitting on an apple box against the wall. "Marlin and I hand-built the bones, the legs, the skin, the shapes; Tyler painted the decay. When we were done, it was good. We knew it was good. But it wasn't what we wanted to do with our careers."

Tyler: "I don't remember which one of us thought of it."

Marlin: "I know that it happened at the Half King, at one of the outside tables, because in those days we all smoked. It was October, months after graduation, when we shared the living room of our apartment as a studio. Jes, we'd met earlier that year. She was living with us by then."

Jes, sitting alone on the black stage of her theater: "Everybody was telling us to be smart. Galleries were rejecting the same work we were praised for in school—Marlin's prints, my music and films, Tyler and Jack's installations—telling us that they weren't salable. We were told, again and again, that the market needed an easy conversation."

Tyler: "The first months outside of school, in the cold hard world where nobody cared, were a shock. Jes got rejected from one gallery after three months of studio visits and talks about a show. I lost like five bartending gigs. Jack started doing drugs pretty hard. We were going nowhere fast."

Jes: "We tried to talk to one of Jack's professor friends about it. He said that it was a great-looking sculpture, but nobody was going to be impressed by four young rich kids who wanted to romanticize death. He talked about Rachel Whiteread, how

House got torn down right away because people were so insulted that some privileged elite artist wanted to fetishize other people's pain."

Jack: "He asked me about it years later. I said he must have mis-remembered."

Jes: "We were pissed off. We thought that the whole world was our enemy. We wanted to turn it upside down."

Marlin: "We entered *HARD BODY (7 TIMES A DAY)* into the Young Foundation show, with a made-up backstory and a fake person, the whole thing. If it got any press, we were going to say right then and there that it was a hoax."

Jack: "It was Jes's idea to give it this, like, political dimension."

Jes: "It was the '90s. Everyone loved stories about women suffering. The history of art is littered with the bodies of dead women. That's always been true. Think about Paris in the last century. *L'Inconnue de la Seine.* Every artist had this woman's death mask on their wall, like it meant something that she looked happy when she drowned." She sniffs. "But it didn't mean anything."

Jack: "We felt that our class position was holding us back. Class was a construction, we told ourselves."

Tyler: "Everything that was selling was hyperrealistic figurative sculpture. We thought it was complete garbage. And even if we could have put our names on it, we didn't want to. We wanted to make fully experimental works that could not be commodified. We thought we were Marxists."

Marlin: "I couldn't believe it when it won. That was—I mean, I was so surprised."

Jack: "The prize was twenty thousand dollars. That was enough." He shakes his head and lights a cigarette. There's a brown drink in his hand. "That was all it took." He takes a big swallow; it foams. It's Coca-Cola. "I'm so ashamed," he said.

Cut to Tyler. "We told ourselves that it didn't matter. We thought we needed the money. We agreed to reveal it someday and then…we didn't ever have a plan, actually. We always called revealing it 'Plan A.' 'Plan B' was to see where it went. We just kept saying, let's use plan B for a little while longer."

Marlin: "I honestly thought that someday it'd all be worthless. It was trendy, you know? Calculated. We didn't believe it would go the distance, like it did. That's—I mean, for me, that was why I didn't want my name on it. I wanted to grow, as an artist. It's hard to be rigorous *and* profitable. So . . . " She shrugs. "We separated the two."

Jack: "It was easier to pay somebody else to deal with the brain damage of it all. And when it was done, they could go back to being themselves." He stubs out the cigarette. "That was the plan, anyway."

Jes: "Maria Clarke used to hang out with some of the theater kids from Juilliard. She was totally untrained, this runaway kid from upstate, and she'd been taking Method classes out of somebody's apartment."

Marlin: "Eliot&Sprain kept writing and writing to the email address we'd put on the entry form."

Jes: "We thought about coming clean, but . . . then we figured out how to keep the money. The check would go to Carey Logan. Carey Logan, the business, could deposit the check."

Tyler: "I assisted for a guy who had a great accountant. He set it up for us. A four-way partnership."

Jack: "Maria was into the whole thing. Always. She told us that she was an experimental performer. She wanted to push boundaries."

Tyler: "There are things you think about yourself at nineteen, and things you say about yourself, that have nothing to do with living a real adult life."

Marlin: "We had no idea how vulnerable she was. We thought class was this, like, idea, that you could change, that you could cast off. We genuinely didn't get it. She didn't have the tools we did. No home at Christmas was the tip of the iceberg. She didn't have the basic building blocks of what you need to be a successful

person—time management, emotional regulation, the ability to re-
flect on hindsight..." Marlin trails off. "She was not emotionally
adept, or mature, in the ways we had been raised to be. She lived
in one long reaction. That was invisible to us at the time. All we
saw was how charismatic she was."

Tyler: "I was so in love with her."

Jes: "She was my best friend."

Marlin: "I mean, I was in love with her. In the beginning. Like
crazy."

Jack: "We lived together, you know? We took care of each other.
It felt like it was meant to be." He lights another cigarette. "That's
probably the thing I want my children to understand. I loved her."

Jes, briefly pictured picking up trash on the shoulder of the
thruway in an orange vest labeled DUTCHESS COUNTY
CORRECTIONS: "Oh. The practical stuff? When we signed
with the gallery, I hacked into the recently connected Dutchess
County public records database. I made a birth record for Carey
for the same town Maria was from, so it would be easy for her.
Same birthday, but 1970." She spears a seltzer can, pushing until it
crumples against the dirt. "That was a crime. I freely admit that.
The DA gave me three months of community service." She looks
out at the highway. "We never registered Carey for a Social; we
used the business tax ID for everything. Maria used her own ID
whenever, booked her own travel. In public, she paid for things
in cash or charged it to the company. That part—that part was
easy. It's astonishing how willing people are to believe in someone.
Anyone."

The film cut through a composite of Maria's early days as Carey.
Her first show, *BODYWORK*, was followed by *CAREY 2*. There
was footage of Pine City making the work, filmed by Jes on a
Handycam. Maria comes in the door and coos. She's wearing a
frilly, frothy dress—very un-Carey.

"It looks so good," she said. "What should I wear tonight?"

Marlin throws her a plain t-shirt and jeans. Maria sticks out her tongue. "Carey Logan is boring," she yells, right before shutting the bathroom door.

Jack: "She moved into the loft in Long Island City. We were all in love with each other." He exhales and looks offscreen.

Tyler: "I wrote a whole manifesto on it, early on. Richard Prince and Damien Hirst and Jeff Koons don't make a single thing. They have assistants. This was *exactly* like that. It's the exact same thing. Except that in those cases the labor is executed by someone interchangeable but the idea-machine remains the same, and what we were doing was the opposite of that."

Marlin: "What was the labor? Was the labor the work itself, or was it the identity, the standing in the gallery, being small and blond, working-class and nonthreatening? Was the labor being the object of other people's fantasies? Was it the emotional labor? Or was it the sculpture?"

Jack: "Carey got famous pretty fast. We were special by association. The galleries opened doors for us—residencies, institutions. We didn't have to figure out how to sell work until after she died. I spent fourteen years making exactly what I wanted."

Marlin: "I honestly believe that without our connection to Carey, we would not have had the careers we did. Especially me. I was a bisexual girl from the suburbs who liked to draw. There's a million of me. My success was one hundred percent because of her."

Jes, back in her studio: "I would have been fine in my career, but without the money we made from Carey Logan, we never would have been able to buy the place upstate. I got to spend a year cutting my last film. Millions of dollars changes things."

Tyler: "I never would have figured myself out if it wasn't for her." He looks down, away from the camera, and his voice breaks. "Maria taught me how to be a person."

There was footage from THE BURIAL PROJECT, that night on Grand Street. You could see me in the corner of the frame, standing in a line, scratching my arm awkwardly.

Tyler: "*THE BURIAL PROJECT* was great because it gave us forty-two fresh casts to work from, and all these people who had 'seen' her 'work.' After that we made whatever we felt like, and all Maria had to do was show up for studio visits and openings and stuff like that. That was easy because she was with us all the time, anyway."

Jes, her face flat: "She was in love with Tyler. Absolutely, unequivocally. She didn't want to share. Him, or her. They became a unit."

Marlin: "Problems began to appear—tiny little cracks—things that were inevitable. Tyler and Maria had this intense relationship. Jack and I split off. Jes was left all alone. We fractured. We became afraid—of being accused of being dishonest, of stacking the deck, so to speak, with five minds pretending to be one. Of being fraudulent."

Tyler: "That's an important technicality. It would have rendered us ineligible for nearly every solo show Carey was in, every prize she won, all of it. We were breaking the rules, and the older we got, the more important those rules seemed to be. When we were young it didn't matter, but when we were older . . . it began to eat away at us."

Marlin: "We met with a lawyer and talked about how to unravel it. The problem was that we'd sold all this work in her name, and if the value of the work plummeted, we'd be exposed to that liability. And of course, it was illegal."

Tyler: "We decided to at least start making our own money. We started to give in to the market. We were going to kind of ease out of it."

The film cut to Charles Eliot, standing in Eliot House. "There was no one else we wanted for this house. We asked her over to drinks and she agreed right away. We were thrilled."

Jack: "We were floored. How were we supposed to get in there if she was the only one who could be in the space? I mean, she was not—Maria did not have the skill set that Carey Logan had. I don't want to say she wasn't an artist. But she was a *performance* artist."

Marlin: "That was the beginning of the end."

Tyler, now smoking. "The house took five years. It was sup-posed to take two. She and I broke up. She took up with Charles. His marriage ended. She thought they were going to run away together. Then—he married Max, who was staying with us that summer. Maria was devastated."

Max went rigid.

Jes: "By the time the house was done—work we had not agreed to, for which we received no credit, that had to be done through an increasingly demanding intermediary—we, Pine City, were ready to retire Carey Logan."

Jack: "The vote, among the four of us, was not unanimous. Mar-lin thought it was the wrong thing to do."

Marlin, looking frustrated: "I envisioned it working out poorly. That's all I can say. I was outvoted."

Tyler: "Carey was going to simply cease to make new artworks—she would fade into the distance. At first it would be a long vacation, and then rehab and a romance in Thailand, or whatever. We would pay her for five more years to do nothing but acknowledge she was Carey Logan and make zero artwork."

Marlin: "She agreed to it pretty reluctantly."

Jes: "She was instructed to alienate and insult everyone she'd met through us. Slowly but surely, people would stop wanting to see her, and then they would forget about her. It happens every day. After a few years, we would spread the rumor that she'd gotten married and moved to the suburbs, and Maria would dye her hair a different color and start her own life."

Tyler: "We were pretty surprised when Eliot&Sprain announced that Carey Logan would be exhibiting a new performance piece, standing in the gallery, holding strangers, like a fucking graduate student."

Marlin: "I called her right away. I said you can't do this. You can't be Carey Logan. Give it five years and you can be yourself. Just—just go to a beach or something. Read books. Go to therapy.

Untangle all of this and get back to your life. We'd talked about that several times. And then she said, and I'll never forget this, she said, 'Who is ever going to care about Maria Clarke? Who is ever going to want a washed-up fake like me?' I mean, that broke my heart. We had—we took her life away, in some respects."

Jes: "We couldn't stop her from performing. The boundaries identifying who owned Carey Logan had shifted over the years. She'd done so much work to pump up Carey's career. I thought it was okay that she tried to make it her own."

Jack: "I didn't like any of it. But I respected her need to try."

Tyler: "Sometimes it was interesting. *OTHER PEOPLE'S RULES* was pretty strange."

Jes: "I think it was the reviews for *OTHER PEOPLE'S RULES* that pushed her over the edge. She wanted to make a mark."

Marlin: "The problem with killing yourself and calling it an artwork is that you're asking the people who loved you the most in the world to validate it."

Tyler: "We had a hard time doing that."

Jack: "I felt very, very guilty. I felt like we had killed her. That we were responsible for her death."

Tyler: "We probably were."

Jes: "I don't feel responsible. It was her choice. As the only member of Pine City who was also a performer, I unequivocally respected her right to define her performance. It's not that I don't miss her. But I won't undermine her decisions."

Marlin: "We didn't tell her family." She taps her fingers against the window. "I think about that every day when I wake up."

Jes: "Maria's parents were upstate alcoholics who used to beat the living shit out of her. She hadn't spoken to them since she was seventeen. I don't feel any obligation to them whatsoever."

Tyler: "I saw the cameras on the beach and I knew." He reddens, then chokes. "I tried CPR but she was already gone."

Jack: "I don't know if *DROP OUT* is an artwork. She said that it was."

Marlin: "We're in a weird position. It *is* fraud. If the value of the work plummets, we could be held liable for damages."

Max de Lacy, pictured in the elaborate gilded egg of her office: "I wanted to write about *DROP OUT* in *The Art of Losing*, my memoir that releases next month, because I deeply loved the woman whom I knew as Carey. She was a friend. I wanted her to have what she wanted. To be seen." Max glimmers. The thing about Max is that she means it when she says things like this. The camera allows the light to bounce off the peonies painted on her wall, and cuts back to Max smiling; it's an effect that makes her look as gauche and out of place in this film as a diamond bracelet in a homeless shelter.

It cuts back to Tyler in his studio. The camera zooms out to show an empty room. "We've sold Pine City to Eliot&Sprain and consolidated our assets." He looks around. "Today is our last day here."

Charles Eliot: "We have no legal action to pursue against Pine City at this time." The camera zooms out to show him standing in front of the Mission, directing workers.

Helen Sprain, sitting in the office of their Chelsea gallery: "This extraordinary property will become a true center for the arts in upstate New York. Performing arts space, a permanent collection, rotating exhibitions, funded residencies for marginalized artists—the Maria, as it's now called, will be an anchor for the community."

Marlin, exiting her empty studio: "The next thing is the retrospective. We've loaned the museum everything we have."

Jack: "It's not only the Carey work. It's the work we made about her."

Jes: "I don't care about the retrospective. We got what we wanted. Bring on the future."

Tyler: "I want to move on."

The closing credits dedicated the film to the memory of Maria Frances Clarke over a photograph of her standing in Tompkins

Square Park. In a floral dress, holding a skateboard, grinning ear-to-ear, her hair long, dark, uncombed, she looked like a nineteen-year-old girl with everything ahead of her—and absolutely nothing like Carey Logan.

The audience was spooked. Some people were yelling into their phones and shoving past each other for the doors, while others stood, struck dumb, looking around for Pine City, who were not in the room. Most people didn't seem to know whether they should be angry or outraged or excited or confused or what, and so they typed into their phones, searching for an article or a recap or anything that would tell them how to feel.

Max, beet red with discomfort, stayed still. She hadn't known a thing about Charlie and Maria.

"I'm sorry," I said to her, simply.

"It's fine." She gritted her teeth. "That's his job. To make people love him. He's—he's too good at it, sometimes."

Charlie appeared at the end of our row, all sorrow and regret, beckoning for Max with a furrowed brow. When Max stood I noticed that she was pregnant.

"Oh my gosh," I said instinctively. "Congratulations. I didn't even notice."

"No, no, I'm carrying small, she could be a burrito," Max said.

"She?"

"She."

"Congrats," I said. She straightened up, then looked at the ceiling to force a tear to dispel over the surface of her eye.

"Okay. I'm fine. It's the hormones."

"Don't worry about the photo," I told her, impulsively giving the forgiveness she so craved. I had a thought in the moment that if I were ungenerous, it would be bad for the baby. And—I signed the release. I did. I was young, and I didn't know better, but I did it, and I profited from it, too, in one way or another. I can confess that, now. I should.

As Charles moved toward us, she took my hands with her tattooed fingers. "I think about it all the time. I think about it every day," she said, urgently, squeezing my fingers. "I do. I do."

I looked into her big blue eyes. "I don't," I told her. "Not anymore." When her husband was only a few steps away, I took back my hands and walked in the other direction.

🌲 🌲 🌲 🌲 🌲

The galleries, unlocked after the end of the film, were already packed. I pushed my way through, holding my dress in one sweating fist, and found myself back in their wonderland, though Pine City themselves were nowhere to be seen. The whole atrium was filled with *FORGIVE/FORGET*, rotten flower petals coated the floor, and the ceiling was draped with one of Jack's ethereal nets. Carey's bronzed heart, broken in two, stood gleaming on a pedestal. Every room contained a central work of Carey Logan's, mixed with those by the other members of Pine City. Side galleries, drawn with velvet curtains, showed recordings of Maria Clarke's performance works. The *DROP OUT* piece was playing, separate from the documentary, in a side gallery, and there was already a long line of people who wanted to watch it again.

Then I saw a flash of pink and green.

Prudence.

She was on loan from a British collector. The wall text said she was the last piece of art made at Pine City. I reached up and touched her. This time, nobody stopped me. Instead, someone asked me to turn around and smile so that they could take my picture.

That's when I saw him in the crowd, watching me, in that same threadbare tuxedo. People were speaking to him urgently, tugging at his jacket. He kept his eyes on me, didn't acknowledge anyone else, and pointed toward the exit.

Outside? he mouthed. I nodded.

The crowd was suffocating. I was pushing, shoving, squeezing to get through, as was everybody else, when I passed a room where Charles Eliot was holding court. "Well no, we had no idea," he was saying to a group of people, looking elegantly disappointed. I paused, safe within a scrum of strangers, to watch him play this out.

"Isn't it fraud?" someone demanded.

"There have to be damages. Right now—everything is fine. The work continues to hold its value."

Helen Sprain stood behind him, back-to-back, so they could work the largest number of conversations in the smallest possible square footage. She was elegant, with soft red hair, hard black eye-glasses, and a slightly oversize mauve wool suit.

Charles said something out of the side of his mouth to Hen; she reached back and brushed his leg with one burgundy finger; he tapped her with his elbow and said a name; she leaned her hair into his and nodded in such a way that he could feel it—and all the while, they were carrying on multiple conversations with collectors, curators, artists, and the various personalities who had been issued a ticket. The Young Museum, I realized, was merely a venue. Eliot&Sprain had orchestrated everything: the work, the guest list, the timing—even, I realized, the seat assignments in the theater.

Charles and Helen symphonically directed the futures of Carey Logan and Maria Clarke. Two artists for the price of one. Max appeared at Charlie's side, hand on her big belly, and he brushed his cheek against hers. Max smiled. Hen turned and hugged Max, like she loved her—motherly, almost—while Charles looked on, something haunting his elegant face.

Then I didn't hear the noise in the room anymore, or feel the bodies shoving against mine. I thought only of Susan Bricklings-Young saying, the night of the turtle party, "He was so very in love with her. It was all so upsetting," and I understood that she meant Charlie, and the breakup of his marriage. "She didn't know what she had," Susan said about Carey. *Maria wanted to be with Charlie, but couldn't, or wouldn't, tell him the truth about herself.* And so—he married Max, after six weeks of dating.

Charlie wasn't Max's prize, like I'd always thought. She was his consolation.

And with that, the spell was broken. It didn't matter anymore, not to me, what Max and Charlie did to each other, because I never wanted to see either of them ever again.

I fought through the crowd until I burst through a fire exit, onto the sidewalk. Tyler was nowhere to be seen; the street was filled with occupied taxis and throngs of people. A group of partygoers next to me lit up in a cloud of cigarette smoke. I bummed one, then held it between my fingers, unlit, while the city around me, dark and damp, honked and blinked and squealed.

When the traffic moved, I spotted him—leaning, in that way that he was so good at—on a wall across the street.

His hair, combed back, had turned almost completely gray. His beard was enormous; it hadn't been trimmed in months. There were more lines on his face. He looked older, but the unhappiness he'd carried, the worry, the tender charge of fear and anxiety—that was gone.

"You sold it," was the first thing I said.

"We did." He shrugged. "You were right." He took the unlit cigarette from my hands. "May I? I know you don't want this."

"You're right. I don't." My dress was still balled up in my other fist, and I let go of it, watching the wrinkled, sticky fabric tumble to the ground.

He lit up and exhaled. "*The Maria,*" he said, shaking his head. "You were right about everything—about the retrospective, about Charles, about the film. He bought it from us shortly after you left, over market value, on the condition that we do the retrospective. They even liked the name. *The Maria.*"

"Did he agree not to sue?"

"No," Tyler snorted. "He's holding that card. But he's as deep as

we are. Now—he's digging in deeper." He looked at me with ad-
miration. "You were truly right about all of it."

"That's the thing about being cynical," I said sourly, staring at
the sidewalk, the smoke from his cigarette. "Sometimes you get to
be right."

"When do you think people will start going there?"

"The second it opens. Charles will wrap it all up in so much
marketing, publicity, complicity—the next generation will stay
there, show there, refer to it. Carey will become a romantic myth,
like Joseph Beuys and his fat and felt and mountain people. Even
tomorrow," I told him, gesturing toward the crowd across the
street. They were mid-twenties, stylish, curious; one of them
watched us. I pretended not to notice.

"I know," he said, shaking his head. "We should have done this
years ago."

I had no response. It wasn't funny.

"I didn't think you would come."

"I didn't either."

"Was it enough?" he asked.

"I'm glad you used my film."

"We couldn't—not in the end. We couldn't do that."

"No. I understand."

A glossy town car squished to a heavy stop. The passenger-side
window rolled down. "Savage?" asked the driver. Tyler popped off
the wall, sauntered over the curb, and opened the door. I clutched
my heart, fingers working their way up to my clavicle. I didn't want
him to go.

"Can I give you a ride?" he asked.

"You don't know where I'm going."

"I don't care," he said. "How's Berlin?"

"What would you do in Berlin?" I asked.

He leaned in, toward my ear. Out of habit, I angled my neck,
and then we were touching, and I felt that old feeling, the golden
warmth of him.

"I'll be your assistant," he whispered.

"I already have one of those," I said.

"I'll be your boyfriend."

"I have one of those too." He blinked in surprise. "I—I meant to write and tell you. But somehow I never did."

"Who is it?

"I'm sorry."

He blinked again and shook his head. "I waited too long," he said.

"It's not that." I steeled myself to say the thing I had mumbled to myself a thousand times, in bathrooms, in backseats of cars, in the airplane, in the taxi, in my seat as the film played. "You told a lie that changed my entire life. Something that was a crass joke to you, a con to make money, was something I believed in. And I understand how it happened. I'm glad you told the truth. But I don't think I will ever, ever forgive you."

An anguished moment stretched between us before he finally spoke. "I know," he replied. Then he kissed me on the cheek, and I walked away.

♣ ♣ ♣ ♣ ♣

A year earlier, in a café in Neukölln, someone tapped me on the shoulder. Someone with big brown eyes and curly brown hair that poked every which way, like Kramer.

"Pearl," he said, pointing to himself.

"Jonah," I said in wonder. "How are you?" We kissed twice, like Germans.

"I'm good. I saw your show in Paris," he said. "Exquisite. I can't believe you pulled it off. Spectacular, even."

I blushed. "Thank you."

"Can I buy you a drink?"

"Oh no," I said. "I still owe you one."

"You bought me a dozen!"

"But none of them were in person." He begrudgingly agreed and pulled out a chair as I hailed the waiter.

"Are you living here?" I asked.

"I guess so." He smiled. "I'm doing a language course. I have a yearlong visa."

"That's the scam," I said, laughing. "Me and you and everyone we know." I added, "I never asked you what you did outside Pearl."

"I was working on a PhD in applied mathematics."

"Holy cow," I exclaimed. The waiter brought our drinks. "For how long?"

"Uh—fifteen years." He laughed. "I know. It was too long. If I'd left Pearl I probably would have finished earlier. I liked being around all of you."

"I never would have guessed that," I admitted. "You don't seem very math-y. I thought you were some cynical arty downtown critic who'd seen it all."

"God, no. I like art, but I love math," he said sincerely. "It has rules. It's the one thing in the world that tells you what the rules are."

"Did you give up on it? I mean—why are you in Berlin?"

"Oh, I'll get a job," he said, reassuring me. "I could have a job now. I—I don't know. I wanted to see a world that wasn't New York. Everybody's leaving. I mean, look at you. You never came back."

"I discovered that there was more world I wanted to see," I said.

"Me too." It turned out that Jonah, too, was a different person, once you got to know him.

After that—we were inseparable.

I never told Jonah, or anyone, about what happened at Pine City that summer. It took months to sort through it all. I was so lonely, so desperate for a hero, that I looked up to a hoax. I carried her with me like a talisman, like a saint, like an instruction manual, when she was a fraud, calculated to support the ambitions of privileged young people as they sailed around Manhattan, shooting rubber bullets at a world that for them would always ripple, and never break. But there was nothing in this world that could make my compulsion less lonely. There was no one who could show me how to be the person I wanted to be. I had to do everything for myself.

Carey—Maria, I still have to remind myself, after all this time—was, in the end, so much like the woman she pretended to be: uneducated, vulnerable, damaged—and like me, or at least who I was before the Academy. Yet her lines were merely that: lines. Maria didn't write the story, and she didn't learn the lessons. The tragedy was that she never learned to pick herself up after a failure. She never outed Pine City while she was alive; she was brave only in death. It was a shame. She should have been here tonight. She shouldn't have been afraid to feel like a fraud.

I feel like one every day. It's the cost of doing business.

I checked my watch, hailed a taxi, and scooted across its vinyl seats, the stuffing coming out beneath my fingers. I gazed out the window toward the life that waited for me—the one that I had built, and would keep on building, piece by piece.

Acknowledgments

Thanks to:

Grand Central Publishing, especially editor Lindsey Rose and creative director Albert Tang and his team for the cover.

Rose Tomaszewska, my indefatigable editor at riverrun, for her love and enthusiasm for this project, and the rest of the riverrun team for their tireless labor on behalf of my work.

My agent Victoria Sanders, and her right-hand women Bernadette Baker-Baughman and Jessica Spivey.

As an amateur artist (I can only claim an undergraduate minor in drawing, and even then, my own hand is drawn to the banal architecture of banks, hotels, and office buildings, and my years in ceramics have yet to result in the perfect bowl) but a professional-grade enthusiast, my work on this book has benefited from many hours of conversations with my husband, Ian, and our beautiful friends, especially David Brooks, Fabienne Lasserre, and Christine Manganaro.

This book, a love letter to the labor of artmaking, also owes a deep debt to all of the artists whose studios I have had the privilege of seeing in past years, either through friendship, the Maryland Institute College of Art, the Penland School of Crafts, or the Wassaic Project in Wassaic, New York, where I completed a bulk of the edits for the manuscript and acquired a great deal of priceless verisimilitude. In no good order, that especially includes: Eve Biddle, for speaking so openly about the development of TWP and her line about being young and stubborn. Denise Markonish of Mass-MoCA for her observations about the qualities that make up the difference between art and entertainment. Leya Evelyn for her remarks about the gesso. Wim Botha for showing us his "hot knife." Ryan Ketchum for all of the conversations about his work in the old days. Nicole Dyer for the wonderful drawing on page 59 of this book. Lena Schmid for showing me the "Wild Hearts" video and telling me that "a third of American women watch this every day." Katy McCarthy, August Thompson, Eman Alshawaf, Lucinda Dayhew, Will Hutnick, Allie Hankins for our excellent talks and for their friendship, and all of our fellow residents during the winter of 2017–18 at the Wassaic Project, founders Bowie Zunino and Jeff Barnett-Winsby, and staffers Jenny Morse, Paloma Hutton, and Jordan Hutton for their support and dedication to TWP. Special thanks to MICA for bringing us to Baltimore and all that you gave us, including the wonderful Ruth Toulson, the original blond Wednesday Addams, all of the faculty who so generously allowed me into their classrooms, including Sarah Barnes, Joshua Hebbert, and Robert Tillman, and those I have met through MICA and MICAZA, including Ledelle Moe, Jared Thorne, and David Southwood.

Fictional reviews in this book were influenced by actual reviews of the work of Lucy Dodd and Marina Abramovich, and a passage on a particular type of brush is directly inspired by the words of Jack Whitten in an interview with Robert Storr, from *Jack Whitten: Five Decades of Painting*. Other works that I found valuable during this process include: "Women, Art and Ideology" by Griselda Pollock; "Tune in, Turn on, Drop Out: The Rejection of Lee Lozano" by Helen Molesworth; "The End of Painting" by Douglas Crimp; "The Untroubled Mind" by Agnes Martin; "Making Waves: The Legacy of Lee Lozano" by Katy Seigel and David Reed; statements from Robert Motherwell, Helen Frankenthaler, Anselm Keifer, Elizabeth Murray, David Reed, and Joan Mitchell in *Theories and Documents of Contemporary Art* by Kristine Stiles and Peter Selz; *The Collected Writings of Robert Smithson* edited by Jack Flam; *Bas Jan Ader: In Search of the Miraculous* by Jan Verwoert; *Art Talk: Conversations with 15 Women Artists* by Cindy Nemser; and *Lee Lozano: Dropout Piece* by Sarah Lehrer-Graiwer, among others.

To my good friends and dedicated readers Abbe Wright, Jane Orvis, Fabienne Lasserre, and Alfred Bridi, for their incisive notes.

To Ian, who never tires of being my own personal encyclopedia, my biggest champion, and the love of my life. Especially, on the ego front, for letting me swerve into your hard-won lane.

And the Laura Owens show at the Whitney in the winter of 2018 was a necessary reminder of how innovative and exceptional painting can be, so thanks to Owens for setting the bar.